# Sābanto

## Book Two

## The Copper Briar

### ewa anderson

Published in 2024 by Ewa Anderson



Edited by: Maylon Gardner www.rightyourwriting.com

Cover Design by: Umbrella Squared Design Group Inc.  www.umbrellasquared.com

Publisher: Catalie Press www.cataliepress.com

Ebook ISBN: 978-1-7780186-5-7

Paperback ISBN: 978-1-7780186-4-0

Hard Cover ISBN: 978-1-7780186-6-4

Sābanto "The Copper Briar" is the second book in the Sābanto trilogy.


While reading Book One: "The Crimson River" is not required
in order to follow the story,
you will have a deeper understanding of the characters and
the world of Sābanto if you read it beforehand.

Rose blooms in summer
Fragrant, beautiful flower
Winter's shrub of thorns

# PROLOGUE

A YOUNG WORKER WOKE up to a short but piercing whistle, and opened his eyes to a room that was almost pitch black. Neither sunlight nor moonlight reached this far beneath the surface of the earth. The chamber that held him had been dug into the coal rock, more than a kilometer deep in the mine. Only a small kerosene lamp, turned to the lowest possible setting to conserve precious oxygen, lit the place which housed a hundred men cramped inside. The air was thick with black coal dust that found its way into his mouth, crunching between his teeth, tasting of nothing more than moistened rock. It surrounded everything like a fog, entering his lungs with each breath.

He brought his hands, blackened with coal dust, in front of his face. All around him were other miners, every patch of skin grimy like his. Only the whites of their eyes were distinguishable in the near-total darkness. His hair was naturally black, but it was even darker now, and heavier, caked in dust.

He climbed down from his bed, which moaned metallically from the strain, and put his bare feet onto the hard, cold, and slightly damp stone floor.

He hadn't slept well. There was a constant sound of distant drilling and hammering as people worked around the clock. He couldn't fall asleep, tossing and turning, too tired to sleep, not being able to find a horizontal position that would relieve him from the pain of his muscles and joints. People around him coughed and moaned as they lay in their dirty bunks, slowly spitting their lungs out onto the floor. After he finally did fall asleep, he was woken up by loud voices in the corridors. There had been another accident—a worker had collapsed at his station and been mutilated by a drilling machine. They killed him out of mercy.

He coughed and spat on the ground. He'd fallen sick two weeks ago. When he was last outside, up in the village, he thought he'd seen blood in his spit. That had been four long shifts ago and he felt the sickness progressing. He was already thin from the hard work—skin and bones, really—and the worsening cough was eating him alive. His clothes were dirty, just like the rest of him, and they hung on him like a sack.

Two more shifts, and he'd line up at the rusting elevators to go up to the surface and be allowed to breathe the fresh mountain air in the town nearby. That's how it worked here. Six days of work and one day off. Back in town, he would collect his weekly payout of ten flicks. He could spend them on anything the company store sold, but there was no doctor to treat him. He'd go to the mine director's office instead, and if the guards didn't kick him out and hit him across the ribs with their batons, the man would see him. He'd ask for a few days off to get better. He'd exchange the flicks he saved for tickets—real currency—and the guards who blocked the roads to prevent contract breakers from fleeing would let him through. There might be a doctor in the next town, although it was quite far to walk. If the director rejected his time off request, he'd endure the remaining four weeks of his three-month contract as best he could. Many were able to finish it, so why shouldn't he?

He left the room with the rest of the men, and the armed guards marched them through the dark corridor to another chamber dug in the rock that served as a kitchen. There were many already standing in line to get their ration of food. Once his turn came, he picked up his breakfast and sat down at one of the long, crooked tables with the rest of the workers. Two free meals a day had sounded perfect when he'd signed the contract, but they gave him only a bland watery soup in a tin bowl and a piece of dark bread that turned even darker when the coal dust settled on it.

He coughed again, grabbed the corner of the stale bread with his dirty hands, and ate most of the piece. He didn't know if the dust on his food would make him sicker, but he couldn't afford to leave it uneaten. After this morning meal, he'd work hard, breaking the rock and pushing full coal carts for twelve hours, with no breaks. He threw the small piece of remaining bread onto the floor for good luck, as the other workers said to do. Feeding the rats was useful. They detected poisonous gas much quicker than humans. Who'd be first to flee when it was too dangerous to continue working, the rats or the guards?

A loud cough rattled his lungs.

He got up, returned the empty bowl, and made his way to the assembly point in the black corridor to meet with the other workers who were lining up and waiting for the guards to allow them access to their working stations. He didn't speak to anyone. The silence between the men was broken only by their coughs.

A few minutes later, a loud whistle sounded. It marked the start of the next shift. The column of a hundred men shuffled slowly forward. He walked, dragging his feet. The workers were indistinguishable—dirty, and wearing rags. The men blended into the dark walls that surrounded them. The sea of heads moved deeper into the mine, fading into the darkness and the lingering dust.

# 1

V IOLET WOKE IN THE middle of the night. She was cold and curled up on a hard concrete floor. Her bare legs were bent and feet tucked into her body for warmth. Her arm served as a pillow.

She hadn't covered herself with anything. Everything she owned she already wore—a knee-length robe, gray from wear and washing. She hadn't brought anything else with her when the Sābanto soldiers forced her from her old home in Riverlea. It had only been a shack in the former town square, but it had been home.

She sat up, shivering from the cold. She rubbed her hands against her arms. Where was she? She scanned the dark room waiting for her mind to fully awaken. There wasn't much light coming through the only window, but she noticed the contours of a narrow bed shoved into the corner. She recalled it had been pristine, with a crisp bedsheet and she hadn't washed the previous night. Her robe was dirty, and her hair was crusted with dust from being on the road the day before. How could she lie in it and ruin the white fabric?

She had traveled in the back of a truck with other women, kids, and the elderly. The shouts of refugees and the Sābanto guards had rung in her ears, and the constant noise of the tires had exhausted and agitated her. Despite what had been happening around her and what little she had known about their destination, she'd watched, amazed at the changing scenery, as the armed men had pressed the convoy south, away from Riverlea. The familiar hills were now far away.

She turned her body around and glanced behind her at the crib. She stood up, making as little noise as she could. Seb was sleeping. His breaths were slow and rhythmic.

Violet had named her son Sebastian after her late father. She'd been just seven years old when wandering bandits had killed her parents.

Mike, her younger brother by two years, had hidden and survived. Violet recalled the meadows behind their farmhouse. The goats and the chickens. Her eyes moistened. She'd lost so much in the past thirteen years. She could never turn back time and be there again, in their village. She wouldn't even know which direction the golden fields were in if someone were to give her a chance to see them again.

A woman screamed, startling Violet. Where did that noise come from? It was somewhere outside, not right by the building she was in, but close. Was that what had woken her up earlier? Violet immediately turned towards Seb. He was still sleeping, unmoved by the noise. He was peaceful, bundled in a soft blanket and firmly hugging a stuffed auburn monkey. It had been waiting for him in this crib when they'd arrived. It was his first real toy. Rocks and sticks had been all he could play with before.

Some shouts followed the screams outside. There were multiple people arguing; some louder, some quieter. A kid was crying. The voices echoed from the buildings just like they had from the ruins in Riverlea at night. Assaults and rape had been common in the overpopulated city, and no one came to help. Sticking up for strangers only brought misfortune. Everyone in Riverlea lived by this rule. But Violet also recalled the time she had broken it and helped someone in need. The woman had become her friend and helped her out in return.

*Where was she now?* Violet wondered as she hugged herself. She rubbed her hands against her body for the warmth. There was comfort in knowing that whatever the trouble outside was, it wasn't affecting her. She glanced at the closed window, but the night outside was still.

She turned her eyes back to Seb and smiled. Violet adjusted the blanket on him. She stroked his short, pale blond—almost white—hair that curled in all directions.

The shouting faded as the voices became more distant. What kind of place was she in? Many things had happened the night before. There wasn't enough time to get herself familiar with her new home.

She'd been exhausted upon arrival. A boy had greeted them in the Sābanto compound. Robert was his name. She recalled his dark hair and olive skin. He had been nice. She remembered being very tired, barely moving her legs, as she'd followed a woman in a navy uniform. There was grass everywhere, fresh and soft under her bare feet, unlike the gray, hard concrete that had surrounded her shack in Riverlea.

Was the grass still there? She could look through the window and see, couldn't she? Foolish thoughts. The night was still dark.

Silence fell on the other side of the window. The trouble was over, and the night weighed on her again. She quietly lay down on the floor and drifted back to sleep.

A shriek of alarm from a speaker near the ceiling in one of the corners violently woke Violet. The room was lit with faint sun rays coming from the window. She jumped to her feet seeing Seb stirring in his crib. He watched her with his deep blue eyes, fearful of the sudden loud noise.

"Morning, big guy," she said and smiled, comforting him so he wouldn't cry. She noticed his face was dirty. It needed a quick wipe.

The alarm shrieked again, and a calm, cheerful voice spoke. "Good morning! We request everyone assemble outside in fifteen minutes for a meeting."

Seb twitched. He was about to cry, so she scooped him up into her arms. "All's fine," she cooed, and held him close.

With the boy on her hip, she quietly opened the door and peered outside into the empty corridor. She stepped out and silently closed the door behind her.

Instead of turning right, towards the exit, she turned left. Wasn't there a water pipe in a room down the hall, in the common area? As she drew up to the room, she passed a door to her left. She could hear some commotion as well as a child crying behind them. She didn't want to see who was in there and be forced to introduce herself. In Riverlea, minding one's own business was the best strategy for staying out of trouble. That was the safest way forward here as well, she figured.

The corridor opened into a large open area with a table in the middle and some shelves and counters along the wall to her right. On the far end, there was a bathroom where she had seen a water pipe. Violet opened the door, but the inside was dark. There were no windows to let the light in. *Oh well.* As she turned around to leave, Seb stirred in her arms and waved his monkey, and suddenly the lights turned on and the room lit up. It was very clean. The glass door at the far end of the room was so pristine, was it even there?

"Was that you?" Violet quietly asked Seb, looking around her. Her voice bounced slightly from the shiny walls of the room. They were alone. The lights had turned on on their own. She placed him on the floor before turning the knobs on the water pipe. A stream of water came out of the end. It was crystal clear, almost invisible, and it lacked the chemical odor that the river water in Riverlea had.

She washed her face first and noticed her reflection in the mirror. Her blond hair was in disarray. Her gray eyes had dark circles under them.

"We'll start in five minutes!" the voice from the speaker exclaimed. There was one mounted in the bathroom as well. Violet picked up Seb and quickly washed his face before darting out, not wanting to be late. The door to room C was now open and whoever had been there earlier had already left for the meeting. There was no time to throw Seb's toy back into the crib on the way out, so she let him carry it.

People had already gathered outside on the grass covering the open field of the compound's public square. A few older couples stood in between many families with children of different ages and single mothers like herself. Most stood quietly, but there were some heated conversations happening. Everyone wore whatever they had traveled in the day before. They'd been woken violently in the middle of the night by Sābanto and hadn't been permitted to take anything from their shacks. Soldiers in black uniforms had dragged people from their houses, beating them and forcefully rounding them up into groups ready for transport. The people of Riverlea were nothing but beggars, gray and tired, huddled against the pristine white of the buildings.

Violet shied away from striking up any conversations of her own. She took a good look at the place she was in. Small buildings, like the one she had slept in, were placed in eight neat rows. Each had a number on top of it. If not for the numbers, they were all identical in shape and size. They stretched forever. Her house had a big number thirty-five written on it and stood almost in the middle of the second row.

Only one building was unique. Violet recalled having entered through it. It contained a large space where she'd received a thick soup the previous night. The extensive building had a big sign reading *Sābanto* on it, and most of the crowd gathered underneath that.

The display suddenly changed, and the letters were replaced with a woman's face. Violet stared at it with her mouth open. People around her grew quiet and raised their heads.

"Welcome to Sābanto Compound 10 Unit 23," the woman spoke in a thunderous voice. "We hope you've settled in and are enjoying the facilities we have provided. It's currently eight o'clock in the morning and your first of three daily meals will be served shortly in the cafeteria."

The woman on the screen was then replaced with a different woman wearing a navy uniform. "If you have questions or require help, please reach out to any of us. We'll also help you locate those you may have been separated from." The display changed again and a handsome man in a green uniform appeared—attire like what Robert had been wearing when they'd arrived. "Our uniformed guards are here to keep peace in the compounds so that you can feel safe."

Someone threw a rock. It came from behind Violet and collided with the display, cracking the screen. She brought Seb closer to her and scanned the crowd. She recalled the chaos of the evacuation from Riverlea and how scared her son had been. What was happening around her didn't feel any different.

Another rock flew past Violet, but from a different direction.

Through the now-cracked display, a group of people of different ages appeared, wearing sky-blue uniforms. "You all deserve clean clothes, so we'll provide a set for you and everyone in your family."

"Let us go!" a woman shouted beside Violet, making her jump.

*The Sābanto soldiers hadn't allowed them to leave the transport, why would they now?* Violet wondered, recalling those who had tried to escape, but had been captured and put back on the truck with their hands bound.

"Feed us!" a male voice from another part of the square shouted in reply.

Seb stirred in Violet's arms, clinging to her. She squeezed him firmly against her chest and walked backwards, away from the center of the crowd.

"Take us back!" they chanted. "Food!"

Violet was already at the edge of the gathering when men in green uniforms walked in. They were holding batons and wearing helmets. The angry crowd noticed them as well and turned in their direction.

Fights had erupted back in Riverlea during the evacuation. Angry people had attacked the troops, who had responded with force. Many people had been severely hurt. Violet turned around and ran as fast as she could, carrying Seb in her arms.

At the end of the main building, she stopped in her tracks. A tall double fence topped with barbed wire blocked her way. In the distance, on the other side of the wide dirt road, there were more white buildings organized in neat rows. It was another camp, just like the one she was in.

"Where are we?" Violet asked under her breath.

The shouting and screaming of the crowd were getting closer. A man in a green uniform threw a woman down to the ground and cuffed her hands behind her back. The woman screamed and cursed the guard while he kicked her repeatedly.

Violet could see a small shed near the building, so she adjusted Seb on her hip and eased closer to it. She pressed the handle. The door wasn't locked. She opened it slightly and listened. There was no noise coming from the other side. Her heart raced. Violet opened the door wider and walked inside.

The shed was only slightly bigger than their shack in Riverlea. The inside held some tools she recognized—a rake and a shovel—but most of them were unfamiliar to her. The interior was cold and smelled of the damp earth that remained on the tools after they'd been used. It was dark with only a small window near the ceiling allowing some daylight in.

She closed the door behind her, then found a spot on the bare floor and sat down. It gave her an unobstructed view of the door in case someone entered. She held Seb and his monkey in her arms and waited, listening to her quick heartbeats.

"We're safe," she told Seb. *Of course we are.*

Violet didn't know how long she sat there before the muffled shouts and cries in the distance eventually faded. She noticed the shadows on the floor moved with time and the place darkened. Seb fell asleep in her arms almost immediately. He was hungry and weak, but it wasn't the first time they wouldn't be eating for a day. *All the hard times will pass.*

For now, they were safe. No one would look for them here. She waited as her eyes became heavier.

The door suddenly opened with a loud squeak that Violet woke up. She jumped up to her feet. She had been lying on the floor curled up around a sleeping Seb. A man in a green uniform stood in the doorway. "House number?" he asked with authority.

"Thirty-five," Violet replied quietly. Her voice was shaking. These were the men she'd seen beating people earlier. Seb held his arms around her leg for comfort.

The man was calm. He waved his hand at her. "Get outta there." He stepped aside and held the door open. He didn't seem like he'd take no for an answer. She grabbed Seb in her arms and slowly exited. Once outside, she turned towards the middle of the compound, where the morning trouble had started.

The man caught up with her. "Follow me," he ordered. He walked quickly, and Violet was having trouble keeping up with him.

It was already getting dark, but she still noticed the destruction around her while walking across the compound. People had trampled the beautiful grass she'd admired earlier and dented the façade of the main building. The now-black display had more cracks. Some of the small houses had broken windows, and their walls were damaged as well. They no longer looked new and identical. She turned her eyes to her building and the number thirty-five above the door. It was still standing, but there were signs of fire on the walls.

An older woman with short gray hair and a navy uniform came out of the main building and the soldier spoke to her. "Thirty-five's ruined," he said. "Find her a place." He then turned towards Violet. "Go with her," he said, and left.

She followed the woman into the main building. The fans on the ceiling were spinning, creating a faint breeze. Tables and chairs had been overturned. Many of them lay broken on the floor. A small, slightly cracked display panel hung near the ceiling. It showed an enormous fire, and the announcer was talking about it animatedly. The sound bounced between the empty walls and Violet was having trouble hearing where the fire had taken place and what had caused it.

The woman pointed at the bench and left the room, her steps echoing through the hallway.

Violet, left alone with Seb, sat down at one of the remaining long tables. Seb smiled and held up his toy, showing it to his mother. He was relaxed, unconcerned about where they were, and Violet let her guard down a bit as well.

"Monkey," she said. She had heard of monkeys, but had never seen one. *They couldn't be real animals,* she thought. They must be the creation of the puppet maker.

"Mo-kee," Seb attempted to repeat. Violet smiled warmly. He loved learning new words.

The woman came back with a metal bowl full of soup and placed it in front of Violet, whose stomach grumbled at the sight.

"I'm Carol," the woman said. She pointed at the bowl for Violet to start eating. "How old's he?" she asked.

"Eighteen months." Violet picked up the metal spoon and tasted the soup. It wasn't hot, so she gave some to Seb.

"Do ya know how much eighteen is?" Carol asked skeptically.

Violet nodded. "I been to school," she said, proud of her accomplishment. Mr. Rodden had run free classes for the poor people in Riverlea.

Carol left again and came back with a jug of milk in her hand. She handed it to Seb and sat down beside them on the bench.

Violet enjoyed every sip of the soup. Seb loved the milk he got and tried to hold the jug by himself. Violet helped him, preventing him from spilling all over the table and onto himself. She didn't want to be wasteful. Violet couldn't recall the taste of milk. Last time she'd had it had been at the family farm before the evil men had stolen their goats.

"Ya remind me of ma daughter when she was younger," Carol said. "She ain't in Sābanto yet, but she'll get here eventually."

"Ya from Riverlea?" Violet spoke and quickly rescued Seb's monkey that he was trying to dunk headfirst into the milk.

"Mo-kee," Seb said, laughing as though it were a joke.

"No." The woman shook her head. She was smiling, entertained by Seb's silly talk. "But all the cities are getting rid of the poor and sending them here. Ya group is first."

"Where's everyone?" Violet scanned the empty hall. She didn't see anyone outside either.

"On a lockdown, back in their homes." Carol sighed heavily. "Too many emotions. They don't understand."

"Where are we?" Violet wiped the milk dripping from Seb's mouth with her hand, which she then wiped on her clothes.

"Sābanto. A refuge."

Violet shook her head. She didn't understand what that meant.

"They made it for us," Carol started. "Here we got a warm bed, food, clean water."

"Why the fence?"

"So we not leave."

*Just like in Riverlea,* Violet thought, *where the river prevented people getting to the other side to Clamerton.* "They never told us where we're going," she said.

"It upsets people," Carol replied. Violet waited for her to explain, but the woman changed the subject instead. "We'll send food to houses until the lockdown ends."

"Thank ya for the soup," Violet said and smiled, continuing to eat. She was grateful. Seb finished his milk and insisted on having more of the soup as well.

"Did ya arrive with someone?" Carol asked.

Violet shook her head. It was just her and Seb.

"Family?" Carol asked after a moment of silence.

Violet nodded. "Brother. He signed with Sābanto."

"Excuse me." The woman got up and left, disappearing again through one of the doors at the end of the hall.

Violet looked up at the display. The segment about the fire had ended. It now showed two people having some sort of discussion.

Carol came back and put a tablet she'd brought with her onto the table.

"What's ya brother name?"

"Mike."

"And last name?"

"Stone."

Carol poked the device she was holding in her hand a few times with her index finger. She then turned the tablet towards Violet and showed her a picture. Violet's eyes brightened at seeing Mike's face, looking just how she remembered him. Her mouth was full, so she nodded at Carol. It was him. She'd have recognized her brother's face anywhere. Maybe Carol could help her find him. There was a chance she could bring the family together again.

"Not with Sābanto anymore," the woman said. "He left ten months ago."

Violet's eyes welled up with tears. She turned her face away from Carol. The happiness of having a full stomach suddenly evaporated and was replaced with the emptiness of still not knowing where her brother was.

Violet looked at Seb. He was happy, oblivious to what was happening around him. She smiled through her tears. They would make it without Mike. They would have to.

"Ya said ya read?" Carol asked.

"A bit," Violet replied, composing herself. She took the last spoonful of the remaining soup and left the utensil in the bowl. She wished she'd been able to study more, but taking care of Seb didn't leave her with much spare time.

Carol poked her tablet again and placed it in front of her. "Can ya read here?" she pointed at a specific line of text.

The letters were small and Violet carefully traced each word with her index finger, stumbling over some words she had trouble pronouncing. "In a saucepan, heat oil over medium heat." She paused and looked at Carol. "What's a saucepan?"

"Come, I'll show ya," the woman replied. She grabbed the empty dishes off the table and smiled at Violet. "I'll show ya where ya will sleep tonight," she added.

Violet got up, picked up Seb, and followed Carol.

# 2

ANOTHER SMALL CONFERENCE ROOM cramped with reporters. The air was stuffy from all the people who had been sitting inside for hours. These places came with their own distinctive odors of sweat, perfume, and disinfectant. A more intimate interview would have been preferable. Then Anita could've asked all the questions she wanted, without the crowd and time restraints.

Anita had asked her news agency, The Citizen, if she could be the one to cover Sābanto and her office had not objected. No one else wanted to go to Clamerton where the new Government had its offices for the North American continent.

She'd flown from Durban and had arrived late in the afternoon because the jet she'd borrowed from her father had encountered some turbulence on the way, and they'd had to adjust their course. She had rushed straight from the jet to the conference without even changing clothes, and had still missed the start of it. She had on a pair of black pants and a yellow cotton top she liked to wear because it contrasted perfectly with her dark skin.

Anita looked around the room when she walked in. *Who had chosen the paint in this room?* The oppressively dark navy only made the place feel narrower and more claustrophobic. The only chairs left were at the back, and the speaker was in the process of answering a question as Anita squeezed through so she could sit down. His surly bodyguard, a young man in his early twenties, wearing the black Sābanto uniform, followed her with his eyes.

She sat down in a plastic chair. She could barely see the speaker and his dark, neatly trimmed hair and well-fitted suit from behind the lectern, but his blue eyes glanced her way several times. Anita had seen him on the display, but this was her first time seeing him in person. She scanned the people in the room and sighed. Would she be able to get the speaker's attention?

Those seated closer to the speaker kept asking questions about the amount of money being spent on the Sābanto project, and how much of it would go back to the economy. *Boring.* Some were interested in the logistics of food distribution and medical care. *Irrelevant.* How could they still believe that the people of Riverlea had been evacuated to Sābanto because of a tuberculosis outbreak? Anyone with half a brain knew that wasn't true.

"Mr. Conway!" She raised her hand, but the speaker seemed to only be interested in taking questions from the front rows.

During the war, they hadn't wanted any female reporters at the agency. They'd said there was no place for them. Perceptions had begun to change after the war, however, and that was when Anita had gotten her chance to shine.

"Mr. Conway!" She raised her hand again.

She'd begun as a radio correspondent, traveling to different places chasing news stories about World United, the new government. She'd visited many continents and even spent a few months in Karben, where the new laws were being made. She was already all over the radio when the news stations began broadcasting their first video updates. Anita didn't need an invitation. Why not be the first to show her face on screen in people's houses and businesses? There was demand for anchors with pretty eyes.

"Yes, Miss Gibala," Conway finally replied, motioning in her direction.

At last. She smiled and stood up.

Anita was famous—a recognizable figure—but she introduced herself anyway. "Anita Gibala. The Citizen. There are rumors, Mr. Conway, that World United didn't limit Sābanto to the people of Riverlea. If that's true, who will they force to take part in this project next?" She'd managed to say it all in one breath. Not bad. She immediately sat back down in the uncomfortable chair, waiting for an answer.

A hush went over the room as the speaker weighed his words. "That's a loaded question," he finally replied, and added, "but it's correct." A murmur erupted in the room, and Conway waited for the uproar to subside. "The pilot project has been a great success. The World United Council is currently developing a plan that would allow us to create Sābanto compounds for other areas that are also severely poverty-stricken and would benefit from the extra help." He adjusted the sheets of paper in front of him. "As to the other half of your question, Miss Gibala, the current criteria we're looking at is whether or not people own property."

Questions erupted from the room. The noise level increased as the reporters shouted over each other. "Since when?" "Which areas?" "What are the details?" Through the forest of hands, Anita saw the bodyguard in front of the room become more alert.

Anita smiled. She had gotten some people's attention and prompted them to ask questions about the future of Sābanto. Covering Sābanto compounds would be a career-killer, her peers at The Citizen had warned. They'd said she was too young. That she didn't understand what real journalism was. They had claimed that fighting for so-called "justice" was a trap many young people fell into. It wouldn't get her any advancement in the field. Been there, done that, they'd said.

They knew nothing.

The shouts became more subdued, and an older man sitting at the side of the room asked, "Can you elaborate on that, Mr. Conway?" He was from a small news channel, Asian Report, serving only one continent.

"Certainly," Conway replied. "Those who aren't employed will undergo a wealth review. If they can't produce an official document of ownership of land or property, World United will consider them for Sābanto."

There had been rumors circulating about the new laws, but this was the first time someone had officially confirmed them.

"What about farmers?" another person asked.

"If they don't own the land they're cultivating, they can buy it," Conway said.

Many of these farmers had once owned their land, but the mafias had stolen it from them. The cartels charged them steep rent prices for the small fields they lived off. They were now being told they would have to buy them back. At what price?

"Who will enforce this relocation?" somebody else in the room asked. Anita didn't see who.

"Sābanto will enforce the relocation," the speaker replied, then added, "Black Shirts." With that, Conway thanked his audience and left the room, ignoring all the additional questions that were still being shouted from the audience. His bodyguard followed behind him.

The conference was over, but Anita remained in the building. Other journalists walked out to their expensive cars and drove off. The old city hall was empty, and only the occasional footsteps of an office worker echoed in the hollow corridors.

A door suddenly opened and Conway emerged. A Black Shirt bodyguard followed him.

"Chop-jet is ready," the young man said. He noticed Anita standing against the wall and turned towards her. "Can I help ya?" he asked, and pressed his lips together.

Conway turned his eyes towards her as well. His face was pale, but it might've just been the light in the hall that was different. "Conference is over, Miss Gibala," Conway said, and started walking in her direction through the corridor towards the exit of the building. His steps were uncertain, his posture bent slightly.

"Why are you doing this?" she asked as he approached. She stared at him coldly.

"Doing what?" Conway asked. He stopped in front of her and stared straight in her eyes. Sweat glistened on his forehead.

He didn't intimidate her. "You force people into Sābanto, and then you send them to perform slave labor."

"Miss Gibala," he replied calmly. "That's not my shot to call. If you want to know more, you'd need to ask World United . . . but I'd advise against that." He started to walk away. The bodyguard gave her the stink eye before following. The word "Sābanto" was printed in large white letters on the back of his black uniform. Her eyes followed them as they left. The young man's heavy boots squeaked on the polished floor as he walked.

"People are dying!" she shouted, her voice echoing, but they didn't turn around. "Blood is on your hands, Mr. Conway!" They ignored her and walked out of the building.

She couldn't stop pursuing this. That's what journalism was, wasn't it? What did Conway, the director of Sābanto, know that he wasn't saying? Was he threatening her, or was avoiding questioning World

United genuine advice? Either way, the topic was too important. She couldn't drop it.

Finally back in the chop-jet, Oliver slumped heavily into his seat. He was exhausted. His left side hurt again, and the painkillers had stopped working an hour ago.

He'd let his guard down during his last job. How had he missed the gun in his opponent's hand? *He was getting old and slow*, he thought. If the man had had a steadier hand, Oliver wouldn't have survived the encounter. Instead he'd been wounded, and the wound was now infected.

"Y'alright, sir?" Greyson asked.

"I need a doctor." Oliver said, closing his eyes. He shivered from the cold. He needed help. "Someone we can trust."

"I don't know many doctors, but the one in Covedale seems okay," he said. "He helps people and doesn't charge them if they can't pay."

Oliver nodded. He had little choice.

The light flickered above Bruce Lott as he sat at his desk in his clinic in Covedale, reading about skin conditions. A patient he'd seen a couple of days ago had developed a skin reaction to something while harvesting apples in an orchard. It was likely a chemical rash, possibly from some type of pesticide, but he wanted to be sure.

The clinic was quiet. There was no one bustling around. The new machines Mr. White had provided them with a few years ago, when he'd been running the city, treated patients much more efficiently. An injured person was placed directly between the device's long, all-seeing arms. With a few quiet movements of its limb-like parts, the machine could diagnose within minutes. The machine was able to easily heal almost any injury—even the most serious ones could now be healed in days rather than months.

Bruce got up and glanced at the clock on the wall. *Time to go home.* He put on the light jacket he'd hung on the back of his chair earlier and closed the thick book in front of him and stashed it away in one of the desk drawers. There was a video display in the back of the office. Bruce glanced at it. The volume was lowered to reduce distractions while he researched. The late-night news was reporting on some conference. Whatever they were talking about, Bruce knew it would bring nothing but trouble.

Bruce turned off the display and scanned the room. All was in its place. He walked out into the empty hallway and locked the door to his office behind him. Turning right, he walked out of the building to his car. He unlocked the door and sat on the driver's side. Suddenly he felt the cold metal of a gun being pressed against his neck. He froze.

"I ain't gonna kill ya," a male voice behind him said. "Ya gonna do something for me." Bruce swallowed as he listened. "Turn on the car and follow ma directions."

Bruce nodded. There was no one around that he could turn to for help. It clearly wasn't drugs the man wanted, or else he would've forced him back to the clinic and made him dispense some. Bruce complied and drove away.

They made many turns, moving away from the town center. His abductor finally told him to stop in the middle of a thick, wooded area. "Out," the man said.

Bruce opened the door and stepped out as he was told. The air was cold and he shivered, but there was barely any wind. He scanned the eerie darkness that surrounded him. Did he have enemies he'd forgotten about? Did he owe anyone money? Had he done something wrong? He couldn't think of a reason why anyone would want to abduct him. *What was the man's plan?*

A faint light appeared as the body of a chop-jet showed up at the edge of the clearing. The door opened and his abductor pushed him forward.

Bruce stepped inside and immediately recognized Mr. Conway. The man sat crookedly in his seat and looked pale.

"Thank you, Dr. Lott, for agreeing to see me," Mr. Conway said.

The vessel door closed behind him and he frowned. *He had yet to agree to anything*, he thought. He'd been taken against his will. He said nothing, however. Mr. Conway was a powerful, well-connected person, and it was safer to be agreeable. Bruce couldn't stop the man from putting out a bad word about the clinic if he wished to do so. They would close the clinic and replace the doctor and the staff. The services they were providing would no longer be available to many in Covedale and surrounding areas. Bruce looked at the dome-shaped jammer on the desk. It was turned on, ready to interfere with any recording device within a five-meter range. Whatever this was, it was important. "How can I help?" he asked.

Mr. Conway opened his shirt, exposing the bandages on his wound. It was bad. A yellowish infection seeped through the wrapping. "Can you treat this?" The man started to undress the wound.

"We can go back to the clinic—" the doctor began to say.

"We can't," said the man behind him, still holding his gun.

Bruce turned around and looked at his abductor. "Greyson?" That made sense, Greyson worked for Conway. All of Covedale knew it. Bruce turned back towards the injured man and added, "Our machine will fix the infected tissue in minutes."

"You know this is a gunshot," Mr. Conway replied. The bandages were off now and all could see the infection was extensive, and it was clear that a gun had caused the wound. "Don't you need to report this? Doesn't the machine take a DNA sample from anyone who's treated? You know I can't do that."

Bruce's hands were sweating. He scanned the room for a way out. Mr. Conway was right. He had to report all the people who visited his clinic with suspicious wounds. The machine, as far as he knew, couldn't be reconfigured for anonymous use. He wished he could hack it, disconnect from the network somehow, but he'd studied the mechanism before and it was impossible. His work would be so much easier if he could. There wouldn't be any need to use the old medicines. No more worrying about keeping patients stable during operations. Many more people could be saved if only he could use it undetected.

"You know how to use the old medicine," Mr. Conway said. "Greyson says you help the poor and you don't charge them for the service, which means you can't use the machine on them, and you understand that it can't treat me."

Bruce nodded. If Conway were trying to hide his gun wound, the new ways couldn't be used. Word about the Covedale clinic helping everyone for free and without the machine had, however, spread, and that worried Bruce. He could be stripped of his degree and forbidden to practice ever again. Treating people without being able to buy required medicines and equipment would be even more challenging.

"Mr. Conway," Bruce ran his right hand through his thinning hair. "A lot of the old tools are now gone—"

"All you need to do is get me back on my feet." Oliver took out a cigarette and lit it.

"Please, Mr. Conway," Bruce protested. "I'll help, but please don't smoke." The cigarette smoke made his eyes water. "It's not good for you."

Oliver nodded and stubbed out the cigarette in the ashtray.

The wound looked bad. If Bruce didn't do anything, gangrene would be next and that could be deadly. If the injury had been accidental or if he'd gotten it in self-defense, then Mr. Conway would have simply visited the clinic. Being an accessory to whatever crime the man in front of him had committed was the last thing Bruce wanted, but he couldn't just leave a human being in such a state. He'd never forgive himself for breaking his professional oath.

Bruce pushed the jammer to the side of the table and asked Mr. Conway to lie down. He examined the wound and turned to Greyson. "Got a knife?"

The kid looked at Mr. Conway, who gave him the approving nod, then took a knife from the side of his pants and handed it to Bruce.

"I don't have any anesthetic," Bruce said. "I have some at the clinic if you want to reconsider—"

"Pass me that whiskey," Oliver said, reaching towards Greyson with an open hand. Once he had the bottle, he took a big swig of it, downing large gulps. "Use the rest to disinfect," he said, handing the bottle to Bruce. He took off his belt and put the leather between his teeth.

Anita checked into her hotel room. It was still an early evening for her, but she wasn't interested in exploring Clamerton. She'd been here before, and she hadn't found the old buildings very compelling. They were in the process of building an entertainment district with cafes, restaurants, and clubs. A shiny new hotel was being planned as well, but that was a few months away yet. So she checked into the same hotel she'd stayed at last time, which still offered some luxury, including fresh sheets and decent room service.

She looked at the television screen mounted on the wall. They'd stopped broadcasting the conference now and had moved on to a segment Anita had sent them the day before in which she'd interviewed a winemaker. It was a fluff piece requested by The Citizen, meant to inject some positivity into the coverage of current events.

The post-war world was, after all, healing. The man had explained to her how he grew the grapes and turned them into wine. There wasn't anything particularly newsworthy in the segment. The man was much like other employers these days: constantly complaining about his workforce not being committed or dependable. A pointless rant. Anita turned off the display.

Someone knocked on the door. Anita opened it without hesitation and let in a servant, who set down a thermos of fresh coffee, a couple of small ceramic cups, and a selection of complimentary pastries. She had ordered the coffee for herself, but the staff had assumed she had company. It was unusual for a respectable woman to be alone in a hotel room.

The girl picked up the thermos to fill the cup, but Anita stopped her. "I'll serve myself."

"Yes, ma'am." The maid set the coffee down, curtsied, and left, closing the door behind her.

Anita unscrewed the thermos and poured the coffee into the provided cup. Steam immediately rose from the hot liquid. She grabbed the cup and walked out onto the balcony. The September night air was still warm but came with a fleeting sense that the weather would change in a matter of days. The summer was clearly over.

There wasn't much of a view from the balcony. The parking lot below was mostly empty, and the hotel itself wasn't very busy at this time of year. Only those who came to World United on important business came outside of summer.

Anita stared ahead of her. *Who are you, Conway?* She sipped her coffee, absorbing the view of the forest on the other side of the street. The trees were mostly green, but some leaves were beginning to turn yellow and red. *Who are you?* A robin flew up from the canopies, shrieking in alarm, but the source of the danger wasn't visible.

Anita sipped more of the rich coffee and retreated to her room, grabbed her tablet from her bag, and walked into the bedroom. She sat down on the bed, her back against the headboard, and placed her coffee cup on the nightstand. She logged into her device and scanned through her notes on Conway.

"Two years ago, no one knew who you were," Anita mumbled to herself. "The war created you, Conway." Before that, he didn't exist. There was no record of property ownership or education certificates.

Had somebody homeschooled him? He'd clearly taken more than just basic literacy classes, so he must have had an education, which cost money. If he or his family had money, why couldn't she find anything about them?

She grabbed the coffee from the nightstand and took another sip. The liquid was still warm, but cooler now on her lips.

If he didn't come from money, where had he gotten such a large sum? The war had created a lot of opportunities and some people had gotten richer, but being very smart about it and not getting caught and tried for war crimes was the key. Was that the reason he was friends with the past and current War Crimes Commissioners of World United? Commissioner Leggett had been murdered more than a year ago. It had happened right in the hotel she was staying at. There had been news reports of some jealous boyfriend killing him. The story hadn't added up, though, because Leggett wasn't the only man that girl had been sleeping with. Anita had investigated that months ago, and she trusted her sources.

The newly-appointed Commissioner for War Crimes, Lars Johansen, had paused all investigations into war atrocities. There had been no new developments, and each time the press requested an update, Lars replied that the matter was complicated, and information needed to be verified before being made public. He called for patience and trust. Anita was certain, however, that nothing was actually being done.

Sābanto was most puzzling. Conway had clearly gotten his money from somewhere. There was no proof it was from war crimes, but she wouldn't put it past him. He was smart and educated. He could analyze the risks and opportunities of his decisions, so why had Conway entangled himself in Sābanto? How was he profiting from this? It was a tax-funded operation run by World United and there was no money to be made.

If not for money, then what? Having his face on the displays undoubtedly gives him some fame, but he hadn't seemed to enjoy the attention at the conference. It was possible that he was thinking of himself as a replacement for the Health Commissioner, although he hadn't yet openly opposed Scholtz, who currently occupied the seat, or made any moves to be a possible candidate for the position. He might not have a lot of power outside of Sābanto, but inside the compound walls, he dictated everything. Was that it? A feeling of superiority and the need to take advantage of others for his own gain? His arrogance when she met with him in the hallway had been obvious. He knew very well what was happening in the compounds, and he simply didn't care.

Anita took another sip of her coffee. To her surprise the cup was almost empty. She must have unconsciously drunk it as she was thinking. She put the cup back down on the nightstand. She added another entry to the document on the tablet, starting with a date.

*Mr. Conway appeared at the conference today. He looked cold and hostile when questioned about Sābanto. When talking about Sābanto, he referred to the decision-makers in the third person as World United, removing any responsibility, distancing himself from the new laws that dictated who would be sent to Sābanto. Did he disapprove of what he was communicating, or was he just bitter about being presented with these questions? It was hard to tell. Later, in the hallway, he'd looked visibly sick. The illness and cause were unknown; however, Mr. Conway is known for indulging in tobacco and alcohol . . . but never anything cheap.*

He'd seemed very sick. Anita looked up from the tablet. Whatever it was, he'd need a doctor. Who *was* his doctor, anyway? She got up from the bed, picked up the thermos full of coffee, and refilled her cup.

*Start from the beginning.* "Time to visit Covedale." She sipped more of the steaming beverage.

## 3

IVY'S EYES FILLED WITH tears as Mrs. Harris pulled on her copper red hair that she had foolishly worn down that morning. The woman was in her thirties and had her dark blonde hair fashionably styled into an updo. She stood on a little podium while Ivy knelt on the floor in front of her. She was average in build, not very athletic by any standard, but her grip on Ivy's hair was painfully firm.

They were at the Leggett factory in Covedale. Ivy had decorated the private fitting room in cotton candy pink, with soft carpet and tall mirrors surrounded by expensive wallpaper specifically imported for this space from Asia. The air was lightly scented with floral perfume for the pleasure of the factory clients. She had designed these rooms when she was first put in charge of the tailored luxury clothing line for the upper-crust clientele.

Mrs. Harris had come in this afternoon. She wanted some adjustments to the dress Ivy had made for her the previous year. It was a flowing red dress that ended just above the knees; the perfect length for her. It hid her wide hips and thick thighs while drawing attention to her narrow waist. The shade of red they'd chosen went perfectly with Mrs. Harris's complexion.

"Please, Mrs. Harris. You're hurting me," Ivy pleaded. Their conversation had begun pleasantly, but as soon as Ivy had explained her decisions on the dress's design, the woman had become angry and unreasonable.

"This dress needs to be redone!" Mrs. Harris's face was as red as the dress she was wearing.

"Ma'am, there's nothing wrong with the dress." Trends had changed this summer, and the design had slightly fallen out of fashion, but Ivy had perfectly cut, assembled, and fitted the dress last year.

"I'm telling you to bring it higher!"

Why should she comply with the request? Agreeing and redoing the dress would undermine her and the company. More ladies might come back and demand free alterations. She couldn't allow such behavior. She preferred to make new dresses rather than alter the old ones. "If I do it, I'll ruin the dress," she said firmly trying to free herself from Mrs. Harris.

"Then don't ruin it!" the woman insisted tightening her grip. "What kind of seamstress are you? If you can't make the changes, then get me someone who can."

Ivy was head seamstress. Her opinion should matter, but arguing was pointless. The more she resisted, the more hair Mrs. Harris pulled out, but she couldn't do the impossible. "Ma'am, we no longer have the material to make the changes you're asking for." Ivy's tone had become firmer as she attempted to stand up for herself.

"When Mr. Conway was running this company, I never had these issues! Whatever that new owner, Roberts, is paying you, you don't deserve it!" Mrs. Harris pulled on Ivy's hair harder, and she cried out.

"Ma'am, you're hurting me," Ivy pleaded for the woman to stop. Mrs. Harris had probably yanked a fistful of her hair out already.

"I'll never shop here again," the woman said and pulled Ivy, who was barely able to stand, along behind her as she exited the change room.

Mrs. Harris walked into the waiting room with her head high and a sure step. Ivy was bent over, barely keeping up with the woman.

"I'll find Mr. Roberts and I'll make sure he fires you! Then they can take you to Sābanto and out of my sight!"

*Sure, go and find Mr. Roberts,* Ivy mocked her customer in her mind. *We'll see what he says.*

There were other people in the waiting room, but Mrs. Harris was oblivious to what was happening around her. She released Ivy, shoving her hard into the reception desk.

Ivy gasped as her body came crashing into the polished wooden tabletop. She braced herself with her hands before standing up straight and smoothing her hair and dress, putting everything in its place. She smiled and turned around to confront Mrs. Harris, noticing a strange young man standing in the door of her showroom as she did so.

"Good afternoon, Mrs. Harris," he said. He was smiling, probably amazed by the situation he just witnessed. The man's dark hair was styled and falling lightly in waves onto the forehead of his square face.

"There's nothing *good* about it, Mr. Menken," the woman fumed. Her face went red again, but this time she was ashamed of being caught in a situation that didn't reflect well on her social standing. She glared at Ivy—her eyes were intense, brows drawn together—then stormed out of the factory, muttering something under her breath.

Ivy smiled. A small victory. No doubt her freckled face was red from the pain, and the humiliation, but there was nothing she could do about that, nor about the tears that filled her eyes and blurred her vision. She smoothed her hair down again and turned toward the man at the door. "Good afternoon, sir," she said with a forced full smile. "How can we help you?"

He smiled back at her warmly. "Liam Menken," he introduced himself. "I know my new suit was to be delivered tomorrow, but since I am here in Covedale on business, I thought I could pick it up."

"Of course, Mr. Menken," Ivy said. Ivy's assistant, a girl who had until now been waiting patiently behind the desk, not interfering, disappeared through the shop door in search of the man's suit.

"Is there anything else we can do for you, Mr. Menken?" Ivy asked while they waited. She didn't want to make eye contact with the stranger, nor did she know how to fill the awkward silence after that embarrassing scene with Mrs. Harris.

"No, that'll be all," the man said and smiled widely as he added, "Please call me Liam." Ivy noticed dimples on his cheeks.

"We're glad to be of service," Ivy replied. She averted her eyes as though she were looking at something behind the desk.

Luckily her assistant brought out the suit, breaking the tension that lingered in the waiting room.

"Have a great evening, Mr. Menken," Ivy called.

"Liam," he corrected and smiled. He then turned to the door. Ivy's assistant followed him out, holding the suit in her hands.

Ivy sighed and slumped into one of the waiting room armchairs. She absently watched the display on the wall and listened to the interview.

"You can produce double the amount of steel with the same number of workers," the anchor said. "How do you do that?" He passed the microphone to the man sitting beside him.

"It's easy, you know," the man replied. "I'll explain. They wanted me to give the workers a place to live. I carved out living quarters for them in the steel plant, so now they don't need as much time to get to and from their workstations." The man was gesticulating with his hand that wasn't holding the microphone. "We also provide them with meals, so they don't need to waste hours cooking. But they were bored, and boredom only leads to crime and stupid ideas. So the extra hours saved, they now spend working. They only need eight hours of sleep."

The assistant opened the door and stepped back inside after hanging Liam's suit in his car. Ivy turned off the display. She was exhausted after her eight-hour shift and Mrs. Harris's abhorrent behavior. She was ready to head home.

Ivy's afternoon walk from the factory was quiet. The road parallel to the river was practically deserted, with only a few people hurrying by. There were no rickshaws, no loud conversations or random laughter erupting anymore. No kids ran past her, chasing ducks or geese. The washers, who used to sit under the willow trees, weren't coming to the river anymore. With electricity, everyone who was still around had water pumped up to their houses.

She passed the old barbershop. The owner was no longer waiting for his clients at the entrance. It was permanently closed. The bakery was still there, but the display of pastries in the window was no longer required. No random passersby to stop and indulge in the sugary treats. The kids who once stood in front of the bakery, devouring the pastries with their eyes, were nowhere to be found. All baked goods were ordered in advance now and delivered directly to the customers.

Ivy strolled down the empty street for a few minutes and stopped beside a dirt path leading to the riverbank. The slowly moving water was just a few meters away. She looked at the old bench made from a log that stood close to the shore. She sat there for a moment each time she passed it on her way home. She found comfort in watching the waves hitting the shore rhythmically. They, at least, hadn't changed.

Someone was sitting on one edge of the bench—a well-dressed woman—but Ivy didn't mind. She wanted to spend some time looking at the burned city that reminded her of what she had lost. She walked down the steep riverbank and quietly sat on the other end of the bench, ignoring the stranger. She was not interested in a conversation.

The ruins of the city on the other side of the river towered above her. Just a month ago, they'd been gray and eerie, with concrete and steel sticking out into the sky. Now they were black, darkened from the fire. Riverlea somehow looked more evil than it had before. Ivy remembered walking there through the ruins with Mark beside her before the city had burned. He wasn't here anymore. He'd died there in Riverlea. Ivy's eyes welled with tears.

The acrid smell still lingered. It smelled even stronger on windy days, when the gusts brought the odor in. World United had left Riverlea to burn out on its own. They had only bothered to protect the bank of the river where Covedale stood. Fire brigades had been on constant alert, seeking out and extinguishing any burning embers that traveled across the river. It had taken a month and the city had only stopped burning a few days ago, once the heavy fall rains had begun.

"What happened?" the woman sitting on the bench asked without turning to Ivy. She was looking ahead of her at the ruins as well.

"It burned," Ivy replied and shrugged. What else could she say? How could she explain the pain, the tragedy she was carrying in her heart, to a stranger?

The woman nodded. "What happened to the people?"

"Sābanto evacuated them. Tuberculosis, they said." That was the official answer that the radio had provided.

"Lies," the woman said, as though reading Ivy's mind. "Was it tuberculosis that made them evacuate Covedale as well? That all sounds like bullshit, you know."

Ivy kept quiet. She listened to the river and the waves.

The woman sat up and turned her body to Ivy. "Anita Gibala," she introduced herself and extended her hand.

Ivy glanced at the woman and recognized her. She had seen her on the video display. She shook the reporter's hand out of politeness. "Ivy Roberts."

Anita watched her attentively, but must have noticed that Ivy wasn't very interested in further conversation because she added, "No one wants to talk with me about Riverlea."

Ivy shrugged. "Dreadful memories," she said, trying to dissuade the reporter from asking any questions.

Anita got up from the bench and offered Ivy her business card. "Please, if you need someone to talk to."

Ivy smiled as the journalist thanked her for taking the card. She wouldn't take the journalist up on the offer, but she didn't feel that refusing the card would be polite. She took it from Anita's hand and glanced at it. *The Citizen*, it said.

Anita took her leave and scaled the river bank up to the street. Ivy, left alone on the bench, put the card between the pages of the book she was holding.

She brought her head up and stared at the ruins again. Her mind wandered.

Some thirty years ago, before her time, before she'd even been born, the city on the other side of the river had apparently been full of life. Old women told stories of the grand skyscrapers, parks, shops, and restaurants. The big city, full of glamor. People from Covedale had visited Riverlea for fun. Ivy had trouble imagining how it might've looked. She only remembered the ruins that reached the sky. Between them were people living in makeshift houses. There were some shacks here in Covedale as well. She lived in one of these. It was one room made from wood and metal boards. Down there, however, it was much different. Ivy remembered. She'd been there. She'd seen it. Thousands of people crammed into small alleys and what used to be parks and roads. Their shacks were sometimes so small that they couldn't stand up straight or stretch their legs during sleep.

Ivy opened the book she was carrying to the page where she'd slid the business card. It was a book of poems, written by people who had died a long time ago. She read a random phrase. Her reading was still slow and careful, but the more she read the better she became at it. The heroic men in the poem were rebuilding the world under the light of the stars. She couldn't imagine that the world was as broken then, when the poem was written, as it was now.

A sudden gust of wind turned the page on her as she read. Ivy closed the book. She didn't fight the wind as it grew stronger, but she moved her hair from her eyes, pushing the strands off her forehead with her hand and facing the wind that blew in the moist air.

A strong breeze was coming from the ocean. The sky was dark with heavy clouds, threatening rain. Usually Ivy would sit in this spot reading for some time, but today she couldn't stay here long.

A few months ago, Ivy had been experiencing the best days of her life. She'd gotten her dream job as a seamstress at Leggett factory and fallen in love with Mark Rodden. Had it all just been a dream?

Her memories took her back to Riverlea and to the small apartment where Mark had lived. She smiled to herself, recalling the moments they'd spent together. She remembered being safely wrapped in his warm arms, listening to stories from his youth or reading a book together. She recalled his passionate kisses that had sent shivers through her body. It was obvious to her at the time that he had loved her . . . but had he? He had never uttered those three words she'd longed to hear him say.

Mark had said he was protecting her. That was why he'd sent her away to Covedale, the safe side of the river. He had promised her that he'd follow right behind her and escape as well. They were supposed to reunite, but he had broken that promise.

Mark had written her a goodbye letter and set up a bank account in her name. What for? Clearly he'd known he'd die. Why hadn't he done anything to save himself? Instead, he had made arrangements for her ownership of the Leggett factory, which he'd bought for her from Mr. Conway. Mark had secured her future so that she wouldn't have to worry about money.

He'd taught her how the elites behave and how they carry themselves. She had laughed, with tears in her eyes, while she imagined being someone else in the company of the upper class. Is that why he'd invited her to his classroom? To make a lady out of her? It made sense when she imagined accompanying him to a ball or a casual business meeting. It would have been shameful for a man of his stature to show up for important events with a village girl who didn't know how to behave herself. It would be a scandal.

With Mark gone, everything lost its meaning, but she felt that she must continue what he had started. Why? She wasn't sure why, and she feared what lay ahead.

Ivy felt exposed and vulnerable knowing that Mark was never coming back to protect her. She wanted one more embrace. Was that too much to ask?

Ivy clenched her teeth. Why did she keep thinking about him and reopening the wound she carried in her heart? Mark was gone. "Fuck you, Mark," she mumbled to herself as she sprang up onto her feet. She had to move on. There was no reason to dwell on the past.

Ivy scaled the short but steep riverbank back to the road. She turned left and continued along the river. The wind grew stronger and pushed her from behind. Her hair flew in front of her. She raised her right hand and held her hair together in a ponytail, keeping it out of her face.

She passed some workers on the street fixing the roads and the sidewalks and planting flowers in the big concrete pots. Town council had removed the weeds and discarded them. They'd said they were beautifying the town; that nothing ugly had the right to exist there. The town had changed. The old Covedale was no longer there.

Ivy walked the same path each time she returned home from work. It was a detour, making her afternoon walk longer. She turned right onto the wide street leading towards the town square. She had lived here, right on this street. The packed soil and the concrete pavement slabs had been the floor of her house. She saw the trees and potholes were still there, but the city had demolished the slums, most of which had been falling apart anyway. The familiar chatter of people sitting on the ground in front of their homes and talking with their neighbors was gone. Mothers were no longer shouting at their kids who squealed either with laughter or from the punishment they were receiving. The wind was the only sound that echoed through the emptiness.

The new mayor said he'd make a park here, with trees and walkways. He envisioned people enjoying strolling along or sitting on the benches. This area would serve the community of Covedale, he said. But what was a community without people?

The people who had lived here, probably three-quarters of the population of Covedale, had been moved to the Sābanto compounds down south. Those who remained, survivors of the evacuation they called themselves, worked for a master or a local business. Her friends, family, and neighbors had all grabbed whatever they could carry and left.

There were many who'd resisted. Fights had erupted on the streets of Covedale. Some slums and houses had burned down. People had broken into businesses and destroyed them.

Ivy could've gone with the others, or persuaded her family—at least her mother, who worked as a washer—to stay with her rather than going to Sābanto. She could've provided for her, but her mother refused. She didn't want to be a burden, she'd said. Whatever that meant. Ivy would've preferred to carry that burden than be left alone like she was now.

"The world ain't the same," her mother had said, leaving. "Ya meant for better things. Ya special." Her mother's words still resonated in her mind. "Follow ya heart, girl. Don't ya worry about me," she'd said, dismissing Ivy's concerns with a wave of her hand.

Ivy didn't know where her heart would lead her. It was stuck somewhere in the past, and for the first time it feared what awaited it in the future.

She turned right again onto main street. Another quiet road. Before the forced relocation, kids would play here in the sewers at this time of day. There had been laughter and, despite the hardship of living, there had been happiness. That old world was now gone. Was the new one better with Sābanto?

Ivy stopped beside the row of large windows of her new home. Once she had taken over the factory, she'd bought a house from Mrs. Woodham, whose husband Leo was still missing. People speculated that he had been in Riverlea when it burned and that he'd died in the fire.

Ivy looked up at the facade. She'd fallen in love with the place, especially her namesake climbing up one side of the house and the quiet garden at the back. Was it really hers? It had more rooms than she'd ever need. *Accept this life, Ivy.* Wasn't that why Mark had left her the Leggett factory and all his money? She wasn't sure she could accept it. *Follow your heart.* Ivy recalled her mother's words. She wished it were that easy.

# 4

I VY WALKED UP THE few front steps and into her house. The closed door brought a welcome respite from the glare of daylight and soothed her eyes. She stood there for a moment, looking around at the familiar hallway. The builders had installed two elaborate silver-and-crystal chandeliers in the high hall ceilings, which highlighted the dark wood staircase with carved posts and railings. They had covered the walls in dark navy wallpaper accented with a silver print that reminded her of a sky full of stars.

The house was quiet, but the smell of dinner filled the hallway. Julia, her only household staff member, was in the kitchen preparing it. It was fine that no one greeted her at the door—Ivy could still take care of herself. She didn't need Julia to serve her all the time and follow her everywhere. Her maid didn't have to be like the other maids she'd seen in residences who tip-toed around their masters.

Ivy and Julia had lived in the same slum alley, but had never been close friends. When Sābanto had started to take people away, Julia begged Ivy for some kind of job so she could stay. The girl had said that she didn't want to be forced to leave and lose her boyfriend, Greyson. Why not? Having a familiar face in the house was also a plus. It had been a month now, and they'd both learned to work together even if Julia was a little too bossy sometimes.

Ivy removed her flats, which had been pinching her feet in many places and rubbing against her heels all day. Barefoot, she walked to the stairs to the left side of the hallway and descended the beige marble steps to the basement. The dinner aromas were stronger there, toying with her empty stomach.

At the bottom of the stairs, she glanced right at the long corridor and the doors to the servants' rooms. There had originally been a separate staff barracks here, but Ivy hadn't purchased it as part of the property. Why buy it if she wouldn't force Julia to sleep there, anyway? Julia was needed in the house. She kept Ivy company. Loneliness? No, Ivy wasn't afraid of it. There was already plenty of room for both of them and any other servants she would need to hire.

Ivy turned left and entered the large kitchen. To her right were cupboards and counters at which Julia was busy making dinner. She stood at the stove mixing something in a big pot. Above her hung a large stone chimney which had been used more when the wood-fired oven had been there, but that had been replaced with an electric appliance.

In the middle of the kitchen, above a large island, hung pots and polished skillets shone, reflecting the overhead lights. On her left there was a simple table with six chairs. A young man with short dark blond hair already sat at it. He must have been the new staff member that Ivy had been waiting for. She'd requested someone capable of doing house repairs and preparing the grounds for winter.

The man was watching the screen on the wall above him. It was showing current news. His back was to the entrance of the kitchen, and he hadn't noticed Ivy come in.

"The efforts of World United to end the poverty of millions of people aren't being fully appreciated," the anchor said. "Our reporter, Anita Gibala, sent us this footage last night. A standoff between the villagers of Plano and the Sābanto Black Shirts ended with five dead and many wounded." The display showed civilians being taken away. They were shouting at law enforcement. Their hands were bound behind their backs. A different camera view showed them being shoved into waiting vans. The men in black uniforms who were escorting them had the familiar large print on their backs reading "Sābanto." The news reminded Ivy of the evacuations of Riverlea and Covedale. Those too had turned violent. *They shouldn't be forcing people out like that,* she thought. *They should have a choice.*

"They should just go willingly," Julia commented without looking at the display, but then noticed Ivy in the kitchen and turned towards her. "How was the factory?" she asked.

"It was alright," Ivy replied and walked directly towards the man, who got up. She extended her hand towards him across the table. He shook it gently, taking a quick up-and-down glance at her.

He was just slightly taller than Ivy and narrow in the shoulders. She thought of Mark when she first saw the stranger in front of her, but she couldn't pinpoint exactly why. This man bore little resemblance to the man she loved. He was of similar build and height, but that was where the parallels ended. The stranger's eyes were lighter in color and not framed with thick, black eyelashes. His skin was also a darker shade that contrasted more with her own.

"Ivy," she introduced herself and smiled.

"Taylor," he replied.

"I'm guessing you're the man that Sābanto said they were sending us," Ivy said. "I hope you're good with a ladder. There are many high places in this house."

"I'm capable." Taylor smiled.

Ivy sat opposite him at the table with her back to Julia and the kitchen. She leaned forward and rested her elbows on the tabletop. "Did Julia give you a tour of the house?" she asked.

"Yes," he said, and sat down himself, dragging the chair noisily on the floor as he pulled it closer to the table. "Some things need work."

Ivy leaned back in her chair as Taylor sat down. He was a bit too close. The extra space made her more comfortable.

The news continued, and they glanced up together at the display.

"World United is meeting this week to discuss people's proof of employment," the anchor said, and passed the microphone to the guest speaker in the studio.

"Every employee outside of Sābanto needs documents signed by their employers as proof of work. We're phasing out this impractical process in favor of a system using bracelets that employees can't easily remove. Stay with The Citizen for—"

Julia set a plate full of soft buns on the table, then walked up to the display and turned it off. Without making eye contact with those sitting at the table, Julia retreated back to the cooking area of the kitchen.

"First time in Covedale?" Ivy asked. She noticed how interested Taylor was in the food in front of him. White bread. Many people had never tasted it in their lives. Ivy could afford it now and treat herself.

"I'm not familiar with town," Taylor replied. "What's with the burned city?"

"We don't talk about it here," Julia stated, coming over again and putting a shiny box of butter on the table.

Ivy agreed; she wasn't in the mood to talk about Riverlea. She continued the conversation but changed the topic. "Welcome to Covedale, then. What did you do before?"

"I did a couple years in a quarry," he replied.

Ivy felt Taylor's eyes fixed on her as she grabbed a bun and ripped it in half with her hands, then covered it thoroughly with a thick layer of butter. She'd loved butter ever since she'd first tried it and, much like a child, she had a hard time restraining herself.

"This summer I did some garden work," Taylor continued without breaking his stare. "But the doctor in Sābanto said that I shouldn't carry heavy things regularly; old leg injury from the quarry days. I got assigned to the service."

Ivy took a bite of the soft roll and gestured to Taylor to help himself to the buns as well. They were still very warm. There was no reason for him to be shy. Plenty of buns for all of them. She smiled at him and encouraged him to follow her lead, but quickly averted her eyes from his stare.

"I need to talk to the neighbors tomorrow and figure out how they order parts," he continued. "I'd like to ask them for maintenance tips." He grabbed one of the buns and followed Ivy's example of ripping it open and buttering it.

"Dinner's ready," Julia called from the other end of the kitchen. An announcement about dinner. That was new. Ivy turned and looked at Julia, but the maid wasn't looking at her. Julia was looking in Taylor's direction. "Come help me carry the soup," she ordered, pointing at the terrine on the counter with her chin.

Ivy frowned. Normally, the maid brought the food over herself, and she didn't need any help. Julia was already trying to boss the new guy around.

Ivy got up and said, "I don't mind helping." She picked up the terrine from the counter and carried it effortlessly to the table. Julia sighed and followed Ivy with a set of plates and spoons. The maid didn't protest Ivy's help, but she muttered something under her breath.

At the table, Julia grabbed Ivy's plate and spooned the soup into it without even glancing at Taylor. Ivy sat back down in her chair and the maid put a full plate in front of her.

"Anything new?" Julia asked while serving Taylor.

"Mrs. Harris came in," Ivy replied. "She asked me to ruin the dress I made for her last year." She grabbed a spoon, but waited for Julia to finish plating before she began eating.

"What do ya mean, ruin?" Julia sounded curious. The maid served herself as well and sat down, and they started eating. The soup was nothing fancy—Julia wasn't a great cook, but the meal was adequate.

"She told me the dress was no longer in fashion and she wanted me to shorten it," Ivy replied.

"Can't ya?" Julia asked.

"I don't have that material anymore. A shorter dress would also look terrible on her."

"Is that so?" Julia commented. Contrary to her words, she no longer showed interested in the story. She was more absorbed with the food in front of her.

Ivy brought her head up from the soup and met Taylor's amber eyes. She blushed as she did so, and he smiled slightly. "I can't make changes that'd look ridiculous and jeopardize the good name of the factory," Ivy replied to Julia. She averted her eyes, but couldn't shake off her embarrassment. It was foolish of her to be so conscious of Taylor's attractiveness. These thoughts were intrusive and inappropriate. Was she betraying Mark somehow? Mark, who was no longer there. Why did she still care so much about him? She brought the full spoon up and glanced at Taylor again. His eyes were still fixed on her. Suddenly she lost her grip and the utensil almost slipped out of her hand. She recovered at the last second and avoided spilling soup all over the table.

"What did she do when ya told her no?" Julia asked, oblivious to the tension around her.

"She left furious," Ivy replied, composing herself. "But I know she'll be back soon enough for a new dress. She won't find better craftsman-ship anywhere."

"I bet. The factory has lots of other customers," Julia replied.

Ivy agreed with her. "We don't need Mrs. Harris's money—"

"What do ya make?" Taylor interrupted. "Dresses?"

Ivy nodded, then put a spoonful into her mouth and swallowed. "But we mostly make the clothes for the Sābanto residents, the staff, and the Sābanto Green and Black Shirts. I'm sure you've seen our Leggett trims on them." The contract with Sābanto would keep the factories going for many years. "Oh, there was a new person in the store today," Ivy added, looking at Julia. "A young man. Mr. Menken, I think he said. Liam Menken." She recalled the man's kind smile and his gray eyes which looked straight through her.

Julia said nothing. The maid probably hadn't even heard what she'd said.

Once they finished eating, Taylor broke the silence by saying, "I got a document that needs to be signed by Mr. Roberts."

"Show me." Ivy extended her hand and grabbed the document that was handed to her. The bracelet system was still in being implemented, and the authorities required paperwork to be in order. If workers had a missing signature, they risked being held for questioning at the Sābanto offices.

"How's he, anyway?" Taylor asked.

"I like him," Julia replied with a malicious grin, "but Mrs. Roberts is best."

Ivy lowered her head to look at the document in her hand and smiled. She couldn't help herself. She didn't approve of Julia lying, but the situation was rather amusing.

Taylor adjusted his position in his chair. "They feed well." He smiled. Ivy made sure Julia always put generous amounts of meat in their meals. The soups were thick and nutritious, though a few more herbs wouldn't hurt. Ivy was happy that Taylor liked the food. "Is it just three employees here?"

"Just us three," Julia replied. She enthusiastically got up and started to clean the table, starting with the empty plates.

"I normally don't sleep in the house," Taylor commented. "The rooms are big too. Last place we all lived in a shed. We had to fight to get a stove for the winter. Living here will make me feel like I'm the master of the house." Taylor laughed.

"Told ya, Mrs. Roberts cares for us well," Julia said loudly from the other side of the kitchen. She noisily set the dirty plates down on the counter.

Ivy looked up from the document in front of her and sighed. "I guess the master of the house has to sign it," she said. She grabbed the pen from the counter behind her and scribbled her name at the bottom of the page.

Taylor sprung up from his chair, making a lot of noise as he did. His hands were behind his back, and he'd lowered his head. All this time he'd truly had no idea who she was.

Ivy smiled at him. There was something comical about his reaction. "You can relax, Taylor. Please sit down." She wasn't mad at him. Many masters were gravely insulted if a servant even looked at them, but Ivy wasn't like that. Her staff didn't have to pay her these kinds of respects. She was no different from them. Ivy laid the pen down on the table and lightly pushed the signed document towards Taylor. "Please sit," she said again. "I'm sorry. I assumed Julia told you I'd be dining with you."

Julia, however, was absent. It wasn't unexpected that the dishes were right at this moment in need of special attention.

Once Taylor sat down, Ivy added, "You can speak if you like."

"I'm sorry, ma'am," he said.

"There's nothing to be sorry about," Ivy said. "Just a misunderstanding. It's all right to look at me."

"I was told . . ." He trailed off, bringing his head up. He met Ivy's eyes.

Ivy smiled widely. She felt bad, but it was funny. "As you can see, Julia doesn't curtsy in front of me. I don't want you to, either." Her voice was calm.

Taylor contemplated this for a moment. "Yes, ma'am," he said and lowered his head again. He grabbed the paper from the table, folded it, and put it into his pocket without saying a word.

The maid returned and sat down beside Ivy. Julia didn't apologize for her behavior at the table. They'd spent a few hours at most together and there was obvious friction between them. Something had made Julia sour. She broke the awkward silence by changing the focus of the conversation as though nothing out of the ordinary had happened. "I packed ya bags for the trip."

"You probably packed more than I need," Ivy replied.

"Just the essentials, and ya won't be carrying them anyway. I'll tell Taylor and he'll load the car in the morning when the driver gets in. Servants will unload them and put them in ya room at the hotel."

"I'm only going for a week," said Ivy. "I don't need much."

"But I heard there's a heated pool and walking trails. Ya also need something nicer for the evening. I thought of everything."

"I'm too tired to argue with you, Julia. If I don't wear it, I'll just bring it back."

"Exactly ma thoughts."

"Thank you," Ivy replied. "I'll go upstairs and pick some books to take with me."

Taylor was still sitting silent and motionless at the table. Ivy turned towards him. "It was nice meeting you, Taylor."

"Yes, ma'am," he replied formally. He now avoided eye contact with her at all costs. Taylor would need some time to recover. *Guilt and embarrassment take time to fade away.*

Ivy got up to leave and Taylor sprang up as well, out of respect. "Sorry, ma'am," he said again.

"I hope you like it here," Ivy replied, and walked out of the kitchen. She ascended the dark wooden stairs to her bedroom and glanced out the wide window. It was wet. The rain had already begun.

It wasn't ten yet, but she undressed and put on her silk pajamas. She then brushed her teeth and lay down in her bed under the soft covers. Ivy curled up and hugged herself. The sheets would warm up faster that way. She had no interest in reading tonight. She was feeling the weight of everything. Even the ceiling above her seemed closer than it really was. She lay paralyzed, motionless, listening to the rain. The drops hit the window and the roof above her.

Ivy was alone in this enormous house. She had no family or friends she could turn to. There was no one she could call or visit. No one to accompany her to the market for the evening's discounted loaf of dark bread.

Julia would finish cleaning the kitchen now that dinner was over, and then she would probably leave the house to meet with Greyson. He worked for Mr. Conway and it wasn't far for Julia to walk, though on rainy evenings like this one, she would likely take a rickshaw to his place. She'd spend the evening there, then come back late or before dawn so she could start breakfast.

Taylor seemed nice. Younger than she'd expected. Sābanto could've sent someone more experienced. She smiled, recalling how awkward Taylor had been at dinner. It was Julia's fault. He'd learn to relax over time. Ivy was a person, not a master.

She was no longer the girl from the slums. She was someone else. A factory owner with thousands saved up in the bank. *So impressive,* she thought, mockingly. But really, who was she? An illiterate. Nobody. A freak with red hair, a pink face, and skin so pale one could see her blue veins. A tear rolled down her cheek.

She got up and grabbed her stuffed doll from the shelf. She had made it herself from some old rags as a child. It had been one of her first sewing projects. Its fabric was no longer colorful, but grayed from constant use.

Ivy lay down under the sheets and held the toy close to her as she curled up again. She squeezed the doll tightly against her chest. For some reason the comfort she craved from the toy didn't come. Everyone who really cared for her was gone. "Where are you, Mark?" she called out softly. "Why did you abandon me?"

She quietly sang a lullaby in between her sobs and sniffles. The song her mother had sung to her as a baby. The lyrics were an assurance, an agreement that those she loved would never leave her. Now it seemed like an empty promise. There was, however, something soothing about the song that Ivy had trouble putting her finger on. The comfort of something familiar. An anchor to the past. She kept singing the words from memory until she sang herself to sleep.

# 5

C AT WAS IN A large gym with a soft floor that muffled the sound of heavy footsteps and protected the trainees from unnecessary injuries when they hit the ground. The air in the room was thick with the smell of sweat from all the bodies that had exercised there that day.

"Ya choice," said Ken, the Green Shirt officer in her compound. He pointed at the wall of different exercise weapons. The previous day, Cat had met Ken and he'd had said he could get her into the Green Shirts if she showed him her skills.

Cat walked up to the wall. The selection of handheld weapons at the gym was pretty good. She knew she could fight him with any of those on display. There was an assortment of training weapons of different sizes—swords, clubs, ropes, and more. She grabbed a bō staff. Nothing beat a familiar weapon. She held it right in the middle to weigh it. It was adequately balanced.

Cat returned to the center of the room with the bō in her hand. She faced Ken and placed her staff in a vertical position to her right. Ken went to the wall and grabbed the same weapon that she had chosen. *Let's see who's weak.* The fool actually thought he could beat her. Ken had chosen the place and time, and mocked her for not having what it took to be a Green Shirt. Overconfidence, the undoing of many a good fighter.

They started by avoiding each other's swings. Cat refrained from showing off her advanced skills. She tested the waters and blocked his moves rather than attacking him. Much as she'd expected, Ken was taking it easy on her. He'd assumed she was a weak fighter, that he would be better than her. What he didn't realize was that she'd barely even broken a sweat yet.

Soon Ken grew tired and became sloppy with his moves. Cat began to attack him more often and it angered him. Emotion now drove his actions, not discipline, and he was using more force than necessary. Cat blocked and dodged most of his swings and took advantage of his incorrect posture to get hits in. His desperate attempts to shield himself were imprecise, and she struck him where it hurt. Often.

As they fought, more people came to watch the spectacle. A large audience filled the room and circled them, loudly cheering on both sides. Ken had invited his friends to watch, and most of them were now rooting for Cat. They could see Ken's chances of winning were becoming slim.

Drops of sweat rolled down Cat's back and her muscles ached, but the man in front of her had blood slowly dripping from his broken nose onto his shirt. He no longer had the strength to shield himself from her blows, so Cat concentrated more on defense to tire him. A little bit longer and he would be forced to quit. She took another stance and waited for Ken as he readied himself for his next attack.

"What's happening here?" An angry voice shouted from the open door.

Cat recognized the uniform of a commander. She straightened herself and got into a waiting position with her bō on her right. The fight was over, but Ken hadn't noticed that the room had suddenly gone quiet. He *had* noticed Cat was no longer protecting herself, and was charging towards her.

Not much time to decide. She could either take the hit or dodge it. Cat met the attack with her extended bō. The two wooden staffs made a loud hollow sound in the otherwise quiet room. The blow hadn't disturbed her balance, and she remained in her standing position.

"Sorry, sir," she said as soon as she could, directing her voice to the commander who stood in front of them, watching their performance. He was a bald man in his sixties, wearing a Green Shirt uniform with distinct markings indicating his higher rank. Ken also now stood rigid beside Cat. An assault in front of his superior. Ken was sweating even more.

"What's happening here?" the commander repeated.

Cat stood still. The crowd quickly dispersed in fear of being found at the illegal fight and possibly punished for it. Only the three of them remained in the gym. The silence rang in her ears.

The commander turned to his officer. "Explain this to me." His voice was calmer now.

Ken glanced at Cat, then back at the commander. "She wanted to fight me, sir."

"Why?" the commander asked.

Ken didn't reply. Cat clenched her teeth, suppressing a smile as the commander came closer and looked at her. The commander had seen her skill. Today was her chance to get to the green shirt she'd been vying for.

Since the first day of her arrival more than a month ago, Cat had repeatedly applied to become a Green Shirt. They'd rejected her each time. She'd been marked as available for work placement, and they were considering sending her to some factory that was probably thousands of kilometers from where she was now. The women at the work placement laughed at her—a former prostitute wanting a decent job. Was it really that funny? She could work as a guard, but no one was interested in giving her a chance. Eventually they told her that they weren't hiring women. Why the hell not? There were women-only compounds just like this one.

"Why did you fight him?" the commander asked her.

"I was trying out to become a guard. Green Shirts, sir," she replied.

The commander examined her carefully, then turned to Ken who swallowed audibly. "Is that true?" he asked, but didn't wait for an answer. "I select the Green Shirt candidates in this compound." The commander clearly wasn't pleased. "Wash your bloody nose," he told Ken, then turned to both of them. "I'll see you both here tomorrow morning."

Cat sat down on the wooden bench in the changing area adjacent to the gym. She held her head up, leaning against the wall behind her, letting her body rest for a moment. Her breathing was still labored from the exercise. She closed her eyes.

Sweat drips down her back as she sits down on the hard floor of the large gymnasium. Tiny slivers of light pass inside through a row of large windows high up by the ceiling. The old green paint on the walls is peeling all over.

"I didn't ask for this," Cat says to her trainer. A few days of training, and she's already had enough. "Can't you just teach me how to use a gun? That's all I asked!"

"Anybody can shoot a gun," he says. "I don't know if ya wanna kill someone or if ya like to learn self-defense. I don't care." He shakes his head, circling the room as he continues, "Let's say ya meet ya opponent face to face. What if they have a gun too? Who do ya think would be faster?"

*Me, you fucking dumbass!*

"What if ya opponent is stronger and takes ya gun away from ya?" he continues. "Poof, ya gone." He stops beside her and looks her in the eyes. "What if there's someone else? Now ya have no gun, they have three."

He walks to the side of the room where different exercise aids sit on the concrete floor, away from the matted area. He picks up a weapon and tells her to get up. He throws it towards her and she catches it. It's a smooth wooden stick about two meters long with a clearly-marked center.

*What the fuck is she supposed to do with a stick?* she wonders.

"Wanna survive?" he asks. "Ya got to know how to fight and how to get ya gun back. Then ya shoot. Shooting is the easiest part." He chooses a similar stick for himself as he waits for Cat to respond, but she stays silent. "We only have a few months. Not a lot of time."

He's right. Her enemy isn't stupid, and she needs to be ready for him.

The instructor takes his place in front of her, then charges at her. She raises her stick and blocks him.

Cat absentmindedly scratched her left temple. Ever since she'd left Riverlea. She'd felt an itch there from the surgery. Was it a real or phantom feeling? She wasn't sure.

"Where did ya learn to fight like that?" Ken asked.

Cat immediately lowered her hand from her temple and opened her eyes, surprised to hear Ken in the changing room. She looked at him as he sat beside her. He had tissues hanging from his nostrils to stop the bleeding. Cat laughed out loud. His entire face was bruised, but his ego was the most battered.

Cat struggled to stop laughing, but she cooled down enough to reply, "Been around."

"Are ya always this much of a bitch?" he asked. His face had a crooked sneer. *Oh my.* When was the last time anyone had laughed at him?

"Yes," she said, and it angered him more. He got up from the bench and left with the tissues still in his nostrils.

Cat smiled widely at the door closing behind him. "Don't fuck with me!" she shouted after him. She was a bitch. A real fucking Covedale Bitch.

Cleaned up and bandaged, Oliver finally got home late the following evening. He was tired, but the pain was mostly gone thanks to the pills the doctor had given him.

The house was quiet. Only a single servant girl awaited his arrival. She helped him out of his coat, curtsied, and quickly left to put it away.

Oliver walked up the stairs to the bedroom. Sophia was already in bed. Recently, she'd say she was sleepy as soon as the sun went down. She blamed it on her pregnancy of twenty-one weeks. Grieving her father's death was also contributing to her lower energy levels. Doctors had concluded that Steven White had died of a heart attack. The man had gone peacefully, they'd said, but it had had a tremendous impact on Sophia. She'd been on edge ever since.

Oliver quietly undressed in the bedroom and lay down beside Sophia in bed, between the golden sheets, trying not to wake her. He put his arm around her, pressing his body close to hers. Sophia stirred. She was facing away from him, but he knew she wasn't sleeping. He propped his head up on his right arm and moved her chestnut hair off her face. "I'm sorry I couldn't be home earlier," he said. "I had to attend the conference and take care of things."

"Why couldn't I go Clamerton?" Sophia asked. She didn't even glance in his direction.

"I need you to be safe, Sophia." He bent down and kissed her hair. The thought of taking her with him had crossed his mind, but he'd decided against it. He didn't know what to expect anymore. Sābanto had created a lot of enemies for him.

"I've been stuck in this house ever since Riverlea burned. Stuck in this room with wet cloth hung over the windows to keep the smog out. It's been a month!" Sophia let it all out.

"I was trying to protect you and the baby," Oliver said. His eyes traveled down Sophia's body and rested on her full belly, admiring her curves showing under the covers on the way. "It would've been dangerous for you to breathe that air—"

"I could've gone to Clamerton, breathed the fresh air, and been spared this prison."

"I had to make sure you were protected. I promised you I wouldn't let anything happen to you."

Sophia uncovered herself and sat up at the edge of the bed with some difficulty. Her belly was getting bigger each day. Her back was to Oliver, away from his embrace.

"You leave me alone for days," she said. Her voice was breaking up. "Sābanto is more important to you than your family."

"That isn't true, Sophia. I'm equally responsible for you and for those people."

"When we owned the Leggett Company, we had some income," she replied and stood up. "You sold the business to that girl—"

"I told you. I couldn't run it and Sābanto at the same time. I sold it to Mark, and he wanted Ivy to be the owner instead of him. You agreed."

Oliver sat down on the edge of his side of the bed and watched Sophia shuffle towards the balcony window. She stared outside at the darkness in the distance. She was bent slightly back to balance her pregnant belly, propping up her spine with a hand on the back of her hip. The hem of her silk nightgown was slightly raised in the front, and longer at the back.

"You know how much I care about these people? . . . They are nothing to me."

"Please don't say that," Oliver pleaded in a hushed voice, burying his face in his palms.

"Why not?" she replied angrily. "They're breaking our family apart."

Oliver got up and walked towards Sophia. She didn't have to be angry with him. He tried to comfort her and kiss her beautifully curved neck, but she turned around and faced him before he could reach her. Her cheeks were red.

"It would've been dangerous for you to go anywhere," he said. Was this still about the trip? "What if someone wanted to use you against me?" There were thieves on the road and people were often abducted in remote areas. Also, there was Friends. They were too big and too influential. What if they learned he was working against them? He had to be cautious.

"So turning this house into a prison was easier, right?"

Oliver had done Sophia wrong. Her security and well-being had been more important to him at the time than her feelings. She was right. Maybe he was too paranoid. He could send her on vacation with bodyguards who would protect her. "I'm sorry you feel that way. I didn't know that going to Clamerton was that important to you. Please go—"

"*Graciously* the master of the house allows me to go. And what do you think I'll be doing there? I'm already five months pregnant!" she burst out. "Dragging my ass around on swollen ankles?" Oliver remained quiet. What was he supposed to say to that? "Now it's too late," Sophia continued. "I need to be at home taking it easy, with Dr. Lott close by in case something happens."

"I'm sorry," Oliver said and mindlessly touched his signet with the dragon, the one that his father had given him.

Sophia glanced at the ring on his finger. "I remember you saying that your father didn't love your mother. Is that why you keep wearing that cheap thing? To be just like him? If you loved me, you never would've cared about Riverlea."

"They cut all food shipments going into the city. That'd mean slow death by starvation and cold for all the people there—"

"And you were the only one who could save them," she said mockingly. "You should've let them all die—"

"Shut up!" Oliver tensed. "You don't know what you're saying!"

"Sure," Sophia replied with a fake smile on her face. "It's so much easier to have an obedient, stupid wife who does exactly what you tell her to do. Isn't that how your father was? A control freak!"

"When it was about charity work, you loved collecting money for the poor. You praised the cause!" he shouted. "Now, when they really need our help, you just turn your back!"

"They mean nothing to me!"

He grabbed her by the arm, squeezing it tightly. Sophia gasped.

"You're no better than the other ladies," he said. "Are your pretty dresses the only things of value about you?"

Sophia grimaced and her eyes widened. "You're hurting me!" she cried. Her voice was shaking.

Oliver said nothing, but released her arm immediately. Why did he use the same grip on Sophia as his father had on his mother? Maybe there was some truth to what Sophia had said. Maybe he was becoming like him.

Sophia stormed out of the bedroom and slammed the door of the guest chamber down the hallway. Oliver didn't stop her. He couldn't make things right tonight. No point in trying.

Of course Sophia was upset. He'd left her alone and neglected, but World United kept adding more and more to his plate. Commissioners had implemented bracelets and tracking devices. He was unable to change their minds. For the security and well-being of everyone, they said. But Sābanto wasn't intended to stand for surveillance. Tracking people hadn't been his idea.

He went to the jacket he'd left on the chair earlier, taking his cigarettes out of the inside pocket. The pack was nestled against a red velvet box with earrings he'd bought for Sophia in Clamerton. Gifts wouldn't fix their fights, but giving up wasn't an option.

He opened the glass door to the terrace and walked outside. The September night was dark and quiet. There was no wind disturbing the peace. Even the crickets were silent. *The calm before the storm.* He lit the cigarette and looked at it. He had promised he'd stop smoking. "I can't just quit when everything's on fire," he mumbled to himself, taking a long drag of nicotine.

# 6

AMY SCANNED THE PITCH-BLACK apartment. It was late in the evening and overcast. There was barely any light coming in from the windows, even with the curtains open. She turned on the flashlight she'd brought with her and scanned the room quickly to orient herself. The place looked exactly as it had weeks before. Same messy bed on her right and kitchenette at the back wall—a bachelor's room with an overflowing garbage can and the stale smell of unwashed clothes and dishes hanging in the stagnant air.

Greyson had left earlier to see Julia. The place was empty, and Amy expected Greyson would be out late. She could sneak in and do some investigating, but she wasn't sure what she was looking for. Greyson had been acting weird recently. He'd been sneaking out at all hours of the day and night, alone or with Conway, then yesterday Greyson had said he needed help. Why all of a sudden was he dragging her into things?

She soundlessly approached the desk in the corner of the room and searched the drawers. They contained nothing but junk. Greyson didn't use the desk much. Did he even know how to read? Amy couldn't recall ever seeing him with a book or a document in his hand.

She slowly closed the desk drawers and moved to the bedside table. Socks and underwear. At least they were clean. She checked for false bottoms, but all of the drawers were solid.

Amy turned around and looked at the kitchenette. Dirty dishes sat in the sink. She searched through the cupboards, but all she found were some cans and open boxes of dry food. The inside of the small fridge stank from the spoiling leftovers on the shelves and dead vegetables in the crisper. What the hell did Greyson eat? Did he even live here?

She went back to the bed, got on her knees, and carefully checked under it. The flashlight illuminated only dust and garbage. *Can't the dumbass spare a broken ticket for a maid?* She got up. The search was pointless, but she wanted to be thorough.

She quietly opened the chest of drawers and checked between the clothes. There were a few complete sets of Black Shirt uniforms, not much else. None of the drawers had false bottoms or backs.

As she closed the drawer, she heard faint footsteps outside and froze. *Go away whoever you are.* The steps, however, were getting closer. *Too early for Greyson to be back.* Maybe someone had seen something or heard her shuffling inside. She couldn't risk being caught snooping in his apartment.

There was a closet beside the door. The only hiding place. She got inside and slid the doors behind her. Through a small slit between the door and the frame, she could see a small portion of the room. She waited.

Greyson walked up to his apartment, unlocked the door, and walked inside. He took his gun out of his holster and threw it on the unmade bed.

The night hadn't gone as he'd planned. He had been looking to spend time with Julia. All he wanted was a couple of hours cuddling together. But no, she had no time for him. She wasn't in the fucking mood. Greyson took off his black Sābanto shirt and threw it onto the bed. *I gotta clean and make dinner*, Greyson replayed Julia's words in his head mockingly. *The new guy, Taylor, needed a tour of the house. It took a lotta time.* He walked into the kitchen and turned on the light above the stove. Julia had said her days would be lighter this coming week. She'd promised she'd come and spend a night or two at his place. But Conway had a project for him, and knowing his luck he'd be away when Julia was in the mood. Inside the cupboard he found a pack of cigarettes. He took one out and lit it.

"I'm sorry if I'm imposing," a woman's voice said behind him. Greyson jumped and spun around quickly towards the intruder. It was a girl with long brown hair, tied in a ponytail, and dressed in baggy clothes. *Oh, Amy.* What was she doing here? He inhaled from his cigarette.

"I'm sorry. I saw ya come in, and the door was open," she said with a grin, and pointed behind her at the entrance.

He must not have locked the door when he'd come in. It was all Julia's fault for pushing him away. Taylor, what kind of name was that, anyway? Julia had said that she wasn't interested in the new guy, but what if she was?

"Anything I can do for ya?" Greyson asked Amy formally. He put his cigarette on the edge of the sink so that the ash fell into it, then took a few steps into the middle of the room.

He followed her with his eyes as she walked up to him slowly and touched his bare torso with her cold hand. She smiled at him and bit her lower lip. *Damn, that smile.* Her eyes were dark and hungry. "We should be together," Amy said. She leaned closer and kissed him.

Greyson didn't flinch and kissed her back. Maybe he'd get lucky tonight after all.

She pressed him against the wall. They kissed madly. Why not? Julia didn't need to know. Fuck Julia! She didn't have time for him.

Greyson kissed Amy harder. He squeezed her hips. Her body was putty in his hands. If he picked her up, he could carry her to bed. It wasn't that far. He'd take off her clothes slowly . . . no, he'd do it fast. What shade of brown would her nipples be? Or maybe they were more pink in color.

Suddenly he felt cold steel pressing against his neck, and froze. Amy's kisses had stopped, but she still had him pinned to the wall.

"What the fuck?!" he said. What the hell was she doing with a knife in her hand?

"What are ya using me for?"

"What are ya talking about?" It had been her who'd come into his apartment. Fuck, she'd even kissed him first!

"The plan," Amy hissed at him.

So that's what it was all about. Bitch hadn't come because she wanted him. "I told ya all ya need to know," Greyson replied. The plan was simple: they were to retrieve an item from a chop-jet. Conway had gone over all the steps with them.

"Stop bullshitting me," she replied, a weird smile on her face. "Why am I to kill the people in the chop-jet?"

"That's the order," Greyson replied coldly. What had happened to subordinates never questioning their orders? Greyson's eyes darted around the apartment. Could he free himself without anyone getting hurt? Amy noticed him stirring and pressed the blade harder against his neck.

"Fucking bullshit," she said through gritted teeth.

"Calm down," he said. "Let's talk." At least she had closed the door, but had she locked it? How would this look? He, Greyson, was being pinned to the wall by a woman.

"What's Conway up to?" she asked.

"Stay out of it." He'd be in trouble with the boss if the plan fell apart. Everything had been on track until Amy had started to fucking question it.

"Too late. I'm already too fucking deep." She pressed the knife harder still. Greyson felt pain where the knife touched his skin. Had the bitch drawn blood?

"It's dangerous," he replied.

"So is the fucking plan." Amy released him and moved back towards the bed. Greyson touched his neck with his hand, then glanced at it. There was no blood. Amy picked up and inspected his gun, a gift Conway had given him a year ago, which he'd carelessly thrown onto the bed. She put it on the nightstand away from him and sat down on the edge of the mattress. The bed springs moaned.

"Don't be a fucking fool!" he shouted.

"Ya've changed, Greyson. One day ya too sure of yourself, the other ya keep looking behind ya back like an animal. What's going on?" She was still holding the knife in her hand.

Greyson slid down the wall and sat on the floor. Amy was right—he'd been on edge lately. Working with Conway was stressful. All the secrets kept him awake at night. Nightmares haunted him.

"We don't need to kill to steal that thing—"

"Ya don't understand," he broke in. He shook his head, which was hanging between his legs. His elbows rested on his knees.

"Explain," Amy replied, making herself more comfortable on his bed. She'd given him some room to sit down beside her as well and he reluctantly joined her.

They spent at least an hour talking. Greyson had explained things to her five times now, but the bitch was still confused.

"I don't get it," she said. "This is all fucked up. Are ya telling me we're working for a hit man?"

Greyson got up and paced the room. Once she knew what she was up against, she'd go along with the plan.

"Not a killer," Greyson said finally. "*The* killer."

"What do ya mean *the* killer?" She rolled her eyes.

"Any high-profile murder; it was him." Greyson met Amy's eyes. She frowned.

"Ya shitting me." She shook her head in disbelief and grinned nervously.

"Ma hands are shaking, and ya laughing." He extended his hands to her, so that she could check for herself.

"Why did ya agree to this?" She smirked at him like he was an idiot.

"I had no choice."

"I'm sure ya did. Why should I believe ya?"

"The alternative was death," Greyson replied. "Fuck! I'm a dead man for telling ya any of this." He paced back and forth again, sweating profusely. He was done for. He had to disappear tomorrow. Hell, he couldn't even say goodbye to Julia.

"Tell me what happened," Amy insisted.

She already knew too much. She could have this story as well. "I was working for White," he started. "They told me I'd be a guard for Conway. When I started, his house was nothing but ruins."

"Yeah, I remember. He was renovating it for months."

"I was told not to report to Conway," he began. "I was to report to ma officer. Only him. All was great until one night. Here's where things got weird." Greyson had more energy in him now, and he became more animated, moving his hands as he explained. He had never told anyone his version of events. He'd kept it secret for more than a year. "We went with Conway to Clamerton. He was on some business there. There was some trouble with the chop-jet, so we stayed in for the night.

"Well after midnight strange men arrived at the hotel and ma officer nodded towards them like they all knew each other. I'd never seen them before . . . but orders are orders . . . Conway's body was a limp thing lying on the bed and he was fucking heavy to carry, but we got him out of the room and into the basement—"

"Ha! Then he came back as an assassin?" Amy mocked him with a laugh.

"Even if I swore it, ya wouldn't believe it," said Grayson, hitting his chest with his fist. "After a while, we carried Conway back to his room. He'd been given sleeping pills or something . . . I don't know." He shook his head. "When he woke up, he was furious, like a wild animal in a cage. When he cooled down, he got out of the hotel room and all he said was, 'We're leaving.' Just like that, we're going home. *What about chop-jet troubles,* methinks—"

"There were no chop-jet troubles!" Amy interjected

"Exactly!" Greyson nodded. "Conway took us somewhere with the chop-jet, and he told us, 'Put ya gun down on the table.' So, of course, I wouldn't disobey. There were only four of us in the chop-jet, so I put ma gun down, but ma officer and the pilot were standing still. I had no clue what was happening. No one told me anything."

"So, what did Conway do?"

"He waited. Eventually, the other two put their guns down, but the stupid pilot had two guns with him. And while Conway asked questions, the moron tried his luck—"

"And he got killed."

"Listen . . . not just killed." Greyson walked up to the table. He picked a paperweight and placed it in front of him with a thud. "Think of this as a gun that's turned off." Amy nodded while Greyson quickly picked the paperweight up and pointed to his right in one swift move. "Bam, the guy was dead."

"Ya said the gun was turned off." Amy furled her forehead.

"He explained to me later that it was all about precision." Greyson pointed at his eye. "Hitting the guy in the eye with a partial charge of the gun."

"What did ya do?"

"Me? I was sweating and shitting maself. I've never seen anyone kill so quickly."

"The officer got killed too?"

"Right, but Conway didn't kill him. The officer broke the poison capsule in his tooth."

"That's sick." Amy turned her head away, disgusted.

"I had no choice but accept this work."

"Ya went with him and started killing? Who did ya kill?" Amy faced him again.

Greyson nodded. "Leggett."

"The War Crimes Commissioner was ya job?" Amy's eyes were wide open, following him as he was pacing the room. "Why?"

"He got too nosy."

"Conway is a war criminal, and ya fine with it?"

"He isn't." Greyson shook his head as he walked.

"I don't get it." Amy seemed more confused the more he talked.

Was it that hard to understand? "The war criminals made him do it."

Amy was rolling her eyes. "He's a killer, ya said. He can just go after these crooks."

*The stupid bitch thinks she has a solution.* "Who do ya think he should kill?" Greyson stopped in front of Amy.

"Ya said it . . . the bad guys." She looked at Greyson like he was a fool.

"Exactly. And they are . . . ?" He gazed into Amy's eyes.

"Ya don't know?" Amy concluded, surprised somehow, and burst out laughing. There was nothing funny about this.

"If we knew, Conway would've killed them already."

"Okay" Amy calmed down and looked serious. "What if we fail to get that item, whatever that is?"

"I wouldn't wanna be on Conway's bad side."

"I'm not scared of him." She shrugged, got up from the bed and strode around the room. "What's in the box?"

"Dunno. Boss never said," Greyson replied, shaking his head.

"Will that box help Conway find the war criminals?"

Greyson nodded. "It'll get him closer," he said. "We have no choice but to follow orders. If we don't do it, there won't be enough time. We won't figure out who the enemies are, and they'll become stronger."

"All right," Amy said. "I'll do it." She walked towards Greyson until she was in his face, but Greyson didn't move. "Sure. I'll get him the box" *Just like that, she agreed.* She turned her back on him and walked towards the door. Before leaving she faced Greyson again. "Next time tell me the truth," she said. "I ain't a fool."

The door closed behind Amy. Bitch better get that box and do it right. How could she have humiliated him like this? He'd keep a closer eye on her. She had to have a weakness, and he'd find it. *We'll see who's the fool.* For now, she had to stick to the plan and not fuck it up. *Fuck!* She was supposed to be the reliable one on the team.

"Thank you for staying for dinner, Liam." Sophia extended her hand, inviting their guest further into the dining room. Oliver's wife was in a somewhat better mood today. The visit had made her more noticeably radiant and animated; she loved entertaining. Having Liam over wasn't very convenient for Oliver, but if he tolerated the man's presence for a couple of hours, his relationship with Sophia might improve. He didn't think she'd pick a fight in front of company.

The servants had already set the table for the two of them, but they rushed around adding a table setting for the guest.

"It's my pleasure," Liam replied. "My father is very sorry that he couldn't make it to your father's funeral. He sends his condolences."

"Thank you," Sophia replied, sitting on the long side of the table. The staff dispersed. "Your father was always a very valued friend of our family. Please let him know he can come for a visit anytime."

Liam sat opposite Sophia, leaving the head of the table for Oliver.

"How was the trip?" Sophia started. "I can't believe you drove." She put the napkin on her lap.

"My father needed the jet, and it's not that far," Liam replied.

"The roads are treacherous these days," she replied. "Bandits are roaming the woods."

The displays had been reporting all month about people living in the woods and were discouraging any road travel between cities. They claimed that those who were hiding from Sābanto were attacking travelers, stealing from them, and even killing. The reports were nothing but more fuel for the already tense situation with those refusing to join Sābanto.

"It's not as bad as The Citizen says," Liam said. "A couple hours of solitude helps to clear my mind."

"I still don't understand," Sophia said, turning to Oliver. "Shouldn't you do something about it?"

*For fuck's sake!* His jaw tensed. Thoughts of getting up, throwing his napkin onto his plate, and leaving crossed his mind, but the servants rescued him by coming in to serve the first course. Oliver cooled down while they quietly set bowls of soup down in front of everyone at the table. "I'm sure World United is doing something," he said politely.

"Sābanto should just comb the woods," Sophia replied. "They're under your command, aren't they?"

"It's not that easy," Oliver replied calmly, taking a spoonful of the calamari soup in front of him.

"Sābanto is useless," she concluded. "I still don't understand what kind of pathetic role you have there—"

"I think the problem is with punishment," Liam said, saving Oliver from replying to Sophia.

"My father knew how to punish the degenerates. There was no crime in Covedale," she said. Her father had performed public whippings in Covedale.

"The problem is that Sābanto doesn't have a jail yet," Liam said, spooning some food into his mouth.

"Why's that?" Sophia turned her head again towards Oliver.

Why was she badgering him like this? "It is being built, but funding is low," he said.

"You should've used some of your own money and gotten it built," Sophia said. Just a few days ago, she'd been angry with him for spending so much money on the project. Why the fuck was she now urging him to spend more?

"I'm sure Liam understands all the challenges we're facing." Oliver turned towards him. Sophia couldn't fight them both on this.

Wasting more money wasn't on Oliver's agenda. World United had promised they'd fund a jail, and contributing to this was the last thing he wanted. When they'd asked his opinion, he'd told them that a separate compound for those convicted of crimes should be enough, but most of the chancellors disagreed. They wanted a proper building with cells and bars on the windows.

The staff collected the plates and brought the next course in. It was trout, caught that day, on a bed of fragrant saffron rice.

And who would they keep in this jail? Masters accused the maids of stealing extra bread from their table. Employees blamed their workers for the broken tools, which fell apart from lack of repairs. Workplaces accused steelworkers of stealing the missing iron, as though they could do anything with it after their twelve- or sixteen-hour shifts ended.

Liam took the first bite. "You have a talented chef," he noted.

"He worked for my father for many years," Sophia said. "His skills are unmatched."

"Putting together a tasty meal is an art." Liam turned towards the serving girl who stood by the wall in case there was a request or something needed attention at the table. "Compliments to the chef," he said.

"Thank ya, sir," the girl curtsied but stayed in the room, not leaving her post.

Liam turned back to the conversation. "They're building a big restaurant in Clamerton. They said it will be a few more months before they can open."

"That's exciting!" Sophia engaged Liam in a discussion about the project, and Oliver relaxed.

The rest of the evening finished on a pleasant note. Sophia nagged Liam to stay until morning rather than driving through the dark forest at night and in the rain, but he politely refused. They said their goodbyes and Sophia retreated upstairs. It seemed normal now for Sophia to sleep in the guest bedroom rather than share the bed with Oliver. He didn't protest.

After a quick cigarette outside, he also went up to his room. He locked the door, took off his shirt, and untied his bandages. The wound was healing well, but it would leave a scar.

**7**

T HE DRIVER CAME EARLY in the morning, and Ivy was on her way soon after. There was no sense in delaying the inevitable. She was going on a trip and she wouldn't chicken out now. Of course she was nervous leaving what was now a familiar house, but she needed a break in her routine. It was only a week. She'd be back before she even knew it.

The sidewalks and roads were still wet from the overnight rain. Taylor had packed the car with three large suitcases that Julia had prepared. Her maid had gone overboard with packing, but it would've taken too long to unpack what Ivy didn't need. She'd sort it out once she reached her destination.

"I'll be back soon," Ivy said as she got into the car. She gave Julia a big hug and shook Taylor's hand. He'd been stiff and nervous at breakfast again, acting unnaturally. It would pass. She was certain of that.

The road was empty of other cars. Most people were traveling by air these days, but Ivy was terrified of not having the ground underneath her feet. She felt she was safer traveling by car, even though the news was advising against taking such trips. She wasn't going alone—a driver at the steering wheel kept an eye on the road.

The Château de la Belle Cascade was two hours' drive from Covedale. It was situated just north of Clamerton, between picturesque mountains. The owner had advertised the beautiful fall scenery this time of year, which had attracted Ivy's attention and helped her decide where to book her getaway.

It had been Mr. Conway's suggestion that she take a break and relax a bit. He told her she was working too hard and burning herself out, acting as both owner and worker at the same time. "The factory will be fine while you're gone," he had said. She knew she'd worry about what was happening at Leggett while she was away, but she decided she'd give it a shot.

A butler in a pristine uniform accented with white gloves came over immediately as the car pulled up. He unpacked the trunk and carried the suitcases inside. Ivy absorbed the view around her before entering the building herself. The tree-covered mountains in the distance were changing for the fall. The trees were dripping with colors, shining in the sun that had come out after the morning rain. Birds argued noisily, flying between the branches and throwing down droplets of water from the leaves. The place was beautiful. Ivy smiled.

She kept looking up at the tops of the trees, until her eyes rested on the old stone building. It was at least five stories high with even rows of large windows. The roof was steep, with smaller windows sticking out of it. It reminded her of a castle she had once read about in a book. Her smile grew wider as she recalled the story.

"Adventures await," she said to herself and smoothed the thin coat she was wearing. She walked up a flight of stairs and entered the building through the heavy wide wooden doors.

A servant rushed to meet Ivy to relieve her of the coat.

The vast and spotless hall inside had an elaborate chandelier hanging in the middle, between dark marble walls. The wide dark wood staircase led to the upper floors. A tall stained glass window gave the space splashes of gold, red, and blue, as the sun shone through.

"Miss Roberts!" An older woman came out from the hallway to her left and greeted her. Ivy recognized Mrs. Ouellet. She was the owner of the chateau.

To Ivy's surprise, the lady was wearing a dress that Ivy had made for her at Leggett just a couple of months ago. It fit Mrs. Ouellet's large frame perfectly.

"It's a pleasure to have you with us," the woman said. "Please join us for lunch." She gestured for Ivy to follow her.

They went through a short corridor and entered a huge dining room. There were some people already sitting at the long table who stopped their ongoing conversation, interested in the newcomer. Mrs. Ouellet introduced Ivy to an older couple, Mr. and Mrs. Blazer, owners of a jet factory, and two sisters, Calista and Sarai Tari, from a plantation situated not too far from the chateau. The young sisters came here often, the lady of the house claimed, and enjoyed their stay each time. Ivy shook their hands, and Mrs. Ouellet gestured for her to take a seat opposite the sisters.

"Miss Roberts has recently acquired the Leggett Company," the lady explained to all the guests, forcing Ivy into the conversation at the table.

"That sounds like a major purchase," the jet factory owner commented.

"Yes, it is a big enterprise," Ivy replied and lowered her head.

The servants entered, pausing the conversation. They set the table in front of Ivy quickly and with precision. They poured coffee into a cup and some champagne into a prepared flute. They served everything so gracefully that it almost seemed as if they were trained in ballet. Ivy smiled, enjoying the performance, but the rest of the table was oblivious to it. No one found the behavior of the servants unusual, and she realized that her delight was out of place. She suppressed her smile and lowered her chin a little, looking at the setting in front of her and hoping that no one had noticed.

Behaving like the elite still required a lot of work and attention, but she just needed more practice.

"I heard, Miss Roberts, that you came by car," Mrs. Blazer said. Ivy just smiled, so she added, "There are new cars being produced. Driverless. They still have the steering wheel in them, but the newest model doesn't require anyone to operate it."

"How does it know where to go?" Mrs. Ouellet asked and leaned forward to hear the conversation better.

"They put a very complicated brain into it," Mr. Blazer explained. "You punch in the address, and it just takes you there. Way more advanced than the navigation systems we currently have."

"That sounds very convenient," Ivy replied. She was trying to contribute to the conversation, but she knew next to nothing about new technology.

"The teleporters are getting better," Calista said, taking a sip of the champagne in front of her. "Soon cars won't be needed. Plus, why travel by road when bandits roam the forests?"

"Teleportation is still risky. They might not get it right for decades," Mr. Blazer replied.

The servants brought in fresh bread and Ivy pointed at the white bun. She always asked Julia to buy similar ones from the Covedale bakery, even though her maid insisted she liked the dark bread better and that it would save the household some money. The serving girl picked one up with the tongs gently and put it on Ivy's side plate. She thanked the servant, but she felt Calista staring at her while Sarai averted her eyes. What had she done wrong?

"As for the outlaws in the forests, we shouldn't allow them to terrorize us," Mr. Blazer added. "They want us to bow to them, consent to their ways, and we can't let that happen."

Ivy picked up the bun from her plate—it was still warm—and halved it with her fingers as she always did. She then grabbed the knife and put butter on it. *Too much butter.* Was everyone at the table suddenly looking at her? Her face turned hot. She kept her eyes down, lacking the courage to look up again until the embarrassment passed.

Meanwhile, Mr. Blazer continued his rant and the rest at the table nodded in agreement as he spoke. "Sābanto is taking care of these criminals, finding them and putting them away, and we should support these efforts. That way we won't live in fear."

The servants came in again, carrying large individual plates and putting them in front of each person seated at the table. The salad was a mix of lettuce and vegetables with delicate pieces of perfectly grilled chicken and shrimp, drizzled with a lemon vinaigrette, and sprinkled with nuts and dried fruit.

"The Citizen said the other day that the bandits held a woman for a week and she now requires constant psychological care for what they've done to her," Mrs. Ouellet recalled with outrage the recent accident that had been reported in the news. Ivy had seen the interview and the details of the encounter had shocked her as well.

The Tari sisters sat quietly listening to the conversations and not contributing their opinions. Ivy noticed them looking directly at her more than once, and she smiled shyly. She knew her face was red. It always was when she was self-conscious. Feeling the girls' eyes on her, Ivy paid extra attention to what she was doing. She hoped her actions seemed natural as she ate and listened.

"Salt!" Mr. Blazer said before even tasting the meal. "They never add enough," he added as one of the serving girls wearing a navy apron ran up to him carrying a salt shaker on a silver tray. Everyone at the table overlooked his sudden outburst.

"These attacks were still happening during the war, but the media never reported on them. They still don't tell us everything," Mrs. Blazer commented before shoveling a large portion of the salad into her mouth.

Her husband shook some salt onto his food and put the shaker loudly back onto the silver plate without looking at the girl, who curtsied and quickly left. "Something needs to be done, or they will start attacking our houses," he added and sipped his wine.

"That Gibala," Mrs. Ouellet said. "She twists the truth."

"A liar who wants us to pity the *free*," Mrs. Blazer replied.

"Sābanto was created for them, and my taxes pay for it," her husband said with annoyance, "but they resist the help."

"Such ungrateful creatures." Mrs. Ouellet shook her head indignantly.

After lunch Ivy went back to her room to freshen up, reapplying her makeup and brushing the hair she found a little out of place from her trip. She spent the rest of the afternoon following Jane, a personal assistant Mrs. Ouellet had assigned her. The young servant, no older than twelve, showed her the grounds and amenities of the grand property. Anywhere they went, Ivy was treated like a princess in a castle. She found the attention pleasant. She liked this trip already.

Ivy had a relaxing massage and spent some time soaking in the hot tub. Later she sat on the cozy deck chair beside the pool, absorbing the sunlight from the still-warm September day. Nothing beat breathing in the fresh mountain air. Ivy hadn't forgotten to bring a book to read in her downtime.

The Tari sisters were outside as well. They sat in the heated pool with wisps of steam surrounding them. They were discussing something and occasionally erupting with laughter. Calista was the taller and slimmer of the sisters. Ivy deduced that she was the older of the two. She wore a bright pink bikini that contrasted nicely with her tanned body and blonde hair. Sarai was shorter and brunette, but equally attractive.

Ivy didn't join them. She wasn't a skilled swimmer and she was still a little embarrassed about the mistakes she'd made at lunch. She didn't want to do any more stupid things in front of these women, so she buried her nose in a book. She was reading about a crime investigation from pre-war times in a faraway city she knew nothing about. A woman had been murdered, and the detective couldn't rest until he found the killer who needed to be punished.

After a while she brought her head up from her book and noticed the sisters looking at her, but they quickly averted their eyes. It would take some time for her to fully integrate into her role as a factory owner and into the society of rich and successful citizens that was so new to her.

What was happening at Leggett? Her heart skipped a beat at the thought that she'd temporarily forgotten about her company. She'd told Julia and the factory staff that if there was anything out of the ordinary happening, they were to call her immediately. No one had called. It had to be a good sign. She dismissed her fears and buried her nose in her book again.


Ivy wore one of the green dresses that Julia had packed to dinner that evening. Like most of her wardrobe, it was her own design and creation, and she loved wearing it. The assistant, Jane, helped her get ready.

"You look beautiful," the girl said while brushing Ivy's hair.

Ivy smiled. The servant was just trying to be nice. Her hair was coarse like wire and got in the way of everything she did. Mark had said that he loved the color; he'd just wanted to make her feel better.

At dinner, she sat in the same spot at the table. The meal was festive with multiple courses and wine pairings. Everything at the Château de la Belle Cascade was beautifully served and tempted her with its aroma. There were lots of items that Ivy hadn't tried before. Mark had money, but the meals they'd had together in Riverlea had been simple, and she had no experience with fancy foods. In the company of strangers, Ivy pretended she was just like them and ate everything that was served. In the end, it was all food, and she would try anything once.

Her favorite was meat, which she'd previously eaten only on special occasions. It was very expensive, but it was easy to eat. *Knife in right hand, fork in left*, she recalled Mark teaching her. *Cut into small pieces that will fit comfortably in your mouth. Chew and swallow before getting another piece. If there's a bone, cut around it with a knife and don't pick it up and nibble on it, even if there's still some meat left.*

Ivy paid little attention to the conversation at the table that was mostly about the lazy workers that Mr. Blazer employed, and Mrs. Ouellet agreed with him on all points. Ivy kept watching everyone at the table to see how the unknown foods were meant to be eaten. How were the tasty crabs and lobsters opened? How were the shells removed from the soft, buttered shrimps? How was the napkin she placed on her lap meant to be used? She hoped she wasn't drawing too much attention to herself, but her actions definitely amused the ladies opposite her. Was she doing a good job, or had she made too many mistakes? Ivy would never know, but she hoped it was the former.

"Miss Roberts," Mrs. Ouellet said, turning to Ivy. "Have you found an activity for tomorrow? Don't waste your time with a book again." She picked her wineglass up by the stem and had a small sip of the ruby liquid.

"Yes," Ivy replied. She had some food still in her mouth. *Finish the food then speak,* she heard Mark say in her head. She quickly swallowed and continued, "I found some walking trails. I'll go and see the mountains. The trees are turning."

"Please feel free to use the amenities here as well," Mrs. Ouellet said.

"How about horseback riding? Join us tomorrow," Sarai said.

"I'm sorry, but I've never ridden a horse," Ivy replied. She didn't even know how to mount one.

"It's easy," the other sister, Calista, told her. "You sit on the horse, and it walks. We'll show you."

That sounded like fun. Ivy smiled and thanked the ladies for the invitation. She was here to have a good time, make friends and try new things. There was no point in rejecting the sisters' offer.

After dinner, Ivy followed the other guests to the basement of the chateau where the staff had set up game tables. It was an elegant room. Small, dimmed chandeliers lit the space without making it too bright. The light was slightly amplified with the help of the mirrors that covered the walls. Red and gold drapes surrounded them as though they were windows. Heavy tables with thick wooden frames were scattered in the middle. The tops of these tables were covered in felt, either green or red. Chairs covered in golden fabric surrounded them.

"Let's play some roulette," Sarai said, pointing at one of the tables. There was a murmur of approval and all guests circled around the game. The seats filled quickly and Ivy carefully sat down on one of the chairs. On one side of her sat Calista, on the other side a man. Ivy slowly turned to look at the stranger. It was Liam Menken. She froze. It seemed like just yesterday she'd seen his face at the Leggett store. Ivy lowered her head, embarrassed by the circumstances under which they'd met.

"Have you played before?" Liam asked.

Ivy shook her head. She'd never played any of these games.

"Take this to start." Calista put a stack of green chips in front of Ivy. "Ten tickets each."

Ivy's eyes lit up. One of these chips would have cost her a week's salary if she'd still been a seamstress at the Leggett factory. There were at least fifty of these chips in front of her. Five hundred tickets. Ivy felt lightheaded for a moment, but blamed it on the wine she'd had at dinner.

"They're from us," Sarai said from across the table.

The waiter put a drink in front of Ivy. She hadn't ordered anything, but it would have been impolite to send it back. The staff had already prepared it. *Let it be and don't drink it.* She'd had enough wine already. Everyone around her, however, grabbed their drinks almost as soon as the servants delivered them.

"The rules are easy," Liam said, sipping his amber drink from a short glass. "You put the chips on the square here—"

"Then this young boy,"—Calista interrupted and winked at the roulette croupier who smiled back mirthlessly—"will spin the wheel. If the ball sits on your number, then you win your bet times thirty-six."

Ivy nodded, but didn't understand the game. She looked around the table and noticed Mrs. Blazer sitting with them as well. It couldn't be that hard.

"You first," Sarai told her. "Choose a number."

Ivy took a chip from the pile and put it on twelve. Her hands were sweating. Everyone was watching her. The sisters, the Blazers, even Mrs. Ouellet. Liam had to be watching her as well, but she didn't dare look up at him to check. She took a sip of the cold, fruity drink beside her. It was sweet but refreshing.

The girls then put much larger stacks of chips on different parts of the table.

The croupier set the wheel in motion, and the ladies cheered for their numbers. Ivy joined them, clapping as the ball rested on twelve and the stack of thirty-six chips was pushed towards her. She blushed. Just like that, she'd won three hundred and sixty tickets.

"You're a natural," Liam said. His voice was soft.

"Thank you," Ivy uttered.

"How did you come to own Leggett?" Sarai asked.

"My boyfriend bought it for me from Mr. Conway," Ivy replied without hesitation.

The sisters glanced at each other across the table before Calista replied, "Who doesn't love rich boyfriends?"

Ivy hadn't loved Mark because he was rich, the truth was that she'd only found out about his fortune after he was already gone. Knowing about the money wouldn't have changed how she felt about him. Liam saved Ivy from replying by urging her to make the next move, "Lay down your bet."

Ivy put a chip, one from her winnings, on number twenty-six. The other guests at the table made their bets as well, and the wheel spun loudly.

"I heard you worked at Leggett," Calista said.

"I still work there," Ivy replied. It might've been the recent win or the alcohol, but Ivy began to converse with increased confidence. "I enjoy being a seamstress."

The wheel stopped on twenty-six. Ivy smiled uneasily looking at another thirty-six chips in front of her.

"Where do you work?" Ivy asked, collecting her chips from the table. They clinked as she stacked them.

Calista laughed. "Work? We don't work."

Ivy smiled. "I'm bored at home when I don't go to the factory."

"We have others who work for us," Sarai chipped in. "I don't mind being bored." She shrugged.

"And there's always sex," Calista added, and winked at one of the serving boys in the room. Sarai rolled her eyes at her sister's behavior.

Ivy looked at the roulette table. *Why not?* She took ten chips and put them down. She grabbed her glass, which was almost empty, and finished the rest of it. Before the ball had even settled on a new number, a fresh drink was already in front of her. Ivy mindlessly picked it up and moistened her dry lips. She won again.

"Told you it was easy," Liam said. Ivy found the courage to turn her head towards him. He was looking at her and smiling, his lips slightly parted with his dimples clearly showing on the sides of his square face. His hair curled softly on his forehead. Ivy smiled back.

The guests again made large bets, but Ivy was no longer winning so easily. The sisters explained the other variations of the game, but none of the other winning options were as profitable.

The excitement of this game waning, the sisters suggested they play something else. Poker didn't work well for Ivy. She wasn't good at card games, and her brain was foggy. It had been a long day and the complicated rules weren't sticking. The girls eventually moved to the craps table to continue the fun, and Ivy enjoyed that game more.

After many rounds, Ivy felt the night weighing on her. As she got up from her chair the room began to spin, and she steadied herself on Liam's shoulder. "Oops!" She giggled and Liam smiled. *Those dimples.* How come she was drunk? She'd only had one drink. Only one! Ivy said goodnight to everyone and looked around for Jane. She wasn't there. The girl was probably already sleeping. One of the staff members came over to Ivy and offered her an arm as the world swayed around her, and led her out of the casino hall and through the maze of corridors to her room, leaving her at the door.

What a great night. Ivy had lost the fifty chips the Tari sisters had given her and she'd even spent some of her own money hoping she could turn her luck around. She'd give back the money that was lent to her. Tomorrow her luck would turn around. Would Liam be there again? He was so nice, leaning closer to her, explaining the games and helping her choose bets. *Those dimples . . .*

She entered the room to find Jane staring at her with wide eyes, wearing one of the silk scarves Julia had packed. It was cream-colored with lilies printed on it. Ivy reserved it only for special occasions.

"I'm sorry, ma'am," Jane said, lowering her head and not looking her in the eye. She slowly took the scarf off and put it back on the hanger neatly.

"How dare you!" Ivy clenched her teeth.

"Please, ma'am!" Jane dropped to her knees before her. "Please forgive me. I need this job. Mrs. Ouellet will kill me."

*What's gotten into you? It's only a scarf.* Ivy calmed down. "How old are you?" she asked.

"Fourteen, ma'am," Jane replied, remaining on her knees. Her voice shook and her head was lowered.

"How did you leave Sābanto at fourteen?" Was fourteen the new working age? Ivy couldn't recall.

"I was born here, in Menken Mines. I was never in Sābanto," she said. "I won't find another job like this. I'm taking care of ma mother."

Ivy couldn't think clearly. Her mind was tired, but it was odd that a young girl like Jane was supporting her parents if they worked for a large industry. She'd try to find out more about it in the morning, following a good rest. "I won't say anything," Ivy said, then added, "but don't do it again."

"Thank ya, ma'am." Jane said as she got up off her knees. "I heard ya going horseback riding. I'll find ya the gentlest of the mares."

Ivy had almost forgotten about the outing. It would be fun. Staying here was the best decision she had ever made. She still had six fun-filled days ahead of her. She smiled to herself.

Jane helped her undress and as soon as Ivy lay down, she fell asleep.

# 8

IVY ARRIVED AT THE stables early the next morning, even though she was still feeling the aftermath of the previous night. Her head was throbbing and her body needed a bit more time in bed, but she didn't want to change her plans with the Tari sisters. They'd been so nice to her by suggesting the trip, and it would've been unkind to cancel on short notice. What if she never got another chance to sit on a horse ever again? She'd never forgive herself. Jane had given her something to ease the hangover, and she hoped it would start working soon.

Ivy had dressed in long, slim pants and tall boots for the ride. Jane had also given her a properly-fitting helmet for her safety. Ivy wished she could see herself in the mirror again. It was the outfit for a real horse rider. She smiled.

The sisters were already waiting for her inside the stables. The girls were very relaxed and giggling cheerfully. They both looked fresh and radiant even though they'd also stayed up late last night and had drunk even more than she had. What was their secret?

"Where are we going?" Ivy asked them.

"There's a very nice waterfall not too far from here, and the trail is gentle," Sarai replied.

Taking it easy for her first ride appealed to Ivy. There were no waterfalls in Covedale, so Ivy had only read about them. Today she'd see one with her own eyes.

The horses were ready for them. The stable workers had paired Ivy with a gorgeous chestnut she immediately adored. She stroked its mane as soon as she was helped into the saddle, which was uncomfortable to sit in, but Ivy didn't want to complain. Jane had arranged for Ivy to ride this one, and the workers confirmed it was a good-natured horse.

They soon headed on their way, moving slowly along the path towards the woods in the distance, the horses swaying underneath them as they walked. This place was beautiful. Ivy took in the view around her and the rocky face of the cliffs towering above. Occasionally a startled bird flew away. In the distance she could hear the sound of the wind between the tops of the trees, and a raven call. Her horse walked rhythmically, its hooves hitting the packed dirt of the path in a plodding beat.

It was still morning, but the day was already warm. The sun rays warmed Ivy's helmet and she found herself sweating underneath it. She realized why the sisters weren't wearing any protection. Did she stand out too much with a helmet on?

"How was your night?" Sarai asked politely. "I hope you had enough time to rest."

"I shouldn't have had all that alcohol," Ivy confessed. "But thank you for the games. I had lots of fun."

"That roulette boy was so good," Calista bragged, fanning herself with her hand as she rolled her eyes up. "Those young ones can go forever. I only slept a couple of hours."

"You only care about one thing," Sarai criticized her sister. After a short moment of silence, she changed the subject. "Did you hear they're setting a minimum age for maids?"

"They gotta be fucking, what? Seventeen now?" Calista replied. "Beating these bitches until they know their place is hard when they're that old."

Why did this upset them? Ivy didn't care about the age restrictions. Sometimes girls as young as six had been sent to work for masters to help bring money home to feed their brothers and sisters. It had been normal for families to sell their kids to ship operators or send them to do hard labor loading cargo at the docks. Food was expensive and it was only recently that World United had mandated that factory owners maintain a standard of living for all workers.

"On the other hand, seventeen-year-old *boys* are too young," Calista added. "They get horny as fuck, but they're too scrawny."

"You like them with big muscles and thick cocks," Sarai teased, rolling her eyes at her sister.

"Damn right. Why compromise?" Calista laughed.

Ivy kept quiet. What could she possibly add to the conversation? It was normal for masters to choose and then sleep with the boys and girls who worked for them. Many girls were let go from their jobs for getting pregnant, then fell out of favor with their families for bringing another mouth to feed into the world. There had been a pretty girl in her neighborhood who'd taken her own life after her mother had banished her from their shack and into exile.

"Adult workers are too entitled," Sarai said.

"That's why we have whips," her sister replied.

"Like, to whip people?" Ivy frowned. She hadn't attended the public whippings in Covedale. Watching them was painful and she avoided them.

"You're not disciplining your workers?" Calista replied wide-eyed. She was clearly exaggerating her surprise. "You gotta start, otherwise their brains will rot."

"They need to know their place," Sarai added. "They'll walk all over you if you don't."

"I don't have problems with my workers," Ivy said firmly. Julia was Julia, and she hadn't formed an opinion of Taylor yet, but hitting them had never crossed her mind.

Calista shook her head. "Start now before it is too late."

"Don't let them get to you," Sarai added.

"See, for example, in our house no one speaks up unless asked to," said Calista. "If they forget, then they get lashes."

That would never be an issue with those who worked for Ivy, but then what did she know about keeping staff? It was all new to her. Maybe there was something in what the sisters said. All masters had some way of punishing those who stepped out of line.

They entered the forest, and the path became narrow. They rode silently in a single file, with Ivy in the middle. As they rode, Ivy scanned the forest floor, which was covered in a fresh carpet of fallen leaves. She noticed a startled chipmunk running away into the greenery. Ivy admired the big ferns springing up in areas where the ground was wet. She raised her head to look at the sun peeking in from between the branches and leaves that hadn't fallen yet. The brief flashes of silver rays were mesmerizing.

After about fifteen minutes, they arrived at a big clearing and the sisters jumped off their horses.

"Come, Ivy." Sarai held her hands up, encouraging Ivy to jump off the horse as well. "We'll help you up again before we leave."

Ivy swung her left leg towards the right, feeling the soreness in her muscles from the trip, and found herself back on the ground, steadied by Sarai's hands. She took her helmet off and hung it on the saddle. Her hair was damp with sweat. It was a summer-like day and slightly humid.

Once they hitched the horses, they took a short stroll to the base of the waterfall. It was a beautiful place. Ivy had never seen anything like this. The water crashed loudly into the plunge pool, creating a short-lived foam as the river rushed further, on its long journey to the sea. The falling water created a wide veil on the side of the mountain that was a few stories high. Like a wisp of cotton candy she'd bought once at the market with saved up money she had. She had shared it with her friends and they'd each had just a small piece. It had tasted so sweet.

Sarai called out over the roar of the waterfall from somewhere below. "Come down here!"

Ivy followed Calista towards the voice, carefully walking down the slippery rocks before pausing on a small ledge. A cold, wet breeze blew on them as they stood looking at the falling water. It was so close. If only Ivy could stretch her hand further, she'd touch the strands of water. Her headache and the heat, however, had made her dizzy, and she stepped back a bit where it felt safer. The sisters followed her shortly.

"I don't know about you two, but I'm hungry," Calista said and wandered off to her horse to grab the picnic basket that had been prepared for them at the chateau.

Of the two sisters, Ivy liked Sarai most. Calista's occasional rude attitude puzzled her, so Ivy was glad that she was left with Sarai to find a suitable area to sit and eat, which they cleared of rocks and sticks. Once Calista returned with the basket, they laid the blanket down and sat on it comfortably. In the distance, the waterfall thundered and birds sang in the trees above them.

The wicker basket had a selection of different buns and cheeses, and two bottles of wine. The chateau staff had wrapped the white one in a cooling blanket. Ivy knew she shouldn't drink more. Her head was still spinning slightly, but it was impolite to refuse when the sisters passed her a full glass.

As they ate, the sisters chatted more to each other about their boyfriends and people Ivy didn't know, arguing at times. She nodded and smiled when it felt right and kept the buzzing flies away from the food. She answered sporadic questions about her own life and work at the factory.

After lunch they decided to return to the chateau and the ladies helped Ivy back onto her horse. She was thirsty and the afternoon was hotter than the morning had been. There was barely any breeze. The horse had walked gently as the stable workers had promised and Ivy left her riding helmet hanging on the saddle. She'd put it on again when it got cooler.

They took a different path home through the forest. It was narrow and close to the cliff towering above her. This time Ivy was at the front, enjoying the views. She brushed the neck of the horse with her hand. It was soft. She'd come here again someday, just to take another horseback trip. Ivy didn't want a horse of her own, not yet. She didn't know how much care horses needed. Maybe one day she could hire someone. She'd buy a pair, so they didn't feel lonely.

Suddenly the mare jolted, taking Ivy by surprise. She instinctively tightened her grip on the reins in her hand, trying to hold onto the bolting horse.


"Mrs. Woodham," Anita said as she walked into the lady's house. "Thank you for agreeing to speak with me. I wanted to ask you a few questions." The woman pointed at the sofa with her bony arm for Anita to sit down.

"My husband is still missing," the woman hissed. "When will you find him? And where is that disgrace of a girl with our tea?" She added, loudly enough to be heard from the other room.

Anita hadn't been assigned to investigate Leo's disappearance. She was here for slightly different reasons, but she went with the flow of the conversation. "Can you recall the day he went missing, ma'am?"

"I've told you so many times," said Mrs. Woodham, pursing her lips. She was a woman in her thirties, but the crow's feet on the sides of her eyes made her look older. Recent events must have taken a toll on her complexion, which was more gray than vibrant, and aged her. "You only ask questions. You never do anything to find him." The woman sat down on the sofa and cooled herself down with the fan in her hand. "It was last summer," she began. Anita took notes as the woman talked. "It was just an ordinary day. There was nothing about Leo or his routine to suggest anything was wrong."

A servant girl came in and brought a tray with some tea and biscuits.

"Finally! What took you so long?" Mrs. Woodham exploded.

The girl set the plate and cups on the table in front of them. She said nothing in reply, just curtsied hurriedly and left as quickly as she could.

Anita ignored Mrs. Woodham scolding her staff and looked around the house. It was small, with little of the luxury she had expected. The woman was a citizen, but she could hardly be called rich. The house showed a lack of repairs that suggested inadequate funds, and it was likely going to continue deteriorating. The woman had sold as much as she could, saving herself from ending up on the street or in Sābanto. She was too respected to pick up any work after her spouse's disappearance. Even for Anita, the daughter of a rich poultry tycoon, having a career—especially as a reporter—was unheard of.

"Did anything happen between the two of you that could have caused him to leave?" Anita asked.

"What kind of insinuation is that?!" the woman retorted angrily.

"I'm sorry, ma'am. I'm just verifying the information that I have so far." Anita picked up the cup in front of her, but the liquid was too hot to drink yet.

"I don't understand why they keep changing the investigators on this case." She looked Anita up and down. "And sending someone as young as you?"

"Please, ma'am," Anita said, ignoring the woman's stare. "It's very important."

The woman averted her eyes. She took a handkerchief from the pocket of her dress and pressed it against the corners of her eyes. "I know he was sleeping with the village girls, but he'd been doing that for years." The woman turned towards Anita and explained herself. "I encouraged him to explore, you know."

"Of course, ma'am," Anita replied. "Open marriages are quite common."

Mrs. Woodham huffed at the label, but said nothing in return. She drank some of her tea.

"Did your husband have any enemies?"

"Leo was the head of security under Steven White. Rest in peace. What a tragedy," the woman digressed. "Leo had to do everything to protect Covedale. Did that earn him some enemies? Of course, but I couldn't tell you who they were. I never pried into my husband's work."

Anita took a sip of the tea from the cup in her hand. "Anyone you could think of as a potential kidnapper?"

"No one asked me to pay any money for his release."

"So you're ruling out kidnapping?"

"If someone kidnapped him, Mr. White would have immediately paid any ransom. My husband would have been back within weeks."

"Do you think someone killed him? Any idea who it might be?"

"I don't think anything," she replied. Having Leo return alive would have been best for her. If he was dead, she'd need to put a lot of effort into finding a husband, and her options for a second marriage with any older man who might want to combine his assets with hers were probably few.

"How long did your husband work for Mr. White?"

"As long as I can remember," Mrs. Woodham replied. "When I met Leo, before we even got married, he was already working closely with Mr. White." Her face brightened a bit as she added, "What a handsome pair we were at our wedding." She pressed the handkerchief below her eyes.

"Mr. White didn't like strangers in town and any trespassers were severely punished. Was that true?"

"Strangers are very dangerous to the well-being of Covedale. Who knows who they are and what they bring. My husband took pride in enforcing the laws set by Mr. White."

"Do you think those he punished might have retaliated against him?"

"I guess that can't be ruled out." Mrs. Woodham paused to think, then said, "No, I don't think so. They were all driven to the town borders with no way of returning."

"Were there any exceptions to this treatment of strangers? Have you heard of anyone who wasn't expelled?"

"I never pried into my husband's work, but I have not heard of such exceptions."

"How about Oliver Conway?" Anita asked. Mrs. Woodham gave her a blank stare, so she clarified. "Little of him was known when he arrived in Covedale."

"What does he have to do with my husband's disappearance?" the woman scolded her, drawing her brows together.

"Do you remember what the relationship was like between your husband and Oliver Conway before your husband disappeared? Were they close?"

Mrs. Woodham reflected on the question. "I think so," she finally said, but she sounded uncertain. "Mr. Conway visited our house many times, but always by my invitation, not my husband's."

"Did you notice any friction in their relationship?"

Mrs. Woodham quickly dismissed this idea. "Conflict between them? Nonsense!"

"Can you describe the first time you met Mr. Conway?"

"He came to Mr. White's fundraising event to reopen the power plant." That fit his profile. Conway had appeared in Covedale with money, and he hadn't hesitated to spend it on charities.

"Was there anything unusual about him?" Anita put the cup with tea down on the table.

Mrs. Woodham paused. "He definitely stood out in how he dressed, but I don't see how that has anything to do with my husband. Mr. Conway is an outstanding member of our community, and I don't appreciate such insinuations in my house."

Anita nodded, then changed the subject. "Did you know about your husband's cocaine addiction?"

Mrs. Woodham sprang up from the sofa. "I think you should leave now!" she shouted, putting her tea down on the table and pointing at the door. Anita noticed that the woman didn't seem surprised. If Leo was alive, he would likely have surfaced somewhere to feed his addiction. Lack of information about him suggested he was probably dead. Hiding such a dependence wasn't impossible, but it was extremely hard.

Anita got up and left the room. The woman didn't even glance at the reporter as she walked out into the hallway. Anita was about to show herself out of the house, when the girl who had brought in the tea stopped her by the door.

"Please, ma'am," she said. "No one in Covedale wants Leo back." Anita wanted to ask the girl some questions, but the girl turned around quickly and left as Mrs. Woodham called after her. Left alone, the reporter mindlessly scanned the empty hallway. The place was miserable with its dark and bare walls. She opened the front door and let herself out.

Ivy woke up in a room she didn't recognize. She was lying on a soft bed on her side under warm covers. The room was dark, but she saw some daylight coming through the cracks of the drawn curtains. She stirred, trying to see where she was, but suddenly a sharp headache hit her. She felt as if her skull was splitting open. A young servant girl rushed to her side and smoothed the sheets.

"Please, don't get up, ma'am," she whispered.

"Where am I?" Ivy asked in a similar hushed tone. The girl didn't look familiar. Her servant's dress was dark in color, black or navy, different from the light gray that Julia wore.

"Mr. Menken's estate, ma'am."

"What happened?" The name Menken. She'd heard it before, but was having trouble remembering where.

"Ya fell off a horse, ma'am. Doctor said ya has con-sion."

Ivy tried to remember what had happened. She had been on a horse. She had seen the waterfall with the Tari sisters. It had been beautiful. Her memories, however, were incomplete. Where exactly was she? Concussion? How?

"I'll let Mr. Menken know ya up. He's very worried," the girl said.

"Mr. Menken?"

"Yes, he brought ya here yesterday ma'am. Ya slept for a long time."

"Why are the curtains drawn?"

"Doctor's order. He says it helps with them headaches." Ivy said nothing so she added, "I be back," and left.

Ivy closed her eyes. The headache was indeed strong, even in the dark room. She tried to wait for the girl to come back, but shortly after she left, Ivy drifted back to sleep.

The shade of the room was different when she woke up. She didn't know how much time had passed, but her headache persisted. She lifted her head up to see if the girl was back. Her lips were dry and she wanted a sip of water.

The servant wasn't there, but another person was sitting in an armchair deeper in the room. The stranger got up, hurried to Ivy's side and sat down on the edge of the bed beside her. It was Liam Menken. The man who'd been at the factory the other day picking up his suit. The man she'd played games with at the casino. He looked at her and smiled. She noticed his dimples again.

Ivy scanned the room. What had happened? Why was she here? Where was everyone? Where were the Tari sisters? What day was it? Something was missing from her memory.

"I'm sorry about your accident," he whispered.

Ivy nodded her head slightly and the headache rushed in again. She closed her eyes, trying to get the room to stop spinning. "The servant told me I fell off a horse."

"Do you remember what happened?"

"No," she replied. She knew better than to shake her head again.

"The doctor said you might not remember," Liam said. "He said that a concussion is not a visible injury and it can't be instantly treated with the machines. He left some pills for you for the headache. Would you like some?"

Ivy opened her eyes and tried sitting up in bed.

"Would you like me to help you?" Liam offered and jumped to his feet.

"Please," she replied after a moment of hesitation. She couldn't do it on her own.

Liam helped her sit up and adjusted the pillow against the head-board. He put her right arm around his neck and slid his hand under her knees. He picked her up with no effort and moved her up on the bed so that her back could rest against the pillow. His cologne had a faint note of cinnamon.

"Thank you," Ivy said as he adjusted the covers around her and sat back down beside her. He picked up a glass from the side table and filled it with fresh water from the carafe. He offered her the water and a pill, which she swallowed with no hesitation. She wanted the pain to go away.

"The doctor said you need to rest," Liam added. "He said not to move you for a week. He'll be here later today to explain."

"I'm doing fine," Ivy tried to argue. "I don't need to be in bed for a week." Her head, however, disagreed and she was overcome with another wave of intense pain. She didn't have the strength to protest this decision at this moment. She'd try to make a point of it when the doctor came.

"It'd be an honor to have you stay." Liam smiled. "I'll make sure you're comfortable."

Ivy lifted the corners of her lips shyly. He was making this promise on his own behalf, and not the staff's. "Thank you," she replied.

Ivy was tired and hid her yawn with her hand. Her eyes filled with moisture and became heavy. The pills had made her drowsy.

"I'll let you rest," Liam said and smiled at her before leaving.

# 9

T HE ROOM WAS SMALL. There was only space for ten lockers and no more than five people changing at a time. The smell of sweat and dust permanently lingered inside. Cat sat down in the middle of the wooden bench and put on her finest dark green pants. The straight-cut fit her legs perfectly. She stood up and put on the black leather belt which went with her uniform. The polished brass buckle shone in the October morning sun rays coming in from the only window on this side of the room.

She glanced at the uniform cap that hung on a hook inside her locker. Cat was now forty, and she could see the odd gray hair standing out amid her black curls. She used to wear her hair long, cascading down her back. These days she kept it shoulder length for convenience and tied her hair in a low ponytail so that it didn't interfere with her cap, which she put on last.

As she was grabbing a leather leg strap from her locker, Robert, a young man in his early twenties, walked in. His black hair was wet from the shower and he looked the worse for wear following the training they'd had together. He still had a long way to go before he'd be fit enough to make a worthy opponent.

When Cat had joined the Sābanto force a month ago, the superiors had assigned them to each other as partners. Initially, Robert had assumed the position of enforcer on the team, but quickly learned that they would need to switch roles. Cat was better prepared to handle even the biggest men who gave them trouble, pushing them to the ground and restraining them. Robert was the nice guy, talking kindly to women and explaining the rules of the Sābanto compounds to them, or scolding the ill-behaved kids.

About a week ago, Robert had asked Cat for some training tips. The superior officers considered Robert too soft. He'd ended up here with Cat after barely passing his strength exam. He wanted to train with her and improve. Cat was getting her exercise practicing with him every morning at six before their shift started at eight. She was glad for the opportunity to continue to use her bō with someone.

"Thanks for the workout," Robert called, interrupting her thoughts.

She smiled at him and continued dressing. Cat fit the straps of the thigh holsters around each of her legs and attached them to her belt. It'd stay put even while she walked. She did a quick squat and ensured everything was in place and that her movements were unobstructed. She then loaded the sides of the strap with a baton and a stun gun. The radio unit went on her back, attached to the belt; the receiver she placed closer to the front for easy access.

"Someone said that ya were in Riverlea before it burned," Robert said. He was standing beside her and was also in the process of dressing in his uniform.

"Stupid rumors." Cat had spent almost two years in Riverlea before it had been evacuated by Sābanto, but she didn't want anyone to know. The office had written Riverlea in her documents, but only a handful of people in the compound could access that information. Why would anyone care? Cat felt the familiar itch on her temple, but she refrained from touching it. Any interest in her might jeopardize her mission in delivering the blueprints. She couldn't wait for an opportunity to leave the compound and complete the task she was entrusted with.

Cat was ready, but she waited patiently for Robert. Once he finished dressing, they walked out of the changing room together and started their morning routine with a quick look around the compound. There were close to a thousand people under their protection, mostly women, kids, and families. They occasionally had to break up fights between residents during food distribution. On top of that, people rioted often, demanding to be let out of the compounds or complaining about the living conditions.

Cat's superiors didn't allow her to work in the more troublesome male-only compounds for fear she wouldn't be able to perform adequately and would thus put others in danger. It was foolish of them, but she didn't protest the matter. There was no reason to complain.

She enjoyed working as a Green Shirt in the Sābanto compound she'd been assigned to. She and her partner did plenty of work.

"The usual route?" Robert asked.

The day was nice—it was warm and didn't call for rain. They wouldn't have to rush with their rounds and take shelter from the elements along their way. "I wanna check on the Atkinsons first," Cat replied.

They walked along the dirt path through the grass field to one of the white compound houses with a number fifty-eight above the door and knocked.

A middle-aged woman opened the door. "Ya again?" She scolded them as if they'd woken her up. Her hair was a mess. Was she even fully awake? There were large, dark circles under her squinting eyes.

"We just wanted to talk with Nick," Cat said politely. Her voice was as soft as she could manage.

The woman inspected her, then turned back into the house. "Nick, they came for ya!" she called.

A moment later, a fourteen-year-old with unkempt hair showed up. Cat immediately noticed a new bruise above his right eye.

"I'll be back," he barked at his mother who shrugged and retreated into the house. She closed the door behind her with a thud.

The boy walked out, and they slowly moved together away from the house and the curious ears of his parents and siblings.

"How ya doing?" Robert started without commenting on the kid's injury. Cat let him speak. He was better at finding common ground with teens.

"I'm okay." The boy shrugged. "Mole got it worse." He spoke of his older brother, who was sixteen and getting the brunt of the beatings inflicted on them by their father, a man with a history of domestic violence. Unlike Nick, Mole—real name was Jeff—didn't want any pity or attention from the Green Shirts. He wanted to solve his problems on his own by standing up for himself. However, despite many of these incidents, he wouldn't incriminate their father. Their mother also stood behind her partner. Just like most of the people in the compound, she saw any interest from the local guards as a threat to her independence.

Green Shirts couldn't do much without the family's cooperation. They'd have to catch the man red-handed and navigate the lies that would surely follow. The family would defend him.

"How are the girls?" Robert asked. Nick had three younger sisters. The smallest of them was just three years old.

"They hid," the boy replied and shrugged. "They're fine."

Cat sighed and scanned the sun-filled compound which was already buzzing with people on their way to the cafeteria for their share of food, or coming back after grabbing their rations. Nothing was out of place.

"They're opening a school in a month or two," Robert mentioned, squatting in front of the kid. "Ya should sign up."

"I dunno." The kid shrugged. "Am too old." He scratched the back of his leg.

"Who told ya that?" Robert laughed. "Ya smart. Ya should go."

The boy wasn't convinced. At his age, being smart didn't earn a kid the respect of his peers, but knowing how to read and count opened many new opportunities for the future.

Robert reached into his pocket and took out a handful of white powdered mints and pressed them into the boy's hands, and the boy's eyes lit up.

"Share them when you get home," Cat suggested.

The boy nodded and ran back towards the house.

Robert got back on his feet. They walked slowly, following their usual morning route. Robert broke the silence between them. "Sorry for asking ya about Riverlea," he said, returning to the previous conversation. "I'm looking for someone."

"Did you try the registry?" Cat asked. There were thousands of people that had been rounded up in Riverlea and brought here. They'd made note of everyone, so it wouldn't be hard to find someone. There were, of course, delays, due to the sheer number of displaced people and compounds Sābanto could have sent them to.

"I did," he replied. "Nothing."

"Not everyone made it here. Some escaped," she said, and Robert shook his head as though disagreeing with her.

Before she could ask him for more information about the person he was looking for, the radio cracked and a woman's voice sounded. "Unit C, please check in."

Cat grabbed hold of her radio and pressed the button on the side to speak. "Unit C."

"Report back to the command center," the woman replied.

Cat shrugged. What did they want now?

They quickly retraced their steps back to the offices in the main building of the compound to find out.

The secretary had gray hair and a wrinkled face and hands. She was sitting at the counter on a high swivel chair watching the display mounted on the wall when Cat walked in with Robert trailing behind her.

"Regulating industries is the best resolution," a program guest on the screen said. "World United is there to make sure that every business conforms to the best established practices in terms of production."

The secretary noticed them and turned in her chair. "We need you two outside today," she said formally. "Black Shirts sent a lot of men to resettle the town of Fairfield. There was trouble, and they asked for a hand with transport."

"We cannot have millions of these small businesses that produce nothing," the conversation on the display continued.

"Who are we picking up?" Cat asked. They didn't often collaborate with the Black Shirts who maintained order outside of the compounds. There was a clear division of labor.

"Two men."

"Investment into big businesses is the only way," the speaker on the screen said.

"Crime?" Cat asked.

"Unauthorized fishing. They used their boat as a home," the secretary replied.

"Non-property owners," Robert said.

Cat glanced at the display and the talking head. A person she'd never seen joined the discussion, saying, "These small producers need to be eliminated."

"The truck's ready. The Black Shirts coast guard team put ankle bracelets on them already," the secretary added.

Robert and Cat nodded in unison. The bracelets would come off inside Sābanto.

"Here is the address." The secretary pointed it out to them on the tablet, and they were soon outside on their way to the old truck. It was an hour's ride to the coast. If they timed it right, they'd be back for lunch.

The trip was uneventful and bored Cat. Robert drove. He didn't revisit the conversation about the person he was looking for and she didn't press. There was nothing interesting outside the window besides the big forests they drove through. The road was old and full of holes. Every so often the truck's wheel fell into one and the old rusty suspension moaned loudly. There were no other cars or trucks. The radio continued rambling on about Fairfield for a while, then moved on to an interview with someone whom the Free people had allegedly abducted, but Cat didn't pay attention to the story.

When they arrived in the coastal town, it was quiet and deserted. Sābanto had done evacuations here a few weeks ago and its citizens had no reason to stick around in a former industrial port city like this one. The fate of the abandoned town buildings and infrastructure was unknown.

The only place that showed any signs of life was the Black Shirts' police station.

As soon as they entered the building, a man noticed them and waved them over. The station was busy with people sitting around waiting. There were no windows and the place was stuffy, with air having no way to pass through. A woman at another desk was loudly discussing the fate of her son, whom Sābanto had apparently rounded up and held for questioning. Her voice was muffled, but filled the space. Cat didn't catch what crime he had committed.

The officer who had waved at them introduced the captives. "The younger man is David Rosten, he says. Age forty-five. Born in Dunnville. I couldn't find the town on the map, so I'm guessing it might've been one of those ones that got leveled during the war."

"And the older guy?" Robert asked.

"We don't know. He's illiterate and a mute. The other guy doesn't know him either, but calls him Doug. He says they aren't related."

While Robert spoke with the Black Shirts and gathered paperwork, Cat ventured into the other small and windowless room where the two men were waiting. The place reeked of rotting fish and Cat gagged, but quickly recovered. *Don't let the smell get to you.* She took out a scanner from the back of her belt and looked at the old man. He had long gray hair falling down his shoulders. His white beard contrasted with his tanned skin. He was at least sixty, so he wouldn't have to work once he got to Sābanto. He might even be assigned to their compound. There were still some rooms available for the elderly.

"Got yourself picked up, old man," she said, probably a little too loudly. The guy was mute, they'd said, not deaf. She kneeled down on one knee and scanned the bracelet already on his ankle. She checked that the number registered properly on the device. "Going home for a nice bath and a good meal," she told him with a small smile. She was glad they'd be riding in the back of the truck. The smell would make her sick by the time they got back to the compound.

"The old man wants to know where his boat is," the younger man, David, said.

Cat glanced at the man and her heart skipped a beat, instantly recognizing the dark eyes staring at her. She'd never mistake them for someone else's. He clearly recognized her as well.

Cat turned away from David's gaze, back to the old man. "Gone, sir. No more boats. No more fishing for you." Markets in the cities were also disappearing with no people living there, so he probably wasn't selling much of what he caught at sea these days. It was hard making a living.

What possible reason could there be for a Gutter to be here? Cat thought, returning her thoughts to the other man in the room with her. Didn't the Black Shirts know who he was? They clearly had no clue, Cat concluded. Back in the compound, they would check him thoroughly and interrogate him. The truth of who he really was would come out. No, she couldn't deliver him to the compound. She had to think of something, and fast.

She scanned David's ankle without looking up at him and returned to her feet.

Robert had finished doing the necessary paperwork and they were ready to go. Cat helped the old man into the back of the truck. "Got to move or your bones will get stiff again," David told him and laughed, seeing him struggling a bit with the height of the vehicle and the small ladder on the side. The metal clinked under the strain.

Cat noisily secured the latch on the truck door before jumping into the driver's seat. Cat insisted on driving back—she couldn't bear another boring ride as a passenger. Soon they were on their way and Robert closed his eyes and snoozed.

The truck rolled over the holes in the road until Cat reached the middle of a wooded area. She remembered it from earlier in the day and stopped at the side of the deserted road. Robert was still sleeping, and she didn't wake him up. She shut off the engine and quietly slid out of her seat and the warm cabin. She left the door open behind her. It was quiet outside. There was little sun coming through the trees and the fall dampness lingered along with the smell of pine resin. She scanned the road and the forest, making sure they were truly alone, and hugged herself, feeling the slight chill of the air.

She walked around to the back of the truck and quietly unlatched the back door. She let David disembark without exchanging any words. As she was cutting David's restraints, she noticed movement from behind the truck. *Fuck!* Cat turned towards Robert. He was supposed to be sleeping.

"What's going on?" Robert gazed at her with wide eyes. "His hands can't be untied." Robert walked towards Cat and reached for his stun gun, looking at David, but Cat got to him faster. She punched him in the nose, right between his eyes, knocking him out.

"Sorry," she said as Robert swayed. Cat caught his falling body, laid him gently on the ground on his side, and took his knife from his holder.

The old man was laughing out loud at the scene, as though he'd never seen such comedy in his life. "Do you vouch for him?" she asked, looking at David, but pointing at the amused man. "Will my partner be safe with him?" Cat had no intention of freeing the old man.

"That guy?" David said, pointing at Robert. "Yeah, he won't harm him."

"I owe you," Cat said quietly to Robert and stood up.

"Which way?" David asked as she took a quick look at her partner.

"That way," she replied, and pointed with her chin.

"When they ask, did you see which way we went?" David asked the old man. Cat didn't hear a response, but David must have been satisfied because he said, "Let's hope that'll slow them down."

David slapped the side of the truck, sending an echo through the trees, then ran to catch up with Cat to disappear into the woods together.

It was midafternoon, and the cook was already busy preparing dinner in the kitchen in the basement of Conway's house. He was a man in his fifties in a white chef's coat that was tight around his large waist and stained with whatever he was cooking. His white hair was topped with a white chef's hat. The man worked noisily with the metal rotisserie rod, standing beside the long countertop and skewering four small birds to put in the oven. The dinner he was preparing only had to feed three, but he always made extra just in case one didn't turn out the way he wanted.

As he weighted the rod so it would turn smoothly, cooking the birds evenly, a young girl—a couple years shy of twenty—came into the kitchen. She was wearing a black knee-length dress and a white apron that marked her as a servant. She slumped down onto a chair beside the long scratched up table next to an older woman wearing the same servant's uniform.

The girl grunted with relief at being off her feet for a moment and removed her flat shoes. She raised her hands behind her head, untied her bonnet, and removed it too. Her dark hair was neatly tied in a bun. "One more call and am gonna lose it," she said, placing her head cover on the table. "Bring this. Do that. Like she can't do it herself."

"Watch ya mouth!" the woman said with disapproval. "Ya have nothing to complain about." The older servant's full attire was still on, including the shoes and the bonnet. She had completed her chores in the morning, and as usual, was spending the afternoon helping the cook and doing minor chores. A set of silver spoons lay in front of her, and she was rubbing them with a gray cloth to keep them shiny.

"Glad ya didn't serve last night," the girl said. She brought her feet up on an empty chair beside her. There had been a baby shower for Mrs. Conway last night "Some people even traveled from Karben to be here yesterday."

"Couple hours of walking around with a tray and you're tired?" the cook barked. "Two days on my feet to prepare."

"That's why ya making an extra bird," the girl said matter-of-factly. She knew how the cook worked, making himself an additional helping whenever he could get away with it. Everyone saw how high the cook carried himself. It wasn't a secret he benefited from his position.

The girl took another glance at the food. There were four birds on the skewer, which meant there would be three people at the table today. "Guests again?" the girl said and wrinkled her nose. She rolled her eyes and slid down further on the chair.

"Ya stop doing that," the woman scolded her as though Mr. Conway himself would enter the kitchen and see the young servant.

The walls, however, had ears, and such disrespect would only bring trouble for everyone in the house. So many perks the master might forbid the rest of the servants. What would happen with the soap scraps they sold behind the master's back to the women working at the local factories? None of the staff could live without the leftovers from upstairs that would otherwise be discarded as waste. Would the master even go so far as to forbid this old woman from polishing the same spoons repeatedly?

"No guests, just Mrs. Woodham," the cook replied and shrugged. He'd been told to make dinner for three and that was all that mattered to him.

"What's for us?" the girl asked. It was usually some leftover soup prepared that day, and there was always plenty of it. The servants shared it late at night once they'd completed the after-dinner cleanup.

The cook turned away from the stove and glanced at the two women. "Gazpacho," he said, and turned back to what he was doing.

"A what?" the girl wrinkled her nose.

"Cold soup," the cook explained.

"That's the thing with them rich." The woman paused her polishing, looking at the cook whose back was turned to her. "They have a fridge, so wanna eat their soups cold." The woman was clearly forgetting herself.

"That's the whole point, for it to be cold," the cook replied, busily preparing the meal. "The problem, though," he added, "is Mr. Conway hates gazpacho."

The young girl laughed out loud.

"Then why are you making it?" the woman commented.

"Mrs. Conway's *special* request," he replied, emphasizing the word special. He then added, "But the fault will be mine."

"Now I don't mind serving tonight," the girl said with a smirk on her face. "All those teeth clenching and grinding will be funny."

The woman polished the spoon more vigorously.

The masters would be in a bad mood and they'd probably sleep in separate beds again. That meant extra work for her cleaning up tonight and making beds in the morning.

"Wish I was rich," the girl said and smiled to herself.

"And whatcha gonna do with the money?" The woman laughed.

"Hire a maid to bring ma stuff so I don't have to get up." The girl looked at her tired feet.

"Be glad ya not," the woman replied. "Is Mrs. Conway happy? I don't think so."

"Nothing's wrong with being bored and a little demanding when ya rich," the girl replied. She wouldn't mind changing places with the lady, even just for a day. She imagined herself lying on the sofa, maybe holding a book—she wouldn't read because she didn't know how—or she could do a little knitting instead.

"Devil's in idle hands," the woman commented without looking up from polishing the spoons. "That's why they fight like that."

The girl didn't respond. The old people were spoiling all the fun. And how many of them had seen the devil they spoke of? None.

There was a moment of silence that was only interrupted by the cook setting the partridges up in the rotisserie rack in the oven. Soon the smell of roasting birds filled the kitchen.

"How long 'til dinner?" the girl asked, stirring in her seat. She felt as though her stomach had wrapped itself around her spine. Her last meal had been a few helpings of appetizers last night, not counting the two sunny-side up eggs she'd had in the morning. "I'm starving." Without waiting for an answer, she took her feet off the chair, put her shoes on, and got up. "Anythin' left after the party?" she asked as she strolled towards the fridge.

As soon as she opened the door of the appliance and looked inside, the cook shouted at her. "Get away from there or I'll pull your legs out of your ass!"

She grabbed a small, jiggly green cube of something that she re-membered carrying around at the event the previous night before the cook got her with his wooden spoon. She stuffed the food into her mouth so that no one could take it from her. It tasted slightly tart and spicy, but she didn't know what it was made of. The slightly transparent, bouncy appetizer cooled her mouth as it disintegrated, revealing a crispy vegetable inside. She knew that one—asparagus.

"Told you not to open the fridge without permission!" The cook was angry, waving the wooden spoon in front of her.

"What an unruly creature," the woman scolded the girl. "Told ya it costs a ticket each time ya let the cold air out! Mr. Conway will cut it off ya pay if he finds out! What ya gonna do then? Ya won't find work like this in Sābanto!"

A bell on the kitchen wall sounded. It was a call for a servant and it was coming from Mrs. Conway's room. She probably wanted something brought to her, or maybe the pillows on the sofa needed fluffing. The girl ran to the table and grabbed her bonnet. Before anyone else in the kitchen could react, she was out the door, tying her head cover back on.

# 10

I VY SAT UP. SHE was in her own bed. The thunder in the distance had woken her up. She didn't think she would be able to fall asleep again until the storm passed. She brought the white stuffed bunny, the one that she'd been squeezing as she slept just a moment ago, to her face and inhaled the light floral scent that lingered on it. Liam had given it to her, and she smiled recalling the moment.

Liam Menken and his staff had pampered Ivy for an entire week at his father's house. The servants brought her fresh, lightly-scented pillows every day. They'd delivered food to her bed, and she'd had no shortage of fruits and snacks between meals. They'd brought her books from the chateau, but with the darkened room and her headaches, it only strained her eyes to read. She couldn't do more than a few lines at a time and eventually gave up trying.

Liam visited her often, bringing fresh flowers and keeping her company. He didn't stay long during his visits because he wanted to avoid tiring her too much, but each time he made sure that she was comfortable and feeling better. He joked that he had to check on her himself as he didn't trust the serving girls.

At the end of the week, the doctor had finally agreed that she could return home and Ivy was happy she could leave. Despite her injury, she'd had a great time staying at Mr. Menken's, but she felt she had overstayed her welcome. She was eager to sleep in her own bed again and return to her old routines. Liam was sad to see her go as she thanked him for his hospitality. She had invited him to stop by next time he was in Covedale.

Ivy put the bunny aside, got up from her bed, and put on the robe she'd left on the back of her chair. She glanced at the get-well card from the Tari sisters on the table. Everyone was being so kind to her.

Downstairs in the study, there was a book she'd been reading before going to the chateau. She missed curling up and reading for hours. She put on the robe and tiptoed down the stairs. Besides the rain and thunder, the house was quiet.

Ivy found the book on the table, grabbed it and sat down on the sofa. She hesitated before turning the lights on. What if the headache came back? She needed to be patient. Dr. Lott confirmed that the medical machines wouldn't help the concussion. He said that her illness would pass, as long as she took care of herself and didn't push too hard.

Ivy sat motionless with the book in her hand, looking through the window at the storm outside. Big drops were hitting the windows and sliding down the glass, chasing each other to the bottom. She put her feet up and lay down, putting her head on the arm of the sofa.

Suddenly the light above her turned on and she squinted. Julia had probably heard her getting up and wanted to check on her. "Please keep it off," she called.

"Yes, ma'am," Taylor replied. He turned off the light immediately and added, "I'm sorry, ma'am. I didn't know ya were here. I just came out to check if the windows were closed. Lots of rain came with the storm."

"I couldn't sleep," she replied.

"Would ya like anything? I could bring something," he offered.

"No, I'm fine."

"Please call me if there's anything, ma'am," he said as a goodbye.

"Please stay," she called.

"Yes, ma'am."

"Do you read, Taylor?" she asked.

"Not very well, ma'am."

"Come. Sit beside me," she said. She pointed at the armchair on the right of the sofa she was lying on.

He sat where he was told.

She handed him a book. "I can't read. It makes my headache worse," she said. He took a look at the book in the darkness. "You can turn on the side lamp," she added.

He turned it on, showering him with light while she remained in the shadows.

"There's a bookmark." She drew his attention to it and he opened the book there. "Please, read to me."

Taylor scanned the text as though preparing himself before he started reading. He took many pauses and read some of the long and unfamiliar words twice, but he did his best. She was patient and forgiving of his errors. It was a romantic poem for the moon, the beautiful woman of the night, to whom the man vowed his love. Ivy stared out the window. The storm clouds covered her tonight. Had the storm reached Liam? Had it awoken him as well?

"That is a lovely poem," Ivy mentioned, stopping Taylor from reading further. "You should read to me more," she said. Then added, "For practice." She smiled, but he couldn't see. "You know, I only learned to read a couple of years ago. It takes time to master it. I don't think I'm there yet, but I like to read."

Taylor sat in silence. They listened as the storm moved away from them.

"Thank you, Taylor," she said. "I'd like to visit the factory tomorrow. I should try to get up early."

"Thank ya, ma'am." Taylor got up and was ready to leave as soon as she was on her feet. "Would ya need help to get upstairs?" he asked, putting the book away on the side table.

"No, I'll be fine."

She took the stairs up to her room, feeling Taylor's eyes following her.

The chop-jet Amy teleported to was an old model just like the one Conway had, and she knew every corner of that vessel. The lower compartment of this one was empty. She drew her gun and listened, but there was no noise besides the loud humming of the engines which were keeping the chop-jet moving thousands of meters above the ground, and the metallic creaking of the strained steel. No one was around to be alerted by the sound of the incoming teleport.

Amy had to be quick. She still regretted accepting the assignment. She should've said no right there at Greyson's apartment. She reached the metal stairs going up and paused. Everything appeared still. She could see no movement or shadows above.

She slowly climbed the stairs, stopping out of sight, just before reaching the second floor. She peeked out over the top of the stairs, gun ready in her hand. Amy had asked for a better weapon and Conway had approved her request. It was a new model, much lighter than the one that fool Greyson used, and it fit her hand well. Whatever she was stealing must have meant a lot to Conway for him to be so generous.

Amy scanned the big room. The cockpit door to her left was open. There was no one inside—the chop-jet was flying on autopilot. To her right, at the end of the room, was the door to the jet engine compartment. It was closed, as she had expected. Directly in front of her was the entrance to a second room of the chop-jet. The door was slightly ajar, and a faint yellowish light shone from inside. That was the only place that someone could be occupying, and she didn't need to go in there.

Amy slowly walked up the steps while watching the other room. Someone was there with their back to her. The person didn't move as she passed the door and disappeared from their view should they turn around. She tip-toed to the overhead compartment on the side of the chop-jet and opened it up. Here it was, just like Conway said it would be. Amy picked up the small black box. She had no clue what was in it. It had some weight to it, but she didn't look inside. Regardless of what it was, she had to bring it back. Maybe it was better not to know.

Amy put the box into her pocket, then turned to the door of the jet engine room. She turned the knob. It wasn't locked. She entered and found a big panel with information about the operating engines. Amy quickly glanced at the pressure gauge and the temperature indicator. Everything looked in order, but that would soon change. She removed a metal wall cover beside her. Behind it there was a maze of pipes, wires and computing modules.

Conway had said to remove the third computing plate from the left. The pressure regulator. She found it and grabbed it with her fingers. In a few minutes the engines would overheat and the crew, disconnected from the warning system, would be unaware of the danger they were in. The only place they'd be able to see anything amiss was in this direct control room at the back of the vessel. No one went in here unless there was a real emergency. Amy pulled on the plate and it slid easily out of its socket. She hurriedly put it in her pocket and put the metal cover back on.

She emerged from the back room with her gun in hand, but the room was still empty. She just had to go down the stairs and she'd teleport back to Greyson. Her job here was done.

As she passed the door to the other room, she took a closer look at the man sitting at a desk. His head was lowered above a thick book of some kind. She couldn't see his face clearly, but there was something familiar about him. *Focus on the task. Don't let the man see you.* Amy moved away toward the stairs and walked down them back to the empty cargo compartment. Who was that man? Amy stepped into the teleporter space. Where had she seen him? Her eyes widened. *Fuck!*

Instead of initiating the transfer she whispered. "Greyson, are ya there?"

"Do ya have it?" he replied in her ear.

"Yes, I got it, but we have a problem."

"What is it?" he replied.

"Dr. Lott is here."

"So what?"

"We need to save him." Amy was trying to shout at Greyson but needed to remain quiet. "I can't let him die," she whispered.

"Stick to the plan. Just bring that thing over here."

"I can't."

"Stick to the plan!" Greyson repeated.

"Fuck the plan!"

His body jerked. Bruce had drifted off again trying to read. He was struggling to catch up with his studies. Maybe on the way back from Karben he'd be more rested. *Don't lie to yourself.* He was getting old and his body didn't have the energy it used to have.

He got up from the chair and walked to the main room. His muscles and bones ached from the strain of sitting too long. His eyes noticed the food replicator on one of the walls. He'd forgotten it was there. *Coffee sounds good.* Maybe that would help his concentration.

He pressed the buttons on the machine and it hummed as it worked. Bruce loved the aroma of coffee. The dark liquid had helped him through the long nights while he was studying for his medical degree, and then through the short breaks between surgeries at the front. It had always been his friend and he cherished every cup. One day, however, he'd need to start cutting back on it.

He heard a noise behind him and froze listening. The noise stopped. He turned towards the stairs that led down to the cargo compartment.

*You're alone.* Bruce wasn't afraid of ghosts. It was an old vessel, and just like an old house, it had its unique noises.

He grabbed the waiting cup of coffee and retreated to the other room where he'd left his book on the table. He was taking a sip when he heard someone running up the stairs. He jumped, spilling the coffee on his book.

"Dr. Lott!" A young girl emerged from downstairs. Her steps were hurried. "We gotta leave!"

"And who are you?" he asked. "Where did you come from?"

"Amy. Don't you remember me, sir?" She did look familiar. Amy. The tomboy from Covedale who he had treated years ago for a broken arm after she'd challenged a boy to a fist fight. She had grown a lot since then, he noticed. Had she snuck into the chop-jet before it had lifted off without him noticing? "Please follow me!" She scanned the room and grabbed his jacket hanging on a hook.

"I'm on my way to Karben," he said. He took the jacket away from the girl and hung it back.

"No, no, sir, please listen to me. The chop-jet will explode!"

"What are you talking about?"

"We have reliable intelligence. The chop-jet has been compromised." Amy gazed into his eyes. She didn't appear to be lying, but he'd been flying for two hours already. If there was something wrong, the autopilot would have alerted him during takeoff.

"Are you sure?"

She ran out of the room and Bruce followed her. She opened the door to the engine room. He looked at the gauges on the wall. The temperature of the engines was close to the critical line. How was that possible? As though Amy heard his question, she opened the metal latch by the floor.

"Here," she said, and pointed at something between the wires. "The computing module is missing. Whoever it was, they knew what they were doing."

"Do we have a replacement?"

"I don't know, but there's no time. Please evacuate with me."

The girl was right. If they knew for sure that the spare plate was on-board they might've been able to replace it. They would, however, waste the precious time they needed to evacuate. "How?" he asked.

They were above the ocean. The parachutes would take them down to the icy waters. That was as dangerous as staying here in the chop-jet.

"We teleport," she replied. "There's one downstairs." He had totally forgotten about the teleporter. Was that how she'd gotten here? "Please hurry," the girl urged.

Bruce went into the room and grabbed his jacket and briefcase. The coffee-soaked book was lying on the desk. He closed it and put it under his arm. He'd dry it out at home.

They were already descending the metal steps down to the cargo compartment where the teleporter was when he remembered the box. He'd left it in the overhead storage. He tried to turn around, but the girl was behind him.

"No! We need to go!" she said.

"I forgot something."

"There's no time!" She pushed him forward to the teleporter and initiated the transfer.


Greyson stood at attention in Conway's office. The black box was laying on the top of the desk. Beside him stood Amy, the fucking idiot. Conway sat on the other side of the desk and stared at both of them in awkward silence. At least the boss didn't have a gun with him. Although Conway hadn't said why he'd called them in, Greyson knew. The reason someone formulates a plan is for others to follow it. Amy had fucked up and now he'd pay for it as well. Greyson's legs ached already, but he didn't dare relax his posture. He didn't dare to move until he knew what her punishment would be . . . but the boss had said nothing so far.

The display in Conway's office began to show a news segment. "The jet carrying Dr. Bruce Lott to the Science Conference in Karben disappeared from our radars above the Atlantic Ocean. We feared the worst, but this story has a happy ending." The anchor turned towards Dr. Lott. "What happened?"

"I was flying to Karben when the cockpit gauges showed weird readings from the engines. It was an old chop-jet, more than thirty years old, and it wasn't that reliable anymore," Dr. Lott digressed. "The engines were going critical. I didn't have much time. I put on the life vest and the parachute and jumped out. The chop-jet exploded before I hit the water."

"Then you were rescued," the anchor urged Dr. Bruce Lott on.

"Yes. Another vessel saw my life vest beacon and rescued me before I froze—"

"Thank you Dr. Lott," the anchor interrupted. "It must have been a scary experience. Experts were dispatched to the site, however not much was left of the chop-jet. They believe there was a critical malfunction in the engine compartment that caused the explosion. Foul play is unlikely."

The display changed to the next news segment. "The authorities confirm that the fugitive from the Sābanto transport we reported on earlier today had taken a Green Shirt officer hostage. The man is described as white, slim, and about one hundred seventy centimeters tall. Last seen with black hair and matching beard. He's considered armed and dangerous, and shouldn't be approached. A search party is being organized—"

Conway turned off the display. "Anything you want to tell me?"

"It's her fault, sir," Greyson started. "I told her to stick to the plan." She was obviously a coward, too scared to speak up. She should be the one explaining herself. He shouldn't even be here.

Conway took out a cigarette and lit it. Then the man took a few breaths full of smoke. His movements were slow, dragging the time. "Bruce Lott never travels anywhere," he finally said. "He's needed at the clinic all the time. Jeopardizing the health of his patients is not in his nature. One of his office assistants was supposed to make that trip in the chop-jet, not him. I don't know why, but Lott made the last-minute decision to go himself." He slowly puffed the smoke, extending the pause. "Why did you save the doctor?" Conway asked.

*Yeah, why did you, Amy?*

"I have respect for Dr. Lott, sir," she replied.

Did she even know what that word meant? Respect. Conway needed respect. Couldn't she see that?

"Why?" the boss asked.

"He saves lives, sir," Amy said.

Another long pause.

Greyson watched Conway smoking. Who cared about some doctor? Medicine was becoming obsolete anyway. Machines were replacing them. Amy's reasoning for her decision made absolutely no difference. She had no argument in her defense.

"I didn't know Lott was in that chop-jet," Conway finally replied. "I missed that possibility. Saving Bruce Lott was the right decision."

*Fucking what?* Greyson's face grew hot. Had Amy just been praised for her insubordination? He clenched his teeth, but otherwise didn't move.

"Is there any reason he might suspect that I have this?" he pointed at the box on the desk.

"No, sir," Amy replied. "He never knew I had it."

"Thank you," Conway said. He put the box into the drawer of his desk and turned to Greyson. "You're dismissed."

What fuckery was this? Conway had something to discuss with Amy behind his back. That was bypassing his authority. Nevertheless, Greyson clicked his heels together, turned around and left the room. Maybe her strategy of disobeying orders was working in her favor, but that wasn't him. He cared about this job.

Greyson left Conway's residence and turned towards the nearby forest instead of heading home. His steps were hurried but steady. His ears were pounding. Conway had a target shooting range in the woods that would have to do for now. Amy would eventually pay for how she humiliated him. He'd find something on her.

Amy sat down when Conway told her to stand down. Greyson would be mad as hell. In a way he had been right to want to follow the orders to the letter at all costs. That was what good, reliable soldiers did. She was different and she couldn't let Dr. Lott be killed. How could she have lived with herself if she had?

"I like how you handled this situation," Conway continued. "Telling Lott to be quiet about the incident was a good call as well, but don't pat yourself on the back."

Amy had no such plans. She was in trouble with Greyson. He'd lost his trust in her, and now her commanding officer was probably furious that he'd been dismissed while she stayed. What did Conway want from her?

"I like people that think out of the box," Conway said and took out a tablet from a desk drawer and put it on the desk in front of him. He slid it towards Amy. "A good friend of mine gave me this a couple months ago," he said. "I listened to them a hundred times, but I cannot make out who or where these people are."

"Why should I help ya?" Amy said, looking at the tablet. "I know who ya are."

"What did Greyson tell you? I doubt it was accurate." He inhaled more of the cigarette smoke, then exhaled slowly.

"He told me enough," she said and shrugged.

He nodded. "I see that you've made up your mind about me based on what he told you." That wasn't hard. Even if Greyson's story was exaggerated, there had to be a lot of truth in it. "You don't need to help me, but hear me out." He leaned back in his chair and crossed his legs. "There was a meeting in Karben, right before Sābanto entered Riverlea."

"Yah, ya called them to liberate the town," she replied. She had been there when the town was evacuated. People had been packed onto the backs of the trucks and taken away.

"That was never my idea." Oliver shook his head and pointed at the tablet. "These are the conversations of the higher ups about that infamous vote and what happened during that time. Hours of discussions with different people, but nothing that could identify any of them."

Amy directed her eyes to the device on the desk.

"Listen to this," he said. "Give it a chance."

Amy didn't mind just listening. There was no harm in that. Maybe the information on the tablet had something that could incriminate Conway. Without saying anything, she pulled the tablet close. She'd listen through the audio files.

"Thank you for allowing me to speak with you, Mrs. Conway. I know it isn't a great time," Anita said as she walked into the sitting room at Mr. Conway's residence. She scanned the soothing light beige decor of the room. The tall windows faced the sun-filled terrace.

"Oh, please," Sophia replied with a smile. "Is that why I get visitors so rarely? I'm only pregnant, not feeble. Please sit down." She pointed at the sofa and armchairs at the side of the room.

"I'm sorry," Anita said, sensing that the lady of the house was a little upset. She took the armchair to her side. Sophia sat awkwardly opposite her with the help of her servant, who placed a large golden silk pillow behind Sophia's back for additional support before quickly leaving the room. Anita wanted to ask about the pregnancy and how far along it was, but she didn't know much about babies. She didn't want to make a fool of herself. Anita had always focused on pursuing her dream. As the only female reporter at The Citizen, she had broken barriers and glass ceilings. Kids and marriage were unimportant. She stuck to the script. "I'm doing a documentary about your husband's charity work. He's made a big difference for the poor."

"I'm so proud of his accomplishments." Mrs. Conway smiled.

"He's a veteran of the fifty-year war, correct?" At the side of the room Anita noticed the fireplace mantle with the dragon heads carved into it. She had heard about it, and that Mr. Conway was very fond of it.

"Yes, but he doesn't like talking about it. I don't think he ever wanted to fight. That's not in his nature."

"He was new here in Covedale the first time he showed an interest in charity, isn't that right? This town is wary of strangers, but it quickly embraced the idea of donating to your husband's charity. Why do you think it was so easy for him?" No one had heard of Oliver until he'd set foot in the town. Sophia's father had severely punished any trespassers, but he had made an exception in Conway's case. Mr. White had allowed him to operate within the town limits. *Would Sophia know anything about the reason why?* Anita wondered.

"Everyone loved him. The townsfolk, the elites. He has a way with people."

"Did he tell you how he got his fortune?" The citizens always took great care in making sure their bloodlines weren't spoiled. Mixing blood with commoners was unheard of. Steven White, Sophia's father, couldn't have been any different.

"He's a good man, and people are interested in the cause and willing to donate," Sophia replied without addressing the question. The charity money had come in much later when he'd already invested the bulk of the money he possessed. Donors and donations weren't what had made Conway rich, but it was a good story and it made sense that Sophia brought it up. Maintaining a good image was very important.

"Recent changes that he's making to Sābanto, like the creation of the Black Shirt police, are worrying to some people," Anita said. World United liked the idea of them policing their own. "Do you think he could lose support for Sābanto?"

"I think saying that *he* is making changes is an incorrect statement. There's a team working on the laws, including the World United

Health Commissioner. Oliver is only on the advisory board and he never has the final say," Mrs. Conway corrected. "Regardless of what decisions were made, there would always be those who would oppose them."

"Do you think the changes have created enemies for your husband?"

"That's the craziest idea I've heard," Mrs. Conway said and laughed. "These new rules benefit everyone. They're for everyone's safety. Theirs and ours," she added. "Enemies? That's such a strong word. Oliver's never had any enemies." The sweetness and kindness of her expression didn't fool Anita. It was all superficial.

"I agree," Anita replied. "The word enemy is not appropriate here, but I don't think Leo Woodham and your husband were ever close."

Mrs. Conway gazed off into the distance for a moment. "I don't know." She shook her head. "Leo's been missing for more than a year now." She sounded a little sad recalling his disappearance.

"I'm sorry for bringing him up," Anita said. "Did you know him well?"

"We grew up together," Sophia replied. "I sometimes think of him and I hope he's alive and doing fine. I hope he comes back. This is his home. But I fear the worst."

"Do you think his disappearance might have something to do with your father's death?"

"Of course not. They worked closely together. Leo spent more time with my father than I did. Maybe if he'd been around, he'd have noticed that my father was getting older, getting sick."

"Leo went missing not that long before your wedding. Do you think his disappearance might have something to do with your relationship with Oliver?"

"You mean like was Leo jealous?" Sophia laughed. "No, that wouldn't be like him at all."

Anita got up from her armchair. "Thank you for your time, Mrs. Conway."

"Anytime," Sophia replied with a smile. "If you have questions, please don't hesitate to visit me again."

"Of course." She shook hands with Sophia, but made sure the lady of the house didn't get up. There was no reason for her to see Anita to the door in her condition.

# 11

CAT AND THE MAN she'd freed were deep in the forest now. They had walked in silence until they were a fair distance from the road and out of earshot. They'd focused their eyes and ears on their surroundings in case they were being pursued. Cat wasn't fooled by the new name and identity the man had assumed. She had known him as Max. She'd recognized her perpetrator, the man who'd made her life miserable in Riverlea, as soon as she'd laid eyes on him. There was no way she'd ever forget his face.

"Do you still have it?" Max asked suddenly, breaking the silence that surrounded them.

Cat turned on her heels to face him and slapped him. Her hand stung from the impact, but she did not grimace. Yes, she still had the blueprints of the device with her. She smuggled it for Max out of Riverlea, but how easy did he think it was to reach Oliver?

"Nice to see you too," Max replied. Her slap didn't faze him. He grinned at her.

"You were supposed to be fucking dead, Max," Cat hissed. She wanted to shout at him, but it wouldn't be wise. Sound traveled far in the forest. They had no idea where they were or how far away people lived or worked. Her hands curled into fists. "What the fuck is wrong with you?"

He brought his hands up and stepped back from her, giving Cat extra space.

Max, the last person she wanted to see, had appeared out of nowhere. He was back in her life, uninvited. "I wish I could kill you right now," she said through her teeth. But she couldn't even deliver him to the compound. She had witnessed Green and Black Shirts using truth serum. Max would have had no choice but to tell them about her.

"But you won't." He smirked. Cat hated that crooked smile on his face.

"I can't," she corrected and started to walk again. Max trailed behind her. The freshly fallen leaves crunched under his boots. "Dead or alive, you're a fucking problem."

"Thanks," he said and sighed heavily. "I thought you'd be fucking happy to see me."

Cat stopped again and turned around to look into his face. "Happy?" She squinted. "You give me no reason to be fucking happy right now." Max's mouth opened, attempting to say something, but Cat didn't give him a chance. "Just keep your mouth shut," she ordered.

Max closed his opened mouth, then walked ahead, passing her on the path.

She couldn't kill Max. If anyone found his body, it would be made public that he hadn't died in Riverlea. His enemies would start looking for any other abnormalities in the cover story and eventually they'd connect her with him. If they found him alive, his forced confession under the truth serum would be enough to cause serious trouble for her, and possibly get her killed.

She followed him, looking around the forest. It was mostly quiet. The wind was light, gently swaying the tree canopies. The occasional squirrel disturbed the leaves on the ground, hiding their stash for the winter. Somewhere a bird above them, seeing intruders, sounded an alarm.

They'd made good distance walking from the road and they hadn't seen or heard any signs of pursuit. By now, Robert would have either woken up or someone would have found him with a broken nose at the side of the road. Although the roads were deserted, Sābanto might've sent a patrol.

The October days were short and the forest got dark quickly. They didn't know the terrain or what lay ahead, so there was no point in risking traveling while it was dark. They moved away from the path they were following and found a hiding spot between the trees where they could still see the trail. They sat on the ground and Cat leaned her back against a thick tree trunk and stretched her legs. They couldn't risk setting up a fire even though the night would be freezing, but at least predators wouldn't be a concern. Lots of animals had been hunted down for food during the war, so Cat didn't think they had to worry about any of them attacking.

Cat sat in silence, listening to the sounds of the forest. Max was still complying with her request and keeping his mouth shut. She wasn't sure where they were exactly, but she knew the general direction they were going. They were south of their destination and heading north. Eventually the landscape would start looking familiar.

Cat finally broke the silence. "Once we get to the river, we'll head west. We have lots of ground to cover—at least several days' worth." Cat recalled the time she'd been transported on a truck to Sābanto. It had taken them about a day to drive to the compound. This time she didn't have the luxury of a truck. They were heading back to Covedale on foot.

There was a light rustling behind them, and they slowly turned around and waited in silence, scanning the woods for any other movement or sound, but there were none. Everything was dark. No flashlights in the distance, barking of search dogs or people whispering. The sound didn't repeat and they concluded it was probably some animal. If Sābanto were already looking for them, they'd first deploy drones.

"Cat?" he asked, pointing at her name badge.

"Catherine," she replied. She'd changed her name when she'd arrived at Sābanto. She'd hidden any connection to Max for her safety. It felt silly now that she'd gone through all the trouble.

"I like that."

She couldn't see his face, but she was certain he was grinning again. "Why aren't you dead?" The news had said that they'd found his burned body in Riverlea.

"I staged my death," Max replied as though it was normal. "I didn't wanna fucking die like that, in flames."

"How did you get out?" Sābanto had patrolled every inch of the river looking for anyone who tried to swim to the other side.

"The fires in the city made it fucking unbearable to be inside," he recalled. "The subway tunnels were no longer safe. It wasn't hot there, not yet, but the falling buildings collapsed on some of the exits and the tunnels became fucking death traps. I left them, hoping to get off the island, but there weren't many ways to do that. I saw some swimming into Covedale, but Sābanto most likely apprehended them on the other side. If they were my people, the Gutters, White probably had them killed."

Cat remembered. The trespassers from Riverlea had been hanged on the tree by the River. All courtesy of the cartel leader, Steven White, and his officer, Leo Woodham. She hadn't forgotten that Leo had killed her husband, Tom, and thrown his body into the river. He had then given her hope that Tom was still alive and that he was in Riverlea. She had gone there, to the slum city, looking for him, and had almost died herself. Although her rage had cooled down in the past few months, she hadn't forgiven Leo. She'd just put it on the back burner.

"Some were swimming out into the ocean," Max continued. "Don't know if you remember, but the next island is just a small gray outline by the horizon. No way for a person to fucking swim the distance. So I waited, not being entirely sure what I should do. When I could no longer breathe—the smoke and heat were unbearable—I jumped into the water. My destination was that fucking shadow of an island. Insane of me, but I couldn't go to fucking Covedale. Too risky. I chose the option that gave me a better chance of survival. I blacked out at some point while swimming. My limbs stopped working. I woke up on the fishing boat with the old man."

"That explains why you reek of fish," Cat observed bluntly. There had to be more to the story than he cared to share with her. She was skeptical that he had staged his death without a plan to get out of Riverlea before it burned. That a fisherman had saved *him* out of hundreds that were desperate to flee. What was he hiding?

"I helped the man catch and sell fish at local markets," Max explained. "That wound down once the people from the coastal towns disappeared. The markets were closed, and only ghosts occupied some towns." After a short pause, Max asked, "Did you ever go back to Covedale?"

"No." Cat lowered her head. While in Riverlea, all she'd wanted was to get home to Covedale, but she wasn't allowed to leave Sābanto. There was no one waiting for her anyway.

"Can you take this off me?" Max pointed at something in the near total darkness. Cat knew he was pointing at the bracelet on his ankle.

"Nope." She didn't have the tool to remove it. Forcing it caused serious injury, and it wasn't worth the risk. "I don't have the key, but I didn't scan your bracelet at the station," she said. "They can't track us with it." Cat had scanned the old man's bracelet twice and dismissed the error on the device. She'd been afraid that the Black Shirts at the station would check the prisoners and discover her deception. She'd prepared her best confused face in case they caught her, but fortunately for both of them, the soldiers didn't have time for an inspection.

"I'll take the first watch," Max decided, and Cat took his offer. She was looking forward to a few hours of rest.

She leaned her head back against the tree and closed her eyes, but the position was straining her neck. She stirred, unable to fall asleep. "Lay on my lap," Max offered.

She hesitated. Laying her head on Max's lap suddenly felt too intimate. Could she let go of her personal space so easily? She recalled them sleeping together a few months back, her head on his chest as though they were lovers, embracing each other. The nightmare of Riverlea was still fresh in her mind, but her need for sleep was stronger.

She carefully put her head on his thigh and lay on her side on the forest floor. It wasn't a comfortable arrangement, but better than sleeping sitting up. She closed her eyes.

Somewhere in the middle of the night, Cat took watch. All was calm. There were no signs of anyone following them or looking for them.

The faint daylight eventually broke through the trees. Max was still sleeping, resting his head in her lap now. She took a moment to look at him before waking him up. His straight hair was longer than she ever had seen it and it covered his ears.

The October dew was on their clothes and her green coat hadn't kept her warm at night. A sudden chill went through Cat's body and woke Max, who sat up, feeling the cold as well. They needed to keep moving.

"We should find a place where we can light a fire tonight," she said. They needed water and food. She was starving. A small animal like a rabbit might feed both of them; the trouble was catching one. Cat recalled the brief survival training she'd gotten in Sābanto. She wished she'd paid more attention to it.

Before the sun was fully up, they came across an abandoned town. The forest path continued on to a dusty road that divided the settlement. From the shelter of the trees, they noticed that some buildings were burned and others had no glass in the windows. Whatever window coverings hung inside were fluttering in the wind. Cat couldn't tell how long ago the people had left these houses, but the front lawns were already overgrown.

"What happened?" Max asked, looking at the town in the distance.

"Sābanto happened, I guess," Cat replied, and glanced again at the burned buildings.

"Was that his plan?" Max looked off into the distance, inspecting the place.

"Whose?" Cat asked.

"Oliver's. He took the people out of Riverlea, but I thought he'd stop at the city. Why here?"

Cat didn't know. "Do you think someone might still be there?" she asked.

"Only one way to find out." Max got up and Cat followed.

They didn't take the main road, but circled the town a bit and approached the first house from the back. No one was in there. They walked inside the single room farmhouse, the floor creaking under their weight. Everything inside was in disarray. The cupboards in the kitchen had been left open. The dresser drawers were mostly empty with only some rags remaining. The occupants had left the place hastily, on short notice, packing as much of their valuables as they were able to carry. Cat checked all the cupboards in the kitchen storage. Besides a few utensils and broken ceramic vessels, they were all empty.

"We should check other houses," Cat said. "We need food."

They moved to the second farmhouse. It was bigger than the previous one. There were multiple rooms, and a wall separated the kitchen from the common area. It even had a proper pantry shelf. Cat opened it and found it empty. The shelves were bare as if someone had gone through them. It didn't surprise her they weren't the first ones pillaging this place.

"There's someone in the house on the other side of the street," Max said as he came over from checking the rest of the rooms, but he didn't look concerned. "Anything here, or shall we keep moving?"

Cat bent down to the floor and looked under the shelves and found nothing. "We should try the next one," she replied. They had to keep trying.

As they were moving outside, Max monitored the other house. He said that the curtains behind the closed window had moved again, but whoever was there clearly wanted to be left alone.

They searched a couple more houses. Cat found a tin of beans stuck in the back of the cupboards that someone had missed. In the overgrown gardens, they came across some carrots hidden in tall grass. A crooked apple tree still had some yellow apples hanging from it. Max climbed it and brought them down. They immediately started on the fruit, feeling the satisfaction of putting something in their stomachs. The apples were slightly tart and refreshing. Cat couldn't remember the last time an apple had tasted so good, although she'd had plenty in Sābanto.

They left the town, not wanting a confrontation with the hiding stranger. They walked a few kilometers and found shelter in a small cave surrounded by woods that was away from the road. Max quickly scouted the area and reported a waterfall and a pool of water up the hill. He said it didn't look like anyone could come and disturb them at the cave from that direction. They cooked the beans in their can over a small fire on the rock floor and ate the carrots raw.

"I'll go wash up," Max said. There were still a couple hours of light left in the day and the weather was unusually warm. Cat went with him to keep watch. Finally, the stench of the fish would be off him.

The waterfall Max spoke of was just a small chute that moved quickly, without much noise, down a not-so-steep rock face surrounded on each side by trees and shrubs. The water navigated around boulders in its way, splitting, then meeting again as it hit and disturbed the still surface of the pool. The water was pristine. Cat could see the pebbles at the bottom of the small lake. She decided to wait and let Max go first into the icy water. As he washed, she found a spot with a good view of the road and the forest. Sitting on a fallen trunk of a tree Cat rested her elbow on her knee and put the palm of her hand against her left cheek. Her fingers touched her temple. There was no scar there. She had checked it in the mirror, looking at the spot from various angles. There was no bump she could feel under her fingers either. Invisible, untouchable, like there was nothing there, but she remembered the surgery she underwent. The thing was certainly still there. Only a couple of days and she'd be finally freed from it. Fulfilling her side of the deal she had made with Max would set her free from him.

The water splashed as he got out and she unconsciously turned her head around and stared at him.

They're sitting on the bed, Max's back against the cold concrete wall. She nestles in his arms while she inhales from a slug of hand-rolled tobacco, then passes him the rest to finish as she exhales the smoke. She places her hand on his torso.

"Your hands are cold," he says. He reaches for the blankets and covers her naked shoulders.

"We should go to the beach," she says as she draws circles on his hair-covered chest. He is slim and not muscular. She brings her eyes up and looks at him. He's smiling.

"You know I can't," he says.

She looks down at her finger, pausing on the two freckles under his left breast. "Not even at night?" It disappoints her they always meet in the same place, his bedroom. They don't always have sex—sometimes they just snuggle, like today, sharing their warmth and talk—but it is always within the same four gray walls.

"Not even at night," he replies and kisses her forehead.

Cat averted her eyes. She didn't want Max to think she was staring as he let the warm breeze dry him off.

He walked up to her sometime later, fully clothed. "Can I borrow your knife?" he asked.

Cat hesitated for a moment, but Max had no reason to harm her. She reached into her pants pocket, took out the knife she had stolen from Robert, and handed it to him.

He grabbed the knife, walked over to the pool, and sat down at its edge to shave. This was the first time she'd seen him with a beard—she'd noticed some silver threads in it—and it made him look like a different person. If it hadn't been for the dark eyes she knew so well, she might not have recognized him at the station.

His moves were clumsy. He was blindly trimming his hair, and he wasn't doing a good job. She smiled widely, watching the performance, but then got up and walked over to him.

"Need some help?" she asked.

He smiled. "Please." He handed her the knife, even though she'd threatened to kill him.

She knelt beside him, took strands of his beard, and trimmed them as close to the skin as she could manage. Once she finished with his facial hair, she started to trim the hair on his head, which wasn't as black as she remembered either. The low sun was reflecting on it and she noticed thin strands of shiny brown hair.

Cat recalled meeting Max for the first time. His men—they'd called themselves Gutters—had abducted her from the street and dragged her through the dark and smelly tunnels to be used and humiliated. She'd been petrified, not knowing if she'd live another day. Everything had been in Max's hands. He controlled everything in Riverlea: the money, food, his army of Gutters walking around with guns . . . this man had held power over her just a couple months ago, but now he needed her help cutting his hair.

"Cat?" Max asked, bringing her back. She'd gotten lost in her thoughts and stopped her motions. She nodded and concentrated on finishing her work on his hair. It wasn't great—she didn't have the skills for cutting hair with a knife—but it'd do for now. The smell of the fish was mostly gone and lingered only on his clothes. He wore pants that hung on him and were tied with a rope around his waist and an oversized shirt under a long coat. His rubber boots were tall, covering most of his shins. He no longer had the look of someone important.

Max promised to keep his eyes averted while she bathed, but she was sure he wouldn't. The day was at its end and it might be a while before she'd get another opportunity to wash. There was no time for hesitation if she still wanted to catch the warmth of the fall sun after her bath. She stepped into the freezing water.

They lit a small fire in the cave when they got back, then quickly reduced it to embers. Just enough to slightly increase the temperature around it, without making them visible from afar. He let her rest first and, without asking, she laid her head on his thigh.

"Remember Brian?" Max started saying as she was falling asleep. "You gave him a bloody nose with your stick"

"A bō," she corrected.

"A bō," he repeated with mock seriousness.

"I gave him a black eye," she said and smiled. The man had been training with her as a potential opponent. He hadn't done too badly until the trainer asked her to use the new trick she had learned. Brian didn't know the move. He'd failed to protect himself and ended up with a nasty-looking injury. Cat hoped her partner, Robert, was found and that he was doing alright after the punch she'd given him.

"Your hair grew long," he said, stroking it. "I like it."

Cat didn't reply. She pretended to be asleep.

The evening was chilly, so Anita hugged herself to keep warm. She rarely smoked, but it would be hard to blend in without doing so while standing at the back of the clinic in Covedale. She pretended to be busy, as though she was on a short break, finishing her cigarette in a hurry. She didn't know how many people worked at the clinic, but she hoped a new face wouldn't be a surprise. Dr. Lott had little time to meet with her, so once a few days passed without him committing to an interview, she decided to find information on her own. She wore a white shirt under her jacket, which resembled a medical gown. She hoped she'd blend in.

As Anita expected, a woman—a nurse—came out the door and lit a cigarette.

"New?" the woman asked. She stared ahead of her, at the woods in the distance. The tall pine trees were mostly bare, with green needles only at the top of the canopy.

"Yeah, first shift," Anita went with the flow, but didn't turn to look at the woman, hoping not to be recognized from the displays.

They stood there smoking, without conversation. Anita had thought of some questions to ask the staff ahead of time, but now they seemed silly. Not asking anything, however, would be stupid.

"How is the Doc?" she asked.

The nurse initially said nothing while inhaling some cigarette smoke, but then she replied, "He's okay."

Okay? That was it? No details about his work, social life, nothing? No complaints about the work at the clinic, no dirt? He was just okay?

"There was an old man that came in today." Anita had noticed him entering the clinic. He was at least sixty or seventy, which would have made him eligible for Sābanto. Why hadn't he been sent away? What value or expertise did he have to offer his master?

"I wasn't the one helping him," the woman said, dismissing any further questions that Anita might've had about that visit.

She wondered what else she could ask, but was distracted by a lot of commotion at the front of the building. The nurse threw her cigarette onto the ground, smashed it with her foot, and hurried to see what was happening. Anita followed her steps.

*Oh, God!* Those were the only words that came to Anita's mind, seeing the amount of blood. A couple of men were carrying another man on a stretcher into the clinic. His left leg was missing. They had tightened a homemade tourniquet above his knee, reducing the blood flow, but it had soaked through the sheets they'd wrapped him in. Anita had learned some first aid in her youth, but this was beyond any training she had.

The nurse ran up and checked the man's vital signs and directed the people and the stretcher to enter the clinic. There was a procession of some other people holding a crying woman who appeared on the verge of losing her mind. The nurse told them to remain outside.

Anita was more interested in what was happening in the building, so she followed the men and the stretcher inside. Bruce Lott emerged immediately from one of the rooms and led them into an examination room across the hallway. The men carefully transferred the patient onto the table. The nurse was already running the blood tests and checking the pressure, and setting up an IV.

"What happened?" Dr. Lott asked. He cut the layers of cloth and bandages that covered the wound with scissors.

"The potato harvester got his leg," one man said calmly. "The belt caught his pants."

Anita was aware that she should help, but she didn't know what exactly she should do. She didn't want to get in the way of the nurse who was now connecting some device to the injured man.

"Blood pressure is critically low. Heartbeat one hundred and fifty a minute," the nurse said. "Pass me the blood." She looked at Anita, then added, "It's behind you."

Anita turned around and opened the huge fridge door. There was a stack of bags with blood in them. A marvel of the technologies developed during the war, a truly universal blood type. She picked one up, closed the fridge, and handed the packet to the nurse who quickly connected it to the patient. The little tube turned red as it fed the blood into the veins of the man lying on the table.

"Please leave," the nurse calmly asked the men who were still standing beside the door of the room. "He is stable for now." There was no sound of panic in her voice.

The men hesitantly retreated into the hallway, leaving only the three of them in the room.

"Miss Gibala," Bruce Lott turned towards her for a moment, then went back to the work he was doing on the patient. The nurse was securing an oxygen mask, not paying attention to either of them. She knew what the patient needed and concentrated on her task. "Is this what you wanted to see?" the doctor asked.

"I—"

"Stand there, where you are," he ordered without giving her a chance to answer. He turned towards the sink, not looking at where she stood pressed against the wall. She wasn't comfortable leaving her spot anyway.

"Why not use—" Anita began.

"Yes, the new machines. They need authorization from the employer. The employer handles any fees required to use them." He washed his hands thoroughly as he spoke. "You know they're quite expensive."

"Why not wait for the authorization?" The man was in stable condition. They'd said so. How long could it take? Couple of hours at most.

"I'm not so optimistic the authorization will come in time, if ever." Dr. Lott replied and glanced at the reporter. He dried his hands with paper towel and used a disinfectant, ensuring his hands were sterile. The smell of alcohol filled the small room.

"It's the employer's responsibility." Surely they wouldn't just leave the person to die with no help.

"Miss Gibala," Dr. Lott replied, picking up some medical gloves. In the background an old machine beeped rhythmically. The nurse had her back to them and was preparing something on the table in the far corner of the room. She kept quiet. "You wanted to meet me and learn what I do," he said. "Here it is. I save lives."

"Behind the employer's back?"

"Whatever it takes. I don't ask questions," he said. "I worked at the front during the war. I never asked anyone's permission to do whatever was necessary to make sure a soldier would live to see their family again. I don't see how this is different."

"So you treat people using the old skills?"

Dr. Lott didn't reply. The nurse laid out a range of metal tools beside the doctor, then helped him into a robe.

"Do you know how to treat gunshot wounds?" Anita asked.

"Patient's stable. One hundred and forty. Pressure still low," the nurse said.

"Seen lots of them at the front," he replied.

"Did you treat one recently?" Anita asked.

"Scalpel," Dr. Lott said to the nurse who handed him the tool. He ignored Anita's question as he made the first incision.

# 12

THE NEXT DAY THEY found train tracks running north. Cat squatted in front of the old rails. "Do you think anyone uses these?"

Max bent over. "The subway lines in Riverlea were all rusted. These are not." The top of the rails was slightly shiny. Maybe not used often, but something had come through recently.

"They transfer stuff via these new teleporters," Cat said. "There's not much land transport anymore."

She stood up and looked around. The sky was overcast and the wind was slowly pushing gray clouds of various shades through the sky. It felt oddly quiet. She was becoming concerned that they weren't being pursued. There were no drones flying low with thermal cameras to find them. The trees were the only things moving in the slight breeze, sending some turned leaves down to the ground.

"They might still use trains to transport bigger stuff," Max replied, and Cat nodded. It was a good theory. She recalled her compound having trouble teleporting in an excavator. It was too big and too heavy. The staff had ended up towing the equipment into the compound on a flatbed truck.

They followed the tracks under the cover of the nearby trees. Their steps made light crunching sounds on the forest floor. They walked for at least an hour until a weird noise in the distance behind them made them stop and turn around. Some birds flew from their shelter in the trees at least a few hundred meters away from them.

Max and Cat moved deeper into the woods and hid behind the shrubs, but they still had a clear view of the tracks.

In a few minutes, an old diesel locomotive appeared to the south of them, spitting black fumes. It was slow. It took even longer for the rusting locomotive to pass them. It was a short train, about twenty boxcars. Some of them had open doors.

Suddenly there was a piercing shriek of metal scraping metal. Cat covered her ears until it stopped. That was the strange sound they had heard earlier: the train braking.

"Wanna grab a ride?" Max sprinted towards one of the open cars in a risky move. They didn't know if anyone was guarding the train, or if someone was inside, but Max was already grabbing the handle of one of the boxcars. Cat had no choice but to follow him.

Max pulled himself up, not getting caught on the rusty metal. He then extended his hand to Cat who was still running. Cat grabbed the handle with one hand and Max's hand with the other. She had trouble getting herself off the ground, but he pulled her up and helped her swing her body into the car. She fell directly onto Max who grabbed hold of her firmly, stopping her from falling onto the hard floor of the car.

They were both out of breath. Cat rolled immediately onto her back and off of Max for a quick rest and to wait for her heart rate to slow down.

"No one else is here," Max said.

Once Cat recovered, she got to her feet and scanned the inside of the car. It was dusty, with metal shavings and oil smeared on the floor. They had to be transporting some large machines or metal parts on this train. Cat didn't know much about the teleporters, but the cargo was probably not suitable for them.

Max sat down and rested his back against one of the walls. He followed Cat with his eyes as she inspected the inside.

She eventually sat down by the door, looking in the direction they were going. A cold breeze hit her face, blowing her hair back. She didn't think the train would take them all the way to their destination, but it would save them a lot of walking. It would also be harder for anyone looking for them to know how far from the road and from Robert they were.

"You're mad at me," Max said.

*Captain Obvious.* "Why wouldn't I be?" she replied.

"What's wrong?"

Cat laughed. She couldn't believe him. How could he not know what had he done wrong? She turned around and met his blank stare.

She shook her head derisively and turned her eyes back to the view outside.

Cat is on the ferry. The one that takes people from Covedale to Riverlea. She looks up at the darkened ruins of the skyscrapers towering above her. She is looking for her husband, Tom, who is missing. Leo says he's in Riverlea. She'll find him. Otherwise . . . there's no otherwise. She dismisses other possibilities.

"You can go," the ferry operator tells her as the ferry opens. Cat can disembark, but where should she go?

Cat steps onto the solid ground. She can't remain on the ferry without paying for a return trip. The armed men stand around and look at all who have arrived, but they don't stop her or apprehend her. She walks. A random street takes her deeper into the ruins of the city.

"You knew everything that was happening in Riverlea," she said.

"Not everything, just the important stuff," he replied.

"Tell me." She turned her body towards him. "You knew about me when I stepped out of the ferry, didn't you?"

He said nothing.

"Didn't you?" Cat pressed.

He nodded. "Yes."

"Was that when you decided you wanted to fuck me?"

"I couldn't do anything for you then."

"You don't deny . . ."

Max didn't respond. He leaned his head against the wall he was sitting against, and gazed up at the ceiling.

Cat turned her back on him. He was lying. He could've taken her off the street anytime, rather than waiting until she'd lost all her money and been assaulted. He'd done nothing when she was starving. Cat took an apple out of her pocket and took a crunchy bite. She sat listening to the rhythmic sounds of the wheels and the cargo car they were in, clicking as it was pulled along by the boxcar in front of them. The train was now maintaining a steady speed.

She is walking through the alley, passing men clearing rubble off the street. She feels weak and lightheaded, dragging her legs, slowly moving towards the Bayside Inn. Bam . . . bam . . . bam . . . she feels the pounding in her chest as the men work rhythmically, hitting their metal tools against the concrete, breaking it up. Or is it her heart beating faster at the thought of what she is about to do?

She touches her sunken cheeks with her bony hand. Her skin is rough under her fingers, but it used to be smooth and radiant. Riverlea has changed her. Forced her to adapt, to survive. She needs money so desperately now. She needs food to stay alive. She can't wait any longer or she'll be gone. If she doesn't do anything, she'll have only a few days. Safety and dignity no longer matter.

She wiped a tear from her face before Max could notice.

He spoke. "I took you off the street. I couldn't stand knowing that you were even considering selling yourself."

"Is that what you think? You think that you saved me?"

"You were better off with me."

Cat laughed. Her laugh echoed through the empty car. She was quiet for a moment. "You used me," she said. "Humiliated me. Should I thank you for it?" Cat watched the world outside the train as it passed them by. The forest scenery changed to fields. The clouds remained as gray as before.

"I was trying to help," he said.

Cat turned towards him. His blank eyes stared at her.

"Did you forget I was your 'Covedale Bitch?'" she exploded. "Do you remember the first time you used me? When you got between my legs like you owned me? What the fuck are you talking about?!"

Max lowered his head and sat motionless while she talked. When she was done, he brought his head up and spoke slowly. "Showing that I fucking cared about you would have made me look weak."

"Weak?"

"Weak leaders aren't respected. What do you think the guys would have said? I asked for a bitch from the inn and I didn't fuck her?" Cat rolled her eyes. "I did a lot for you to make up for it."

She looked away from him again. He truly had no fucking idea what he had done, and how it had made her feel. What had he done to make up for it? How did he think he had accomplished that?

She visits Max. He is sitting at the table with a nearly-empty plate of food in front of him. He smiles at her and gestures for her to come over as he pushes the chair away a bit, giving her space. She does not hesitate to sit on his lap, her hands around his neck, giving him a long kiss. Max's hand travels up her skirt, touching her bare skin. She breaks the kiss and smiles at him. If she acts right, he'll allow her to stay for the night. There's a storm outside. Freezing wind pushes cold snow around the city, creating drifts. She doesn't have proper shoes or a coat, and his bed is warm and dry.

Max bends forward and grabs a fork with a piece of food from his plate. He holds it up to her mouth.

"Try it," he says.

She hesitates, but takes a small bite. It's real meat. She can't remember the last time she ate it. Her eyes widen. "How did you get meat?" she asks.

"I have my ways," he smiles at her. "Have the rest." He pushes the fork towards her again.

She eats it and closes her eyes. The meat is good, tender, tastes just right.

Meanwhile, Max kisses her neck. Cat allows him to hold her close as she relishes the taste in her mouth. Is it wrong that she'll open her legs for him, let him do what he wants, for a treat?

"I fucking cared for you," Max added. His voice was calm. He didn't seem upset that she disagreed with him. "I never stopped."

Cat stared at the lake they were passing. The golden reflection of the sun, which had found its way through the heavy clouds, cut the gray of the water. She looked at the tracks in front of her. They continued north. "You never cared for anyone," Cat replied with disinterest.

She looks into Max's eyes. There's a deep sadness in them.

"What's wrong?" she asks. Max does not reply, he just shakes his head, but Cat knows about the accident that happened the previous night. A Gutter had been killed. She had seen the young man at Max's place many times. Always a wide smile.

Max recalls enjoying working with him. "I planned to promote him soon," he says. "Keep him closer to my command."

Cat sits beside Max and presses his head against her chest. "It's okay to cry," she tells him, and she feels his body shaking. "I won't tell anyone." Only in her arms can he mourn his loss. She hugs him and strokes his hair as he cries.

"You never cared for *me*," Cat added, correcting herself. She turned her body towards him. "Paying me an extra ticket so I could have extra food or make shack repairs was not caring."

"Why do you think I did what I did in Riverlea?!" Max exploded. "That I reigned to become fucking rich? Look how well that turned out for me!" He grabbed his baggy clothes in a fist. "The nights I spent trying to find new sources of income or the days securing food shipments, that means nothing to you, right? Bitch about how hard it was for you to be with me 'cause you'd have preferred to be fucked on the streets by ten guys every night. Guess what? All you had to do was tell me you didn't want to come. You never did."

"Right, I had a choice," Cat replied calmly, and turned away from his gaze.

"You did, and I know you chose what you thought was best," he replied. "Don't tell me it's all my fucking fault."

"Was that you following me everywhere in Riverlea?" she asked. "Why didn't you save me earlier? You wanted to wait until I hit rock bottom before you rescued me?"

"Mark was following you. Not me," he said. His anger had begun to cool.

"Mark? What for?" Cat turned and looked at Max with wide eyes. In Riverlea, everyone knew who Mark Rodden was. Max had said that they were working together to get the food shipments for the city. Cat had only found out who Mark was later.

"Weren't you asking about him?" he replied, then added, "If I'd known he'd stopped with the surveillance when he brought his girl-friend into the city I might've done something. I thought you were safe. No fool would have crossed Mark's men. When I heard what happened to you, I was mad. I blamed myself for not doing more, but it was too late."

"You know who hurt me," Cat said.

Max nodded. "He bought cocaine with the money he found on you. I made him keep taking it until he had fucking seizures."

"You killed him." Cat was surprised by this development, but nothing was really shocking to her anymore. Of course he killed him.

"Don't tell me you never wished for his death," Max said.

Cat turned back to the world outside of the train car. They were back in the forest. The trees grew closer as they rode north. It was true. She'd wanted that man dead for what he'd done to her.

Cat is left alone in Max's room. She slowly walks up to his desk. There's nothing but papers on top of it, and none of them interests her. She walks to the other side where the chair is and looks at the drawers. She hesitates and looks around the room. Max can come in at any moment and find her prying in his business, but she takes the risk and slowly opens the drawer.

There's a knife in there. She places her hand on the smooth wooden handle and picks it up. It's not a huge blade, only fifteen centimeters. She touches the shiny metal with her other hand. It looks sharp. She doesn't need to test that it will draw blood.

She looks at the room again. If she conceals the weapon in the bedroom, under the bed, she can use it when the opportunity arises. She can slit Max's throat while he's sleeping. Push it right into his heart and finish him off.

She looks at the knife again and places it back into the drawer just as she found it. Killing Max will bring nothing but trouble. *He wants you,* she thinks to herself. *He's not pushing you away.* She knows she needs him too. She understands that she can't survive alone. She needs to get out of Riverlea, and Max can get her out.

Cat closes the drawer and walks away. She won't use it. She'll never forgive herself for killing him—and, with him, the only chance she has of getting home.

"I thought you accepted me," Max rejoined.

"I tolerated you," she replied immediately. Yet . . . just a week ago she recalled dreaming about having Max beside her, his warm arms embracing her, making her feel relaxed as she drifted off.

The rusty brakes screeched loudly again, bringing Cat back from her thoughts. Max came over and joined her by the boxcar door. They kept looking ahead and, after a while, they noticed the train was turning. They needed to leave. They had no reason to go east, and there was no guarantee that the tracks would go north again. As soon as a suitable place showed itself, they jumped.

They landed a few meters apart from each other. First, they stayed low, waiting for the train to disappear around the bend, then sat up and assessed their surroundings. The countryside they were in was quiet, with only the wind rustling through the wheat in the nearby field.

"Shouldn't they have harvested the wheat a long time ago?" Cat asked. She recalled the farmers in Covedale working hard and getting the grains ready for sale in July and August. It was already October.

"I have no clue," Max replied as he got up. He was ready to go.

Anita sat down on the leather sofa. Her body sank into the soft cushions. She didn't like being enclosed in so much furniture. She preferred the hard surface of a wooden chair, or at least something firmer than what she had under her right at that moment. It made her feel vulnerable somehow, like it might swallow her up at any moment into some dark place with no escape.

"You wanted to speak with me?" Mr. Theodore Menken said, walking in. He was an older man, not very tall, with thinning gray hair.

"Yes, and thank you for seeing me," she said. She got up and shook his hand. He then gestured for her to sit back down. "Your company is running very well, and you show consistent profits." Anita stated the intention of the visit. "It's remarkable how successful the Menken Mines are, and you have many locations around the world. I'm doing a segment on how Sābanto works for you and for your business."

"I'm an open book." Theodore went over to the side table and grabbed a drink. "Would you like one as well, Miss Gibala?" he asked, but she refused.

He came back to the table, sat down opposite her, and placed the glass in front of him. "What would you like to know?" He smiled encouragingly.

"Menken Mines employs a lot of workers," she said, then looked up at him from the notepad in her hand. "Can you explain how difficult the hiring process is?"

"I find it quite easy," he said without adding anything more to his answer.

"Are you getting the right workers?"

"Most of the time, but not always."

"Can you elaborate?"

"I need strong, healthy men, but sometimes Sābanto seems short on the exact type I need." He picked up his drink and took a sip of it.

"How could this be improved?"

"They say that they want people properly trained before working outside of Sābanto. That takes too much time, and as of right now it gives me fewer options for workers."

"World United is doing a lot of research on genetics and robotics. Do you think that could make a difference to Menken Mines?"

"I don't know a lot about these projects," he replied, but sounded interested.

"Let's say you could select the exact workers you wanted and however many you want?"

"Can I make them obedient?" Mr. Menken leaned forward.

"I don't see why not." The science conference in Karben hadn't directly discussed those types of experiments, but Anita was certain that it was something the scientists were interested in exploring as well. Obedient workers were the key to success for most companies. No one wanted riots and strikes that would affect production and lower their profits.

"That'd be an incredible improvement," Mr. Menken said.

"The engineered workers might come at a steep price," Anita added. "How likely are you to buy them rather than taking the free workers from Sābanto?"

"I think it all depends on the price, Miss Gibala. If they never get sick, for example, it could save money in the long run."

"There was an accident at one of the Menken Mines not too long ago," Anita reminded him. "A shaft collapsed, if I remember correctly. I couldn't find records on the authorization of treatments for any of the workers that were injured."

Theodore Menken leaned back in his chair. "These kinds of accidents are difficult to discuss," he said with seriousness in his voice. "Most of the workers perished that day under the collapsed mine section. The rest had only minor injuries, and our first responders were able to treat them in the village."

Anita hadn't been able to find any records for the past six months of any medical authorizations. For the fifty mines that Mr. Menken operated around the world, no employees had recorded cuts, broken legs, muscle strains, or burns. Although he had voiced his displeasure regarding workers who got sick and weren't able to work, there was no evidence of anyone so much as taking a sick day.

Anita recalled the farm worker she'd seen on the operating table. He had died that day. When he arrived, his hours had been numbered. The nurse had run around the table helping with the IV and oxygen and had kept pumping more and more blood through the man's veins. Nothing had helped. When his heart stopped, they'd tried to bring him back, but eventually reality set in. Dr. Lott covered the patient's face with cloth. The man had been in his late twenties, too young to die, but there was nothing else they could've done without authorization for the machine treatment from his employer. The medical machine could save anyone with broken bones, deep cuts or even burns. The second Lott put the patient into the machine, the bleeding would have stopped and his heart rate stabilized. Permission for this treatment, however, had never come from the farm that employed him.

Anita thanked Mr. Menken for the meeting and excused herself. The butler escorted her to her car, but she waited to turn on the engine. She sat there for a moment with big tears rolling down her cheeks. She cried for the young man.

# 13

IT WAS POURING OUTSIDE. Cold sheets of October rain banged against the windows and the roof above. Violet put some bowls out on the floor where the water dripped from the ceiling, finding its way through the holes in the rusting metal that covered the cabin. She wore an old beige sweater that insulated her from the wind and dampness coming through the walls. The small fireplace in the corner of the room didn't provide enough heat for the entire cabin. They'd need to move their beds closer to it for the winter.

Violet stood beside the counter over the basin she'd filled with warm water. With circular motions she cleaned the chipped mugs and plates from the lunch she and Seb had eaten. Her mind wandered back to when she was still in Sābanto. The work in the kitchen had been hard and the hours long. She'd started getting breakfast ready at six in the morning and wouldn't get home until eight or sometimes even ten in the evening. She prepared, served, and cleaned up after each meal. During the day, they'd also have deliveries, and the fresh, canned, and dried foods were put away into storage. There had been quite a few women working with her, preparing the meals and taking care of the kitchen, but Violet would still get home exhausted.

Despite the hardship, she'd liked what she did, but she also wished people in the compound had appreciated her efforts a little more. Some of her neighbors had accused her of stealing food while she worked, which had been a lie. She'd done nothing like that. Others would shout names like "whore" as she passed them on the grounds, hurrying home. They'd said she was sleeping with the compound director who'd given her the job in the kitchen. One day, someone had thrown a rock at her, bruising her shoulder, but she'd protected Seb who'd been in her arms.

Violet hadn't felt she had the right to complain. She didn't mind working hard, and she couldn't expect everyone to like her. She'd kept herself busy and believed things would change for the better. She'd been making friends with the women she worked with and ignored anyone who acted hostile towards her or her son. Seb had also been getting used to his new home. He had loved playing with the other kids. He'd become happy and more talkative as the days passed.

Violet had been called to the Sābanto office more than a month ago. She had a visitor, they said, but she hadn't been expecting anyone. She walked into the small room where a figure sat waiting for her. *Mike!* She couldn't believe her eyes. She had run up to him and held him in her arms for a long time, not letting him go. "Forgive me," Mike had said, his voice shaking. Big tears had fallen down his cheeks. "I wasn't thinking," he'd added as he'd knelt in front of Seb and hugged him.

Violet closed her eyes and stopped washing the dishes for a moment. She smiled to herself. The family was reunited again.

It had taken them a couple of days traveling—walking or catching a ride on the backs of trucks or horse driven carts—to get to Mike's. Some drivers had asked for money from them, others had let them ride for free, seeing Seb. While on the road, Mike had told her about the hard work he'd done for Sābanto, which had left him with some savings. "I got a property," he'd said. "For us three." Property made him a citizen, and so he'd taken Violet and Seb under his protection and out of the compound. At first she hadn't believed his story, but when they hadn't been bothered at the Sābanto checkpoints, it had reassured her he'd been telling the truth. His documents were in order.

Violet looked through the small window in front of her at the dark forest outside while she dried the mugs with a cloth. The rain was rhythmically hitting the glass and creating its own melody.

Her brother had told her that the cabin wasn't perfect, and that turned out to be an understatement. It had two spacious rooms, just as Mike had promised, but that was the only positive about this place. Bringing the family together was what Violet had always wanted, so she didn't complain about the cabin and its state of disrepair. She didn't mind the hard work and cleaning that lay ahead to make this place livable. She found her new routine and became accustomed to the crackling of the cabin at night and the sounds of wolves far in the distance.

Violet put the dried dishes away and turned around to see what Seb was doing. She'd left him playing on the floor with his stuffed monkey. He had taken his favorite toy from Sābanto and he didn't leave anywhere without it. While playing, he always talked to it in his own toddler language, but he seemed a little too quiet now.

He was sitting on the floor where she'd left him, but he wasn't playing. His eyes were fixed on something in front of him. As Violet's eyes moved to what he was looking at, she noticed a man leaning in the doorway. She gasped, surprised to see a tall figure with messy hair. She hadn't heard him open the door.

The man stared at her, grinning, holding something thin in his mouth like a blade of grass, playing with it between his teeth. His long coat was soaking wet and dripped onto the rough wooden floor she'd recently washed.

Violet took a step backwards, then ran up to Seb to protect him if she needed to.

"Where's Mike?" the man asked and walked towards the middle of the room, leaving muddy puddles behind him.

Violet took another step back, holding Seb close to her. "He ain't here," she said.

The man brought a gun out from behind his back and put it down on the table. He took off his wet coat and hung it on the back of a chair that stood beside the table. He then sat down as though he owned the place. "When will he be back?"

"Dunno." Violet wanted Mike to walk in right then and explain to her what was happening.

The man adjusted his hair and she noticed that a piece of his ear was missing, and she froze. She stood there holding Seb close, not sure what to do or say. The only sounds in the cabin were the drops falling into the dishes on the floor, now partially filled, and the hollow thuds of rain hitting the roof.

"Make me something to eat," the man ordered, breaking the silence. He got up and moved to the cupboard and took out a bottle of alcohol. He knew where things were kept here.

The man got himself one of the chipped mugs from the counter, one that she'd just washed, and poured some of the alcohol into it. He then looked at her. "Deaf?" he said. The stranger moved away from the kitchen counters and back towards the middle of the room. He put the bottle on the table and sat down again.

Violet moved to the space the man had just recently been occupying, keeping him in her sight. They had little food. Mike had said he would bring some when he'd left that morning. Last time he'd brought a rabbit he'd killed in the woods. She'd made a stew from it that had fed them for a couple of days. The cabin was in the middle of a thick forest that stretched far in each direction, and Mike said there were plenty of small animals that he was free to catch.

Violet stopped beside the kitchen shelf. There was some flatbread left which she'd made the other day with what Mike had brought home. She'd learned how to make cornbread in Sābanto. She didn't, however, have anything to put on the bread. There was no butter or jam to go with it. Violet missed the salty, nutty spread that Seb had loved having on the sandwiches at the compound. They called it peanut butter.

She grabbed one of the flat pieces and handed it to the man, trying not to get too close. Seb clutched at her leg.

"That's all you got?" the man asked, turning towards the door as Mike stepped in.

"We got some chicken," her brother announced and nodded to the stranger. Mike then walked up to Violet and handed her the two birds he held by the feet. "Make something good outta them." He reached into his pockets and took out some potatoes and turnips. He placed them on the table.

"Robbing people, aren't you?" the stranger commented.

Her brother brought his eyes up to look at the man. "What's it to ya?" he asked.

The man shrugged, taking a bite of the flatbread.

"So ya met my sister," Mike said.

"I just got in," the stranger replied. "We didn't get a chance."

Mike turned towards Violet. "Leo is living with us," he said.

Her heart sank. Mike hadn't mentioned that there would be someone else they'd be sharing the cabin with. It was supposed to be just the three of them.

"Go, cook us something," Mike ordered and took Seb from her side. Violet wanted to protest, but she was certain her brother wouldn't let anything happen to his nephew. She needed to accept the new situation with dignity. She couldn't show that she was scared of Leo.

She put on a thin raincoat, grabbed the old pot, and left the cabin. A small creek ran behind her new home and she hurried there to fill the pot.

She was back inside as quickly as possible to check on her son and avoid getting soaked from the rain. The men were still sitting at the table talking, and Seb was sitting on Mike's lap. Her brother also grabbed a fresh mug for himself and poured some alcohol into it. Everything seemed in order. She took off her coat and hung it on the nail beside the door. She put the pot on the old stove which she fed with the firewood that Mike had split and brought inside earlier in the day.

Violet's back was to the men, but she listened to their conversation as Leo continued, "I need to get him here—"

"Like, *here?*" Mike replied, hitting the table with his finger.

"Not here. Into the woods," Leo said. There was annoyance in his voice.

"Oh, okay," her brother said.

Violet blew into the stove to get the fire started. Mike took a loud slurp from his mug and set it back down on the table.

"I need to lure him out," Leo said.

The fire engulfed the wood, so Violet closed the iron door of the stove to keep the ashes and embers off the floor. She walked to Mike and took Seb from him without making eye contact with the stranger, but she felt his gaze on her.

"With what?" Mike asked.

"I might have an idea . . ." Leo said and relaxed in his seat. He didn't elaborate.

Once the water was boiling, Violet plunged the chickens into it for a minute, then took them and Seb outside. She sat down under a small overhang above the entrance and plucked the birds. The rain outside continued. The world smelled of wet earth and the decaying leaves that covered the ground.

Mike was making friends with the wrong people again. She should talk to him and explain that what he was doing was probably not right, maybe even illegal. Had he really stolen these chickens and turnips from someone? Mike was on the wrong path, but would he listen?

She looked at Seb sitting beside her and playing. She hadn't listened to Mike when he'd told her to not fall in love with a man she knew nothing about. How could she expect Mike to listen to her now?

Once she finished cleaning the birds, she brought them and Seb back inside. Leo wasn't at the table. He must have gone to the other room. She cut up the chicken. In Sābanto, the chickens had come in headless and without feet, but her mom had killed an old rooster at the farm once. She had used it all, the head and feet. Just like her mother, Violet didn't waste anything and threw the meat together with the turnips and made a stew.

After the meal, the men went outside for a smoke and she busied herself with the cleanup. As she washed the dishes, they argued. The conversation was muffled, but understandable.

"You asked me to help you get your sister out. I fucking did!" Leo said. "You didn't tell me she'd come with a fucking kid! Sell this shack if you have to, but I need the money. I'll be gone for a couple of weeks, maybe. When I'm back, you better be ready to pay."

Leo walked away. Violet followed him with her eyes as he disappeared down the forest path. Mike came back into the house. He sat down at the table and buried his face in his hands.

"How much did ya borrow from him?" Violet asked.

"Not ya business," Mike barked at her. He got up from the chair and went outside again.

Whatever the amount of money was, they didn't have it. She shivered.

It rained the following afternoon as Cat and Max pressed north. Waves of moving droplets fueled by the wind cut at their face and hair. They were both soaking wet and cold. Cat's teeth were chattering. Her body temperature was dropping with each gust of wind, but there was no shelter anywhere.

Cat's mind wandered as she walked. She thought back to what they'd said to each other on the train. Had there been something between them back in Riverlea? She showed up; he fucked her; she got paid. That was it. Had there been anything else to the relationship?

She recalled Tom, her late husband, back when they'd lived together. The small apartment had been the only thing they'd had in common for many years. It felt normal to say that she and Tom were a loving couple—an expected lie from a married woman. But she hadn't stuck around because she'd loved him. There had been no love between them for many years. She had just been afraid to leave. She'd feared being alone.

Cat is with Max. He lies beside her, propping his head on his elbow.

"I heard your training is going well," he says, tracing his finger along her ribs and noticing the new bruise. Her trainer had hit her this morning with a bō, which she didn't properly shield herself from.

"I'm not very good at it," she replies and shrugs. She'd just started training and handling a bō was still difficult.

"I want something different tonight," he says and grins at her. Cat looks at him and their eyes meet. She tries reading him and deciphering what he means, but he smirks wider at her and quickly looks back at her body. "I want you in control," he adds and looks at her again. "What do you think?"

"Hmm . . ." she bites her lower lip and smirks back at him. "I don't know." It might be fun. Is it wrong that she enjoys being with him, even looks forward to the nights they spend together? Just a few months ago, she was pushing him away. She'd never succeeded. What was she afraid of when she stopped herself from saying no?

Now it's too late. He's cast a spell on her. Cat is aware of it, aware that there's no way back. Every day, like a fool, she looked forward to his embrace, knowing that the time she'll leave him is getting closer. They'll be going their separate ways as soon as Sābanto comes to Riverlea. There will only be loneliness waiting for her. She promises herself she'll enjoy the time they still have together.

She quickly pushes Max onto his back, taking him a little by surprise. They laugh at their own clumsiness in bed, untangling themselves from the bedsheets. She mounts him, holding his hands up, restricting his moves. He complies and doesn't resist. She kisses his neck and feels aroused as she tastes the saltiness of his skin on her tongue.

The rain was hitting her face again. She turned her head to avoid it.

"Look!" Max bent over towards her, shouting over the wind and rain, and pointing at something in the distance.

She turned her head and followed his finger. The day was gray, but it was turning even darker as night approached. A small row of houses—a shadow in the distance—was, however, still visible. Was it safe? They couldn't possibly know, but they had no choice. They risked it.

Their walk to the houses was longer than they expected. Cat was shivering all over by the time they got there, unable to control it. Max wasn't looking any better, with pale skin and blue lips.

They rushed towards the first house, a small bungalow, with all the strength they could still manage, but they remained careful. The village seemed abandoned like the other one they'd passed the day before, but bandits roamed the countryside and squatters could've moved in. After a quick search they found no one inside. The place was unkempt and dirty, but it was dry.

"Good enough for me," Max said, and Cat nodded. She was still shivering. Her wet clothes clung to her body. The absence of rain and wind was an improvement, but it wasn't making Cat any warmer.

People had looted the two-bedroom house, but Max found a couple of broken chairs and a blanket that wasn't yet eaten by rodents. Max broke the furniture further and threw the pieces into the fireplace in the main room. "Got a light?" he asked.

"Isn't it risky?" Someone could see the smoke, or the light in the windows. They could sell their location to Sābanto in exchange for money.

"Not as risky as hypothermia," he said.

She handed him the lighter. He was right, without the fire they might not survive the night. It took a moment, but the wood eventually took it with a faint glow.

"Take off your wet clothes," Max said as he took his jacket, shirt, and pants off. She watched him take off his underwear, but didn't move herself. "Please, you'll feel warmer," he urged.

She slowly undressed, putting her clothes beside his by the fireplace.

Max took her hand. "We need to do this together," he said, guiding her to sit on his lap as he sat on the blanket he placed on the floor. She froze, not understanding his intentions. "We need to hold on to each other and share the heat of our bodies while we wait for the fire to warm the place up," he clarified.

She sat on his lap, facing him. Her legs hugged his hips. Max pulled her to himself pressing his torso against her naked breasts. He rubbed his hands on her back, moving them back and forth, creating friction, his cheek resting against her shoulder. His eyes looked away from her.

At first his body was icy on hers, but eventually she relaxed, feeling warmer. Cat hugged him as well, moving her hands on his back in similar movements. She felt calm in his embrace. Her shivers faded as her blood got warmer.

She paused and pushed him slightly away from her. Their eyes met. A faint glow from the fire reflected in his dark irises. Her breath became quicker, and she felt the familiar squeeze inside her belly. Cat needed to have Max right there right now. She needed to check if his lips were as soft as she remembered. She kissed him and he didn't budge. There was no need to take it slow. They were both ready for lust to drive the moment. She grabbed his hair in her fist, not letting his lips part from hers as she raised herself up on her knees and slowly guided him in. The floorboard cracked with the shift of their weight.

Cat recalled the time she'd started enjoying sex with Max. She let her mind wander back to that day at the beach, the sun, the extra meal she'd had that day. Cat had always been fond of rice, but it was hard to get it in Riverlea. When it was available, it was expensive, but she could never resist getting some and tasting the soft grains melting in her mouth. She daydreamed with her eyes closed and forgot for a moment that she was with Max, and that her body was reacting to his increasing movements inside her. Her muscles flexed and tightened. Her nails dug into his skin.

Cat moaned quietly, holding Max by the nape of his neck, squeezing him closer to her as her muscles spasmed. Her legs could no longer continue the up and down movements. Her body relaxed, satisfied. Cat opened her eyes. She noticed their faint shadow moving on the wall; the fire was bigger now. The heat licked her back, and the fire crackled quietly in the room.

She released Max slowly from her embrace as she loosened up.

"We're meant for each other, Cat," Max said. He gently pulled away from her and their eyes locked. When she said nothing in reply, he added, "Please, love me again," and kissed her, slowly this time. He then turned her around, laid her down on the blanket, and slid into her. She didn't resist. Max wasn't finished, and he knew her weakness. Was it wrong that she wanted more as well?

Cat woke up on the floor beside the fireplace, alone, but covered with a blanket. The morning fire in front of her was just a few glowing embers that would die soon. They'd added some wood later in the night and Max had held her close, burying his face in the nape of her neck as they fell asleep.

She turned around to get a better view of the room and found Max standing beside the window, hiding from being spotted from the outside. He was naked. She rested her eyes on his rear for a moment—well rounded; firm. What had she been thinking last night? One look into his eyes, and she'd given him what he wanted. Cat, dripping wet like a cheap whore at a roadside brothel. She could do better. *One day you'll find someone that will care for you. Don't settle for a dick. Don't let him ruin any more of your life.*

Max noticed her looking and held his hand up so she wouldn't speak. He was observing something outside.

A moment later, he held two fingers up. There were two people out there. She couldn't hear anyone, but she waited, motionless, not making noise.

"They left," Max eventually said and walked over to her. He lowered his body to kiss her, but she turned her head to her side.

"I was cold," she said. She brought the blanket closer and covered her nakedness. If Max thought they were back together, he was deeply mistaken.

Max seemed to want to say something, but he didn't comment on her words or behavior. He explained instead what he'd seen outside, "There were two men. They walked through the center of the town. Not hiding. They both had guns."

"You think they live here?"

"No, I don't think so. They didn't enter any buildings. This might be part of their territory they're patrolling."

"Free men, maybe?"

"Whoever they are, we should stay away from them," Max said.

Cat agreed. Best to not mingle with locals, regardless of whether they're friendly or hostile. She got up and touched the clothes they had spread out on the floor to dry. They were still wet. Cat sat back down in front of the fire and Max joined her shortly after, adding another piece of the broken chair. They covered their bare shoulders with the blanket without making any attempt to get close again.

# 14

I T WAS PITCH BLACK, with no moon rays coming through the heavy clouds above them or the canopy of trees in the forest. Cat stumbled over the forest floor. Were they even still following the path or going the direction they were supposed to be? Each shadow of the greenery around her appeared new, but also strangely familiar. They'd better not be walking in circles, she thought.

They left as soon as their clothes were dry. With a knife, they'd cut holes in the middle of old blankets which they'd found in the settlement and made themselves ponchos. The extra layer gave them protection from the chill outside. They hadn't managed to find shelter for the night that would keep them adequately protected from the cold, so they'd decided to press on. At least it wasn't raining.

"Turn on the night vision," Max said.

Cat stopped in her tracks and hissed. "When you implanted this thing into my brain, you said never to turn it on." Hadn't he said it was dangerous? "What do you want from me?"

Max paused as well. "Are we even going in the right direction?"

Cat sighed and gazed into the darkness where Max stood and focused. *Turn on. Map view.* She turned her head around. "North is that way," she pointed. They were already heading in that direction. "There are no clear paths or roads through this forest, but if we continue north, we'll get to the river, which is about twenty kilometers from here." If they continued at a steady pace, they might get there in the morning. Once at the river, it was still a long way to Covedale. At least a couple more days walking. *Night vision on.* The world around her turned green. Cat walked forward in sure steps and Max followed her closely behind.

They hadn't gone far when Cat suddenly stopped. She turned around and surveyed the bright green shrubs. Something wasn't right, but she couldn't put her finger on what was out of place. She turned around towards Max and saw concern on his face. Although he couldn't see a thing in the darkness without night vision, he was looking around the forest attempting to spot the anomaly they had both felt. *Infrared vision*—she started but didn't finish her thought. Someone firmly pressed an unknown object against her back.

"This is what I was talking about." Ivy grabbed a large sheet of paper that lay on the sofa in the sitting room and showed it to Julia. "Look at this design," she pointed at the pencil drawing. "Like the angels from the old paintings."

"Do ya think she'll like it?" Julia asked, taking the paper from Ivy's hand and looking at it. She didn't seem convinced. Julia wasn't in a good mood and Ivy attributed it to another fight with Greyson.

"I don't know." Ivy shrugged. Mrs. Conway hadn't been happy with her lately, but she hoped these designs might change her mind. It had been Mr. Conway's idea that Ivy decorate the nursery for their baby. He trusted her skills, but as the deadline grew near, Ivy became more nervous. She hadn't made the final decision on the wall paint and drapes, and the workers were eager to start.

Julia walked to the table and checked the other drawings. Ivy had come up with too many ideas and she was having trouble choosing the one that she liked the most. She had her favorites, but she laid all the drawings out for Julia to look at and give her opinion. There was paper everywhere, and a faint dusting of graphite and charcoal lingered on the flat surfaces in the room.

"Methinks this one with the flowers," Julia said. She was about to say more, but the doorbell rang. She gave the paper back to Ivy and walked out of the room.

Ivy glanced again at the flower design and grimaced. She heard voices coming from the hallway, but ignored them. This drawing wasn't her best. If she knew whether the baby would be a boy or a girl, it might've been helpful, but Mrs. Conway didn't want to tell her.

The door opened and Julia stepped in. "Mr. Menken came to visit, ma'am," Julia said formally.

"Please," Ivy said mindlessly, still staring at the drawing. Immediately her eyes widened and she wanted to call Julia back and revoke the invitation, but she was already at the door. Ivy should've said one moment to give herself time to change into something nicer. All she was wearing was a simple cotton housedress. She'd braided her hair this morning for comfort, preventing it from falling in her face while she was working with the pencils.

She'd only had enough time to smooth her dress when Liam walked in.

"I'm sorry I came unannounced," he said from the doorway. His eyes wandered around the room.

She followed his gaze. Her face immediately turned red. She'd made a mess. "Please excuse me." She grabbed the sheets of paper from the sofa and put them on the coffee table. "Please sit down."

"Would you mind if I looked?" he asked as he slowly sat down. His eyes were fixed on the drawings on the low table.

"Not at all," Ivy foolishly agreed. She smiled widely at Liam. He picked up one of the sheets of paper. Ivy bent over and took a look at the drawing he was holding. She got a faint whiff of the cologne he was wearing. It was pleasant.

"These are amazing," he said. "Are these all yours? I didn't know you drew." Ivy blushed. "What are these for?"

"Designs for a nursery. This one has playful patterns on the drapes." She pointed at a drawing, then picked up another. "And here is something I think would look nice on a wallpaper."

Liam grabbed another drawing. "Little fat angels." He stared at them, studying. He brought his head up and ran his fingers through his hair before letting it fall back onto his forehead. "These are beautiful," Liam said. "I didn't know you had such talent."

"Just occupying myself since the weather is terrible outside," she said. It had rained almost every day and what little sun they had was no longer warming and comforting. Suddenly Ivy's heart skipped a beat. *No, she hadn't drawn these for herself.* "Mrs. Conway is expecting," Ivy clarified. "I need to give her the best designs soon, so that everything's ready before the baby arrives."

He grabbed a different drawing from the pile. "I like this one," he said. It had jungle animals on it, playful monkeys swinging from branches and parrots watching from tree canopies. Behind the trees, majestic lions and playful tigers were hiding.

"One of my favorites as well," Ivy replied. The idea had come from a book she was reading. She'd even done some research on the different animals that lived in the faraway tropics. She was proud of her creation but wasn't convinced that Mrs. Conway would like it. *Liam likes it.* She'd present it as one of the design options.

He smiled at her. "I'm sorry for the surprise visit. I was passing by and I thought I'd stop in. I wanted to know how you were doing." He studied the drawings again. "I wanted to check if you're doing alright . . . you know . . . after the accident," he said, then quickly added, "Calista and Sarai are also asking about you."

"Thank you," Ivy replied with a smile. "After all your care, I'm healing quickly. Dr. Lott says that I should be able to resume my regular work soon." Was it stupid that she was looking to return to the factory? She scanned the room. She realized she hadn't offered her guest anything. "I'm sorry," she stirred in her seat. "Would you like something to drink? Tea maybe?"

"That'd be wonderful." He smiled at her, showing his dimples.

Ivy pressed the button under the table and asked Julia to bring them some refreshments.

"Thank you for stopping and checking on me," Ivy said.

"I couldn't come earlier, I'm sorry. I'm helping my father now. He's passing the business on to me and my days have gotten busy."

"What brings you to Covedale?"

"I'm meeting Mr. Conway. My father says we need some more workers from Sābanto."

"They say that good workers are the key," Ivy replied. She didn't have much of an opinion on that topic. Her factory employed few people, and they usually stuck around once they were trained. Their turnover rate was very low. Many employers, however, as the news said, had a lot of issues with their workers.

Julia walked in carrying a tray with tea steeping in a ceramic teapot and two cups on saucers. Ivy jumped up seeing her and moved the drawings away from the coffee table to make space.

"Thank you, ma'am," Julia said in acknowledgment and put the tray down. She placed the cups in front of Ivy and Liam, poured some of the tea, curtsied, and left.

Liam waited until Julia closed the door. He then turned towards Ivy and stared into her eyes. "I couldn't stop thinking about you." Ivy opened her mouth slightly to say something, but no words came out. "That day when I found you on the ground, I held you in my arms. Do you remember what you said?"

Ivy shook her head. She didn't remember that moment at all, it was as though it had never happened. Dr. Lott had said that it was normal to lose time during a scary accident.

"You asked me if I was an angel." Liam moved closer to Ivy on the sofa without breaking eye contact with her. He was so close that she could almost feel his breath on her. Had she really said that? She smiled a little.

"You said that I was bright as an angel." He smiled.

Ivy's face burned. Angel? That was silly. She scanned Liam's face and his eyes. Was that how angels looked?

Liam brought his lips to hers, briefly. A gentle kiss, just barely touching. It left Ivy paralyzed. Her eyes remained locked with his. She smiled each time she recalled Liam's gentle arms scooping her up in bed, helping her sit up. Was this it? Was he the man who would rescue her from her grief and memories of Mark? Free her from the loneliness she had in her heart? Was he the angel she was waiting for? She fixed her eyes on his lips, wanting to experience them again; their taste, their softness.

Liam read her mind and kissed her again. Ivy closed her eyes as their lips slowly moved. A relaxing warmth spread through her body.

Ivy opened her eyes as Liam paused. "I should go," he said all of a sudden. He looked a little shaken. Had she offended him somehow? Had she done something wrong? Why the unexpected change?

Liam got up and nodded goodbye to Ivy without a smile as she sprung up from the sofa. He exited the room in a hurry. She heard the front door close behind him.

Ivy stared off in the direction he'd left. It was her fault, she was certain of it, but she wasn't sure which of her actions had made Liam leave so abruptly. *Why can't I be just like other people?* She slumped back down onto the sofa.


"I'm sorry I kept you waiting," Mr. Conway said as he entered his study. Liam Menken was already sitting comfortably in a leather chair at the huge desk in the middle of Oliver's study, but he got up and greeted him.

"That's not a problem. I'm not in a hurry," Liam replied politely. "Thank you for agreeing to see me. My father regrets that he couldn't make this trip and visit you in person."

"Please sit down." Oliver pointed at the chair his visitor had previously occupied. "Can I offer you a drink?" Without waiting for a reply he walked towards the carafe on the side of the room and poured a couple of fingers of whiskey into two glasses. He put one of them in front of Liam, then circled around the desk and sat down on the opposite end.

Liam took a sip of his drink. "That's very smooth," he said.

"Life's too short to drink the cheap stuff," Oliver replied, taking a sip of the fiery liquid as well. "How can I help you?" He wanted the meeting over with. He had an idea what this visit was about, and prolonging it wasn't worth it.

"As you know, the demand for coal is quite high, and Menken Mines is one of the few companies that can provide adequate supply," Liam started. "That means we must dig further down. Our main mine is over 1.5 km deep. This, of course, comes with some consequences and dangers." Liam took another sip of his drink and nodded his approval of the liquid. He put the glass down and continued, saying, "As you know, we implement all the required security precautions, but despite that, we had an accident a couple weeks ago. A tunnel collapsed and buried some of our workers." Liam reached into the inner pocket of his jacket and took out a folded piece of paper. He put it on the desk.

Oliver grabbed it. It was a list.

"With your approval, we'd like to hire replacements from Sābanto," Liam said.

Oliver nodded, looking at the names in front of him. Not all of them had birth dates beside them, but everyone's death was listed as a couple of weeks ago. Oliver turned the paper around. There were more names on the other side. "How many?" he asked rather than counting them.

"Eighty-seven," Liam replied.

*Eighty-seven.* Oliver kept his eyes on the paper in his hand. "We'll let the families of the dead know," Oliver said. "And we'll work on getting your father some additional help." He put the paper down on the table.

"Thank you," Liam replied.

They talked a bit more about the rebuilding process of Clamerton and the new entertainment district that was opening soon. Oliver didn't care about these developments, but he didn't want to seem rude. He followed along politely. Liam sipped his drink every so often. *Finish and leave,* Oliver urged the man in his mind. He wished he'd given him a smaller drink.

Oliver finally escorted Liam to the door and wished him safe travels. He was glad they didn't run into Sophia. She might've insisted on inviting Liam for dinner again. Last thing he wanted was a repeat of that evening. He returned to his study and picked up the list from the table. Eighty-seven strong, healthy men had lost their lives for the greater good of the new world.

He walked to the safe at the side of the room, punched in the code, and opened it up. Inside was another piece of paper, similar to the one he was already holding. He took it out and examined the list, comparing the two. Within a couple of months, there had been two major accidents at Menken Mines. Last time they'd asked for one hundred and fifteen new workers. Now old Menken had sent his son to request another eighty-seven.

They could've gone and gotten them straight from Sābanto, but coming here and speaking directly with him was safer. It reduced the paperwork as well as the number of people at World United who knew about the deaths and the constant need for new workers.

He put the two lists together, put them into the safe, and locked it.

"Miss Gibala." An older man, a security guard, spread his arms across the gate blocking her way. "I cannot let ya in."

Anita wouldn't take no for an answer. She tried to bribe the security guards at the factory, but they refused the money and soon two men approached her from behind.

"We're arresting you for trespassing," one of them said.

They grabbed her with their muscular arms. She braced her feet on the dirty floor but they pulled her away from the entrance of the factory.

She'd spent some time and done additional research on the rate of usage of medical machines by various companies. Much like Menken Mines, this was yet another factory that hadn't spent a ticket on its workers' healthcare in over six months.

She'd hidden a small camera in her jacket to take some pictures, but she needed to get inside this steel mill to take them. Looking at the building and even talking with people on the outside hadn't yielded any results. The ones who did talk to her said only good things about the place. The employer had built housing quarters directly on the grounds, preventing them from leaving. The workers stayed at the plant even during their time off. The only way to speak with them was to get inside.

If she couldn't access the factory via the front door, through the security gate, she had to find another entrance. The manufacturing plants employed their own security teams, and they paid these men well to keep the workers in and the nosy people out.

The men dragged her away from the factory to the sidewalk in front. Anita curled up, protecting her face with her arms as their batons came down on her with full force. *Fuck it hurt!* They didn't care who she was. *Ahh!* She didn't dare scream from the pain. She'd worn simple clothes today, not her usual fancy outfit, but she was still recognizable. They knew exactly who she was. *That was my kidney! Motherfuckers!* Were they ordered to be indiscriminate and rough with those who were too nosy?

Suddenly they stopped.

"We'll take it from here," someone said. Anita took a peek from between her arms, afraid that the hits would come again. A man in a black Sābanto uniform stood above her. His hand was extended towards her like an invitation, a promise that he'd help her get up. The other Black Shirt was talking with the factory guards. The security men that had been beating her went back into the factory. She was alone with the two Sābanto men.

They led her to their car and shoved her into the back seat. Anita was enclosed in a metal cage, separating her from the officers. The two men got in front, and the car began to move.

Anita didn't ask where they were taking her. They'd find her hidden camera, then interrogate her. She'd be charged with some crime. *Once they found out who she was, they'd drop the charges. Not a huge deal.*

Sābanto had no jurisdiction over the citizens. Word about her arrest would get out. The other media outlets would use it as proof that she'd gone a little too far with her side investigations. The Citizen was already talking about moving her out of the field.

A few minutes into their journey, the man in the passenger seat turned towards her. He wasn't anyone she recognized. He had a long, weathered face and was in his fifties.

"Ya won't get anywhere trying to force ya way in," the Sābanto soldier said. *What was he babbling about?* "Forcing ya way in will just get ya hurt. Ya need a better plan."

"What do you want from me?" She asked defensively. Who were these men? What if they weren't on their way to Sābanto station? A cold shiver ran down her spine.

"There are some who hate ya guts," the man said calmly. "The legwork ya do will never be on the displays. They want ya gone. Be careful. Next time, we might not be there to rescue ya. There are places where no woman like yaself should be."

The car stopped and Anita looked outside. They were at the downtown hotel she'd checked into earlier. Why hadn't they gone to a Sābanto station?

"What do you want me to do?" she asked. They must have wanted something from her. A favor of some kind.

"Be smart," he said. "We need people like ya." The man turned back around and faced forward. The locks on her door disengaged.

Was this a trick? Anita slowly opened the door. She was certain that they'd be locked again as soon as she reached for the handle, but the two men in the front didn't stir. She carefully got out and closed the door behind her. The car took off immediately, leaving her on the sidewalk. She watched it disappear as it turned right at the next intersection.

They only wanted her to be smarter, sneakier. Wasn't that weird?

No one around her appeared concerned. Even the doorman at the hotel didn't notice anything unusual. Anita casually walked into the lobby. She was in pain, but she forced a smile. She'd inspect her bruises later and see how much damage the batons and kicks had done to her body.

Once she was in her room she locked the door. She took the device out of her coat. It was still recording. Who were these people and how much did they know about her? Who was after her? She was in danger. She believed the Sābanto men. Those who hated her could be anywhere. Who could she trust? Who should she avoid? *Be smart, Anita,* she thought. *Be smart.*

She took the memory card out of the device. All of the day's events had been recorded on it. Anita had proof of what they'd done to her. A recording showing how she, a citizen, had been mistreated by security guards at the factory. Anita walked to her tablet. It was good that she'd left it in her room—it would have been damaged otherwise. She opened it up and sat down in front of it, waiting impatiently for it to turn back on. No doubt she'd missed something important during the struggle. The recording would give her all the details.

She began to put the card into the device's slot, but froze. *Be smart, Anita. How many times have you left this tablet unattended? You have no proof someone else hasn't used it.* If the recordings leaked, there would be an outrage at first over the security guards beating a journalist, but the shock of the events would quickly fade. The factory owner would have to settle with her and pay her money for the harm she received from the hands of his employees who would continue what they were doing without punishment. She didn't need the money.

Was there anything else on the card that she could use to move forward with her investigation? Anita didn't think so. The goal of the recording was to get inside the factory and get proof of the owner's abuse of the employees. The guards, gate keepers, were well fed and treated right. Their role was to keep the unwanted visitors away from those that were exploited. They did their duties well, but she had no proof that was the intent.

The Sābanto men were on the recording, Anita recalled. The camera must have captured their faces and the message clearly. Would anyone be interested in them? Would someone try to find them, investigate what they need people like herself for? Clearly, they hadn't followed the protocols. It didn't feel like it was an accident that they were there to help her. They dropped her at the hotel entrance rather than the Sābanto station. Insubordination like that might cost them their jobs, maybe even their lives.

*Be smart,* Anita told herself, and she got up and walked to the foyer of her room. She wouldn't be able to sleep knowing that this recording in the wrong hands could be used against those who wanted to protect her. She dropped the memory card onto the tile floor and crushed it with the heel of her shoe.

Greyson walked into the old warehouse at the edge of Covedale, far from the city center. The windows had been broken for years, and the roof had caved in in many places. Even though the moon shone outside, the inside of the warehouse was completely black. No one in town seemed to remember this warehouse existed, or if they did, they had no reason to come here.

He heard footsteps in front of him. Someone was already inside. There was no guarantee that it was the person he was expecting. He drew his gun. The steps grew closer, crunching on the glass that lay everywhere.

"Do you have it?" Leo Woodham stood before him in the moonlight.

"Yeah," Greyson replied, seeing the familiar face. He turned around and scanned the darkness. No one had followed him here, but Conway was a sneaky bastard.

"No one else is here," Leo reassured him. "Show me." Greyson put away his gun and reached into his pants, took out a bag, and handed it to him. Leo opened it and checked the contents inside. "Did you get it all?" he asked.

"Two hundred grams. Just as ya asked." He wasn't foolish enough to shortchange him. That's how people got murdered.

"Very well," Leo said. He took one hundred tickets out of his pocket and handed them to Greyson. "Same time. In four weeks."

Greyson nodded, pocketed the money, and left in the direction he came from.

# 15

AMY PARKED THE CHOP-JET in a clearing in the woods and got out. She hated November. The days were wet, cold and short. It was only a matter of time before there'd be snow on the ground. She longed for spring.

A short walk down a muddy path led her to the village. Amy had been here many times. The people were used to seeing her around and ignored her whenever she arrived. She'd left her Sābanto clothes behind so that they wouldn't associate her with the organization.

Amy looked around at the women busying themselves cooking on fire pits or washing. Their pots steamed in the cold air. Some men were sharpening their knives and hunting tools, warming themselves by the fire. Inside one of the open huts, an old man was cutting leather for clothes or shoes. Kids ran around chasing each other and slipping in the mud between the buildings.

Living outside of Sābanto and the World United's reach had its benefits. They didn't report to anyone, and they worked only for their own small community. The downside was that they lived off the grid. With no roads leading here, no electricity and no easy access to water, they lived very simple lives. They got their water from wells and burned wood they gathered in the forest. They ate the animals they raised, hunted, or caught in the traps they dug. They didn't cultivate the land because they were afraid they would get caught in the open.

Amy walked up to one of the huts in the center of the village. She kicked her boots against the door frame, releasing most of the mud, and entered. She welcomed the dryness and warmth inside, which smelled of burning wood. Richard, the chief of the village—and her uncle—sat alone in front of the fire.

"How have ya been?" she said.

The man looked at her, got up from his place near the fire, and sat down at the table. He was in his sixties and had mostly gray hair and dark circles underneath his eyes. He was the village chief, selected by the inhabitants to be their leader. "Surviving," he replied. That was his usual response.

Amy reached into one of the pockets of her winter jacket and took out small packages of loose tobacco and matches. Her other pocket held various bottles of painkillers and antibiotics that she'd bought in Covedale for a steep price. She put all the items on the table. Isolation meant that the village had no access to basic medications, and Amy helped them replenish their stocks each time she visited.

She sat down at the table opposite the chief.

"What's new?" he asked.

"Outside of the ankle-attached tracking bracelets I told ya about last time, there ain't nothing," Amy replied. She scanned the cabin walls, trying to think of any other news. "They still haven't found these fugitives that escaped a few weeks ago."

"What fugitives?" Richard was suddenly alert.

"Man and woman in their forties," Amy replied. "The woman was a Green Shirt, so she wouldn't be a threat to ya. Black Shirts have stopped looking for them now. They're waiting for them to resurface somewhere."

Richard stared at her with a serious expression, not saying anything. He looked like he was trying to come up with the right words.

Amy eyes widened. Her uncle knew where the fugitives were. "Why didn't ya tell me they're here?" Amy sprang up from her seat.

"We captured them couple weeks ago." Richard was calm, as though apprehending strangers was routine in these parts of the woods.

"Captured?"

"They trespassed," he explained, leaning his back against the chair. The men monitored the land and perimeter of their village to keep the inhabitants safe.

"I need to see them." Amy paced the room. She'd spoken with Conway after hearing the news of the fugitives on the display and he'd told her to keep an eye on any information on them or their whereabouts. He'd told her that he needed them alive.

"What for?" the chief replied. "The village council is making their decision tomorrow."

"What decision?"

"We can't let 'em go," the chief said. Richard was more animated than he had been a moment ago. They weren't making a decision tomorrow—the decision had already been made. "They'd tell everyone where we were. We can't let them stay."

"Death?" Amy asked, drawing her brows together. "Ya can't."

"Listen. We'll do what we need to do. Lives of all ma people are at stake."

There were over a hundred people who lived in the village, but there had to be some other way to keep them safe. The village couldn't be killing others. She would have expected something like this from Conway, not from the chief.

"I need them alive," Amy replied.

"Ya know we can't do that. They've trespassed and they'll bear the consequences."

"Chief, ya have no choice." It wasn't a great time to cross Conway. If he ever found out that she'd known about the village plans and hadn't stopped them, there'd be trouble for her. One thing she'd learned about Conway so far was that he wasn't a fool. "Ya might lose ma protection. I won't be able to alter Black Shirts' search plans and distract them from this area or come here and bring ya the stuff ya ask me for." Amy pointed at the table and the medicine bottles she'd brought.

Richard was agitated. "Are ya blackmailing me?"

"No, I'm being realistic. I need to bring these two alive, and ya have to trust me."

"And what I tell ma villagers?" the chief drew his brows together.

"Let me speak with the prisoners and we'll think of something." Amy paced the cabin trying to calm down. There was a way out and they'd find it. She combed her brain for ideas.

Richard wasn't convinced, but got up from his seat. He walked outside for a moment and spoke with someone. When he returned, he sat back at the table and said, "They'll bring the man in. The woman doesn't talk anymore, but ya won't get much out of him either."

As they waited—and it seemed to Amy that it took forever to bring the prisoner in—she tried to make some decisions. The choice was obvious. She should save the prisoners. But how? She wouldn't be able to simply free them. Amy imagined how people would be gaping at her while she escorted them through the center of the village. Inhabitants would openly protest, knowing that the strangers weren't to be let go. It would burn bridges between her and them if she forced her way. She might never see them again. Could she still protect them?

Amy turned her eyes to Richard. She should do everything for him and the village. She respected him as a family member, but also for being instrumental in creating this community where people hid from Sābanto's reach. He was a smart man. She recalled the times he'd visited her when she was still a child, the meals they'd shared and the countless laughs they'd had while playing games. Amy always had looked forward to a Kalah match with her uncle. They'd made the board from an old piece of wood and small pebbles found on the beach. He was very good at the game and it had always been a joy for her to beat him at it. She longed for another match, but things were different now. The strategic game that she needed to play with the chief would be anything but friendly.

The door to the cabin opened and two men entered. The one being brought in was bent over slightly and walked with some difficulty. The other man, the villager she'd seen before, was tall and held a gun in his right hand as he supported the prisoner with his left.

Richard had gotten his hands on a few solar panels. Not that he could provide power to the village; the sunlight wasn't as efficient as diesel generators, but they needed guns to fight the Black Shirts, and the solar panels meant that they could charge them.

"What's ya name?" Amy asked.

"Who's asking?" The prisoner brought his head up and glanced at her. His face was bruised with some dried blood covering his temples. His hair was messy and dirty.

"It's me asking questions." Amy pulled the chair she'd previously occupied away from the table and sat down facing the prisoner.

"And you can fuck me up again for not answering your fucking questions," the man replied and stared at her. Amy wasn't afraid of him. His hands were bound behind his back, and the armed man held him upright. He had some difficulty standing on his own. He could try to stare her down, but he was more pathetic than intimidating.

"What's ya relation to Catherine Reed?" she asked. The man said nothing, so Amy asked another question. "Why did ya escape?"

"What's with your egoism?" the man said. "You want to live fucking free, away from the politics, but if someone else expresses such a wish, you fucking beat them up and jail them. What are you gonna do? Hang us for wanting to be free? You're worse than fucking Sābanto." The man spat onto the mud-caked floor in front of Amy. This kind of behavior didn't help his cause. The chief and the village had the right to protect themselves.

"I told ya. Ya won't get much outta them." Richard sighed and Amy glanced at him, taking her eyes from the prisoner.

The short break in her attention was enough for the prisoner and the guard to make a move. Before Amy was able to react, a cold metal pressed at the side of her neck, probably a knife. She couldn't see it. She froze and swallowed. Amy glanced again at the chief in front of her. The armed guard stood behind him, pressing the muzzle of a gun against his ribs. The intensity of the blue light increased as the weapon charged.

"Keep still," the guard ordered the chief.

"Ya know what we do with traitors," Richard said in reply. He looked composed, as though it weren't the first time someone had threatened his life.

"We Gutters are not afraid of ya," the guard added, pressing the gun further into her uncle's ribs as the latter grimaced in pain.

*Gutters.* Amy recalled hearing stories of them ruthlessly controlling the city of Riverlea. What business did they have in the village?

"What's a fucking Black Shirt doing here?" the prisoner who now stood behind her asked.

Amy frowned. Only Richard knew about that. "How . . . ?"

"Tell me. How did you explain your fucking tracking device to them?" the man continued.

"What tracking device?" Her uncle stared at her with grave, piercing eyes, as though he were reading her mind directly from across the table. She hadn't told him about the Black Shirts' implant beacon requirement which provided their whereabouts. World United did it to ensure the police force was supervised. If their location was known and recorded at all times, it was harder for them to sabotage the government, or for the troops to hide the Free people just like she was doing.

"I ain't got one—" Amy tried to explain.

"I doubt Sābanto fucking missed chipping you," the man behind her replied. She noticed a shadow of doubt on Richard's face. *Don't listen to them,* she thought. Keeping the village safe was his biggest worry as the chief, but she wouldn't do anything to jeopardize that. She wouldn't be here if anyone were able to track her movements. She would never put the village at risk.

"We're on ya side, chief," the guard added. "We don't want the Black Shirts findings us either."

"Fuck ya are!" Richard exploded, but otherwise didn't move.

"Put your hands on the table, slowly," the prisoner ordered. "Palms up."

Amy was cornered with no way out of this situation. There was nothing in the room that she could use to set herself free. All the weapons that she usually had on her were waiting for her in the chop-jet.

She complied with the request, and the prisoner searched for a mark on her right forearm. The beacon left a small scar, but he couldn't find it. She had told him the truth. Conway had exempted her from the procedure.

"What's so fucking special about you?" the prisoner asked. "No tracking, and an invisibility shield on the fucking chop-jet?"

The guard—the traitor—must be giving him all the details.

"What do ya want?" Richard asked. "Ya didn't come here to this village to ask her questions."

"We thought of ya as a friend," the guard said. "But Gutters take care of their own."

Meanwhile, the prisoner searched her pockets and found a phone in one of them. He threw it onto the table in front of her. The phone was turned off. She always remembered to power it down close to the village.

"Call your boss," the man said.

"Don't ya dare!" Richard exploded. Turning on the phone would announce Amy's location and the village would be destroyed.

"If he's important enough to make you exempt from tracking, maybe we can bargain with him about this hellhole of a village," the prisoner continued. "Who do you report to?"

Amy swallowed. "None of ya fucking business," she said firmly.

The man picked up the phone from the table, and put his finger on the button with the intention of turning it on.

"That'd get us killed!" Richard shouted, looking above Amy at the man who threatened them.

"Who is it?" the man repeated his question.

Amy's eyes concentrated on her phone in his hand. If the man pressed the button, that would be it. Two years of hard work had made this place an oasis for those who ran from their masters. The maimed, sick, and hungry had come here and found a place where they belonged. Pregnant maids with nowhere else to go had sought shelter in this village. It was a place that welcomed and accepted them. A village in the middle of nowhere where people finally felt safe. Pressing the button would ruin it all.

The only way to save the people might be to get the prisoners, the Gutters, out of the village. Her boss had said some time ago that he knew Gutters. He had worked with them on evacuations of Riverlea. Everyone in Covedale knew who she worked for anyway. It wasn't a secret.

"Oliver Conway," she replied.

"Don't fuck with me!" the prisoner said with anger.

"I report directly to Oliver Conway," she calmly repeated, but nervously bit her lips.

The man laughed. "You'll take me and my woman to him."

She nodded to the chief. He had no choice. The prisoner had the phone, and with the press of a button he could determine their fate. Connecting him to Conway meant there was a chance that he would leave them alone, and the community had to take it.


Cat lay on the packed dirt that was the floor in a windowless room, hugging herself to keep warm. Men had ambushed them, coming out of the darkness in the forest and threatening them with loaded guns. The only weapon she carried, a knife, had been taken away from her, but they hadn't found the other one that Max was carrying, the one she'd stolen from Robert. The men had bound their hands, led them into the village, and separated them.

She'd been taken to a wooden hut where they'd tied her to a chair. They'd beat her up repeatedly during an interrogation. Cat wasn't sure how long it had taken, but it was long enough for her to lose all sense of time. The men asking questions had changed, but there had been no break for her. They'd questioned her about her reason for being there and about her escape, which they had apparently learned of on the radio. They'd asked who her companion was and what their connection was. She had answered them truthfully when the questions didn't matter, and carefully dodged those that did. She had to protect the information that she still carried with her, as well as Max's true identity.

They had then thrown her into this room exhausted without so much as a bed. The place was cold and damp and she had no clue how many days she'd spent there receiving the occasional scanty bowl of cold food and water someone would quietly slide under her door.

When she'd regained her strength, they'd taken her out of her jail and questioned her again, but she'd stopped replying. She'd already told them everything they needed to know. Whatever she said wouldn't stop the beatings nor the mental torture she received. Following the second round of interrogations, she was put back in the same room and left alone, nursing her wounds and letting her body rest. Her ribs hurt and were most likely bruised. She didn't think any of them were broken. There was a cut on her temple that hurt to touch. She left it alone, so that it scabbed over and started to heal. Her muscles ached from tensing them to reduce the effects of the blows her captors inflicted on her.

Suddenly, there was a noise outside. It wasn't the food delivery. She heard a male voice speaking to someone. Cat wasn't ready to be taken out again. She wanted a warm bed, clean sheets, and hours of sleep. Not another interrogation. She had nothing else to tell them. They'd heard it all. She closed her eyes hoping that this nightmare would stop.

The door opened and Cat looked up at an armed man.

"Let's go!" he ordered.

She slowly and painfully got to her feet and stepped out as she was told. The man bound her hands behind her back and pushed her outside of the hut. He followed behind her. It was chilly out, a few degrees above freezing, but the sun was peeking out from between the heavy clouds. She squinted as the man shoved her out of the dark. She noticed the hut they used for interrogations on her right, but the man didn't push her towards it. They continued straight.

They crossed the village square. Her feet slipped on the mud from time to time. Some people turned their heads, looking at her with interest. She noticed women waiting in line to pull the water from the well in the center, between the dwellings. One of them spat on the ground upon seeing her. A few men sat around the fire, smoking tobacco. They grinned at her, showing their yellow teeth. Whatever their intentions, they clearly weren't good and she had no desire to find out.

All the eyes of the inhabitants were full of hatred for the Green Shirt uniform she wore on her back. There were no other clothes she could change into. Cat hadn't been able to find anything in the abandoned houses she and Max had passed. She'd stripped the Sābanto markings from her uniform, but the cut and style of what she wore couldn't be mistaken for regular, everyday clothes. Until a couple of weeks ago, the only concern she had was of her and Max being captured by Sābanto, but the Free people who'd brought them here were also unfriendly and dangerous. Was Cat's attire her only crime?

The guard behind her urged her forward through a path into the woods. Her feet now stood comfortably on solid ground. The mud was gone, and the coldness became more bearable as the wind was slowed down by the trees. This was it. Did the Free have a special place? A firing squad or gallows to guard their little secret? Why weren't they doing that in the open for everyone's pleasure, then? Public executions were entertaining.

The door to a chop-jet opened suddenly in front of her, as though the vessel had materialized out of thin air. The guard pushed her forward to get in, but didn't enter himself.

"What the fuck is going on?" she asked, seeing Max inside with three other people. Cat wanted to beat him up for leaving her and not getting her out, but her hands were still tied.

She noticed Max's bruised and blood-crusted face. The Free hadn't spared him either.

"We're getting the fuck out of here," Max said without looking at her, as though that sounded perfectly normal. His body turned towards an older man who also sat in the vessel. "You can go!" He pointed at the door.

It was the man from the interrogation room who had asked questions and ordered the punishments when the answers hadn't pleased him. Cat gave him a hard stare. If her hands were free, she might not have been able to control herself. She would've dealt with him in the same manner he'd treated her, leaving him sore and bloodied. Cat took a step back from the chop-jet doors.

"Don't try anything stupid, *chief*," Max added, emphasizing the man's title. The older man left without looking back or saying a word. He retreated through the path in the woods together with the man who had brought Cat out of her cell. The chop-jet door closed.

Cat turned to Max. He looked composed, and his posture was straight and confident. His eyes were wide, alert. This was the Max she remembered from Riverlea: a leader. The corner of Cat's mouth lifted slightly. Max was back.

"I keep my word," Max said to the young woman standing beside him. She clearly wasn't from the village. She wasn't dressed in rags like them, although her clothes were rather baggy. Cat had no clue who the woman was or what promise Max had made to her, but he was right. He always kept his word.

"Do you know how to fly this?" Max asked the tall man who was pointing a gun at the woman.

"I can manage," the man said. He lowered his gun and entered the cockpit.

The engines turned on and the chop-jet jolted up. The man was obviously somewhat out of practice as a pilot.

Once they were off the ground, Max freed Cat's hands and she rubbed her tired wrists to release the tension in them. Max was cold and seemed indifferent to her clearly-visible injuries, but she knew he cared. His current priorities didn't allow his emotions to take over, possibly jeopardizing his plans. She didn't hold it against him.

"What's going on?" Cat asked again, calmly this time. They were traveling now, and a fair distance from the village and the danger there.

"Sit down," Max said, pointing at the seat behind her. "One of my Gutters is at the stick. We're good." Cat collapsed into the seat, relieved to be off her feet. "It will take some time before we're in Covedale," he added.

Was it that easy? Just grab a chop-jet and fly there? He had no reason to lie to her, but this whole situation was a little strange. Where had he found a Gutter? Whose chop-jet was this?

"Who's she?" Cat asked, looking at the woman sitting in the other chair.

"Mr. Conway's personal guard," Max replied with a grin.

"Oh." The information caught her by surprise. A personal guard? Wasn't she too young for that?

Max took a phone out of his pocket and handed it to the woman. "Call him now and let him know we're on our way."

The woman hesitated, but took the phone from Max's hand. "What if he doesn't wanna see ya?"

"He will," Cat replied as the girl made the call.

Oliver stepped into the chop-jet with his gun drawn and ready to fire. After receiving the call from Amy and learning that Cat was with her, he'd rushed to meet them. He probably should've waited for Greyson and taken him to this meeting for additional protection, but it was too late now. Inside he noticed Cat and Amy. They were alone.

He put away his gun and ran up to Cat and gave her a long hug. The news had said she went by Catherine now, but Oliver recognized her instantly. She was alive and out of Riverlea. "I was worried I'd never see you again," he said, releasing her. "What happened?" He wanted to know her story. How had she wound up in Sābanto, and in a Green Shirt? Why had she escaped, and with whom? Why hadn't she reached out to him sooner? "Do you need a doctor?" he asked, concerned, looking at her face covered with bruises and blood. Her face was also more wrinkled than the last time he'd seen her. Her eyes were darker somehow, sunken deeper into her skull.

"I need a rest," she replied. "The cut will heal." Cat did look tired.

"I'm glad Amy found you," Oliver said and smiled. "You're safe now."

"Amy didn't find us," a male voice said. Oliver turned towards the man who emerged from the back of the vessel. He looked equally beaten up.

Oliver's blood boiled and his breath quickened. He took out his gun and pointed it at the intruder. "You gotta be fucking kidding me!" he shouted, recognizing Max. He then asked Cat for answers while keeping his eyes on his enemy. "Why did you bring me this"—he asked her, pointing at Max with his extended hand that he shook trying to find words—"this man!" Fucking Max! He was supposed to have died in the fire in Riverlea. What was he doing here in his chop-jet? The news had said that Cat had been abducted by some man. Max, who was now standing in front of him, hadn't even crossed his mind.

"Calm the fuck down!" Max replied. He brought his hands up slightly to show he was unarmed.

"I thought I wouldn't see your fucking face ever again!" Oliver replied. "Why aren't you dead?"

Cat walked between Oliver and Max and separated them. "Stop!" she shouted. "Listen."

Oliver focused his eyes on Max. What was Cat's connection to this piece of shit? He had more questions than answers. He wanted an explanation.

"Why burn the city anyway?" Oliver exploded and stepped closer towards Max, the gun still in his hand, ignoring Cat.

"Why uproot all of the towns and villages? I see what your Sābanto plan was!" Max replied, matching Oliver's angry tone.

"That is not what we came here for!" Cat was mad at both of them. "Let's talk," she said, looking at Oliver and then at Max.

Oliver relaxed slightly. The moron in front of him was safe, but only because Cat was here. He put his gun away, but stayed alert.

"Do you trust her?" Max said, pointing at Amy.

"Yes," Oliver replied. He gestured to Amy to take out the jammer from the storage. She knew enough and she'd be reliable as long as she protected the people in the forest. Oliver had known about them for a long time and had turned a blind eye when she'd taken the chop-jet to visit them. He had no business with the Free and their little paradise, but he worried that Cat and Max would want revenge on the village for what had happened to them. Their bruises looked awful.

Amy put a jammer onto the table in front of them, and Max started to explain. "We need your help—"

"You overestimate my kindness," Oliver interrupted dismissively and sat down. He took a cigarette out of his pocket and lit it. He took a look at both of them and how sad their appearance was against the backdrop of the white upholstery of the inside of the chop-jet. Whatever they planned to ask for, there couldn't possibly be any benefit for him.

"Oliver," Cat said. She came closer to him and looked at him directly. She pleaded again with her puppy eyes. "Please, listen first."

Oliver nodded. They were wasting their time, but with an open-palm gesture of his right hand he invited them to talk.

"You know Riverlea had a secret," Max said. "Friends wanted to get their hands on it."

"Just one secret?" Oliver replied and inhaled the cigarette smoke. Riverlea had been full of secrets. The biggest was how to find money and food to feed the thousands in the city. The ruins were special, and Friends were after something in Riverlea. They were trying to infiltrate the island. He couldn't wait to tell them to go to hell with their Riverlea secret. He had enough problems and he didn't want another one.

"I think it might interest you too," Max said.

Oliver focused his eyes on Cat. How had she gotten herself in the middle of this? What the fucking hell happened to her in Riverlea? "What is it?" Oliver asked and gestured for them to get comfortable as well.

"I'll need a doctor to extract it." She pointed at the back of her neck.

What kind of charade was this? Hadn't she just said she didn't need a doctor? He glanced at Cat again. Her face was serious. She was pointing at the back of her neck. There was a slight lump.

"It's hidden under my skin," Cat explained.

Oliver turned to Amy. "Fetch Dr. Lott," he ordered.

Amy started to get up. "Tomorrow," Cat told her. "I've had enough for today."

Oliver sighed. Rest was all he could offer them, and one night only. "You can stay in the chop-jet tonight," he said looking at Cat and Max. No one could know that the two of them were in Covedale, so the chop-jet would be the safest place. Tomorrow he'd drop them off at any location they chose.

"Tell me everything," Oliver said. "From the beginning."

## 16

O LIVER FREED MAX FROM his ankle bracelet using the master key he had borrowed. He was lucky that the village checked first that it was inactive, otherwise they might have tried to forcefully take it off and seriously injured him. Oliver then spent the rest of the evening in the chop-jet with Cat.

He took out the bottle of whiskey he'd stashed away for a special occasion as Cat told him her story. Two long years had passed since he'd seen Cat, and lots had happened during that time. She told him how she'd searched for Tom in Riverlea, then how she'd heard about Mark. How she'd had troubles with money and how Max had helped her through the hard times. Cat also told him about her escape from Riverlea on the back of the Sābanto truck, and about her fight to become a Green Shirt. She explained the device, but Oliver had trouble understanding it. Maybe Bruce Lott would have a better chance at it. He knew how the human body worked.

Oliver eventually arrived home. Sophia was already asleep in the guest room. It was for the best. She wasn't awake to smell alcohol on his breath. He didn't have the energy for another fight.

He spent the lonely night thinking. He couldn't keep Cat and Max in the chop-jet forever. He'd need the vessel for travel. Taking them anywhere with him was out of the question. The chop-jet had a couple of cots, but no proper beds.

Cat and Max, they were fugitives. He had a lot of sway in Sābanto, but he couldn't persuade the Black Shirts to stop searching. There was already a warrant out for their arrest. At least no one was actively looking for them anymore. When Max didn't shave, he wasn't very recognizable, but Cat. . . . She wouldn't be able to hide easily even if she bleached her black curls blonde. She was a Green Shirt and a resident of Sābanto. The compound had many pictures of her.

If Friends had any idea that Max was alive, there'd be a manhunt. There was also the secret that Friends would be after. Riverlea had been of interest to them for years, and now this secret might end up in his hands. What if Cat and Max were right? Maybe whatever the doctor extracted would be of value to him.

The surgery Dr. Bruce Lott performed inside the chop-jet the next morning was brief and minor—even though he wasn't happy about it and talked under his breath about how dangerous it was for him to do such favors—but it was fucking painful. Cat screamed even though she'd gulped alcohol in preparation for it. Finally that tiny memory card was extracted from the back of her neck. *Never again, Cat. Never agree to anything stupid like being a fucking mule again.*

Before Dr. Lott could get up and leave, Oliver turned to him. "They need your help," he said. "Please, we need your expertise." Oliver glanced at Cat. "Please explain."

Cat rolled her eyes. Here it was again. She sat down in a chair. "This thing contains the blueprints." Cat pointed at the tiny, freshly extracted, memory card on the table.

"Blueprints of what?" Dr. Lott asked.

"Some weird device."

"Neurological device," Max filled in.

"What kind of neurological device?" Dr. Lott asked. He showed interest in what they were saying.

Cat pointed at her left temple with her index finger as though discharging a gun. "It goes here."

"What does it do?" the doctor asked.

"You see things," Cat replied and shrugged. It was hard to explain—Oliver hadn't understood any of it the previous night.

"Like what?" the doctor probed. His eyes were wide as he waited to learn more.

"Show them," Max said, pointing at the display on the wall of the chop-jet.

Cat looked up at the display and then at the doctor. "I don't have to say these commands out loud, but I want you to understand what I'm doing." She looked at the display again. "Agent on . . . calibrate display

. . . present on display . . ." The screen flickered. Cat turned her head towards Oliver and the display showed him as seen through her eyes.

Dr. Lott gasped, "Incredible!" Cat turned her head towards him. The display changed and it showed the doctor.

"This is just one thing the device can do," Max added. "It also has night vision, thermal vision, increased sound sensitivity . . ." He counted the functions on his fingers.

"How is it connected?" the doctor asked. "I can't see anything." Dr. Lott studied Cat's eyes and temples.

"It taps into here between your eyes and ear," Max said and pointed at his own temple. "Agent on . . ." he said.

Cat's own implant registered the presence of a nearby active device. She glowered at Max. "Why didn't you fucking tell me you had it too?!" She felt the blood boiling in her veins.

She'd risked her life when Sābanto had evacuated the city. She'd had to stay low. She'd even changed her name. Max had made her believe that she was the only one with the device. The only one who could save it. The fucker was nothing but a crook.

"But how?" Lott repeated his question, but she wasn't listening to him anymore.

She jumped towards Max and raised her fist. "Explain!" she shouted. Her chest was heaving, making it difficult to catch her breath. The advantage of the device was that it was undetectable to the naked eye. Cat couldn't see it on Max, but she knew right away that he had it when he turned it on. Max didn't say anything. "Why?!" she repeated.

"Cut this out!" Oliver shouted at them and jumped in to separate them. Greyson also moved away from the wall and towards them, but didn't get too close.

"Why didn't you tell me?" Cat repeated.

Max brought his hands in front of his chest, palms towards her as he took a step back while Oliver pulled her away from him. "There was no good time!" he said.

Cat collapsed into a chair at the table and buried her face in her arms. What was she supposed to do now? Her stomach hurt.

"I'm sorry. I didn't know you'd be so upset," Max said.

Cat didn't move. He wasn't sorry at all.

"What's going on?" Bruce Lott asked.

"Everything is on this memory card," Max pointed out. "We aren't scientists."

Dr. Lott picked the tiny card from the table. "Not really my area of expertise, but I can look at it," he said.

Cat brought her head up and looked at the doctor. She pointed at her temple. "Please tell me how to remove this thing." Getting rid of the device was the only way she'd finally be free. Free from Max.

The doctor had left the sour situation in the chop-jet, and Cat had agreed to Oliver taking them somewhere they could stay for a longer time. She had no other place to go. The flight was short, just a few minutes, and the chop-jet stopped above a large body of water. Cat peeked through the window of the vessel, but there was nothing around them. Suddenly, the water underneath them parted and the chop-jet descended, revealing dry land with trees and grass.

"What is this place?" Cat asked as the aircraft set down gently in the middle of the island.

Oliver had created this place for himself. Sooner or later he'd have to disappear and go into hiding. Until now, only he had known of its existence. An invisibility shield covered the island, making it undetectable between the many other islands in the area.

He showed Cat and Max the small Sābanto-style house and told them to settle in. The arrangements weren't perfect, but the place was warm and clean. It was also stocked with food that would last them for a long time. Dr. Lott would quickly learn about the device and remove it from Cat, and then she and Max would have to find another place to stay.

Oliver said his goodbyes for the night and was ready for departure. He entered the chop-jet and Amy followed him inside.

"I think I found something," she said. Oliver turned to her. She held the tablet in her hand. The one that contained the recordings he'd asked her to listen to. "Whatever they're discussing makes no sense to me. I have no context, but talking isn't the only thing that the recording picked up." Amy opened the tablet. "I want ya to listen to this." She played the audio.

*"The shipment is coming soon,"* a male voice said.

*"How are you planning to find the nest?" the other man on the recording replied.*

*"Smoke always comes in handy."*

*"But they might leave without us."*

Amy paused the recording. "Did you hear that?" she asked.

"Hear what?" Oliver asked. The conversation was gibberish, a code of some kind.

"Don't listen to the words. Listen to the noise in the background." Amy played the conversation again. "Did you hear that?"

"That faint sound? Yes," Oliver replied.

"It took me a moment to realize what that was. Then it hit me. It's a shift whistle."

"Like to mark the start or end of a shift?" Greyson asked. He walked into the chop-jet and stood behind them, listening to their conversation.

"Correct, but . . . not just any shift whistle. It's a whistle in the Menken coal mine."

Oliver glanced at Amy. Another puzzle. His brain had had enough for one day. He slumped into one of the seats in the vessel.

"One of these men was in the Menken Mines' village," Amy said. She remained standing. "That sound can only be heard there, and it comes every twelve hours. If you look at the timestamp, it's almost exactly eight in the evening."

"No one can access Menken Mines." Greyson watched her with his narrow eyes. They guarded the place heavily and no one was allowed in or out without authorization. "How do ya know that's where it is?"

"I know some people who worked there," Amy replied. "They said it's a terrible place and that they'd recognize that whistle anywhere."

"What do you think that means?" Oliver asked.

"Let's assume that this person is someone important." Oliver nodded and she continued, "Think of who would have a reason to be in the village."

No one important would have been interested in going to where the workers lived. Most of the citizens didn't even know where the mine was. Menken Mines' town wasn't even on a map. If anyone wanted to sneak in, the settlement was far from the main road, and the additional patrols around the town and at the checkpoints didn't allow anyone in without a special pass. There was, however, no coincidence that this conversation had happened right when Sābanto had evacuated Riverlea. What did it mean? Oliver was silent.

"Mr. Menken or one of his associates," Amy answered. She straightened up and grinned with pride.

"Let's say you're right," Oliver replied. "We have no proof."

Amy's shoulders slumped a bit. "I could be wrong. There could be another whistle like this on the other side of the world. We don't know if the person talking is involved with Mr. Menken. Ya right. We have no proof, but it's what we've got to work with." She shrugged.

"Thank you, Amy. It's more than I could have figured out myself." Oliver recalled the lists he had in his safe. So many people had died there, in those mines, during the last few months. Even if Menken wasn't involved with Friends, he definitely had some shady business practices that he wanted to keep hidden.


"Dr. Lott said a couple more weeks," Sophia said, sitting in Oliver's arms on the sofa in the upstairs sitting room in their house. Outside the first snow of the season was falling, one that would melt by morning.

Sophia seemed happy today. They'd been fighting a lot lately. Maybe it was just the hormones playing tricks on both of them. *Give her space and be patient.* Sophia would need time to adjust to the new role of mother. The hard times would eventually pass and she'd become comfortable leaving the baby with the nanny. He could take her out then for a day or two to Clamerton or maybe Karben to see their friends.

"The nursery is almost finished," Sophia continued. She'd chosen the animal patterns for the walls. Ivy had also added some gentle exotic plants which kept the room fresh and fit the decor. Sophia had approved of them and Oliver was pleased. "But we haven't picked a name for the baby."

There had been no time to discuss it. They saw each other very little lately, avoiding each other and staying off each other's nerves.

"Do you have any ideas?" he asked her.

"If it's a boy, I think Steven, after my father," Sophia said.

*Geez!* Why had he asked that question? Steven. That name brought too many bad memories. How could he suppress them hearing the name every day at the dinner table? "I think it's too early," he said, trying to hide his emotions. They'd said goodbye to Sophia's father less than six months ago. It was still too fresh in everyone's mind. It was a good argument.

"I don't think so," she argued.

"What if it's a girl? I like Claire." It had been her mother's name. She'd died when Sophia had been a small child.

Sophia nodded and smiled widely. "Yes, if it's a girl, I'd love that."

"You said you wanted more kids. We'll have a girl." He leaned over and kissed the nape of her neck. Sophia seemed oddly relaxed and agreeable. Maybe it was a good sign that things would turn back to normal.

"Steven and Claire?" She smiled at him.

"I think you shouldn't use both of your parents' names," he replied.

"Then what?" Sophia said. "You don't like my choice and I'm definitely not using your father's name," she added harshly. She was getting upset.

"Hell no," he replied. He'd never inflict that name on anyone. "How about Matthew?" It was a random name. He didn't associate it with anyone he knew or anything that would haunt him forever. It was a safe name. Sophia grimaced at the idea and Oliver tried to come up with another name that she might like.

"Why do you keep wearing this cheap thing?" Sophia asked. She'd noticed him mindlessly touching the ring on his finger. The air in the room suddenly changed. There it was. The peace hadn't lasted long. "Is that even gold?" she added and sat up so he could no longer hold her.

Oliver sighed. It was gold. It wasn't the best quality, but it was gold. Sophia knew his father had given him the ring, and it wasn't the first time she'd picked on it. It bothered her that he wore it, but she didn't understand. He put it on each morning as a reminder not to be like his father. But nothing good would come from him explaining his reasons. What would Sophia think if he told her more about his youth? How would she react, knowing he'd worked with his father as a killer? Would she believe that he'd wanted to quit that job? She wouldn't love him anymore.

"You know," Sophia said and got up from the sofa. "We should take a break from each other. I should go to my father's house." She walked up to the window and gazed in the direction of her childhood house. "There, by the bay."

"Out of the question," Oliver said, trying not to be too harsh. "We don't have enough men to secure both properties." He remained seated.

"All your men are running around Sābanto," Sophia said. She didn't look at him. Her eyes were fixed on something outside of the window. "I'll have my things packed tomorrow," she added.

"I can't let you do that." Oliver shook his head. No. He wouldn't budge from his position.

Sophia suddenly held her belly. Oliver jumped up and hurried to her side. He helped her sit down on the armchair. "What's wrong?" he asked. Sophia stared at him in surprise. There were no signs of pain or distress on her face.

"It broke," she said. "My water broke."


Cat woke up in the middle of the night drenched in sweat. Was the room too hot, or had she had a nightmare? She moved in bed, her body still sore. She was feeling better every day and her strength was slowly coming back, but she hadn't started her exercise routines yet. She was out of shape.

She slid the covers off to cool down and felt a stir on the other side of the bed.

Oliver had prepared the house for someone to live here for an extended period of time, even a year, but with just one person in mind. The two smaller bedrooms were empty. The only room available was the one that would normally house a small family in Sābanto. It had one large bed that Max and Cat were forced to share, but as long as he stayed on his side of the bed, he was safe.

"Don't even think about it," she whispered. If he touched her she'd fuck him up so hard he'd need to be sent to Lott's clinic.

"You know you're torturing me, right?" Max said.

"Oh, please," Cat said. It was dark, but she was sure he was grinning. He knew she slept in just a shirt and underwear.

Max sighed quietly.

Cat sat up in bed looking in his general direction. "What the hell is wrong with you?" she said it louder. "Can you fuck off?"

"Cat, please," Max said. He turned his back on her.

"I can't wait 'til I'm free from you!"

"Why are you so mad at me?"

"You never told me you also had the device. How long?"

Max sighed. "I insisted on having it while I planned the escape from Riverlea."

"What for?"

"In case you failed."

"Thank you for the vote of confidence." Cat turned her back to Max, hit the pillow with her fist to adjust it, and lay down on her side.

"Why are you so cold?" he asked.

"You made me that way."

"Give me a chance," he replied. "Just one."

"I don't owe you shit," Cat replied.

"I know you aren't indifferent."

"Go to sleep," she told him. "I'm going for a run in the morning."

The bed moved as Max adjusted his position.

Cat closed her eyes. She only had to put up with Max a little bit longer. The doctor would soon figure it out and this stupid thing would be out of her body.

Oliver sat in the clinic's waiting room for hours, until Sophia came out holding a baby in her arms.

"It's a boy," she said. She directed her beautiful smile at their son, wrapped up in a blanket. She handed him the baby and Oliver suddenly had a full heart. He felt lighter as though he had no worries in his life. A son. Such a beautiful, tiny thing. Oliver didn't have a good example of a father figure in his life, but he vowed to do his best.

"I've named him already," she added.

Oliver's heart sank. Steven. It was Steven, wasn't it? He should've expected that Sophia would do this just to spite him.

"Matthew," Sophia said.

Oliver exhaled, relieved.

Bruce Lott emerged behind Sophia and congratulated them both. "Sorry for keeping you waiting," he told Oliver. "It was a C-section, but there was no risk. The medical equipment kept both Mrs. Conway and the baby stable at all times."

"I'll get you home, so you can rest," Oliver said to Sophia. "A nanny will take care of Matthew while you recover. I made arrangements—"

"No recovery time needed," Dr. Lott interrupted. "There's barely a scar . . . and thank you, Mr. Conway, for your generous donation to the clinic."

Oliver nodded in acknowledgment. He'd given the doctor a large amount of money. It was well deserved. Part of these funds was payment for using the medical machine on Sophia and successfully delivering Oliver's son.

"Thank you, doctor," Sophia replied.

"I'll come to visit Matthew in a couple of days to see how he's doing." Dr. Lott excused himself and left the room.

Oliver bent over Sophia and planted a small kiss on her lips. She smiled. He'd missed that smile. Pure and genuine. A sight he hadn't seen in a long time. All the tension inside him disappeared and he smiled as well. He was a lucky man to have Sophia and Matthew in his life.

# 17

"PLEASE COME IN," THE secretary said, and Anita followed her into a large, well-lit room. Windows spanned the wall, and the balcony outside overlooked downtown Karben. The busy city was under constant construction. Old houses were being replaced with new. The fresh towers pleased the eye.

Following her encounter with the Sābanto men, Anita had traveled here for a chat with the Health Commissioner. If she couldn't investigate the workers directly, maybe confronting the man at the very top would give her some answers. He was the source of the new legislation, but it wasn't clear how much he knew about the Sābanto workers and their working conditions. The truth might have been shielded from him.

Anita had prepared for this meeting, researching the facts and collecting the proof. Many companies, unlike Menken Mines, didn't hide their stats. Once the commissioner knew the details, he wouldn't be able to turn a blind eye to what was happening.

"Mr. Scholz." Anita approached the large desk and extended her hand.

The man on the other side got up and greeted her, but he shook her hand mechanically and without interest. "Miss Gibala, I hope your trip was comfortable and uneventful," he said.

"Yes, thank you," she replied.

Ben Scholz pointed at the chair beside her and she sat down. She rested the briefcase she'd brought with her on the floor beside her seat.

"What can I do for you?" he asked, sitting down himself and leaning slightly forward, elbows resting on the tabletop.

175

Neither Scholz nor his secretary offered Anita anything to drink. They expected the conversation would be brief. "I wanted to ask you about Sābanto," Anita said. Might as well get to the point of her visit. She wouldn't waste their time, which was evidently so precious to them.

"The project is proceeding as planned," he said as though he'd rehearsed his speech. "The most vulnerable populations are being accommodated. The houses aren't big, but they're new and have all the necessities, including clean running water and electricity. My department sends food regularly and the reports say the amount is adequate. Is there anything specific you wanted to discuss?"

"I hear that the living conditions at the men's compounds aren't up to this standard."

"We can't take responsibility for that, Miss Gibala," he replied, a bit annoyed. "All compounds are built identically. It is not our fault that the houses are being destroyed during the riots. Even if we had the money for repairs, the workers are afraid to enter some of those compounds."

"There have been violent attacks on Sābanto employees, the Green Shirts, and the supporting staff. Is that why the employees are being isolated and moved to a separate location?"

"I don't know the reason for that decision. That is something that you should ask the Sābanto committee, or Mr. Conway." The commissioner sat back, putting himself at a distance from her.

"Mr. Scholz, are you saying that World United has no control over what's happening in the compounds?"

"World United oversees Sābanto, but we don't dictate its every move." His chair swiveled slightly to the right and back as he spoke. Scholz seemed nervous.

"As Health Commissioner, do you think you should have control over the well-being of the people you're protecting?"

"Miss Gibala—" he started, but she interrupted him.

"Did you know that eighty percent of injured workers don't get adequate medical treatment?"

"I don't know where you're getting your numbers from." Scholz frowned.

She put her briefcase on her lap, and took out a few sheets of paper. She passed them over to Scholz. "Normally, for any dead worker, there'd be on average five to ten injured. Your current rate is one dead to two injured. This means that either injuries aren't being reported, or they're being counted as deceased when they die from their injuries. The number of deaths is then much higher than it otherwise would be."

The commissioner leaned forward and picked up the papers and gazed at the numbers as though he were studying them.

"Miss Gibala," he eventually said, handing the documents back to her. "I don't believe these numbers are correct. According to our data, World United has significantly lowered the overall death rate and we're already seeing a reduction in child mortality since implementing Sābanto. As I mentioned, the project is proceeding as planned."

"Are you planning to look into the rights of the workers?"

Scholz got up from his seat. "For that, you'd need to talk with the Employers Association under the Commissioner of Finance."

*Of course.* She wasn't surprised that the Association was created under the protectorate of the Finance Department. "Are you saying that no one in World United represents the workers?" she asked. There was no Employees Association. She had already checked.

"Please excuse me, I'm late for my next meeting." He grabbed his folio from the top of the desk. "Enjoy the rest of your day, Miss Gibala," he said before leaving the room hurriedly.

Anita put the documents she'd brought, back into her briefcase and allowed herself to be escorted out by the commissioner's secretary. Was there any point in talking with the association for the employers? No, it would be a waste of time. All she'd get would be lies and excuses. The Health Commissioner was supposed to give a fuck about the health of the people. He clearly didn't.

What else could she do? The Sābanto men had told her to be smart. Only the workers cared about their own, but they had no voice. Was there a way to become that voice on their behalf?

Bruce got up early and made a pot of coffee for the three of them. Oliver had invited him to stay on the island and study the memory card without fear that someone might see him doing so. He'd heard Cat and Max have another fight last night. They fought all the time, but they insisted that they could work out their differences. Bruce left them alone.

He poured himself a cup of coffee and sat down at the table. Cat was out on her morning run. Regardless of whether it rained or snowed, so far she'd never deviated from this routine while Max slept in. He was snoring in the other room.

Bruce spent long hours studying the information on the tiny memory card, sleeping only occasionally. He wanted to get it over with quickly so he could return to paying all his attention to his patients at the clinic in Covedale. He should be there, not here.

He heard some shuffling in the other room and Max emerged.

"Good morning," the man said. He walked towards the coffee maker and poured a cup as well. He then sat opposite Bruce. "Thank you for making a pot, and sorry about last night. We didn't mean to wake you up."

"I was working on the blueprints," Bruce replied.

"It's fucking neat, isn't it?" Max said. "I could tap in and see how her run is going, but she'd know."

That was a terrible idea, and Max seemed to realize it too because he simply drank his coffee. When both of the devices were turned on, they were able to communicate with each other using many interconnected commands. They could share what they saw and heard, but according to the blueprints, they couldn't share their thoughts.

Cat walked in the door and Max jumped up and poured coffee for her. Bruce watched him add milk and sugar to it. Max placed the cup on the table beside him. Meanwhile Cat took off her coat and hung it on a hook beside the entrance. She disappeared into their room and emerged with a fresh shirt on.

"Good morning," Cat said to Bruce, ignoring Max.

"I got you some coffee," Max said. "Freshly brewed."

Cat glanced into the cup and, rather than sitting down to drink it, she went to the counter and poured herself a fresh cup. She sat down at the table, pushed the other cup away from her, and placed the one she'd filled herself in front of her. She turned to Bruce and pointed at her temple. "Any news on how we get rid of this?" She took a sip of the coffee and grimaced.

"Yes and no," Bruce said and looked at both of them. "The Mafdet has a very specific way of attaching itself to the nerve endings."

"The what?" Max asked.

"The blueprints called it Mafdet. The Egyptian goddess of justice and punishment," Bruce explained, but neither of his listeners understood. "Never mind. It interprets the signals similarly to how the brain does. For example, it intercepts your vision so you can send what you're seeing somewhere else, like to another person or a display. A similar thing happens with sound. What's also interesting is how that information is displayed. My understanding is that when the Mafdet turns on, you see some kind of menu."

"That's correct," Max confirmed.

"That's what fascinates me," Bruce continued. "Normally the brain only returns instructions for eye movements or changes in pupil size. It doesn't project visions to the eyes that could be intercepted by a device. That means that Mafdet feeds the menu you see directly into the brain." He brought his head up and was met with blank stares. "What might interest you, however, is that this device is practically undetectable."

"We know you can't see it," Cat pointed out bluntly. "I would've known he had it if that was easy to notice."

"It goes beyond that," Bruce replied. "There's no device that I know of that could detect its presence."

"No metal detectors or particle sniffers?" Max asked.

"Correct. It leaves no trace."

"Could we create a detector?" Max showed interest.

"Possibly," Bruce said. "I would need to know all of the compounds involved for that, and I haven't studied that yet. An autopsy, however, would reveal the existence of the device."

"How do we extract it?" Cat asked.

"That's the problem." Bruce glanced at Cat. "I don't see how it can be done."

"So once someone has it, that's it?" Cat stared at him.

"I'm afraid so," Bruce said. "It's the truth." He knew she'd be upset, but he was only the messenger. He didn't want to lie to her. "It's even mentioned in the blueprints."

Cat slumped in her chair and stared down at her hands.

"Any attempt to remove the Mafdet," Bruce continued, "will cause permanent vision and hearing loss on the side of the face the device is installed, as well as almost guaranteed brain damage."

"Thank you, doctor," Cat said and got up from the table. She walked into her room and slammed the door behind her, her unfinished coffee still sat on the table.

Max got up to go after her, but Bruce stopped him. "Give her space," he said. There was no reason to make the situation worse.

Max sat back down. The information hadn't fazed him.

"You knew?" Bruce asked.

Max nodded. "I hoped that there was still a chance," he replied. "That it would turn out differently."

A wearer of the device didn't ever need to turn it on, and could lead a normal life, but once implanted there was no return. It connected them forever.


Leo showed up in the cabin again weeks later. He'd been in good spirits getting in and drank with Mike for the whole evening. The less liquid there was in the bottle, the louder they were and the more animated their conversation. Back in Riverlea, they'd had a neighbor who was violent when intoxicated. He would beat his wife and kids. What if Leo was like that? Violet relaxed only upon seeing them finally fall asleep.

In the morning, Mike went out and cut some wood. Leo came into the kitchen as she was cleaning the dishes from breakfast. "I got something for you," he said. He took a green ribbon out of his pocket.

Violet didn't want any gifts or attention from Leo. Those came with strings. What kind of strings? A shiver went through her, but she smiled a little. Impoliteness might upset him.

He came closer and touched her blond hair. Violet froze, feeling his hands on her, stroking her hair gently. She had kept her hair short while living in Riverlea, but with lice under control in Sābanto, she'd let it grow longer. One day it would be long, as long as it had been when she was a little girl.

Leo brushed her hair back, away from her shoulders with his fingers. She stood still and waited. What if resisting made him angry? Seb sat at the table, playing. She couldn't put him in harm's way. Leo tied Violet's hair in a loose ponytail with the ribbon. His movements were slow and it felt like an eternity. As soon as his hands left her, Violet spun around and looked at her son. "Seb, don't put that in ya mouth," she called and ran to him before Leo could notice that she was bluffing.

Leo walked over to the table, pulled out a chair and sat down. Violet glanced at him and he gazed into her gray eyes. "Who's the father?" he asked.

"I dunno," Violet replied quickly while Mike came in and saved her from further questions. He'd brought fresh wood for the fire. Violet busied herself with feeding firewood into the fireplace, but she still felt Leo's gaze on her.


Ivy returned to her sitting room. Liam had come for a visit. She'd found him waiting for her on a cushion he'd placed directly on the floor in front of the fireplace, rather than on the sofa. He turned around upon hearing her walk in.

"It's much warmer here," he said, gesturing for her to join him on the cushion next to him. He'd prepared it in anticipation of her arrival.

On this visit, Liam had given Ivy plenty of notice. He'd apologized for his last unannounced visit and abrupt departure, and said he wanted to spend whole a day with her. Ivy had already had plans for today—she'd scheduled a truck to come in with frozen turkeys for her staff. She encouraged her workers to cook them on their own over the fire in the middle of the workers' village. The winter solstice was coming soon, and Ivy had wanted to distribute the birds herself and show that she cared about the people's festivals. Liam had supported her plans and was enthusiastic about helping her.

The work had gone very quickly with Liam's help and there was still lots of daylight left when festivities wrapped up. There wasn't much to do in Covedale anymore, or at least nothing Liam would be interested in, so Ivy had taken him to a place that she loved to visit. A small path led to the top of a cliff overlooking the ocean. When she was younger, she'd often go there and sit staring at the golden glimmer on the water, catching the last rays of the day.

The afternoon had turned out to be quite cold. There was snow in the mountains already, but this morning was the first major snowfall on the Covedale coast. Liam had wrapped his arms around Ivy so they could share each other's warmth as they'd stood at the top of the cliff watching the ocean in front of them. They watched the sun slowly hiding behind the horizon as though it were sinking into the water until it was dark.

Chilled through, they had retreated to the comfort of Ivy's house.

"I was a brat when I was young," Liam started as Ivy sat down on the cushion beside him. The logs crackled quietly in the background. It was quite warm sitting close to the fire.

Julia had put out small snacks for them when they'd arrived. There was a bottle of red wine as well as some cheese and dried sausages on the coffee table. Liam filled the two prepared wine glasses and handed one to Ivy. The fire reflected in his eyes.

He held the other glass in his hand as he continued, "None of the governesses could keep up with me."

"I think I can believe that." Ivy smiled then raised her glass of wine to her mouth and took a sip.

"One day I climbed a tree," Liam said. "But I had trouble coming back down." He grabbed a piece of smoked sausage from the tray and put it into his mouth. He finished chewing, then continued, "The tree gave me a superb view of the house and the estate. I liked my vantage point, but I knew I couldn't stay there forever." He sipped his wine. "Once the staff realized I was missing, they started a search. Some even passed right under the tree, but they didn't notice me. It took a lot for a kid like myself not to laugh and give away my hiding place."

"Did they eventually find you?" Ivy brought the glass to her lips and had another sip of the tart wine. Her movements were shy and unsure due to the company. Ivy was watching what she was doing. She didn't want Liam to run away like he had the last time. He'd never explained what had happened. She wouldn't press him for answers.

"Yes, but everyone got punished for losing me." Liam smiled.

"What punishment did you get?"

"Me?" Liam laughed, surprised. "Why would I be punished?"

Hiding from others on purpose was disrespectful, or at least that was what Ivy had learned from her parents. She couldn't claim that the neighborhood brats always did the right thing, but they always got punished for their behavior. Some fathers beat their kids blue if they misbehaved. Ivy had always imagined the rich kids being different, well-behaved, polite, and not getting themselves into trouble as much. She smiled at him nervously and took a sip of her wine. She owed Liam her story.

"My aunt gave me a necklace," she started. "She made it from seashells she found on the beach. It wasn't much, but it was a gift from the heart, and my mother told me to cherish anything that I was given." Liam leaned over and took the glass out of her hand and put it away as she talked. "I wore it with pride around town. One day other kids went to the old quarry for a swim and I went with them. I forgot to leave the necklace at home. I jumped into the water with it around my neck." Their eyes locked. "When I got out, the necklace was missing—"

Liam kissed her. Ivy had wanted to add what kind of punishment she'd gotten for her carelessness, but she felt his soft, moist lips on hers. It wasn't a small kiss like last time. This was a passionate one; electrifying.

There was a spark in his eyes. They both leaned forward and their lips touched again. Their kisses were more eager now. His hand slid under her hair and rested at the back of her neck.

They didn't stop kissing even when Liam gently laid her body on the soft rug. His body hovered above her, not pressing on her. She touched his back gently and traced it down to his waist. She paused for a moment then slid her hand under his shirt, feeling the warmth of his body.

Liam sat up and took off his shirt and Ivy used the time to free herself from her blouse, the first layer of unnecessary garments. The room suddenly felt hotter, as though the fire in the fireplace burned higher, but no one had added fresh wood. Liam moved his lips to her neck. One of his hands held her waist gently but firmly while the other was planted on the floor supporting his weight. Ivy relaxed, letting her body drive her actions.

Liam was nice, caring, and understanding. Did she love him? Maybe. She'd try. What else did she need in life? She'd let him become part of her world, and time would tell if they were meant for each other.

As Liam's hand traveled down the outside of her thighs—her skin was sensitive to his touch—there was a sudden knock on the door. He stopped the kisses, sighed, and rolled his eyes at the maid interrupting their intimate moment.

"Yes?" Ivy called without getting up from the floor. It was too early for the dinner to be ready, and she'd instructed Julia to sound the chime when Ivy had company. She and Liam were still close to each other, embracing, hoping the maid would go away and they could go back to their kisses while the desire was still in the air. She traced the contours of his square face with her eyes.

"There's a call for Mr. Menken. They say it's very urgent," Julia said. Her voice sounded muffled and distant coming from the other side of the closed doors.

"You can take it in the study," Ivy said, tilting her head in the general direction of the room. Liam still was unhappy about the call, so she added, "She said it's urgent."

He slowly got up and helped Ivy sit up as well. He put on his shirt and went to the room next door. Ivy heard the faint sound of a conversation as she put her blouse back on.

Liam hadn't been on the phone long when he reappeared in the sitting room. "I need to go," he said. There was a shadow on his face. "My father has died."

"What happened?" Ivy asked, springing up from the cushion on the floor.

"I don't know. I need to take care of business." He walked over to Ivy. He leaned over, held her chin with his fingers and gently pulled it towards him so that her lips met his. He gave her a short but strong kiss. "It might be a while, but I'll be back." He released her, turned around, and left.

Ivy ran after him to the foyer to see him out the door. She stood there speechless and paralyzed, watching the door close behind him. Such a tragedy. What should she do? Should she send flowers over? What did people do during such difficult times?

"Should we still set up dinner in the dining room, ma'am?" Taylor said, bringing Ivy back to the present and stopping the racing thoughts in her head. She looked at him and smiled nervously.

"I'm not hungry," she said. She turned around and took the stairs up to her bedroom.


A white blanket covered the forest outside of Violet's window and the rocky faces of the mountains. Another snowy evening.

They were stuck indoors for a second day, and everyone was getting on each other's nerves. Leo constantly followed her with his eyes and Violet was glad Mike was in the house and leaving only to bring in more of the wood they had stored behind the cabin. She never wore the green ribbon Leo gave her, but stopped short of throwing it into the fire. He might get angry with her for burning it. Violet didn't know what Leo would do the next time Mike left for more than ten minutes. She brushed those thoughts aside. She had little control over things. There was no point worrying in advance.

Violet sat beside the table and away from the two men, giving Seb some leftovers from dinner. She'd soon lay him down to sleep. Mike and Leo sat in their usual spots on a beat-up sofa in front of the fireplace and talked while they drank. Their shadows danced on the wall behind them. She didn't approve of how much alcohol her brother drank around Leo, who had brought new bottles when he'd arrived a couple of weeks ago, but she didn't have much say in the matter.

"Whose kid is this?" Leo asked Mike.

"She doesn't know," her brother said and laughed. It wasn't funny.

"How many you think had to fuck her for her not to know?" They both laughed, making Violet uncomfortable. It wasn't just that they were talking about her. It was the way they talked that concerned her. Mike had never been mean like this before. The man clearly had a bad influence on him.

"How is her pussy after she got ripped so many times?" Leo asked.

"How would I know?" Mike replied.

"You fucking never?" Leo laughed. "You lived with a whore for all those years and you never?" He didn't care that Violet was sitting at the table, and could hear every word he said.

"I thought about it," her brother said. He was lying. He'd never dare hurt her. Mike wanted to impress the man no matter what the cost, and that scared her.

Leo slapped Mike on the back. "How about we make a deal?" Leo said. "The money I gave you is only a hundred tickets."

Violet's heart sank. For Leo, it might not have been a lot of money—he'd once been a wealthy man, he'd said so himself. For Violet, however, it was a fortune. One could survive a whole year in Riverlea on that amount. There was no way Mike would ever have enough to repay Leo. Where would he find a hundred tickets?

She thought about the money, not paying attention to the conversation, but realized what they'd been talking about when Leo suddenly appeared beside her and grabbed her by the arm, digging his fingers in. He forced her to stand up and pushed her towards the back of the house. She looked back at Seb. Mike picked him up from the chair at the table and took him away without looking at her. Mike! Mike! How could you do this to me? She wanted to scream, but there was no point. There was no one around that would hear her. He'd sold her. Her own brother had betrayed her.

# 18

ANITA HAD EXTENDED HER stay in Karben to do some research. As usual these days, she spent her evenings in her hotel room. Her fellow reporters kept inviting her out for dinner, but she wasn't interested in spending time with them.

The display in Anita's room was off. She wasn't in the mood to hear the overblown stories about the workers or the Sābanto people not doing their jobs. The stories she'd submitted to the agency had disappeared and were never shown, lowering her popularity as a journalist, but it didn't discourage her. Her work was even more important now. She was on the right track. One day she'd have a story that everyone would be fighting to have on their own news channels.

Anita sat on the bed and looked at the list in front of her. She'd dug into all the major companies and researched their spending, their employee death rates, and how often and in what conditions they returned their workers to Sābanto. The data was staggering, and it surprised her that it was so widely available. Why had no one noticed this problem? They probably didn't care. Just like her reports, it was of no interest to anyone.

What should she do with this information? She wished there were someone she could turn to. A person she could trust. Handling this information alone wasn't safe, and trusting the wrong people could be deadly. They could easily pretend to have good intentions and then backstab her when it was convenient. *Be smart, Anita, be smart*, she told herself. But how?

Each day, Violet thought of escaping, but there was nowhere she could run. She didn't know where she was, and snow covered the ground and all the paths in the forest. If it had just been her, she might've risked it, but endangering Seb was out of the question. What if they got lost in the woods? The forest was a maze where every tree looked exactly the same. There were wolves out there. She heard them at night sometimes.

Spring was coming soon. When the weather got warmer she could escape. She'd be fine until then. She'd have to be.

Seb was oblivious to what was happening. Violet shielded him from everything and pretended nothing was wrong. Maybe if she could get her brother away from Leo, he'd return to being a good and caring man like he'd always been, but how would she accomplish that?

The direction of their escape wouldn't matter. There had to be people around who would help a mother with a child. She cared little about herself. She had to be strong for Seb. He was what mattered.

Violet concentrated on her chores, keeping her thoughts from wandering too much. She swept and washed the floors, cooked, and mended their clothes. When Mike brought home extra food, she made preserves and stored them in the cellar under the floorboards where it was cold.

Looking back, everything before this had been so much easier. Violet thought back to the time she'd worked at the Leggett factory. The tick-tock of the sewing machines in the enormous hall. It was hard work, but she would've done anything to be able to go back to those days. They seemed brighter in the darkness of this cabin.

"Sit," Leo came in and pointed at the table. Mike was out, searching for food to hunt or steal. She'd asked him once where he went to find chickens, but he'd brushed her off without telling her the direction of the settlements.

Violet put down what she was doing and obediently sat down in one of the chairs. There was no point in arguing. He'd just hurt her.

He bent over her, and his face was an inch away from hers. His breath stank of alcohol and rotting teeth. "You know who the father is, don't you?" Leo said. Violet shook her head. He took out a small vial from his pocket and a syringe. "We can do it the easy way or the hard way." He took the syringe, attached a needle to it, and slowly filled it with the liquid.

"One more time," he said. "Who's the father?" He pointed at Seb with his chin. Violet faced Leo, begging him with her eyes not to do it. She knew what the liquid was. She'd heard about truth serum.

Leo painfully pinned her arm to the table so that Violet couldn't move it and injected her with the serum.

The liquid spread quickly through her body. Her vision became blurry from the substance and from the tears that filled her eyes. What scared Violet the most was that she knew people didn't remember what they revealed under the influence of the chemical. She watched Seb's silhouette as her consciousness drifted.

After learning of Liam's father's death, Ivy kept away for over two months. She didn't want to interrupt family matters so she didn't reach out to him. It was a tragedy. Heart attack, the news had said. A few days later, the media had grown quiet, but she'd received no news from Liam.

Ivy took a trip to Clamerton in early March to check on the Leggett factory there and decided to brave it and call Liam. She told him she'd been wondering how he was doing and offered him any help he might need. He was thrilled to hear from her and very sorry that he'd been distant and unavailable. Liam insisted on meeting. He was ready to forget about family and business, if only for a short time.

"I've something to show you," Liam said as he picked Ivy up from the hotel.

The car rose up on the hover mechanism and moved gently forward. It was the newest model. The one that didn't need a driver. "Where are we going?" Ivy asked.

"Surprise!" Liam smiled widely and she smiled back. She liked surprises.

A few minutes outside of Clamerton there was a horse racetrack. Ivy had heard about it from the Tari sisters. Sarai was especially fond of it as she thought of it as a source of infinite entertainment.

Liam parked his car in the middle of the street beside a dark wooden stable with elaborate ornaments and accents painted in white.

"Let's go!"

Ivy followed Liam towards the building and admired the facade and workmanship. "It's nice," she said.

"What?" Liam turned to her and followed her eyes. "The building? No, that's not . . ." The huge door on the side opened. A short, thin man emerged. He wore black boots that went up to his knees, tight-fitting white pants, and a blue shirt. He carried a helmet in his left hand that matched the colors of his attire. With his right hand he pulled a horse behind him by the reins.

"Here it is!" Liam's face brightened. "Here is my winner! Eclipse." He took Ivy's hand and pulled her closer towards the animal. The horse was much different than the one she'd rode to the waterfall close to the chateau. It was all black. Its hair glistened in the sun. It was also smaller with slim but muscular legs.

"It's beautiful," Ivy said and smiled politely.

"Cost me a million tickets," Liam said with a broad grin. "Everyone bets on it like crazy! It brings me a thousand tickets a day."

A million? Ivy was impressed. The sales agreement for the Leggett factory in Covedale had been a million tickets.

Liam walked up to the jockey, shook his hand, and moved to touch the horse's mane, but the animal pulled on the reins trying to get away from him. It stared at him with wide eyes and flared its nostrils. Ivy's heartbeat quickened and she backed away from the animal, giving it space. Liam also abandoned petting the horse and the man holding the reins moved away towards the track.

"Let's see him win," Liam said and grabbed Ivy's hand. The animal's behavior hadn't dampened his excitement about the race.

They entered a large building with glass walls. The elevator took them to a third floor where the staff greeted them and ushered them to one of the small private rooms to the right. The room was elegant with light carpets that complemented the darker walls. Ivy walked up to the glass wall, which tilted away from her. It provided a full view of the racetrack below. A few horses were making their slow rounds.

A server came in shortly with a tray which she put down on the low table, curtsied and left. Liam grabbed the drinks and handed one to Ivy. She took it from his hand with a smile, but as soon as they sat down on the leather sofa, she put it on the table far away from her. It was too early in the day for drinks and there was no reason to repeat her mistake from the chateau. Her face turned red each time she thought about how drunk she'd gotten.

Liam immediately started on his drink. He had a couple of sips, then suddenly jumped up from the seat and approached the windows. Ivy followed him.

"See." He pointed down towards the track with his right hand holding the drink, and slid his left arm around her waist. "The horses are getting ready."

Ivy followed his eyes towards the starting line, but she couldn't see much from this far. She looked at the display on the wall in the room showing a close-up of what was happening on the ground. The horses stood lined up behind metal gates. They had all different colored coats or markings that distinguished them from one another. Impatient jockeys were sitting on their horses, ready to start the race. They each wore colored shirts with numbers on them that matched the horses' saddlecloths. Ivy recognized the only black horse and the jockey sitting on it in his blue shirt. That had to be Eclipse.

The gates suddenly opened and the horses, about seven or eight of them, emerged. Clouds of dust picked from underneath the running hooves. They quickly formed a group, but three horses were taking the lead. Their long necks were extended forward and their slender legs moved rhythmically at a great speed. Eclipse was third.

"C'mon!" Liam shouted.

The horse or the jockey had to have heard Liam, because Eclipse moved closer to the chestnut horse in front of him, overtaking it from the outside of the track. Liam grabbed his binoculars and looked through them attentively. "Yes!" he shouted. The horses rounded the bend. Eclipse was getting closer to the leading horse. "Hit him!" Liam shouted. "Hit him!"

Ivy watched Eclipse, and she didn't see exactly what happened on the track, but suddenly the horses in the middle, behind Eclipse, turned into a ball of dust. A mix of horse hooves and human limbs. Ivy gasped and turned away from the window. Her heart pounded in her chest and she took deep breaths with her eyes closed to calm down.

"Yes!" Liam shouted. "We won!" With a smooth motion, he bent over her and gave her a long kiss. The race was over.

She smiled at him, clutching the edge of her dress. "Can we go?" she asked. She didn't dare look back at the window and the track.

"Yeah." He looked at her with narrow eyes, and added, "Yeah, let's grab dinner." He then smiled the full smile of a winner. "The Jungle just opened."

The Jungle was a new club in the new district in Clamerton. Ivy had heard nothing but good things about it from the Tari sisters, and although Sarai kept inviting her to check it out with her, Ivy hadn't had a chance to visit it before today. Ivy agreed that the place was splendid, and being there with Liam made it even better.

"That was a lovely dinner." Ivy brought her head up towards Liam in search of his eyes. He'd sat beside her in the middle of a private booth, holding her close to him so that she had no choice but to lean against him. One of his hands rested on her knee. Ivy felt like it was just the two of them in the whole establishment.

"I'm glad you enjoyed it," he said and kissed her hair. The food had been very good and presented beautifully. Ivy had savored every one of the many courses that had been served. She'd enjoyed all of the dishes—the beautiful zucchini flower stuffed with ricotta cheese, the beef tartar, the saffron risotto, and the white fish in truffle sauce.

A waitress came by and emptied the rest of the wine from the bottle into their glasses. "The show will start in five minutes, sir," she said, addressing Liam.

At first, Ivy had felt uncomfortable seeing the serving girls mostly naked, wearing only skimpy underwear on their perfect figures. Their breasts full and round and accented with shiny jewelry that swayed while they walked. As the night grew, Ivy became used to it and no longer considered it abnormal. She wasn't even concerned about Liam looking too closely at the staff anymore. She relaxed in the carefree atmosphere.

"I need to visit the ladies' room," Ivy said. She gave Liam a long kiss and left his embrace. "I'll be right back."

Ivy was escorted through the maze of fresh plants and booths where people were enjoying the evening. Like in a real jungle, it was easy to get lost. The second part of the night would be a show and a dance. The only performance Ivy remembered from her youth was the jugglers who were allowed on the square in Covedale to amuse the kids and adults with their skills. This new lifestyle as a citizen had lots to offer. She could get used to having this kind of fun.

Ivy put on some makeup in front of the mirror, trying to cover up her freckles a little more, but no matter what she did with them, they were still clearly visible. When she was ready to get back to Liam, a member of the club staff waited for her, but they didn't escort her to the booth. Liam had moved to one of the stools at the bar.

"Got you a drink," he said.

Ivy sat beside him on the adjacent stool which he had saved for her. She took a sip of the drink. She wasn't tense around Liam anymore. "Thank you," she said as a siren pierced her ears. "What is it?" she asked, alarmed, but no one around them was concerned.

"You'll see," Liam said, pointing at the middle of the club where the now-empty tables and booths were. Suddenly, there was an explosion of colors. The whole place beamed with lights and confetti fell from the ceiling, while the floor of the restaurant flipped itself upside down. The sitting places disappeared, giving way to a flat surface making the entire club an enormous open space.

"Amazing," Ivy said with wide eyes, and Liam smiled at her.

A belly dancing show began. A woman came out wearing bells and decorations all over her body that made lots of noise as she shook them. Her flexibility and acrobatics were impressive. Ivy smiled at Liam every so often, glad that he'd brought her here. It was so much fun. Meanwhile, he replaced her empty glass with another drink.

Once the show finished, the stage turned into a dance floor. Some couples and singles got on it and swayed with the music. The lights flashed, reflecting off the walls around them. The music was loud and Ivy found herself tapping her foot to the beat.

"Shall we dance?" Liam asked, leaning in so she could hear him over the noise. He extended his hand as an invitation.

"Sure!" Ivy put her drink down on the bar top and took his hand.

He led her to the middle of the dance floor. Ivy laughed and spun around in place. The bottom of her dress fanned along with her hair. She brought her hands up and gave in to the rhythm. The music surrounded her just like Liam's arms did. Their moves aligned with the beat.

Beat. She felt it in her chest, a hollow thud. Beat. Hitting her right into the rib cage. Beat. Her heart felt the rhythm. Beat. The lights were vivid around her. Beat. Her body moved faster with each beat. Liam holding her hand. Beat. There were only lights. Beat. Blinding lights. Beat. She turned. Beat. Sweat pouring. Beat. She danced. Beat. Just her and the music. Beat. World swaying. Beat. Beat. Beat. Beat.

# 19

THE CAR HAD STOPPED on its own, but Ivy was oblivious to what was happening around her. Her mind and body were fixated on Liam and the moment they were sharing together. He reclined the seats in a quick move as they kissed. Ivy's eyes were closed, but she felt the weight of her body shifting backwards. Liam's passionate kisses were strong and confident and Ivy returned them. The night had been magical with the dinner and the dancing. She felt the familiar squeeze of arousal low in her abdomen. There was nothing wrong with doing it in the car.

Liam paused the kisses and repositioned her hands above her head. He held them there with one of his hands as the other moved up her skirt and pushed her underwear aside. His wet tongue slid against her neck as his hand gently touched her, sending shivers through her body. She'd missed having sex, and passion rushed through her brain like an electric current. She kept her eyes closed as Liam moved on top of her, resting on his knees and moving her thighs far apart. Ivy was exposed and vulnerable, but she welcomed the intensity of the moment. She was ready for what she expected to happen next.

She tried to move one of her hands and hold Liam's neck and give him a hint that she was all his, but her hand didn't move. Both of her hands were trapped. She tried to wiggle them out. Liam was probably not aware that she wanted to readjust her position. His passion for her must be blinding his perception of things. Liam's hold, however, grew stronger, pressing her wrists down harder, removing any wiggle room that she'd thought she had a moment ago. She moved her legs a bit, but as soon as she did that, Liam stopped kissing her and laid his heavy body on her. Ivy panicked and opened her eyes wide. She was having trouble breathing.

"You're hurting me!" Ivy shouted. She tried to wiggle her whole body, but she couldn't shake him off and make him stop. The inside of the car was dark. She was having trouble seeing anything.

"Relax!" He sounded annoyed.

How could she relax? She couldn't move. She was paralyzed, and Liam was strong and determined that she would stay where she was. He'd trapped her. She could still adjust her legs, but Liam's strong thighs held them apart, restricting how much she could move them. He was urgently fumbling with his belt, trying to unbuckle it. Liam was hurting her with his full weight pressing on her. Her eyes filled with tears.

This couldn't be. Why? They'd had such a pleasant time together. She had planned to let him in, so why was he forcing himself on her? Had there been any clues earlier that would explain this situation? She couldn't recall any. Her mind raced. When had they left the club? What time was it? Where were they? What had gotten into him?

Ivy struggled harder. "Get off me!" she shouted at him again, as he moved his pants down, pressing on her heavier and tightening his grip on her arms like a rope. It couldn't be true. Liam was such a nice person. He cared about her, didn't he? Why was he doing this to her?

"Stop it!" She cried, wanting to escape.

Ivy felt him lifting off her a bit, sliding his underwear down. She couldn't let him win, so she wiggled her body with all the strength she had, like an animal caught in a spring trap. She moved her legs as much as she could, painfully hitting her foot on something in the way. Ivy noticed that her actions had forced him to try and adjust his grip on her arms. He loosened up a little to improve his control over her and get a better hold, but she was quicker. She freed one of her arms and clawed at his cheek, her nails sinking into his skin. They dug deeper and deeper, making him stop.

"You fucking bitch!" he shouted. He moved off her and away from her claws. In almost total darkness, he tried to assess if she had caused any damage with her hand. She was certain she had left a mark.

"Liam?" Ivy asked, timidly, looking for answers and reassurance that she was safe. Big teardrops were now rolling down her cheeks, smudging her makeup. She sat up and put her dress and underwear in place as though it would somehow improve the moment. Surely they could talk this through and figure out what went wrong. There was no reason to get too emotional and jump to conclusions. There had to be some valid explanation. She'd give him a chance to explain.

"What's your fucking problem?!" Liam shouted.

"My problem?" she protested.

"What the fuck was with the nails? You've fucked up my face!"

"I told you to stop!" Ivy was distressed. All he'd had to do was listen. His face wasn't ruined. Ivy knew enough about the medical machines to know that no one would even notice any injury tomorrow.

"All you bitches say that, then enjoy it anyway."

Was she understanding this correctly? She wasn't Liam's first victim. There were others. Liam had been nice to her, or maybe she'd been too naïve to notice anything else. What exactly had he done to these other women? Had it happened here, in this car? Ivy needed some fresh air.

She rushed to the car door, opened it and got out. Liam followed her, buttoning his pants up. The chilly wind hit her face as she stepped out, cooling her down a bit. It was pitch-black outside, and she couldn't see any reference point that would give her an idea of where she was. The night was deep and eerily quiet. She needed to clear her head. She'd insist that Liam take her back to her hotel and she'd have all the time she needed to think this through. There was no rush to make any decisions. It would all make sense in due time.

Suddenly, a bright light blinded her. There was another car parked beside Liam's. Someone got out.

"Hey, Ivy!" She recognized the voice. It was Calista. "Are you leaving us?"

Ivy saw Sarai standing in her sister's shadow, saying nothing.

What were the Tari sisters doing here and how had they found them? She didn't remember seeing them at the club. Did they know that she and Liam would be here tonight?

"I was really hoping for some action," Calista said. She made lewd gestures with her hands as she stepped away from the lights and into Ivy's view.

Ivy backed away from the cars. The girls knew what he was about to do to her. She glanced at Liam and he was grinning. The injured side of his face was away from the light, in total darkness. She couldn't see the damage.

"What did we call her the other day, Sarai?" Calista encouraged her sister, who hesitated before replying.

"A monkey," Sarai said with little enthusiasm.

"Ooh, ooh!" Calista pretended she was a monkey while she and Liam laughed. Their voices echoed and disappeared into the darkness.

"Monkey?" What were they talking about? Sarai had always been nice to her. Why was she here? Why was she allowing her sister to laugh at her?

"Oh, my God! She *is* barefoot!" Calista noticed and they laughed even harder. Ivy hadn't even realized that she'd lost her shoes fighting with Liam until Calista had pointed it out. They'd fallen off her feet while she'd struggled. They were probably still somewhere in the car, but she couldn't retrieve them. Ivy nervously tilted her right foot, realizing she was standing on a cold surface. It was a paved road, cooled by the March night. She couldn't be too far from Clamerton, and seemed to be somewhere on the main route rather than some side dirt road.

"Fucking monkey," Liam added. "Mono Rojo. That's what everyone calls you, even Mrs. Harris. Singe Rouge!"

Was that what Mrs. Harris had called her in her shop a few months back? She'd said something under her breath while leaving, but Ivy hadn't understood it back then. Mono Rojo. Red monkey. Was that really what they all called her?

Calista made the monkey noises again. It was funny to them.

Once they'd had their fun, they would let her be. *Keep calm and let them cool down as well.* It had to be some stupid joke. They would suddenly snap out of it, and all would be back to normal. They couldn't be serious. "Liam?" Ivy called for him, hoping he'd stop this stupidity.

"Oh, Liam, Liam," Calista mocked, sounding like she was in distress. "I have a concussion."

"The horse got scared," Ivy recalled. Why had she brought that up?

"'Cause a monkey rode him," Calista laughed. She was having spasms from her joke, which Ivy didn't find funny at all.

"You can't imagine how much effort it took arranging that," Calista added matter-of-factly.

Ivy retreated, walking backwards away from them. That couldn't be true. The pain? The suffering? Had they been having fun at her expense? Ivy had met the sisters at the Château de la Belle Cascade and she hadn't had much time to really get to know them. They'd known each other for less than two days, and they'd intentionally spooked her horse, scaring her, injuring her? They could've killed her.

Later, after the accident, they'd visited her at Liam's house. They'd seemed concerned and sincere. They'd wished for her quick recovery. Had they laughed when she wasn't around? How could she have fallen for their lies?

"Want us to hold her down for you, Liam?" Calista laughed and moved towards Ivy. Sarai hesitantly took a couple of steps in the same direction.

Ivy moved further backwards. She kept them at a distance, but they gained on her so she turned around and ran. Behind her, they called after her and laughed.

"C'mon, Monkey!"

"Ooh, ooh!"

"Come back to us!"

Ivy ran without looking back.

"Let's chase her!" Calista said.

Sarai quickly replied, "What for? I'm not running!"

Ivy ran into the darkness. She didn't know where she was going. Anywhere was good, as long as she was away from those who wanted to hurt her.

Ivy didn't know how long she had been walking alone in the dark. She could barely see the contours of the trees to either side of her. They parted above her and there was faint light reflecting off the clouds. Ivy was certain that it was the glow from Clamerton. Her feet were still on the paved road, carrying her through the quiet countryside one step at a time.

Ivy walked slowly now. Her feet stumbled on the road, which was cold and hard. Sharp gravel pressed into her soles and hurt her with each step. Ivy was no longer accustomed to walking barefoot. The soles of her feet were much softer than they used to be. She was cold with no jacket on—she must have left that in the car as well—and she hugged herself for warmth. How far from the town was she, and how long would it take to reach it? She continued moving forward.

Suddenly, lights blinded her. It was an approaching car. It was coming from up ahead, not behind her. It couldn't be Liam or the Tari sisters looking for her, could it? The car pulled up beside her and Ivy was relieved it was Sābanto, Black Shirts. Two men got out of the car.

"Papers," one of them said harshly as the other grabbed hold of her arm so that she didn't escape.

"I lost them," Ivy explained. She didn't have her purse with her.

The officer looked her up and down. "Who's ya master?"

"I don't have one," Ivy said.

"That's what they all say," the other officer that held her replied. "We'll figure that one out at the station." He grabbed her hands and handcuffed them behind her back, then shoved Ivy into the back of the car a bit too hard but she didn't complain. The inside of the car was warm. *It would be fine. Calm down.* They'd verify her identity at the station and let her go.

After a brief ride in the back of the car they took her into an old, poorly-lit building that stank of mildew. Her feet hurt. The pain had been manageable when she'd been walking before, but now after allowing them to rest, they were swollen. She could barely walk, but the officers didn't ask if she was alright.

Inside, a man sat at the desk. He whistled at her. "What have we got here?" he said. "Another one?"

"Wait 'til we check her," the man holding her said. "Don't jump the gun."

Ivy ignored the comment. They needed to call her house and Julia would confirm her identity.

"Yer always by the book," the officer at the desk replied. He didn't sound happy, but wasn't pressing the matter.

The officers who'd arrested her freed her hands and asked a few questions about her master and address. They made notes and told her they'd investigate.

"Lock her up with the rest," one of them suggested, and they led Ivy out of the main room. They pushed her into one of the many cells that were in the back of the building. The small, dark room stank of urine and sweat and was filled with women of different ages, as well as children. They were squeezed inside, too many of them in a small cell. The women sat on the benches and floor without enough space to stretch their legs. They were all quiet, not making eye contact with her or the Sābanto soldier that had brought her in. Ivy stood in place, unsure of what to do as the door closed behind her and the lock turned.

"Move!" an old woman scolded a girl that sat on the bench. The young woman moved without complaining. "Sit," the old woman told Ivy, pointing at the empty spot on the bench.

Ivy felt bad for the girl that had lost her spot, but she accepted the invitation. She was tired and needed to rest her feet. "Thank you, ma'am," she said and limped over to the spot the woman pointed her at. She sat down.

"Please, lady. Let me see," the old woman said, pointing at her feet.

Ivy brought her feet up to the woman. "Who are you?" she asked, looking at the rest of the people imprisoned with her. They were watching her closely, interested in the new person, but didn't say anything. They were all quiet.

The old woman didn't reply to Ivy's question. She touched her feet, and Ivy inhaled through her teeth in pain. "It'll heal, lady," the woman said. "No walking for two days."

"Why are you in jail?" she asked.

"We're from a village nearby," the woman said. "The men," the woman pointed toward the closed door, "came in and brought us here."

"Are they sending you to Sābanto?" Ivy asked. She'd heard of people being rounded up everywhere and sent to compounds.

The woman shrugged. "We been here for three days."

Ivy didn't know what else she could ask. She couldn't imagine why they would have arrested an entire village. Three days in this stench and crowd with no window to let the light in. The only light was a small, faint bulb hung from the ceiling. What a nightmare.

Ivy rested her head against the cold wall behind her and closed her eyes. They were supposed to call Julia and have her come pick her up. She would clear up this whole mess. Ivy longed for her warm bed.


Hours passed. The officers walked back and forth. There were occasional noises outside the door. Someone screamed in the distance. A baby cried in her cell. Women whispered to each other and occasionally readjusted their positions. Ivy didn't know when she drifted off to sleep, but she was woken by a loud argument right outside the cell door.

"Ya did what?" Taylor's muffled voice sounded on the other side of the wall. "Do ya know who she is?"

There was a thump, as though there was a fight happening on the other side. Then the door opened.

Taylor ran up to her and kneeled. "Are ya okay, ma'am?" He ignored everyone else in the cell with her.

Ivy nodded and smiled. She got to her feet, but the pain returned.

"Please, let me carry ya," he said.

"No need," Ivy protested.

"Let the pretty boy carry ya," the old woman who now sat on the other side of the cell said.

"Please," Taylor repeated, and Ivy agreed.

He scooped her up off the bench with ease. His arms were firm, flexing under her weight. He carried her out of the cell and into the main room of the station.

"Can one of ya fools open the door for me?" he growled.

They helped him, but they didn't seem in a hurry.

He got her all the way to the car and helped her get in. Dawn was breaking. It was probably six or seven in the morning. Taylor got into the driver's seat and the car moved.

"Julia didn't come?" Ivy asked. She had made Julia a point of contact during the arrest, and had expected she would be waiting for them in the car. It was surprising she wasn't here, helping to bring her home.

"I couldn't find her." Taylor made a turn onto the main road. "I didn't wait."

Julia was probably with Greyson again. She barely spent a night in the house anymore.

"Thank you," Ivy said.

"Please, ma'am. No need," Taylor said.

Ivy smiled to herself. She was safe now. She was heading home.

"Those people, there at the station," she said. "What do you think will happen to them?"

"They're going to Sābanto, ma'am," Taylor said.

"But they've been there for three days already."

"If there are no transports available, some people have to wait."

Ivy noticed the sun was already lighting the tops of the trees. "Anything we could do to help?" she asked.

Taylor kept his eyes on the road ahead. "I don't think so," he eventually replied.

Ivy closed her eyes and rested her head on the back of the seat and fell asleep.

# 20

I T WAS STILL EARLY in the morning when Ivy arrived home. She went to her bed to sleep and recover, but she tossed and turned between the soft sheets, unable to sleep. Thoughts of recent events had her restless.

While at the club, she had thought she'd had a great time . . . but while replaying the scenes in her mind she remembered how the eyes of the other patrons had followed her. She'd brushed it off at the time, but now everyone's curiosity seemed out of place and relevant to what had happened to her later. They must have known she was another one of Liam's victims. Why had no one warned her? Sarai and her sister were complicit in his crime. They'd laughed at her, hurt her. They'd taken advantage of her eagerness to be accepted. She was never an equal. In their eyes, she would never be a citizen. She was no one—a monkey, as they'd called her.

Once she finally fell asleep, Ivy slept a long time. She woke up late in the evening of the next day, sat up in her bed and surveyed the quiet and dark room. She stood up and put her slippers on, found her silk robe on the back of the chair, and put it on. A small stroll through the house and she'd be back. Long enough to stretch her muscles and move her joints.

She was safe in her house, within these familiar walls, even if they felt empty. The bruises on her feet from walking barefoot still hurt a bit. Taylor had insisted that she have her soles checked and Dr. Lott had visited her at home. Like the old woman in jail, the doctor wasn't concerned. He didn't think there was a reason to use the medical machine, but urged her to take it easy for a few days. He said she needed a break to recover from such a traumatic experience of being held by Sābanto.

Ivy wandered aimlessly from one room to another before stopping in front of the grandfather clock in the hallway. It rang nine, and even through the closed windows, she heard the faint tolling of the bell tower at the city square. Her mind traveled back to when she'd lived in a single room with her parents and her brother's family of eight. She had never had a moment alone back then. Sometimes it had angered her that there was no privacy when she needed it, but now she longed for those moments. She scanned the hallway and realized that she wasn't totally alone. She had Julia.

She went downstairs and knocked on Julia's door. There was no answer. Why had she assumed her maid was there? She hadn't seen her when she'd arrived the previous morning. Did she even know Ivy had returned home earlier than planned?

Ivy turned around and knocked on the door on the opposite side of the hallway. There was some commotion, then the door opened and Taylor jumped out. "What do ya want Julia—" he said, but noticed that it was Ivy. "I'm sorry, ma'am," he immediately corrected himself.

"Can I come in?" Ivy asked with a small smile. She stepped into his room without waiting for an answer. She didn't think he'd protest.

Taylor's cheeks turned red. He started to clear the room of his clothes which lay around in disarray.

"No need to tidy," Ivy said and sat down at the edge of the bed. "What did you tell Sābanto?" she asked.

"What do ya mean, ma'am?"

"When they asked why they found me walking down the road."

"Told 'em it was the concussion," he said. Taylor didn't look at Ivy, even though there was no reason to be ashamed of his words. He knew that her horse accident had nothing to do with the reason they'd found her on the street in the middle of nowhere.

She surveyed his room and noticed a stuffed toy on the window sill. She got up and walked to it. "Can I hold it?" she asked.

"Of course, ma'am," Taylor replied.

Ivy picked the toy up and examined it. "You know, I have a similar one," she said. It was still upstairs in her room. Misshapen and made from scraps, tediously sewn together by her inexperienced hand years ago. Two shirt buttons were placed where the eyes were supposed to be, one of them with a piece of plastic broken off. Ivy smiled to herself. She'd spent a lot of time making it. "I made mine when I was still a kid." She put Taylor's toy away, but kept looking at it. "I wish I could be that girl from the slums again," she said and sighed.

"Why would anyone want that, ma'am?" Taylor asked.

"I don't belong here," she said. "I belong with my people. With people like you." She turned around and faced him. Ivy recalled feeling at ease sitting in the dark cell with the other women. It felt natural somehow.

"That ain't true," Taylor replied quickly. He wanted to say something else, but stopped himself.

"You know what they called me?" Taylor shook his head. "Red monkey. Why did I think that they would ever accept me?" Taylor stood quiet with his head low. "Wasn't that silly of me?" Ivy added, trying to engage him. They had been nice to her, Mrs. Ouellet, the Tari sisters . . . Liam . . . but Ivy was new money. She was a stranger, a freak that had never belonged with them.

"I don't have an opinion, ma'am," Taylor replied.

"That's not true," Ivy replied and glanced at the window sill again and the stuffed toy. "Everyone has an opinion. I'd like to hear yours."

She waited patiently for his answer. "Ya are better than us," he finally said. "And them."

Ivy turned her head towards him. Better than the Sābanto poor, better than the workers or the Free, and better than citizens. Was that what he meant? "You really think so?" she asked, and Taylor nodded. She came over and stood in front of him. "Look at me," she asked, and he raised his head. "Is that what you thought of me when you met me?"

Taylor lowered his eyes again.

She grabbed his hand. His fingers were bigger than her own. There was a familiar roughness to his skin. Her father had had hands like that. He'd worked hard with them his whole life. They were so different from the soft hands Liam had.

Taylor didn't move, allowing Ivy to touch him.

"What *did* you think when you first saw me?" she asked, but he again didn't reply. She remembered him staring at her at the dinner table the night they had met. He hadn't known that she was his new employer and his behavior around her had been sincere. Ivy brought his hand up and put it against her chest where her heart was, then met his eyes. He quickly looked away from her gaze. He licked his lips, unable to speak and reluctant to answer her question. Why was she doing this to him? She was looking for a confession of some sort, but why? Why did it matter to her what his thoughts were? It all suddenly felt inappropriate. "I shouldn't have come here," she said and released his hand. She turned around and left the room. The visit had been a mistake.

"That girl, Amy," Julia said as Greyson adjusted himself. His girlfriend put her head on his arm as they lay on the bed in his apartment. He hadn't gone anywhere for the last couple of days. He'd been enjoying some time off with Julia. Conway was busy at home most of the time now with his little boy, Matthew, and there had been no calls from Friends requesting any work. Ivy was away on a trip to Clamerton, so Julia also had extra time for him.

"What about her?" Greyson didn't know what Julia was getting at, asking about that bitch Amy.

"Ya spend a lotta time together," she said.

"We're working," he replied. He fucking had to spend time with Amy. Conway had said that she'd been right in not following orders. The boss had humiliated him in front of his subordinate. Why had he done that? Conway could've easily scolded him in private. Greyson might've been fine with that and forgotten all about the rest. He wasn't a kid anymore, even if Conway thought of him as one. The more time he spent with Amy the more he learned about her. It was a matter of time. He'd come up with a plan to get his revenge on her.

"I heard rumors," Julia continued, "that ya sometimes go somewhere. The two of ya."

"Sometimes that's what I gotta do." Greyson sighed. Why did she care about people talking, and when did she find the time to do it?

"Promise there's nothing between ya two?"

"I promise," he replied and stroked her soft hair. The last thing he wanted was a relationship with a bitch like Amy.

"Ya not sleeping with her, right?"

"What's gotten into ya?" he asked, annoyed but not angry "With her?!" He bent over Julia and kissed her forehead, then added, "Ya know you're the only one."

"Have ya ever kissed?" Julia asked.

Yes, they'd kissed, right before Amy had put a knife against his neck. "We kissed, but it was before I knew ya," he said. In case it came out one day, he wouldn't deny that kiss. A white lie would keep Julia from inquiring further.

"What kinda kisser is she?"

Why did she care? *Damn.* Amy was a much better kisser, but of course he wasn't going to tell Julia that. It'd make her furious. "I don't remember," he said, dodging the question.

"I'm sure ya think about her sometimes," Julia pressed.

"Would ya believe me if I said no?" Poor choice of words, Greyson regretted them immediately.

"Should I?"

"Why shouldn't ya?"

He wanted to relax and cuddle with Julia for the rest of the night, not be interrogated with baseless questions. Couldn't she accept what he said as the truth? What if she pried into his work? Too many things were classified and Julia was too nosy. She'd want information about every minute he spent away from Covedale, especially if Amy was involved.

He'd like to have punched whoever had said something, but then Julia would know it was retaliation for giving her information. That would just make things worse, and she might think about leaving him for it. She was annoying as hell more often than not, but Greyson loved her. He wanted her and he wouldn't let her go. No one would separate them. Julia was his, and that was it.

Amy knocked on the large door of the Roberts house. The morning sun was already up. She examined the gray stucco on the walls and the evenly-spaced white window frames as she waited. Julia opened the door and stared at her with hatred in her eyes. It was still early and the maid was already in a bad mood. What was her problem?

"What do ya want?" Julia asked.

"Here to see Miss Roberts," Amy replied politely. "A message from Mr. Conway."

Julia opened the door wider and let her in. With no other words, she disappeared deeper into the house. Amy waited patiently in the hallway, not allowing herself to enter further without invitation.

It was her first time inside Miss Roberts' house. The place was dark, not only because of the wallpaper resembling the night sky, but also because no one had turned on the silver chandeliers in the high-ceilinged hallway. The place looked gloomy. Not much light came through the large windows with their heavy drapes.

Julia reappeared. "Miss Roberts will see ya," she announced and gestured for Amy to walk into the sitting room. No one had turned the lights on there either, and the drapes were drawn.

Amy entered the room and Ivy stood up. The lady of the house looked tired. Maybe she was sick. She'd had a concussion. It explained the lack of light in the room.

"Please, ma'am, no need to stand," Amy said, and Ivy sat back down. Julia closed the door behind her as she exited, giving them some privacy.

"How can I help you?" Ivy asked and gestured for Amy to sit down as well.

Amy refused the invitation. "Mr. Conway sent me," she said. "He asked me to deliver something." Amy took out a piece of paper from her pocket and handed it to Ivy who took it from her and examined it.

"It's a list of names," Miss Roberts said, looking back at Amy.

"Mr. Conway said he wanted to give this to ya a long time ago, but there ain't never was a good time. He said ya ready now."

"I don't understand." The lady glanced at the list again.

"It's a list of people who died in Menken Mines, ma'am."

"And how does that concern me?"

"I dunno." Conway hadn't told her much about the list. "I was told ya'd know it once ya saw it."

Ivy nodded. "Thank you," she said, looking up and letting her hand which held the paper rest on her lap. "Is there anything else I can help you with?"

"No, ma'am." Amy lowered her head, showing the lady due respect, and left the room.

In the hallway, Julia waited for her with her chin raised. "Ya slept with him," she accused.

"Who?" Amy feigned ignorance. She knew what Julia was like.

"Greyson," Julia crossed her arms in front of her.

Amy took a step closer to Julia. "Did ya ask ya boyfriend about it?"

"He denied it."

*Oh, great!* Amy rolled her eyes. She walked closer and stopped right in front of Julia and gazed straight into her eyes. "Greyson ain't my type," she told her. She put a hand on Julia's neck, pulled her close, and kissed her forcefully.

With quick but sure steps, Amy turned away from Julia and moved towards the door. She firmly grasped the door handle and let the sunlight enter the dark hallway. She glanced behind her at Julia, who stood paralyzed in the middle of the hall with an open mouth. Amy smiled at her and left, stepping down the short flight of stairs outside.

Ivy read the list she'd received one more time. *You'll know it when you see it.* She read the names one by one from the top. She found it three-quarters down the page.

*Daniel Rodden.* The death date listed was this past July, before the fire at Riverlea.

She recalled the goodbye letter she'd gotten from Mark. The one she'd read when the city was still burning. She got up and walked to the study. She looked at the shelf and found the book. "Crime and Punishment, Fyodor Dostoevsky," she read from the spine, taking it off the shelf. Mark had given it to her and said it was a classic worth reading. She'd finished it not too long ago. The story was still fresh in her mind.

The book opened at the page where the envelope was stuck. Ivy took it out from between the pages, then closed the book and put the novel back onto the shelf.

She took the letter out of the envelope and unfolded it. She noted the date. August the second. She stared at the words. "Since my son left . . ."

A tear rolled down her cheek. She recalled what Mark had told her once in his apartment. "I'm looking for my son," he had said. "Riverlea's where we raised him. He'll come back here looking for me." Mark had died waiting for his son, never moving to the relative safety of Covedale. Meanwhile, Daniel had died in the Menken mines. No wonder there was no military record of his death. He hadn't been presumed missing, either. Daniel had returned from war, but had never met with his father again.

Ivy's knees felt weak and she couldn't support herself anymore. She fell to her knees from the pain in her heart. If Mark had only known this sooner, he could have saved himself. She slumped her shoulders. He could have left Riverlea a long time ago, seeing that there was no reason to wait for his son any longer, and he would never have died in the fire. She could have helped him through his grief, hugged him tight, comforted him with all the love she had. Eventually his sadness would have passed—it would have—and they both could have been happy again, together. Wouldn't it have felt right for Mark to share this new life with her? What a sight they would have been, the two of them walking into the dining room at the Château de la Belle Cascade, her hanging off his arm. Ivy's throat tightened and her chin started to tremble. Mark could have still been here with her. She sobbed.

# 21

I VY HAD BEEN MOURNING for days. The information about the death of Mark's son, whom she had never met, had been devastating for her. She had lain for hours curled up in her bed, curtains drawn, sobbing until the tears in her eyes ran dry.

Unable to cry anymore, she stared deep into the darkness of her room. Until Liam had shown her his true colors, she'd considered him a good person. A rescuer. Maybe even an angel, if he'd really been the person he'd pretended to be.

That was why Conway had waited before giving her the list. She'd never have given Liam's family a bad name because of some unverified information. If he'd provided the list with Daniel on it earlier, she wouldn't understand the importance of it. She would've probably taken the news as an attack on her new relationship with Liam.

She'd been looking blindly to high society and citizens for acceptance, ignoring all the red flags. She was now angry and clenched her fists at the thought of what Liam had done to her. Where was the love he had promised? *Wait.* He hadn't promised her anything. It was her imagination. A fantasy of her own creation.

Mistakes of the past. Why be sorry about them? She had to look to the future. What was it Taylor had said? *You're better than them.* What could she do about it? Confront Liam and demand an apology from him? He'd laugh in her face. She would have to force that apology from him or make him pay for what he'd done. For that, she would need some dirt on him. Something she could use against him.

That girl at the chateau, Jane was her name. She'd said she worked in order to send money to her mother in Menken Mines. It was odd. The employers were supposed to be providing all the necessities. Weren't they breaking the law? Ivy could tell Liam that she knew about this negligence. He'd have to take her seriously or risk being exposed. But what if Jane had lied? Ivy had caught her wearing her scarf. The girl might've fed Ivy the story in order to keep her job. The only way she'd know if Jane was telling the truth would be to assess the situation firsthand.

Ivy was convinced that she would have to visit the Menken Mines, and she asked Taylor to accompany her there. Instead of going to bed, she changed into black stretch pants she had found in the back of her closet, a pair she'd worn once a long time ago and forgotten about. She paired them with a long-sleeved black shirt under a dark brown sweater. For convenience, she braided her hair and rolled it into a tight bun.

She took the servant's stairs to the basement and knocked on Taylor's door, and he answered immediately. Julia was out visiting her boyfriend Greyson again. Whatever happened tonight would stay between Ivy and Taylor. No one else needed to know.

"It ain't a good idea, ma'am," he said.

"You know you won't talk me out of it," she replied.

He nodded and followed her outside to the car. They sat side by side in the front. The car shook a bit as the hover mechanism lifted it up slightly, then it quietly glided east towards Clamerton.

Taylor drove, keeping his eyes on the road while Ivy studied the map on her tablet, tracking their progress. They didn't pass any cars on their way, which was exactly what they'd hoped for.

They traveled in silence for more than an hour before Ivy suddenly said, "Stop here. There's a side road through the woods that would put us a little north of the town."

Taylor pointed ahead of him. "The road into Menken Mines is a bit further that way," he said. "It's a safer path."

Ivy was confident in her choice. "The guards there can't know we're heading in their direction," she said. "Here." She handed him her tablet with the map and pointed to where the side road was.

"I dunno," Taylor said and frowned.

"I want to see the town without anyone noticing."

Taylor didn't argue with her, though he was clearly not happy with her decision. In a few meters, he turned left onto what appeared to be a logging road that led between the tall trees. The path which traveled up into the mountains hadn't been used in a long time, and if not for the hovering mechanism, they would have been stuck in the mud and snow.

Ivy monitored where they were in relation to the mining town on her tablet. Once they were close, but still far enough to prevent anyone from seeing the car, she told Taylor to stop.

"Right here in the middle of the woods?" Taylor said, concerned.

"I know what I'm doing," Ivy replied. It was a lie. She was making it up as she went along. "We need to continue on foot."

Taylor turned off the car and they got out. The forest was pitch black and quiet. They turned on their flashlights. Ivy shivered, feeling the chill of the night, overwhelmed by the darkness that surrounded them. *It's just a forest.* There was no need to be afraid. They kept moving.

She opened the tablet again. The town was to their right, so they started in that direction, finding a path between the trees. At first, the forest floor was wet and springy under her hiking shoes, which she'd purchased for the trip to Château de la Belle Cascade the previous year. She walked around any snow or slippery ice patches that still remained under the shadow of the trees from the last freeze. They walked in silence. The soft soil under their feet became hard rock as they continued to climb, tripping every so often on the uneven surface. When the forest parted in front of them they turned off their flashlights so that no one would notice them and walked to the edge of the clearing.

They'd arrived at a small rock-covered lookout point, lit by the faint moonlight coming through thin clouds. The Menken Mines town wasn't too far below.

"Right here," Ivy whispered. She lay down and crawled closer to the edge of the rock. Taylor copied her movements, and they examined the view in front of them.

Ivy took out the binoculars she had brought with her and scanned the settlement. The town was deserted. There were some bright lights at the side of the mountain where the entrance to the coal mine was, and some dim street lights throughout the town, but Ivy couldn't see any people. There was no movement around any of the houses or beside the creek that ran through the area. Ivy sighed and slumped her shoulders. Coming here at night wouldn't give her any clues about the town. Nothing that would prove the claims of the girl at the chateau.

She handed the binoculars to Taylor, but he didn't notice anything interesting either. Eventually, he gave up staring at the town as well.

The trip had been pointless. They might as well head back. Ivy didn't yet have the energy to get up and make the journey towards the car they had left on the old road. They lay at the edge for a moment instead. Ivy was conscious of how close together they were, almost touching, trying to fit together in the narrow space between the evergreens. She turned her body towards him. "You didn't like Liam being around," she whispered. "You were jealous."

She recalled Taylor keeping his eyes on Liam each time he visited her, but there was more to Taylor's strange behavior. Each time Ivy had come into the kitchen for dinner, he'd been shy, averting his eyes, not wanting to look at her. Exactly what he was doing right at that moment, she noticed as the moon shone brighter, breaking through the clouds. When he worked on the house, he avoided being alone with her and didn't hesitate to change a whole day's worth of plans in order to spend the least amount of time possible around her.

Taylor lowered his head. "There's nothing to be ashamed of," she added.

"I'm sorry," he replied.

"No reason to be sorry, either." She hoped he could see her smiling.

Her weakness for Liam and her new lifestyle as a citizen had trans-fixed her. She'd ignored Taylor. He was simply a young man who worked for her and kept the house and grounds in order. He did a good job, and she was always pleased with him. Since parting ways with Liam, however, she had started paying more attention to Taylor. She'd begun to notice how his lips parted when he smiled at dinner, and how his arms flexed when he unclogged the sink after Julia had washed the pots in it.

Taylor slowly raised his eyes, which shone in the moonlight, and their eyes met. Ivy recalled the night at the Sābanto jail and the old woman's words. *Let the pretty boy carry you.* She wished she'd realized this sooner. Taylor had a crush on her, and the woman had been right. He was a pretty boy. Ivy bent closer and kissed him. Taylor didn't protest her lips on him, nor her hand on his cheek touching the rough stubble on his face.

A loud whistle shrieked in the distance, disturbing the moment. It echoed against the stone walls of the mountains surrounding the area. They parted lips upon hearing the noise. "Shift change," Taylor whispered without taking his eyes off her.

Ivy picked up the binoculars, laid back down flat on her belly, and scanned the town again. It seemed more animated.

"Something's happening," she whispered. There were people coming out of the houses, women and children. They were running towards the entrance of the mine. It was a strange sight, as the town had been dead and quiet just a moment ago.

"I heard bad things about that place," Taylor said.

"I met a girl at the chateau, a servant. She was from Menken Mines. She was only fourteen, but she worked. I thought nothing of it at the time," Ivy said. "After I learned about the deaths in the mines, I knew there was something terribly wrong with this place. That's why I wanted to see it for myself."

Suddenly, Ivy felt her body being pulled backwards, sliding on her stomach, scraping the ground. She grabbed branches and blades of dry grass, hurting her hands, anything to stop the movement she couldn't control. Something had trapped one of her legs. She tried to scream in terror, but nothing came out of her mouth.

Ivy stopped as quickly as she had started moving. Her captured leg had suddenly been released. Able to move again, she looked around for Taylor, but she couldn't see him anywhere. The forest was dark. She shivered and slowly got to her feet. Suddenly she heard grunting behind her, but it was too dark to see. She noticed the flashlight still close to the edge of the cliff, briefly illuminated by the moonlight. Ivy ran towards it, grabbed it, and turned it on. She pointed it in the direction of the noise. Taylor had someone pinned to the ground, an attacker. It was the man who had pulled her by her leg into the forest, but Taylor had tackled him and rescued her from his grip. Taylor had no trouble controlling the assailant, whose arms were thin and fragile. He wasn't one of the guards that monitored the town.

Ivy shone the light directly into the would-be kidnapper's eyes.

"Who are ya?" Taylor asked.

"Please forgive me," the man mumbled slowly. "Am a poor man from the village."

"What are ya doing here?" Taylor asked.

"I was looking for mushrooms. Or fiddleheads. Yes, fiddleheads are good too."

"In the dark?" Ivy asked. There was still snow on the ground. Nothing would be ready for foraging in the forest for at least another month.

"I'm used to the dark," the man said. "I work in the mine."

"Why mushrooms?" Taylor was curious.

"I found no rabbits or birds today," said the man. "I set up traps. They'll serve potatoes today. I like my potatoes with mushrooms. Or fiddleheads if I can find some.

"Why did you pull me?" Ivy asked. Something was wrong with the man. He spoke strangely.

"No rabbits, no birds . . ." he replied.

Ivy stepped back and quickly scanned her surroundings. The man had compared her to animals he wanted to eat. Cannibalism hadn't been uncommon during the war, and even recently she'd heard that some people still practiced it. The news constantly warned of such behavior amongst the Free. They claimed they continued doing it for spiritual reasons.

"Who owns the mines?" Taylor asked, still holding the man down.

"Liam Menken. He inherited it from his father," Ivy replied before the captive could say anything. Taylor stirred a bit, but said nothing. "You said they serve plain potatoes in town?" she asked the strange man. "They're a good source of nutrients. Isn't that enough?"

"Did you see any wild ginger on the way here? Maybe it is already popping out," he said.

Ivy frowned. There was something odd about him.

"Why are people running towards the shaft on the shift change?" Taylor asked.

"Sir, they're checking if their men came back alive."

"Why wouldn't they?" Ivy asked.

The man laughed. "Why would they?" he replied.

Ivy felt uneasy. She wondered if it was true what the man said, that the small mining town lived desperately hoping every day that their loved ones came back from work alive. Ivy studied the miner, under Taylor's grip. He was practically a walking skeleton. It fit the story the girl at the chateau had told her—that she worked because the families in the town were going hungry. The potatoes were clearly not enough.

Neither Ivy nor Taylor knew what to do with the man. She wouldn't forgive herself if they harmed him. He was just a crazy man trying to find his fiddleheads. Taylor gave him a ticket for his information and trouble, and they let him go. The man didn't follow them, but they rushed back to the car and made sure they locked the doors. They sighed with relief, feeling safe.

"That was scary," Ivy said as they headed towards the main road. She was a little shaken, but otherwise unharmed. She had scratches and bruises on her hands and arms from the sharp rocks and branches. There was a long red line on her right arm that she'd hide from Julia. Her clothes were wet and dirty from being dragged on the forest floor. Threads had been pulled from her sweater, which had pieces of small branches and thorns stuck in it. Ivy pulled them out carefully. The inside of the car felt a little cold with the adrenaline levels in her blood dropping and her heartbeat slowing down. Ivy adjusted the temperature, then spoke up again, saying, "Thank you for saving me from that man."

"Ma'am, I'll always protect ya."

Ivy turned her head away from him and smiled to herself while looking out of the window. What she needed was right beside her. She could look for something unknown, exotic to her. *But why?* She'd only get herself hurt again.

Before they reached the main road, she asked Taylor to stop. She leaned over and gave him a long kiss. He found his courage and returned her kiss, gently placing his hand on her waist.

They parted and Ivy motioned to Taylor to continue driving forward. She said nothing. She wanted the mood to last for a bit, giving her some time to think about the kiss. She stared outside into the darkness as the car moved again.

She watched the trees they passed for a while, then turned to Taylor, whose eyes were watching the road. "In two days, come to my bedroom," she told him. "In the evening. At ten."

Miss Roberts had called Anita and invited her over for a talk, and Anita arrived in Covedale the next day. They sat opposite each other in the living room. A small low coffee table separated them. Miss Roberts described the living conditions in Riverlea, the makeshift homes under the ruins of the tall buildings. She had, however, escaped before Sābanto had arrived on the island, which gave Anita no insight into what exactly had happened when people were evacuated. She'd gotten nothing out of the conversation so far that would incriminate Conway or Sābanto, unfortunately. People no longer found Covedale to be an interesting topic. It was a thing of the past now. Had it been nine or ten months ago now?

For Anita, chasing her new topic about working conditions was more relevant at this time, and when Roberts started talking about Menken Mines, Anita sat up in her chair. She made detailed notes describing the woman's trip there and her meeting with the crazy man in the forest. Anita was then presented with a list of the dead which she studied carefully, but no names seemed familiar. They were all strangers.

"Such a list could be fabricated," Anita said, putting the piece of paper down and leaning back on the sofa. She could type a list like that herself.

"Mr. Conway wouldn't lie to me," Roberts replied.

"Wait, you got it from Conway? Why did he give this to you?" Anita sat up again. There was a connection between Conway and Menken Mines. Interesting.

"I know one of these names."

"Sābanto and Conway are complicit in these crimes—"

"Are they? The dates are from July. There was no Sābanto then."

Roberts had a point there, but the document Anita had in front of her was useless. "Even if the list is genuine, it's not official and I can't use it. I need proof."

"What about what I saw?"

"From what you're telling me, you saw nothing," Anita bluntly pointed out. "A change of shift, people running around. If you worked there it might be different, but your status disqualifies you." Anita looked around Roberts' house. Ivy was a property owner, and well off at that.

"I know something wrong is happening."

"Just thinking you know something, or thinking you saw something," Anita said, "that's not enough."

Roberts drew her brows together. "I saw it!"

"Yes, but you need proof," Anita replied. She didn't disbelieve Roberts, but any confession from her would be useless. Anita was just stating the facts.

"Like what?"

"Can you find the guy and have him confess that he was foraging 'cause he was hungry?" Anita asked, looking down at her notes. "Can you be sure he wasn't making this up 'cause he was angry at his employer? Maybe he already has a history of insubordination. What if he says that you forced a confession out of him so that his situation doesn't get worse at the mines? Can you explain why you were there in the forest when you met him? What proof does he have that he is hungry? The employer gives him a meal every day. Being thin could be the result of an illness of some kind. How will you get past all the barriers Menken will put in front of you, even if you get his attention? And there are always assassins, people who would do anything for money. Menken can destroy you for even putting any accusations forward."

Roberts dropped her shoulders and looked down.

"We need to act smart about it. We need proof," Anita said. She recalled her mantra *Be smart, Anita, be smart.* "Proof that is strong enough to stand up to anything. Something that would incriminate the employer beyond doubt. I've tried to find something myself, but every time I do, the evidence I find, I can't use."

"Then what do we do?" Roberts asked.

"I don't know," Anita said. The information was interesting, and she didn't want to give up hope of one day getting the owner of the mines exposed. There was, however, not much to go on. "If I had any proof . . . a video, testimony from the citizens that were mistreated . . . I could make a case. But no one cares about workers; there's no mechanism for them to demand justice through World United. Confessions from workers mean nothing. They would laugh at them."

"So you have nothing?" Roberts asked.

"I'll think about it, and I'll tell you if I find anything," Anita replied. "But as of right now, we've got nothing."

# 22

I VY SAT IN THE corner of her sitting room, which was part of her vast bedroom. Shadows surrounded her. A small lamp beside the door was the only thing that illuminated the space and the contours of the furniture where she sat.

When she'd been much younger, everything had seemed so easy. A good paying job, a family maybe, was all she looked forward to. Such a simple life she could've had. Ivy didn't miss protecting her belongings from the heavy rains that came, or the water that pooled up in the middle of the tarp of their poorly built house, or staying warm by the small stove while cold winter winds pierced through the makeshift walls. Every hardship, however, could've been easily resolved back then, but Ivy no longer belonged to that world. There was no point in looking back. But on the other hand, what reason was there to look forward to the fragile, glass-like weavings of hopes and dreams that could so easily be shattered? Ivy couldn't get back what she'd lost.

Liam had deceived her with his pretenses of care and good intentions. Ivy had let her guard down and hadn't seen what was now so obvious. She was no one to him. Ivy could move on, forget about what had happened, and erase it from her mind. Just because she'd been burned in this relationship didn't mean that there were no genuinely good people out there, even among the citizens. Could she ever forgive Liam? No, and that decision was no longer just personal. It wasn't only about her. How could she ever forget about Menken Mines?

There was a light knock on Ivy's door and she smiled slightly. It was already past ten, and for a moment Ivy had been convinced that Taylor wouldn't come, but he didn't disappoint her.

"Come in," she said.

Taylor opened the door and carefully stepped inside. As the light from halfway entered the room, Ivy noticed he was wearing a fresh shirt. A faint odor of cheap cologne followed him inside as he closed the door behind him. Ivy didn't know how much it had cost him or where he'd gotten it, but she'd order something nice for him. He deserved better.

Taylor stopped by the door, appearing to want to be close to the exit. He seemed nervous, avoiding eye contact with her.

"Come closer," Ivy said, and he slowly made a small step forward. She got up from her seat and walked closer to the light as she approached him. Ivy wore a knee-length white silk robe with long, wide sleeves. The pattern on the robe was of blooming cherry branches, accented with golden thread. She was wearing her hair down, and it fell over her shoulders in thick copper curls. She gestured him forward to the table where two documents lay. "This is for you," Ivy said, picking up one of the pieces of paper. She handed it to him when he moved closer, then before he had a chance to read it, added "I want you to sign it."

"Are ya . . ." he said and swallowed. "Are ya firing me, ma'am?" His voice shook a little.

"No," she said softly. "Please call me Ivy." She gestured towards the document. "Please read it."

Taylor took a moment to read the small print, then put it back on the table. "I can't—"

"It's not a big property," Ivy said. "A small house surrounded by a few old apple trees." Taylor tried to say something, to protest maybe, but she put a finger to his mouth for a second, then stepped away from him, giving him space.

He inspected the paper in his hand again.

Ivy walked up to the window and stared off into the darkness outside while Taylor looked over the purchase agreement.

"I can't accept it. I couldn't repay you," he said.

Ivy turned around towards Taylor. "It's a gift, and I think you'll take great care of the property." She smiled and approached the table again. She picked up a pen and gently closed it in Taylor's hands. "Please. . . . It'll make me happy if you accept."

Taylor hesitated. He opened his mouth trying to find something to say. He then slowly bent over the table, put the purchase agreement down, and signed it. When he was done, he straightened up, but didn't look at Ivy. He stared at some spot on the table in front of him, not saying a word.

"Thank you," Ivy said. She picked up the other piece of paper and put it on top of the signed purchase agreement. "I opened a bank account for you and left you some money for upkeep." She looked at Taylor, who stood paralyzed, then added, "Please hear me out."

She gestured at an upholstered chair and Taylor slowly sat down on the edge of it.

"I'm sorry. I didn't mean for this to be overwhelming," Ivy said as she walked to the other side of the table and sat back in the shadows on a firm sofa. "I couldn't do it any other way. You are the only person I trust and can lean on," Ivy added. "I need you to be close to me, to support me, and tell me when I done something wrong." Taylor was quiet, so she continued, "So now, with the purchase agreement signed, we're equal. We're both citizens. There might come a time when you'll need to make the decision to leave me. If that time comes, I want you to go. I'll understand."

"I'd never," Taylor said. He brought his head up to meet her eyes.

Ivy slowly grabbed the cigarette holder from the table. "See," she said, "I can't be the person I used to be." She slowly loaded the glass tube with a fresh cigarette. It was the latest trend among the elite women who visited Leggett. "I need to change . . . I've already changed, Taylor." She lit the cigarette and puffed a cloud of fresh smoke. "What we saw at the mines has changed me. It made me think of the people there." Ivy stopped for another puff. "Fighting for them might be foolish of me, but if I don't try to do something, it will haunt me for the rest of my life. Only monsters don't see the suffering all around us." Ivy focused on Taylor's eyes.

"What do ya plan to do?" he asked, raising his eyebrows.

"I don't know yet." Ivy averted her eyes from his gaze. She didn't know, but it would be big. Something that would knock Liam and his whole high society of citizens off their feet. It would be quick and unexpected so they would have no time to prepare or protect their sorry asses.

"But ya included me in the plan," Taylor said. He put his elbows on his knees and gazed at a spot on the floor in front of him. He was confused, and Ivy understood that the gift made him uneasy, but she needed him. She couldn't do it alone. She needed support, a circle of people that she could rely on. Taylor was an obvious choice. He'd never do anything to harm her.

"Yes," Ivy replied. He was part of the plan. "But you can say no." She pointed at the documents on the table.

"Ma'am," he replied. "Ya know I won't." He adjusted the way he was sitting and leaned against the short back of the chair.

Ivy nodded. She ignored the fact that he'd called her ma'am again. It was obviously force of habit, and it would take some time to change that. Ivy took the cigarette out of the holder and smashed it in the ashtray. She then placed the holder back on the table, got up, and took a stroll around the room. She stopped behind Taylor, bent over him, and put her arms around his neck. She felt his heart racing. "I know," she whispered into his ear. "I know how you feel about me," she said. She released him from the embrace, circled in front of him, and sat on his lap, facing him.

Taylor's eyes were closed. She admired the contours of his face and traced the bridge of his nose with her eyes before leaning over and letting her lips gently brush his. "I want us together," she whispered, then pulled away from him.

Taylor had opened his eyes and was now staring at her. Ivy smiled slightly as he sat up. Their faces were inches apart. Without breaking eye contact Ivy used both hands to untie the knot on her robe. The halves of the sleek fabric separated and rested on each side of her exposed breasts. She raised her hand and touched his cheek.

"I want you to make love to me," she whispered.

A jolt of pleasure rushed through her body as Taylor's hungry lips pressed on the side of her neck. She gasped. His firm arms gently enveloped her and picked her up with little effort. Taylor carried her to bed and laid her down. Her breath quickened as his soft tongue brushed the hardened nipples of her flattened breasts. She pulled up on his shirt and he helped her take it off.

Everything was happening fast. Taylor's wet tongue lightly touched her sensitive skin. Ivy moaned and grabbed his hair, her arms still in the robe sleeves, as he buried his face between her legs. Relaxed, she closed her eyes, allowing him to pleasure her and waiting for the moment she couldn't bear it anymore.

When Ivy woke up, Taylor wasn't with her. She checked the time and got up. It was five in the morning. She didn't know when they'd eventually fallen asleep. She'd probably slept less than four hours, but she felt unusually rested. Her robe hung on the back of the chair. It had ended up on the floor at some point in the night and Taylor must have picked it up before he left. She smiled, recalling the fun they'd had.

Ivy grabbed the robe from the chair and covered her naked body. She admired the garment and its craftsmanship in the mirror as it lay on her. It was beautiful. Ivy walked to the table and found her cigarette holder where she'd left it. She loaded a fresh cigarette into it and lit it.

The chilly March air blew in as she slid the window to the French balcony open, but she didn't flinch. She stood there looking north. Her small yard lay below in the darkness. Taylor maintained it well, and it was ready for the first spring flowers to pop up. Behind the wall, there was another short building. It had storefronts facing the road that ran along the river.

Everything was quiet and still at this hour. The town was asleep, except for some servants rushing around getting the breakfast started, and the workers that were about to start their six o'clock shifts.

There was lots of work ahead in order to break the power of the elite. To destroy those who were full of themselves, walking around with their noses up, and treating others as if they owned them. Most of it would be tedious, frustrating, and of little importance. But there would be danger and excitement. That's what she was looking forward to. Was it wrong of her to drag Taylor along?

Taylor was different. Ivy smiled to herself, recalling the first time they'd met. He had been crazy about her ever since. It had been almost ten months now, and he still constantly followed her with his eyes when she wasn't watching. There were surely many girls who looked his way, admiring him, but he was never interested. He always found excuses to work late and stay in rather than going out with other guys for a watered-down beer at the bar on his days off.

What she'd told him last night had been true. She didn't want to control him. If Taylor ever wanted to leave, she wouldn't hold it against him, but he wouldn't do such a thing. He'd always be there to give her a helping hand, to be a shoulder to cry on, and to tuck her into bed when she felt broken. That's what she needed him for. Someone who would forgive her over and over again. Someone who would remind her who she really was.

Ivy finished her cigarette and slid the window closed. She dropped the glass cigarette holder into the ashtray and walked into the bathroom for a long, hot shower. She then got dressed, picking something new. She needed to blend in, to look like the other citizens, in order to infiltrate them. In order to find their weaknesses, she needed to think like them, look like them, and act like them. She had a lot to learn.

As she walked down the stairs for breakfast, she heard Julia and Taylor in the kitchen. Ivy stopped to listen.

"Where were ya last night?" Julia asked.

"With Miss Roberts," he replied calmly.

"All ya men are the same!" Julia raised her voice. "Who do ya think you are? Ya no one!" Her voice vibrated with anger. "Stay away from Ivy!"

"Or what?" Ivy walked into the kitchen and both Taylor and Julia turned towards her. Their jaws dropped upon seeing Ivy's outfit. It was the first time she'd worn the close-fitting emerald pencil dress, an impulse purchase from a long time ago that she'd stashed at the back of her closet because she felt awkward wearing it. Today, it was perfect. The beige high heels complemented the dress and made her feel taller and more slender. Her hair, worn down, fell like a waterfall onto her shoulders, framing her face, which Ivy had adorned with heavier makeup than she normally did. She'd accented her eyes with black mascara, and her lips with ruby red lipstick.

Julia stood in the kitchen, speechless.

"Or what?" Ivy repeated the question.

"Ivy," Julia finally replied, taking a step forward. "Ya can't ruin your reputation by sleeping with someone like him!"

"It's Miss Roberts or ma'am to you," Ivy said with complete seriousness. She might have been easier on Julia under different circumstances, but Ivy was done with the maid's inappropriate behavior. Until now, Ivy hadn't required the maid to address her formally. She hadn't thought there was any reason to have her call her something other than Ivy, but it had to change. Julia would have to start showing respect if Ivy was to become a full citizen. *Act like them.* "I'll no longer be eating in here," Ivy said, maybe a bit too harshly. This new persona would require some practice. "Bring my breakfast to my room." Ivy scanned the kitchen as though it were the first time she'd laid eyes on the room. She'd miss it. Ivy recalled the fun they'd had eating scrambled eggs salvaged from an omelet that Julia had cooked, or the time when Taylor had accidentally dropped his meat onto his plate, splashing everyone with gravy. She suppressed a smile and regained her seriousness. "I'll eat dinner in the dining room from now on." It was about time she used that huge table.

"Yes, ma'am," Julia replied and curtsied.

"Taylor," she said, turning to him. "Two doors down, there used to be an old building that was used as servant quarters. See if it is still for sale."

Without waiting for his reply, Ivy turned around and headed upstairs, her high heels clicking on the marble floors, echoing in the stairway as she walked.

Oliver greeted her at the door to his study. Ivy had asked Oliver for a quick meeting, but she'd given him no clue as to what it was about. "A few minutes of your time," she'd said. The green of her dress contrasted nicely with her copper-red hair. He didn't know what had prompted such a change, but it suited her. A man dressed in a black shirt and suit followed her inside. He looked familiar to Oliver, but he didn't remember the bodyguard's name. Ivy seemed like the last person who would need someone following her for protection. Maybe she was afraid of Liam Menken. He wasn't sure what exactly had happened between them.

"Looking good," he said. "What can I do for you?" He pointed at the chair by the desk.

Ivy stepped closer, but didn't sit down. "Do you mind if I smoke?" she asked.

Oliver fetched a pack of cigarettes and put it on the desk. Ivy took one from the pack and slowly fed it to the cigarette holder she'd brought with her. She then leaned forward and allowed him to light it. She inhaled the smoke and slowly exhaled. Ivy walked over to Oliver's side of the desk. In one smooth move, she pulled herself onto it, her legs crossed and dangling. Ivy looked perfect in that pose. No wonder Mark had fallen in love with those legs.

"That list you gave me," she said. "It's not enough."

"Not sure what you expected," he said, trying to suss out the reason for the meeting.

"I need something that he can't have thrown out in court."

"In court? You want to fight Menken in court?" Oliver laughed. That was the silliest way for Ivy to get her revenge, assuming that was what she wanted.

"I need something more substantial." Ivy inhaled her cigarette. Oliver couldn't recall having seen her smoke until today. It certainly added to her sex appeal.

"The best revenge is humiliation," he said.

"I talked with Gibala," Ivy said. "She said that she could try to convince her media agency to run a segment, but that it wouldn't be easy and she needed something bigger than a list like this."

Interesting. "Did she give you examples?"

"She said she'd need hard testimonies," Ivy said. "From victims who are citizens, 'cause no one cares about the workers there. A video perhaps?"

"Does Gibala know you're here?"

"I told her I got the list from you."

Oliver didn't reply to that. What was Gibala up to? She'd had a lot of strong opinions about him when they'd met following the conference, but he hadn't seen her since then.

He scanned the room. Ivy was determined to kick Liam's ass. Why shouldn't he entertain this idea? The spoiled brat needed a lesson, and it looked like Ivy was eager to deliver it, but she needed some guidance.

"I'd like for our conversation not to leave this room," he said. Ivy mimed zipping her lips. Oliver glanced at the man at the door and Ivy followed his eyes. "Oh, Taylor," she said, then turned to the man, "Please wait for me on the other side."

The man closed the door behind him and Oliver turned back to Ivy. "There are three kinds of people," he said. "There are those who care, like you and me. We're trying to make things right. The second group is made up of those like Menken who will shamelessly do anything to increase profits, even if people get hurt or die."

"What's the third group?" Ivy asked.

"The ignorant or apathetic, or both," he replied. "That group is by far the largest, but they won't go out of their way to educate themselves. Those are the people you need to target. If you can sway them over to your side, you might win this."

"How do I do it?"

"There's only one way," he said. "You need to put the issue right in front of them. Shock them. Have all the displays in their houses showing one story. A story that'll make them hate Liam Menken, if that's what you want."

"Are you saying that I need to gain access to the Menken Mines? Get proof of the kids with swollen bellies waiting for their fathers to return from their shifts? Count the bodies that are being buried in town every week?"

"It's an idea," Oliver said, nodding. "Add to that proof of the conditions in the mine itself—the dangerous work, the lack of protections Menken claims he's implemented. Only then would you have a good story for Gibala."

"That's impossible," Ivy said and took another breath full of smoke.

"Quitting so easily?" Oliver looked at her and laughed. She'd need some more confidence to match her new look. Always move forward, no matter what.

"You got something on your mind?" Ivy asked.

"Maybe," he told her. "But to pull this off, I might need your help." He looked Ivy up and down again, admiring her new image. "You might be just the person I need."

Ivy nodded then slipped down from the desk as smoothly as she'd ascended it. She turned to him. "Do you know anyone who could teach me to play cards?" she asked.

Oliver raised his brows at her skeptically, but she had a serious expression on her face. He didn't have time for cards anymore, but Max could teach her.

# 23

OLIVER WOKE EARLY IN the morning. The sheets around him were damp and he was a little shaken. He'd been having bad dreams for a while now. Sophia still preferred sleeping alone. He didn't object and left the large bedroom for her. He had hoped the baby would improve their relationship and that Sophia would begin to seek his love and affection again, but she was pushing him away more and more.

He sat down at the edge of the bed for a moment. It was another busy day and he didn't feel ready for it. Recent events weighed on him. He hadn't figured out who Friends really were, nor how he could fight them. Taking care of his home had become his main priority. Sābanto was also time-consuming. He'd underestimated the effort it would require. Mafdet, the device that Cat and Max had, was interesting and had some potential that he'd need to explore as well. An undetectable camera, embedded into a human body.

Oliver dressed in a hurry to start the day on an upbeat note, even if it was forced. Cat had asked for a bō. He was looking for a trader who could get him something like that under the table. The bō wasn't a popular weapon here. It was occasionally, but rarely, used for strength training. World United had cracked down on access to weapons of any sort, and even a training stick might raise some eyebrows if he were to ask for it directly in some official supply store. At least anything could be bought off the record if one had enough money. The black market was flourishing. He'd look into that some more.

He left the guest room and turned towards the main bedroom to see if Sophia was up. He wanted to give her a kiss and wish her a good day. He wanted to show her he still cared.

Oliver paused by the slightly open door to the nursery. Matthew lay there in his crib between his stuffed animals and the jungle that covered the walls. He was sleeping, innocent, not knowing what was happening around him or of the dangers that the world was full of. Right now, these were the best times of his life. Eating, sleeping and exploring the world without a care. When he grew up, the jungle of the world would eventually swallow him up. Oliver would pass his knowledge on so that he'd be ready. Matthew would carry on his legacy.

The nanny was keeping a watch over him. She noticed Oliver peeking inside and rushed to pick the boy up from the crib and hand him over to Oliver to hold. He signaled for her to stop with his hands and refused politely. He didn't want to interrupt Matthew's sleep. Maybe he should carve out some time each day and check on his son more often.

Oliver quietly moved away from the nursery and walked over to the bedroom next door. He walked in, stepping as lightly as possible. The curtains were still drawn for the night, covering all the furniture in shadows. He noticed the bed was empty, but the golden sheets had been slept in. The shape of Sophia's head was delicately imprinted on the pillow. Oliver walked over to the far end of the room, but his wife wasn't busying herself with her morning toilet. He didn't find her in either the bathroom or the walk-in closet. Her running shoes, however, were missing.

It was cold outside, but maybe she'd woken up early and gone out for some fresh air. Oliver walked to the bedroom window and opened the curtains. She sometimes went for a stroll at the first light of the morning. He peered outside, but he didn't see her on the path under the trees. He turned around and scanned the room. Where was she?

His eyes caught something on the sheets. He walked over to it and picked up a piece of paper that had been folded in half and read it.

*I'll be back soon. No one needs to worry about me.*

Where the fuck had she gone? *Don't worry?* He crumpled the note and threw it back on the bed, then quickly left the room.

"Where is Mrs. Conway?!" he exploded upon seeing a servant in the hallway.

"In her room, sir . . ." she said nervously and ran past him into the master bedroom.

"Yeah, go check," Oliver muttered. His eyes hung on the door to the nursery. Matthew. Sophia had left *Matthew?* Where the fuck was she?

Oliver ran downstairs and out the front door. She'd taken the car. Someone had to have seen her leave. He went back into the house. "Where is my wife?!" he thundered. His voice echoed off the marble in the hallway, reaching every corner of the house. There wasn't a soul inside that didn't hear him.

The butler emerged from the servant's staircase, alarmed at his outburst.

"Assemble all the staff. Now!" Oliver said.

Once they'd all arrived in the front hall, he demanded answers about Sophia's whereabouts. Someone had to have seen her taking the car. Which direction had she gone? What time? For what reason did he employ guards and staff in the house around the clock if no one noticed anything? Were they lying to him? There was no amount of money in the world that Sophia could've paid the maids that would save them from him and his wrath.

"Mrs. Conway is to be found immediately!" he fumed.

Some maids went down on their knees wailing that they knew nothing about Sophia's disappearance. Others stood still with serious faces as though they were at a funeral. Tears wouldn't save them if Sophia wasn't found soon.

"Message from Leo Woodham for Mr. Conway!" A pageboy ran in through the door he had left open.

Oliver turned on his heels. "From whom?" Had he heard correctly? Leo? He drew his brows together and clenched his fists. Heat rushed through his body at the sound of that name.

The pageboy gawked at the assembled house staff, then at Oliver. "From Leo Woodham," he mumbled, extending his hand.

Oliver tore the note out of the boy's hand and opened it up. Leo had been gone for a long time. People in Covedale assumed he was dead, but Oliver knew his late father-in-law's former chief security officer was still alive. He should've known the cokehead would be back. Had it been a mistake not to kill him? Maybe he could've ended it back then at the clearing where they'd shot artificial targets sent into the air by a pneumatic machine. It had been a friendly game until Leo had turned it into a contest, a show of skill and superiority.

*Your precious is with me. Let's meet. Wait for details. Leo.* Oliver read the note, then slapped a beautifully painted porcelain vase off its pedestal, shattering it into many pieces. The assembled maids screamed in surprise.

The morning sun peeked through the canopies of the trees as the car took Sophia to the rendezvous point with Leo. She was at least an hour from home, in the middle of nowhere, when the car suddenly stopped. Sophia scanned the dark forest around her, alarmed, but smiled widely upon seeing Leo's familiar face on the other side of the window.

"I thought I'd never see you again." Sophia embraced Leo as soon as he stepped into the car. "What happened? All of Covedale is missing you. Your wife has been out of her mind trying to find you!"

"Let me breathe," Leo said, and she released him from her embrace.

"I told no one, not even Oliver, just like you told me. He'd be happy to see you I'm sure. Everyone will be thrilled." Sophia turned towards Leo. "You know what? We'll have a party. Then when they're all gathered in the living room, you'll come in and surprise everyone."

"Sure . . ." Leo replied. He punched a destination into the navigation system and the car slowly began to move.

"Let me look at you." Sophia held Leo's face in her hands. "What were you doing all this time? You've lost weight! What happened to your ear?!"

"An accident."

"You should've come to me! We could've fixed it while it was fresh."

Leo took Sophia's wrists and gently pushed her hands away from his face.

"You said you wanted to talk," Sophia continued.

"First I'll show you something," he replied.

The car turned towards the woods and stopped. Sophia peeked out the window. The outside was dark and uninviting. She had no clue where she was.

Leo opened the door. "Come with me." He left the car and Sophia followed him.

The stupid mud was everywhere Sophia stepped. She put her head down and paid attention to where she was walking, too scared to look at the forest around her. She was glad that she hadn't worn her high heels. The sneakers she was wearing were now filthy, caked with brown clay. How far were they from the car? They'd walked for at least an hour.

"Where are we going?" Sophia asked Leo again, but he didn't reply, just like the previous couple of times she had asked. He kept going, rarely checking to see if she was still behind him. His steps were hurried and it was taking a lot of effort to keep up with him.

"Here," Leo finally said. Sophia stopped and looked up. They stood beside a small wooden cabin. "It's warm inside," he said and opened the door.

She followed him into a kitchen with some cabinets on her right and a table in the middle. Sophia wrinkled her nose at the smell of smoke and mildew. "Is this where you live?" Her eyes traveled around the rough floor and walls and stopped upon seeing a blonde girl at the stove and a kid, a toddler, clinging to her leg. "At least you have a maid."

"It's a whore," Leo replied.

"Oh . . ." Sophia scrutinized the girl up and down again. That thing wasn't even pretty. Skin and bones. "It's not her that you wanted to show me, is it?" She turned her back to the girl and surveyed the cabin. How could anyone live in such a sad place? Leo had a house in Covedale. A proper one. She'd convince him to come back.

"Sit down." Leo pointed at the crooked chair beside the table. Sophia's feet were tired from the hike and she welcomed the rest ahead of the journey back. Leo then turned to the girl who stood there like a statue. "Make us lunch," he ordered, and the girl began to prepare food. Sophia didn't imagine the whore was capable of making anything edible.

There weren't many people Oliver could ask for help, but Cat knew what kind of person Leo was. The man who had killed her husband and caused her to suffer in Riverlea. Cat would understand the danger of Leo holding Sophia as well as he did. He could trust her. He immediately traveled to the island—Max had named it The Base—to meet with her. Sophia was in danger, and he needed Cat's opinion on how to get Sophia back unharmed.

He didn't know which direction his wife had gone in the car, and the staff weren't telling him anything. Oliver didn't think it was likely that she'd gone unnoticed. He'd find the traitors.

Oliver handed Leo's note to Cat and she studied it for a long time, leaning on the counter while standing in the common room. Oliver sat at the table waiting patiently as she re-read the note a few times.

"What does Leo want?" she asked, walking over to the table and putting the note down.

"He says," Oliver reiterated, "that he wants to meet."

"Yes, I get that," Cat said. "But why kidnap Sophia?"

"That's what I don't understand," Oliver said. "He's clearly trying to get at me. I don't think it has anything to do with her."

Cat gazed at him with narrowed eyes. "What did you do to him that you think he'd be after you?"

Oliver sighed. "I sniped off a piece of his ear in a contest."

Cat laughed loudly as though it was the best joke she had ever heard. It took her some time to recover. "A contest? Were you pointing guns at each other? I guess he missed—"

"Not exactly," he said. "We were shooting targets."

"Leo would make a nice target." She laughed so hard a tear formed in the corner of her eye, which she wiped off with the back of her hand.

"Can we focus on Sophia?" Oliver tried to bring Cat back to what really mattered.

She recovered from her outburst of laughter, picked up the note and read it again. She remained standing but leaned over and rested her elbows on the table. "What's the motive for a one-eared Leo to kidnap Sophia? One thing is certain, Leo won't hurt Sophia," Cat said. She straightened up and pulled a chair out from the table and sat down.

"How can you be so sure?"

"For one, he said he wants a meeting, so I'm guessing that he'll try to turn Sophia against you. If Sophia's mad at you like you say, she might give him some dirt that he can use. Think of what it might be. She's also bait, to force you to meet with him. Otherwise you'd certainly refuse. Second, Leo was always fond of her. Although they didn't hold the same social status, they grew up together. White treated him better than he ever deserved and the two were like brother and sister for many years. There's no reason for him to harm Sophia."

"What do you think we should do?"

"Unless you have any idea which direction she went, I don't think there's much you can do but wait for a meeting"

Oliver didn't think he could sit idly and wait, but Cat was right. He had no trail, no hint of where she was.

What could Leo tell Sophia that might turn her against him? There were too many things to choose from. How could he narrow it down to just one possibility? If he knew, he could prepare for the discussion and maybe prepare some counterarguments. The more he thought about it, the more everything would depend on Sophia and her love for him. He doubted it was strong enough.

The blonde girl gave Sophia a piece of dry flatbread topped with a thin layer of some sort of spread. She took a bite and found it chewy. The topping was mostly sugar with a hint of fruit in it. Way too sweet for her. She chased it down with something that had been presented to her as coffee, but was nothing more than dirty water. She glanced at Leo, who had already finished his flatbread without complaining. That was so unlike him.

"Come home with me," she pleaded. "This isn't food."

"You get used to it," he replied.

Sophia realized she wouldn't be able to persuade Leo to return with her. She'd need Mrs. Woodham's help. His wife knew Leo as well as she did. Oliver might have some ideas. Together, they'd find a way to get Leo back to Covedale. Dr. Lott could cure his head and bring him back to his senses. "What is it you wanted to talk about? My legs have rested, and I need to get home to my son." She glanced at the toddler who stood by his mother's leg.

"You're not going anywhere," Leo snapped at her.

Sophia wanted to protest, but before she was able to find her voice the cabin door opened and a man entered. He was young with blonde, unruly hair that was also dirty. Possibly infested with lice. He was carrying something—the furry carcasses of two small animals. Sophia's eyes widened. Had he killed them himself? The man stared at Sophia for a moment, making her uneasy, but didn't say anything. Just like with the girl, Leo didn't introduce the man. The newcomer handed the carcasses to the girl and went outside. Leo got up and followed him.

The men left and Sophia approached the girl who stood at the counter, working over a large basin. From her vantage point, she couldn't see what the girl was doing. She didn't know her name, either, but it didn't matter. Sophia wouldn't be here for long. "Where am I?" she asked.

"In the woods, ma'am," the girl replied politely.

"But where? Which way is the road?"

"I dunno, ma'am."

"Leo refuses to take me to my car," she said. "I need to get home. I have a son too. A much younger one."

"I'm sorry, I can't help," the girl said.

Was she a liar? "Were you kidnapped too?" Sophia asked.

"No," the girl replied hesitantly and averted her eyes.

Sophia came a few steps closer. The basin was now visible. The girl was cutting one of the furry animals, opening its belly with a knife and removing the insides. It reeked. Sophia had smelled it earlier, but the fetor, a mixture of vomit and feces, amplified when she got close. Sophia gagged and quickly took a few steps back, retreating to a safer position. "What's that?" she asked.

"A hare, ma'am."

"I won't eat that!" Sophia stepped away and sat back in the chair. The foul smell was everywhere around her. It lingered in her nostrils.

Leo and the man returned. The stink of cigarettes followed them inside. Sophia sighed with relief. The stench of the dead animal was subdued.

Leo sat down beside her again. "Why did you bring me here?" she asked.

"Someone hasn't paid for your father's death," he said.

"What are you talking about? He had a heart attack."

Leo laughed. "That's what he wanted you to think."

"Who?" Sophia stared into Leo's eyes.

"Your dear husband," he said calmly.

What kind of accusation was that? That wasn't possible. Leo had always been reasonable and level-headed. That was why her papa had worked with him. The man who sat in front of her was someone else. Not the security officer she remembered. Brain injury? That was the only explanation. Maybe it was related to the accident where he had lost part of his ear.

"Oliver wanted to destroy your father from the first day he set foot in Covedale," Leo continued. "That was his goal. Gutters in Riverlea paid Oliver to kill him."

Sophia jumped up from her seat and leaned over the table, closer to Leo's face. "That's a lie!" Sophia protested, putting a finger in his face. A terrible lie. Why was Leo being so cruel to her?

Leo didn't flinch. He continued in a calm voice. "And you . . . you were just a prize to him; a keepsake he arrogantly shows off after destroying your father. He's proud of what he did. He deceived you and manipulated you into believing that he was in love with you. Meanwhile it drove your father crazy."

"You have no idea what you're talking about!"

"I would've done something about him a long time ago, but he blackmailed your father who forbade me to act."

"That's nonsense!" Sophia shook her head.

"I tried to do something about him without your father's approval," Leo continued. "I went to talk to Oliver. I was unarmed and ready to negotiate a deal that would've worked for everyone, but your loving husband almost killed me. Good thing he missed and only took a portion of my ear."

Sophia straightened up. "I won't listen to this anymore! I demand that you take me home!"

"Sure," Leo replied. "Tomorrow." He got up from the chair and left the cabin, shutting down any further conversation, despite her protests.

Sophia sat at the table until the girl began to clean the floor, then she moved to the edge of the sofa in front of the fireplace. What Leo had said about Oliver couldn't be true. Of course, her father hadn't been very happy about their marriage. She recalled his sour face while he'd watched her new husband on their wedding day. That was normal, wasn't it? Generations always clash with each other.

Sophia turned towards the boy who hesitantly approached her. He had been very shy earlier, keeping close to his mother all morning, but he seemed to have slightly warmed up to Sophia's presence. He tried to hand her a toy, a stuffed monkey, but she didn't take it from him. It was dirty and Sophia didn't want to touch it.

The girl stopped sweeping the floor and came over, not looking up at Sophia. She took the kid's hand. "Come Seb," she told him. "Leave the lady alone."

"Yours?" Sophia asked, looking at the toddler.

"Yes," Violet nodded.

"Doesn't he look familiar?" Leo appeared in the doorway and stepped into the conversation.

Sophia shook her head. She had never seen the kid.

"These blue eyes. I knew I'd seen them somewhere before." Leo sneered.

Sophia glanced at the boy. Leo was right. There was something familiar in the kid's eyes. No. She dismissed the thoughts that were filling her mind. She stood up and walked towards Leo. "I'm done with your stupidity," she said. "It's time you quit playing games and take me home. I demand you send me back to my son"

"There's no rush," he replied.

# 24

OLIVER COULDN'T SLEEP. HE kept thinking about Sophia and where she might be. What did Leo want with her? Did she have enough food and water? As the hours passed with no information, his ashtray got fuller with the remnants of his cigarettes.

The information he was waiting for came at dawn, delivered to him by a page boy. Oliver immediately traveled to the base.

"We have no time," he said as soon as he stepped into the building. "The meeting is at noon."

"Sit down. You look like crap," Max said. He poured a steaming cup of coffee for him. His movements were slow on purpose, as though he didn't care that Oliver was in a hurry.

Cat stepped into the house and read the atmosphere of the room. "Where?" she said and immediately approached the table without even taking her shoes off. She smelled strongly of sweat.

He took out a tablet, brought the map up on the display, and pointed at the location he'd been given.

Cat studied the map. Max poured another cup of coffee and placed it in front of her. She grabbed it and took a sip. "Have you checked the surrounding area? Any clues?" Cat asked.

"There's nothing there," Oliver replied.

"There has to be something." Cat got up and pushed the tablet towards him so that he could better see what she was showing him across the table. "There are no roads that lead to this clearing, which means they must walk. How much walking can he do with Sophia in tow?"

"No more than a couple of hours," Oliver replied. "She's not accustomed to such strenuous walks in the mountains, and she only took her running shoes."

"Through the mountainous terrain, a couple of hours means probably no more than eight kilometers," Max said.

"Let's round that to ten." Cat drew a circle on the map around the meeting place of such a radius. To the west there were high mountains with steep cliffs. The eastern and southern part of the circle, however, was part of a valley that gently sloped down towards the road to Clamerton.

"If he comes from somewhere else by car," Oliver pointed at the map. "There are only three places he could enter the valley." He inhaled from his cigarette and exhaled the smoke.

"And if he is keeping Sophia anywhere else in this area," Cat said and pointed at the eastern side deeper in the woods. "We need to search here."

Oliver glanced at the time on the wall. "It's already seven."

"Then we have five hours," Cat said.

"If Leo sees me, he'll recognize me and change his plans," Oliver smoked his cigarette. He couldn't go running around the forest looking for nothing. "I need to be at the meeting place at noon."

"He knows me well too," Cat added.

"So we send someone else," Max said.

"Greyson is out. He worked for Leo," Oliver added. "If he gets captured, Leo will know I'm after him."

"I'll go," Max said.

"That's the worst idea I've ever heard!" Oliver exploded and stood up.

"Why? Leo never fucking met me in person, and he thinks I'm fucking dead. I won't shave today and he'll think I'm some Free man who lost his way in the woods."

Oliver stared at Max. "You think I've forgotten you wanted to kill Sophia?"

"Why would I ever want to do that?" Max got up from his seat to meet Oliver's stare.

"She could've been in that car!"

"The car explosion?" Max laughed out loud.

Oliver wanted to charge him across the table. "Cut it the fuck out!" Cat intervened. She put her hand in front of Max to stop them from getting any closer to each other.

"It was only to scare you. Your Sophia was safe." Max added.

"Stop!" Cat said. "We have no time for this!" She faced Oliver. "Sophia will be fine, plus we'll be able to see where Max is and what he's doing through Mafdet."

"How can you trust him?" Oliver asked.

"We have no other choice, Oliver," Cat replied. "We gotta trust each other."

Finding the car turned out to be an easy task. Cat smiled slightly, knowing she'd been right about the plan. There were only three dirt roads that lead to the area she had marked on the map, and Oliver scanned them from the chop-jet. The range of the scan was quite small, but it found a large object about a hundred meters from the main road at one of the access points. Amy and Greyson were set to monitor the other roads.

Max turned on his Mafdet and sent the visuals to a display in the vessel. "If you see something I fail to notice, let me know," Max said. "Better yet"—he turned to Cat—"record it."

Cat nodded and started the recording option on the display. It made sense. They could review it again later if they didn't notice anything. She sat down in front of the displays in one of the chop-jet swivel chairs as Max left the vessel. She watched Max reach the old road. It didn't take him long to find the car.

"That's mine," Oliver confirmed.

Max approached it carefully and scanned the surroundings with thermal vision. There was no one around. He peeked through the windows and tried the door. It was unlocked. He carefully slid inside and sat on the passenger side.

"Nice one," Max commented, looking around. "Anything out of place?"

"There are storage compartments under the seat behind you," Oliver said. "Behind your feet and above the driver's seat."

There was nothing there. According to Oliver, everything was untouched, so Max left the car and scanned the ground. The soil around the car was soaked in rain and melting snow. Suddenly, the display changed. The mud was now covered with random circular shapes showing the slope of the terrain underneath Max's feet. He had turned on the 3D option in Mafdet. They watched for patterns in the sludge, trying to find Sophia's footprints.

Max took a few steps away from the car.

"Here!" Oliver said, looking at the display.

Max saw it as well. "This one is large and quite heavy." Max pointed at what he was looking at. "It sank way deeper into the mud than the other one." He pointed at the second imprint beside the first one. "This one looks like a lighter person left it. I don't see any other footprints around, so there were only two people."

"Leo is working alone," Oliver said.

"Hopefully. We don't know if there was someone else waiting in the woods," Cat said.

Max traced the outline of one of the large footprints with his finger. They concluded it must be Leo's and then did the same with Sophia's lighter step. The mud in the forest suddenly showed two different sets of footprints, traced in pink and yellow for easy identification. Max followed them and the device found new ones ahead of him. Whenever Leo or Sophia stepped on a rock, their steps disappeared, then continued further away.

"Isn't this a cool feature?" Cat said without taking her eyes off the display, but swiveled nervously back and forth in the chair. Oliver didn't reply.

Max walked a hundred meters and found a narrow path. Usually the animals that traveled for water used trails like these. The tracks weren't visible here, and the device couldn't capture their footprints. Max turned left first and walked a few meters without finding where the tracks continued. He then went back to the starting point and walked the other way. He again found nothing.

"Not sure which way they went from here," Max said.

"Is there water nearby?" Cat asked. "If Leo were planning on hiding out for an extended period of time, he'd need easy access to a river or a stream."

Max turned on the enhanced hearing and the room in the chop-jet filled with the sounds of the forest. The trunks of two trees growing too close together were scratching each other in the wind. A bird or a small animal rustled in the dead leaves.

"That way," Max said. "There's water flowing." He walked towards the sound and then turned the enhanced hearing off. He followed the path up and down through rocks for less than a hundred meters when he found a quickly-flowing stream.

"This might be a dead end," Max said, but he found new footprints. He followed them for at least an hour. Eventually Max reached another, much smaller stream. He turned right and followed the tracks along the spring.

Suddenly, Max left the trail and hid behind a shrub. He carefully peered out of his hiding spot for a better view of the stream. A person was walking his way carrying something in their hands—a bucket or a pot. Whoever it was, they didn't have a proper coat, which meant that they hadn't come for water from very far.

It wasn't Sophia or Leo. Who was this person? Max watched the stranger kneel on a rock, put the container down, and take off their hood.

"A woman," Oliver said.

Cat opened her mouth, seeing the familiar face. Her heart quickened. "Violet?"


Leo insisted Mrs. Conway stay for the night. The woman protested, screaming at him in the cabin and scaring Seb. She kept accusing Violet of working with Leo and not telling her how to get to the road. She even tried to run away into the night, but Leo had bound her hands. There was nothing that Violet could help her with. She didn't know the way out of the forest and had to protect Seb. Eventually, Mrs. Conway became exhausted from fighting and collapsed on the bed crying.

Violet couldn't sleep. Mrs. Conway was occupying her bed, so she was sharing the other one with Mike. Violet found the arrangements uncomfortable. Thoughts tormented her as she tossed and turned. What was Mrs. Conway doing with them in the cabin? What was Leo planning? Whatever it was, it wasn't good. Violet eventually fell asleep and woke up later than usual. There was lots of light already outside the window, but everyone was still asleep. Violet slid away from the warmth of the covers and put her feet on the cold floor. The room was chilly, so Violet didn't stay motionless for long. She dressed quickly, trying to get her blood flowing. She'd add some wood to the fire in a moment.

Seb was still in his crib, hugging his monkey and sleeping peacefully under a thick blanket. She stroked his hair gently so as not to wake him up and went to the kitchen. Leo was asleep on the sofa by the fireplace.

Violet tiptoed around, avoiding the floorboards that creaked loudly. She grabbed the water bucket and let herself out.

She hurried to the river up the familiar path, knelt on the flat rock beside the slowly-moving stream, and bent over it to fill the bucket. The water hit the container with a metallic sound. She waited.

She heard a sudden noise behind her. Her heart pounded in her chest as she looked around her for an approaching animal.

"It's okay, Violet," a man whispered, raising his hands, showing that he was unarmed. "I'm a friend."

He stood at the edge of the woods, not too close. She got up off her knees, ready to flee, but paused. If the man was here to rescue Mrs. Conway, it might be a chance for her and Seb. He also knew a way out of these woods. "Who are ya?" she asked.

"I can't tell you that," he said, "but we had a mutual friend in Riverlea."

"I don't think we've met," Violet said and grabbed the bucket, but it was heavy.

"Remember the piece of chocolate?" the man asked. Violet recalled holding the dark, rectangular chocolate back in Riverlea. "You tried it, but you didn't eat it yourself. You fed it to Seb," the man continued, "but you cleaned every inch of his face once he finished. You hid it from the neighbors."

How did he know the story? Only one person was witness to that event and she wouldn't have told anyone unless . . . unless it was important. "Who are ya?" she repeated.

"I'm here to help," the man said. He pointed at the pot in her hand. "I can help you carry this thing."

"No!" Violet said through her teeth and took a step back. He couldn't follow her into the cabin. Leo had a gun. He slept with it, ready to use it.

"Who's in the house?" the man asked. "Leo?"

Violet shivered.

"Who else?" he asked.

Violet's hands were shaking. She bent over the bucket. "I gotta go. I been out for too long."

"Is Seb well?" the man asked. "Our friend would like to know."

"He's fine," Violet said. She picked up the bucket from the ground, leaning slightly to one side due to its weight. She hurried away from the stream and the man. Violet glanced behind her as she approached the cabin. The man hadn't followed. She slowly approached the door, not wanting anyone to notice she was out of breath.

Cat looked at Oliver, who wanted to strangle Max with his bare hands.

"You forgot to ask her about Sophia!" Oliver was angry, standing in front of the display like he had Max in front of him.

"Chill out," Max said.

"Don't tell me what to do!" Oliver exploded.

"The footprints show she is there," Cat said, trying to calm him down as Oliver paced in the chop-jet. "Leo has no reason to hurt her."

"Go after her!" Oliver shouted. "Turn the infrared on and see how many people are inside!"

"We can't see through the walls," Cat tried to explain.

"How about enhanced hearing?" Oliver continued. "Can't you fucking use that to listen to their conversations? I'd recognize Sophia's voice."

"Shh!" Max said quietly, and the sound of the forest amplified in the chop-jet. He was on the move, walking away from where the cabin stood and where Violet had disappeared.

"And where the hell are you going?" Oliver exploded again, seeing Max leaving.

"Shh!" Cat hissed at him. "Listen."

There was a rhythmic crunch of leaves and small sticks, and the scratching of gravel on rocks. Occasionally a whoosh of leaves or branches was audible as they brushed against clothes. Someone was walking through the forest.

Max moved closer to the sound. From between the tree trunks, Cat recognized the man. "Leo," she said.

"Does he have Sophia?" Oliver asked.

"He's carrying something," Max said and tried to get a better view, but the greenery was thick. He turned on the thermal view. There were two distinctive shapes visible. He turned it back to regular view and started moving closer.

"That can't be Sophia," Oliver said looking at the display. "Too small."

Cat felt her blood freeze. "No . . ." she whispered.

Violet snuck into the cabin. Leo was no longer lying on the sofa in front of the fireplace. He'd probably stepped away to relieve himself or grab a smoke. He'd be back shortly. Mike had stolen some eggs the day before and Violet was looking forward to making them for Seb for breakfast. She put the water she'd fetched into a pot and onto the stove before starting the fire underneath.

She turned around to check if Seb was up. If he'd soiled himself at night, he might start crying and wake everyone up.

The crib was empty.

Seb was gone. Mike and Mrs. Conway were still asleep. Leo had Seb.

She ran out of the house, but she didn't know which way they went.

"Seb! Leo!" she shouted, but the forest outside was quiet.

Violet ran back to the cabin. Mike was still in bed, so she shook him violently, screaming for him to wake up.

"Where is Seb?!" she cried. "Where did Leo take him?"

"Calm down," Mike replied. Why was he calm? Didn't he love Seb, even a little?

"Tell me!" Violet ignored the look from Mrs. Conway who was now awake as well.

Mike said nothing and slowly got up from the bed and put his clothes on. He didn't seem in a hurry to answer any of her questions or to get Seb back. Violet grabbed the shirt he'd just put on and held it tightly. "Why did he take him?"

"Stop it!" Mike pushed her away from him with enough force that she fell to the hard floor. He was much stronger than she was.

She quickly got up. "Tell me!" Violet insisted.

"He'll bring Seb back when he's done with him."

"Leo has her!" She pointed at Mrs. Conway, who lay on the other bed and was still tied up. Her eyes were open, watching the scene. "He doesn't need Seb for ransom!" Violet shouted at her brother.

"He doesn't want ransom," Mike clarified. "He wants revenge."

"Revenge for what?!"

"Ya lover ruined his life," Mike said. He sat back down on the bed and put his shoes on.

"That has nothing to do with Seb!" Violet shouted.

"It has everything to do with Seb," Mike said.

"It's about Oliver," Mrs. Conway said, stating the obvious.

"Why didn't he take her?" Violet pointed at the nicely dressed woman lying in her bed again. Surely she was a better tool for Leo's revenge.

Mike shrugged. "Isn't Seb his?"

Seb was in danger. There was no other reason for Leo to take him. He was using him as bait for Oliver.

"Where did he take him?" Violet shouted at Mike, standing in the door frame, not letting him out of the room.

"I dunno!" Mike got annoyed with her. "Let it go!" He pushed her away as he moved into the kitchen.

"Why did ya let him?" Violet had no intention of letting go.

"Why wouldn't I?" Mike replied.

"Leo will kill him! That ain't what mama and papa taught us."

Her words angered Mike and his face went red. He swung at Violet, hitting her in the face so hard that it sent her sprawling to the floor. He grabbed a piece of rope that hung on the chair, a leftover piece of what Leo had used to tie Mrs. Conway. He folded it a few times and hit Violet with it with all his strength before she could get up from the floor.

She cried out in pain as the rope struck her. "Mike, stop!"

"How dare ya bring mama into this? Did mama teach ya to be a whore?"

He hit her repeatedly, then grabbed her hair and dragged her across the floor and tied her hands behind her back. Violet was no longer crying; she was too terrified. Leo might kill Seb and Mike wouldn't help to rescue him. If Oliver came, he'd free Sophia. He wouldn't care about Seb.

Mike opened the heavy latched door to the cellar and forced Violet down the steep wooden steps.

"Mike, no!" She begged him one more time, but he closed the latch. He'd left her alone in a pitch-black cellar that stank of dampness and mildew.

As Violet looked around the darkness, trying to figure out her next steps, the cellar door opened. For a moment, she hoped Mike had reconsidered, but instead he'd brought Mrs. Conway with him. He pushed her to walk down as well. He then closed the latch, and dragged something heavy—probably the old sofa—over the hatch, preventing their escape.

They both listened to Mike's steps fading as he walked away. There was no way out except up the stairs. It was late morning, but the cellar was dark inside, with only faint light passing through the floorboards above them. There were no windows.

"It's cold here," Mrs. Conway noticed. Violet felt the chill of the place as well.

"Are ya hands tied at the front, ma'am?" Violet asked her. Mike hadn't had time to untie Mrs. Conway.

"Yes," she replied.

"Then ya can untie me. Please, ma'am," Violet said and turned her back to her.

The woman hesitated for a moment, but then loosened the knot that Mike had made. Violet returned the favor.

Her brother wasn't going to let them out, so Violet walked around the place with her hands stretched out in front of her, looking for something useful. This exercise proved pointless; she found nothing that might help them escape.

She went back to Mrs. Conway, who was too scared to move away from the stairs.

"Anything?" the woman asked.

"No, ma'am," Violet said. "Why don't ya sit down, ma'am." The stairs weren't comfortable, but there was no point in standing.

"I'm fine," Mrs. Conway replied and remained where she was.

Violet sat. Her mind was spinning with thoughts of Seb and what was happening to him. She needed to do something, but what? She was restless, sitting on the hard step, not knowing what to do with her hands. She wanted to get up, but then what? She remained seated. Would she ever see him again? She recalled the last time she'd looked at Seb. She wanted to imprint that memory in her mind.

"Leo won't harm him," Mrs. Conway said as though reading Violet's mind. How could she be so sure? Seb was innocent. He'd done nothing to Leo. Why had he taken him? "Is it true what Leo said?"

"About what, ma'am?" Violet said through her tears. Her mind was filled with worry about her son. Her thoughts went back every so often to the cellar they were in and the escape plan, but there was only emptiness.

"That kid is Oliver's?" Mrs. Conway asked.

What did that matter right at that moment? "Yes, ma'am," she replied.

"How old is he?"

"Two, ma'am." It had been almost three years since she'd spoken to Oliver. It made sense that he hadn't stayed with her in Riverlea. She was no one, only a poor orphan. She'd had nothing to offer him. Violet didn't have what Mrs. Conway had. The woman was a little taller, with shiny chestnut hair. Her complexion was perfect and her skin was porcelain white, unspoiled by the sun. Violet didn't have pretty dresses or any other clothes that fit perfectly and emphasized her curves. No wonder Oliver had chosen the prettier girl.

"Does he know?"

"No, ma'am" Violet replied, shaking her head. "I don't think so."

"And it'll stay that way," the woman said. "Oliver will come and rescue us," she added, sounding very confident. "After we leave, don't try to contact him. You and your . . . Seb. What a ridiculous name—"

"Sebastian. After ma father, ma'am," Violet clarified.

"You and Sebastian," Mrs. Conway continued, saying Seb's full name indignantly. "If my husband ever finds out that your son is his, I'll find you." Her anger increased. "I'll find you both and destroy you. I know people who won't turn down any job, even a murder. There'll be no place for you to hide from my rage." It was dark, but Violet was aware that the woman was staring at her with eyes full of contempt. "Swear that you'll disappear and never show up in Oliver's life again."

"Yes, ma'am." To get Seb back, she'd do anything.

# 25

THE TOPS OF THE trees swayed in all directions, creating noise that masked any footsteps. Cat checked the time with the Mafdet. There were fifteen minutes left before the meeting, but she didn't step into the clearing right away. She kept herself hidden behind the evergreens, looking around for Leo.

This was the best arrangement. Cat could handle Leo. He would be surprised when he arrived at the meeting point and found Cat instead of Oliver, but with Max following him from behind, he wouldn't be able to retreat back to the cabin. As much as she hated hearing Max's voice in her brain, it was some safety that she welcomed. With the Mafdet turned on, Max had her back.

For additional protection, she'd brought along a collapsible bō that Oliver had given her. It was two or three centimeters in diameter and about ten centimeters long when closed, though it featured a button to extend the stick in roughly a meter in both directions. She kept it concealed in her sleeve. Normally a bō staff was tapered at the ends, but this version had been weaponized and ended in sharp points like a javelin. The bō was perfectly balanced and made from a metal alloy which made it incredibly light and easy to maneuver. If she'd brought a gun, Leo would've known right away that she was armed. A concealed bō staff gave her the element of surprise.

"On your left," Max said through Mafdet.

Cat turned her head in the direction he indicated, but all she could see were thick shrubs. Apart from the wind moving the branches, the woods were unchanged.

"Turn on your thermal vision," Max added.

She complied and her vision was filled with varying shades of warm and cool colors. She was able to make out the silhouette of a person.

Leo stopped at the edge of the clearing and waited, holding Seb's hand.

Cat turned off her thermal vision. She needed an unobstructed view of Leo. She then stepped into the middle of the clearing so that he saw her. "No need to hide," she said out loud as she made the first step. "I knocked your pageboy off his bike. Oliver never got your message." Cat raised her hand with the piece of paper in it to show that she told the truth.

"What the fuck do you want?" Leo was angry. He hadn't planned for this development. All she needed to do was to keep him occupied so that Oliver could rescue Sophia from the cabin.

"I wanted to talk," Cat said. She put the trigger finger of her right hand on the button of the concealed bō.

"About fucking what?"

"You and me . . . and Tom."

Leo stepped forward into the clearing and faced Cat, who almost gasped seeing Seb standing beside Leo. It had been such a long time since she'd seen him. She caught herself in time to hide her surprise and keep Leo believing in her indifference to the toddler. If Leo wanted to make a point, shouldn't he have brought Sophia? Why Seb? Seb complicated everything.

"Your husband was a fucking piece of shit," Leo said bluntly.

"You're no better." She couldn't argue with Leo's assessment of Tom. Her husband hadn't been a good man. It seemed silly now that she'd put herself in danger searching for him in Riverlea.

"I scanned the woods," Max told her through Mafdet. "He doesn't have backup."

Cat didn't know if she could handle Leo while he held Seb. She was afraid of hurting the boy. She was glad Leo had no other company, otherwise the situation could've become even more dangerous for Seb. Cat grew slightly more optimistic, knowing that her opponent was outnumbered.

"What's with the boy?" Cat asked. Leo held Seb's hand. The toddler was clearly terrified.

"He's a present for Oliver," he said.

Cat laughed. "You think he cares about kids?"

"His own, maybe?"

"That's not Matthew," Cat said, dismissing Leo's claim. "Oliver has guards all over that boy."

"Tell Oliver to come out and show himself." Leo scanned the woods. "Maybe we can discuss *this* son." He pulled Seb closer to himself. "Raised in poverty by his mother of low standards. He's a monster, not a father."

"He's Oliver's?" Cat kept a straight face. She'd never have guessed that Seb could be his. Was Leo bluffing? There were lots of questions she needed to ask Violet, but regardless of what the story was, Cat didn't love the boy any less.

Leo grabbed his gun and put it against Seb's head. "Tell Oliver to come out!"

"He's not here," Cat said, trying not to panic.

"I want him to watch me put this kid out of his misery." He pressed the gun and started to charge it.

"I guess it'll need to wait 'til you meet up with Oliver." Cat said. She wanted to persuade him to give her more time, reducing the tension, because Leo was increasing the stakes of this encounter with each move.

Cat noticed Max creeping up behind Leo, a piece of wood raised above his head, ready to strike. Leo's gun was charged. It was a terrible idea to attack him now.

Leo noticed her glance behind him and turned around to point his gun at Max, but Cat suddenly had her bō in her hands and was running towards him. She swung her weapon, striking Leo's right ear, the one that Oliver had shot last year. Her opponent winced from the impact to his damaged ear but still fired at Max.

Cat couldn't check on Max, but the wild shot had to have missed him. Leo pointed the gun at her, but her bō whooshed as she swung it, knocking Leo's gun out of his grasp and sending it flying through the air. It fell to the grass a few meters away.

"Let go of the boy!" Cat called again. She brought her bō staff back to her side, being careful not to strike Seb.

The blow to Leo's face hadn't made him release his grip on the boy, so she attacked him again. She swung her bō upward, hitting Leo right between the legs. He snarled through gritted teeth. "Bitch!" Leo let go of Seb and doubled over in pain.

Seb hesitated. He stood frozen beside Leo looking at Cat. *No! Don't run to me.* Leo was still a danger. "Hide!" Cat shouted at the boy who complied and disappeared into the greenery.

It was her and Leo now.

"I learned to fight in Riverlea," Cat said as she stepped in between him and his gun still in the grass. "That wasn't what you wanted me to learn there, was it?"

"You think you can stop me with a stick?" Leo said as he recovered his voice. He charged at her, trying to tackle her. Cat evaded his assault and tripped him with her bō. Leo was back on the ground, so she quickly turned and picked up his gun.

"I've fought better men than you," Cat said. "They were bigger and stronger. I trained with the best. My trainer said," Cat continued, glancing at the weapon in her hand, "that a gun should never be your main weapon. Fight with your skill, he said."

Leo tried to get up and charge her again, but she struck him on the back, right across his shoulder blades with the bō, knocking him sprawling on the ground. "You want your gun back?" she asked mockingly as she bent over him.

"Fuck you," Leo mumbled. He was having trouble speaking.

Cat recalled the pain she'd felt when Tom had gone missing. She remembered being raped in Riverlea, and her constantly empty stomach due to the never-ending shortage of food. Leo was the reason she'd suffered all that pain. Her revenge, however, wasn't only for her. It was for Violet too, and for all the women of Riverlea. Leo, together with White, had held Riverlea hostage. It had been under his eye that the ferry had charged outrageous fees, preventing people from leaving the island.

Cat pointed Leo's gun at him, charged it and fired. She kicked his body to make sure he was dead, but it would be hard for him to live with a smoking hole through his head.

Oliver took Greyson with him. They followed the same path Max had traveled earlier and arrived at the cabin. Thanks to Max's 'stellar' information gathering, they were going in blind. They had no idea how many people were inside. The only person they had seen was a young man with blonde hair who'd come out for a short break, then retreated back to the cabin. Oliver was certain he wasn't holding Sophia in there alone.

It had taken Cat an hour to get to the meeting point and neutralize Leo. Amy had confirmed through the Mafdet stream from Cat that Leo was no longer a threat. It was time for Oliver to move, but not with a full bladder. "I need to take a piss," Oliver said. He should've gone earlier, but he thought he still had some time.

Greyson nodded. "I'll wait."

Oliver took a couple of steps away. The thick forest surrounded by mountains was quiet; even the birds weren't singing. Weren't they supposed to be more active in the spring? Oliver had discussed the plan with Greyson, and had accounted for many different ways that this day might go. He hoped it was enough.

He finished his business quickly and returned to the place he'd left Greyson, but Greyson wasn't there.

"You were supposed to wait, Greyson," he said to himself through clenched teeth. He didn't know which way he'd gone or what he was doing. Had Greyson chickened out and run back to the chop-jet, or was he rushing forward with the plan, thinking it was so easy he could do it alone? This change worried Oliver. It wasn't the time for the kid to try to prove himself.

No matter what the reason for Greyson's disappearance, Oliver had to keep moving and get Sophia out before whoever was in the cabin learned of Leo's fate. He ran to a window and took out a periscope. He peeked inside without allowing his head in view of the frame in case anyone was watching. He was looking into a bedroom with two beds and a crib. No one was there.

He walked closer to the front of the cabin and peered into another window. The young man with blond hair was sitting in front of a softly-lit fireplace, but he could see no one else.

There were no other rooms in the house. Where were they keeping Sophia? Was there an attic or a cellar? Sophia had to be in there somewhere. She could also be under the bed for all he knew. It was impossible to tell with just the periscope. What if they had made a mistake and she wasn't here after all? What if Leo had her hidden somewhere else? What about Violet? She was also not present, but they'd been certain she was inside.

Suddenly, there was banging on the other side of the cabin. *Fuck!* Oliver mouthed. Someone had knocked on the door. Not just a normal knock, but a code knock. Three short and two long.

The man inside got up from his seat. He knew who was at the door. Oliver ran over as quietly as possible to the front of the house. *Fuck!* He mouthed again. Oliver felt his face turn hot as he clenched his fists.

The door of the cabin opened. It was Greyson.

"Hey Mike. Is Leo in?" Greyson asked.

"Nah," Mike replied. "He stepped away."

Greyson had known about this place all along. Oliver fumed. Had he not severed ties with Leo when he'd joined Oliver's team? Had they met without his knowledge? His deteriorating relationship with Sophia and the birth of his son had been all that Oliver focused on lately. If Greyson had given Leo information about Lott's involvement, it might be the end of what Oliver was working for. Friends would have the upper hand over his life again.

Why did Greyson keep his connection with Leo secret only to reveal it now? Was this a part of some kind of a plan of his? What was he up to? He knew the consequences of crossing Oliver.

"He asked me to drop something off," Greyson said and took something out of his pocket. A small bag. Drugs? Greyson was supplying Leo with cocaine? Oliver became increasingly angry. Not only at Greyson, but also at himself. How had he been played so easily, and by this guy? A fucking idiot.

Mike waved Greyson in and the officer stepped inside. The door closed.

Oliver returned to the window that gave him a view of the inside. He didn't set up the periscope. He could hear them talking from outside.

"Not with ya boss?" Mike asked.

"I got a day off," Greyson said. "He had some important meeting." Had Greyson lied just because he expected Oliver to be listening? At least he didn't tell the guy in the cabin that Oliver was outside.

The remainder of the conversation was about irrelevant topics that were in no way related to Sophia or Leo. Oliver waited a moment, trying to put together a new plan. Under these new circumstances, he would have to take down both of them. The other guy, Mike, wouldn't be a problem, however he'd taught Greyson some gun tricks and the kid was a practiced shot. He wasn't as good as Oliver, but he was capable.

A moment later, Mike spoke, "Can ya wait? I'll bring wood."

"Sure, man," Greyson replied. "Got a bottle here somewhere?"

Oliver immediately moved to watch the cabin door. It opened and Mike emerged. He walked to a pile of firewood under a tarp and bent down to grab some. Oliver circled around to keep the door of the cabin in his view, then quietly grabbed hold of the man and brought him to the ground. The kid wasn't very strong. Oliver twisted Mike's hands behind his back and pressed a knee down on him so that he couldn't move. *Fuck!* Greyson was the one with the rope. Oliver looked around for another way to tie the kid up, but just then Greyson emerged from the cabin and handed him the rope.

"Things have changed," the officer said.

"What things?" Oliver asked. He tied Mike's hands. He needed him out of the way before he could confront Greyson, who strangely didn't seem hostile towards Oliver.

"She's not there," Greyson said, and took a long gulp straight from the liquor bottle.

The kid couldn't have checked every corner of that cabin so quickly.

Oliver dragged Mike away from the cabin and close to a tree. He tied him up with the rest of the rope that Greyson had given him. Oliver then took the gun from the small of his back, turned it on, and pointed it at his officer. "Give me your gun," he ordered with his hand extended towards him.

The officer didn't move. He just took another gulp of the alcohol.

"Give me your fucking gun!" Oliver raised his voice. He didn't have much patience left.

Greyson grabbed the gun from the small of his back and threw it into the mud between him and Oliver.

"Now get inside!"

"Sir," Greyson said as nothing had happened. His voice was calm. "They ain't there."

Oliver wanted to force Greyson to get inside, but his phone vibrated. It was Amy, which meant something was wrong. Just what he needed, another complication. He answered the phone while keeping an eye—and gun—on Greyson.

Cat didn't know which way Max or Seb had gone.

"Seb!" she shouted. "Max!" She looked around. The forest was quiet and unchanged. The bare branches, waiting for new leaves, swayed in the wind as though nothing had happened. "It's safe now!" she called.

She heard a rustling to her right. She gripped her bō tight, but immediately relaxed when she noticed Seb peeking out from behind an evergreen. She ran towards him and fell to her knees in front of him. She worriedly touched his face and arms, making sure he was unharmed. He was petrified, but otherwise fine. She smiled at him and kissed his forehead.

"Max!" she called, but there was no answer. Cat got up from her knees and looked around again. "Max!" *Agent location.* A small red dot appeared in front of her. Cat grabbed Seb by the hand and followed the indicator.

She found Max about a hundred meters away. He was lying on his back, his head resting on a fallen tree trunk, his eyes closed. "Max," she said, kneeling beside him.

Max opened his eyes slowly. "The bastard shot me," he said. There was blood on his lips.

"Can you walk?" she asked, but he didn't reply.

Cat studied his abdomen and the burnt hole in his clothes. The wound underneath was serious, but there wasn't much blood seeping out. There was likely some sort of internal damage, which would explain the blood in his mouth. "The chop-jet is not that far from here," she said. Cat urged him to sit up. She held his back. He was weak and had trouble sitting. Max needed to stand up and they had to walk out of this forest.

"You won't be able to carry me and the kid," Max said.

Cat took a look at Seb, who had a tight grip on her clothes and was staring at her with wide eyes. She could take him and meet Amy, who was waiting for them in the chop-jet, and then come back, but she was afraid that when she returned, Max would no longer be alive. She couldn't imagine learning again that he was dead. For real this time. She looked back at Max and forced him up. "I'll get both of you out."

She let Max lean on her for support on her right, and with her left hand she firmly grabbed Seb's hand. "Slow and steady," Cat said as she moved. She wouldn't let either of them slip away.

The trip back took a long time as they tripped multiple times on the roots and stones that crossed their path. Each time Cat forced Max to keep going.

Amy opened the door to the chop-jet as soon as she saw them approaching.

"We need a doctor!" Cat called out once they were inside the chop-jet.

Max was leaning on Cat heavily, unable to stand on his own. Amy extended her hand to Seb, but he shied away.

"Go with Amy." Cat pulled Seb from behind her. "She's a friend who'll take you to mommy."

Amy slowly took the boy's hand while her mind raced. "I don't know who can treat him," she said, confused. Weren't Cat and Max supposed to be in hiding? There was only one doctor who knew about Cat. "Dr. Lott, maybe?" Amy said. She was still unsure if that was the right decision, but Oliver was busy saving Sophia.

"Does he have a teleport pad?" Cat asked.

"I dunno," Amy said. She looked at the teleport controls and the destination map. "Yes, he does," she finally said. "And it's in range."

"Send us there," Cat said, moving towards the chop-jet teleport pad. She looked at Seb and added, "Wait for mommy."

Amy set the coordinates and they were on their way.

With Cat and Max gone, the displays that showed their Mafdet feed went dark, then quickly picked up the first available broadcast channel. A news segment was playing.

"Come on, Seb," she said to the boy. He was quiet, scared of what was happening around him. "It's okay," she added. She wiped the dirt off his face with her clothes, then picked him up and hugged him as she sat down. With nothing else to do but wait, Amy looked up at the news.

"One hundred people were found hiding in the forest, threatening the local population," the anchor said. Amy sat up. The display showed a man she knew well. It was, Richard, her uncle, the chief of the Free people she'd protected. "The leaders of this group are being charged with numerous kidnappings, robberies, and murders," the anchor continued. "The entire list of accusations against them will be known in upcoming days."

*The fucker had promised!* Amy grabbed the phone and called Conway.

Oliver picked up the phone and Amy immediately screamed in his ear. "Ya fucking promised!"

"What's wrong, Amy?" he replied calmly, but her tone of voice was worrying.

"Ya promised ya'd never do anything to ma people! That ya'd leave them alone!"

"What's happening?"

"Ya sent fucking Sābanto and destroyed them!" she accused.

Oliver opened his mouth to reply and say that he hadn't, but Greyson spoke. "It was me."

"What did you do that for?" Oliver asked and put Amy on speakerphone.

"I knew ya weak point, Amy," Greyson said and drank again from the bottle. "I watched ya buy medicines and fuel, then disappear with the chop-jet. I followed ya and found them. I destroyed something ya loved, like ya destroyed me and Julia."

"The lives of a hundred people for ya insecure bitch?" Amy asked.

"She meant everything to me," Greyson replied.

"What's with you and Leo?" Oliver asked.

"Ya praised her for not listening to me." Greyson looked at the phone in Oliver's hand and pointed at it with his finger. "Ya gave her a newer gun and gave her work behind my back. Everyone noticed how close ya kept her. Everyone! Ya were pushing me out of ma duties, and replacing me with her. Leo at least respected me for who I am."

"I gave you a chance to fix what you'd done," Oliver said. "You worked hard to regain my trust."

"Just to keep ya off ma trail," Greyson said and smirked.

"What did you tell Leo?" Oliver asked.

"That they can destroy ya through Sophia." Greyson laughed. "If yer worried about Lott or the island, that's of no interest to me. I didn't tell him about Mafdet either. I wouldn't put Cat in danger. She isn't like ya."

"Where's Sophia?" Oliver asked. He was sick of Greyson's grievances. He'd heard enough. The kid was mad at everyone except himself.

"There was something that ya didn't account for in your plan," Greyson said. He watched Oliver adjust the gun in his hand. "Go ahead. I knew the consequences, but what kinda life is there for me without respect and without Julia."

Greyson put his hand into a coat pocket and took out a pack of cigarettes and matches. He looked around him as he put the cigarette into his mouth. He lit the match and gazed straight into Oliver's eyes. "Ya never gonna find ya Sophia."

"No!" Oliver screamed as Greyson tossed the burning match towards the cabin.

The pressure wave that followed the blast blew the windows out, sending pieces of glass and debris towards Oliver, who turned away from Greyson and covered his face. Once the rush of air and debris had passed he looked back and assessed the damage. His ears were ringing, but otherwise he was fine. The blast inside the cabin hadn't been powerful enough to destroy the building structure, but Greyson was lying face down in the mud. Oliver ran up to him and checked his pulse. It was weak. He turned Greyson over. There was blood on his lips and a puddle of it was already forming underneath the kid's heavy body. Greyson had been standing too close to the cabin and the shockwave had thrown him off his feet.

Oliver looked at the cabin again. There was fire inside, either from the blast itself or because the embers from the fireplace had ignited the dry floorboards.

"Violet!" Mike shouted from where he was tied up. "She's in the cellar."

Oliver ran inside.

# 26

VIOLET HEARD NOISES IN the cabin above her. Someone new was there, and it wasn't Leo. Mike talked with the person for some time. Violet couldn't hear the conversation. Later there was some shouting, but it was muffled and coming from somewhere outside. It must have happened outside since there was no creaking of floorboards. Then there was an explosion, and Violet and Mrs. Conway fell to the ground, covering their heads. Dust and gravel showered them through the floorboards, but they were unharmed. Violet scanned the dark cellar. Nothing had changed. The cabin was quiet. Violet sat down again and buried her head in her hands.

"Can you smell it?" Sophia asked.

Violet brought her head up and faced her, expecting darkness, however a faint yellow light traced Sophia's perfect face. Her hair slowly moved as though there was a slight breeze in the damp basement. Violet inhaled deeply. Something was burning.

The only exit was the hatch right above them. They ran up the steep stairs and tried to bring the hatch up, but it wouldn't budge.

"Help!" Sophia shouted.

Violet ran back down and scanned for something she could use to break the door. The basement was brighter now and Violet could see the contours of everything inside. She noticed a long metal rod she hadn't seen earlier. She took it out from between pieces of wood and rusting buckets, and ran back up to Sophia. They wedged it between the floor and the hatch and used it as leverage. It moved a little, but not enough for it to open. The sofa that sat on top of it was heavy.

"Help!" they shouted together.

The fire got closer and bigger. They heard strange cracking noises above them. Soon the fire would be roaring, and no one would hear them.

All of a sudden, there was a loud noise and the hatch opened from the top. Violet gasped seeing Oliver's face peering down at them. Her throat tightened and she felt a heavy weight placed on her slumped shoulders. Was she delusional thinking that it was Mike changing his mind and opening the hatch?

Sophia left the basement first and Oliver covered her with his arms. They quickly disappeared from Violet's view. When she ascended the wooden stairs, she couldn't see which way Oliver and Sophia had gone. All around there was fire, unbearable heat and smoke that choked her and burned her lungs. She coughed trying to catch her breath. Violet was disoriented, but the thought of Seb brought her back. The exit was that way. She ran towards it, avoiding any obstacles on the floor. If she fell down, she wouldn't get up again. Violet got outside and stopped a safe distance away from the cabin. She was panting, sucking the cool air and oxygen into her lungs.

Violet brought her head up and glanced at Oliver and his wife. Sophia sat on a log by the forest in Oliver's embrace while he carefully gave her some water. He stroked her hair and kissed her forehead.

Behind Violet, the cabin wasn't fully burning yet, but the fire had overtaken a large portion of it. A cloud of dark smoke billowed above. There was no way to extinguish the fire and save the place. The only water nearby was in the slow-moving creek. It was supposed to have been their forever home. Her, Seb, and Mike, reunited and never apart again.

Violet scanned her surroundings in panic. Her heart pounded in her chest. She was safe now, but Seb was still missing. Through a break in the smoke, she saw a large vessel behind the cabin. Its door stood open. On the steps was a young woman holding her son's hand.

"Seb!" Violet shouted and ran towards him. Her child wiggled his hand free and ran in her direction. They embraced each other. "Mommy's here," she told him. Her vision was blurred with tears at seeing him unharmed. Besides a few new scratches and some dirt on his face, which someone had sloppily tried to wash off, he seemed fine. Violet kissed her son's cheeks and hugged him again. She held him for a long time, big tears rolling down her cheeks. "I'll never let ya go," she whispered to him. Never again. She'd never let Seb out of her sight.

Oliver led Sophia into the chop-jet. He sat her in one of the chairs and found a soft blanket in the overhead compartment. He covered her with it, making sure she was warm and comfortable.

"Thank you," she said. She was visibly shaken.

"I'm glad you're okay," he said, tucking the blanket around her.

"How's Matthew?" she asked.

"He misses you and can't wait for you to get home." He smiled and kissed her forehead. "We'll be leaving soon."

Sophia smiled back.

"Where's Greyson?" Amy asked.

Oliver shook his head from side to side. "He didn't make it," he said. Oliver glanced at the cabin. It was still burning.

"Anything we can do for ma village?" Amy asked.

"I don't know. I doubt they can be spared from Sābanto." There was no sense giving her false hope.

Oliver could look into lowering the sentence or assisting with a legal case for the village chief, but there was nothing he could do to have them set free again. He had no such powers.

"What are we doing with that man?" Amy asked, pointing at the tree in the distance.

Violet's brother was still tied up to a tree, sitting in cold.

"He was complicit in kidnapping," said Oliver. "He'll face a trial."

"What's the punishment, sir?" Violet asked.

Oliver had forgotten that the girl was even there. He turned towards her. Violet sat motionless with her head hung low, unnoticed on the side of the chop-jet cabin and holding Seb close to her. Oliver might've felt something for her once, but too much time had passed. There was nothing connecting them anymore. "Minimum sentence is ten years," he said. "But they'll also charge him with illegal occupation of the property and assault. I'm guessing at least twenty years in jail."

"Anything I can do?" Violet asked.

"No," Oliver said and shook his head. "Kidnapping is a very serious offense." Violet lowered her head. "He's lucky he didn't harm Sophia," he added. "Otherwise, he'd be facing death."

"Can I talk to him?" Violet raised her head and looked at Oliver, who nodded and gestured towards the exit of the chop-jet.

"Wait for me here," Violet told Seb and walked out of the vessel.

It was already getting dark, and the temperature was dropping. It would probably frost overnight again. Violet hugged herself. She didn't want to keep anyone waiting for too long. Oliver wanted to be off soon.

"Sis!" Mike saw her walking towards him. "Grab that sharp wood, there."

Violet turned her eyes to where he pointed, bent over, and picked it up. She walked up to him and squatted beside him in the mud.

"They say ya gonna get twenty years," Violet whispered. It was a long time for someone so young. He wasn't even twenty yet.

"Free me," Mike urged. "Use that wood and cut the rope."

"I can't," she said.

"Don't listen to them."

"Ya left me and Seb in Riverlea with nothing to live on, but I forgave ya," Violet said. "I forgave the beatings I got from ya, but ya ain't a good man, Mike. Ya sold me to ya friend!" She slowly scanned the woods and the cabin that was still burning. "When ya took us out of Sābanto, I thought ya grew up and that ya realized we needed to stick together. I worked hard making this cabin our new forever home."

"It was supposed to be our home," he said, looking at the still-burning structure. "We can find another place."

"What for?" Violet asked. "So that ya hurt me again? So ya put Seb in danger?"

"I tried to persuade Leo—" he said.

"Lies. The man controlled ya!"

"Ya blame me for all this," he said. "Why don't ya blame that rich dick that fucked ya?"

"Ya have no right," she said. "He saved us today. He saved Seb, without even knowing Seb was his."

"Tell him!" Mike ordered.

"Why?" Violet asked.

"Look at his wife and her clothes. Look at the jewelry she's wearing. Don't ya want any of that?"

Violet shook her head. "All I wanted was to have ma little brother back."

"Look at ya, Violet. That man did harm ya and all ya can do is blame me. If ya won't tell him about the kid, then I'll do it. I'll tell everyone who he is."

"Ya going to jail, Mike," Violet said.

"That won't stop me," he said. "Everyone in the jail will know what kinda fucking person he is. Then it'll get out from there and everyone will know"

Oliver wasn't supposed to know about Seb being his son. Those were the terms Mrs. Conway had insisted upon, and Violet didn't take that threat lightly. She didn't know what the consequences would be, but the woman wouldn't be happy if Oliver found out.

"Remember mama?" Violet asked. "Remember what she said?"

"Don't bring mama into this!"

"Mama taught us to care for each other. Our parents wanted us to be good people, Mike," Violet said.

"Did they?" he said. "I don't remember. I was too young when they died. Ya just keep telling me about them and ya never tell the truth."

"What do ya mean?"

"They wanted us to fight, Violet," he said. "Fight to be someone in this world."

"Yes," Violet said. "They wanted us to be strong, to be good people and not fall for the empty promises of power or money."

"I don't see it like ya do."

"Mike, please," Violet begged. It might be the last moment they had together. Soon the authorities would be here to take Mike away. She and Seb would probably be sent back to Sābanto. No one had saved her job in the kitchen for her. Violet might not even end up in the same compound. She'd have to start over from the beginning, find her place and make new friends for herself and for Seb.

"I won't stop 'til I destroy that man." He pointed with his chin towards the chop-jet.

"Ya won't," Violet said.

"I promise ya, I will!"

"No, Mike," Violet said. "I'm sorry."

She raised the piece of wood she had in her hand and stabbed Mike with it. The wood lodged itself in the side of his neck. A large amount of blood gushed from the wound.

"I need to protect Seb," Violet said. Mike tried to talk, but the wound in his neck made it too hard for him to make any sound. He kept looking at her, his eyes filled with terror. "Seb's secret stays with me." Violet got up and turned her back on Mike.

She noticed the monkey, Seb's toy, lying dirty in the mud. Boots had trampled it. She bent over to pick it up. She could wash it. Seb loved this stuffed animal and he'd be asking about his Mo-kee. But she steadied her resolve and left it where it was. It'd only bring bad memories.

She turned back to her brother and took one last look at him. He sat under the tree, motionless, dying without making any noise. "Ya never gonna hurt us again, Mike," she said. "Goodbye." She turned around and walked away. Her eyes filled with tears over what she had just done.

# 27

THE FIRST TIME IVY had been at the Château de la Belle Cascade, she hadn't had a chance to enjoy the full experience of the place. This time, she had planned to try everything and taken Taylor with her to help him become accustomed to being a citizen. She wouldn't let him do it alone. Ivy would guide him.

They went hiking up the mountains to the sapphire lake and enjoyed a chef-prepared picnic, then warmed up in the hot tub back at the chateau with champagne, embracing each other and gazing at the snow-covered peaks. The dinner, which they ate in private, was a feast with the best selection of seafood and meats the kitchen had available. After the meal, they ventured downstairs to join the other guests in some casual games. A few rounds of roulette and they would retire to their suite and tango between the warm sheets.

They sat at the bar and Ivy was in the process of explaining one of the games to Taylor when Liam appeared, taking the stool to her right. She turned towards him.

"What are you doing here?" Liam asked in a harsh tone. He stared at her with cold, narrowed eyes, his lips curled in a condescending sneer.

Taylor immediately stood up in his seat. "The lady doesn't appreciate ya company, sir."

Ivy brought her hand up and Taylor sat down. The bartender turned his back to them, busying himself with something.

"I wasn't expecting you here, either," Ivy replied to Liam with a small smile. She inhaled a cigarette through her cigarette holder. "How is your cheek healing?" Of course it was fine. He wouldn't be parading around with visible injuries. People would ask questions. How had the lady's nails ended up on his face?

"I think you should leave," he said. "And take your lover with you." He glanced at Taylor who looked eager to jump up from his seat again.

"Jealous?" Ivy said and looked around. The game room was busy this evening. There were maybe three dozen guests inside and everyone knew that something had happened between the two of them. Gossip and rumors were a pastime for many. At the craps table, she noticed Sarai sitting beside Calista. The younger of the sisters was looking in Ivy's direction open-mouthed. This conversation would only bring trouble. Ivy turned back to Liam.

Liam wrinkled his nose. "My father didn't fund this casino to cater to freaks like you."

"That was your father's accomplishment, not yours," Ivy replied. "I have yet to hear of one of your own." There were rumors that the mines were operating without any oversight from Liam. The managers had trouble getting ahold of him when important decisions had to be made.

Liam sneered. "And what do you know about running a casino? You can't even play."

"I've been practicing," Ivy said with a small smile. "Poker."

"Wanna test your skills?" Liam asked. He had a wide grin on his face.

Ivy smiled. One game wouldn't hurt, would it? Liam would be humiliated in front of everyone if she won and she had nothing to lose.

Liam immediately jumped up from his seat and walked away without waiting for her reply. Ivy followed Liam with her eyes as he approached a free poker table. He signaled one of the staff members to prepare the game.

Ivy got up from her seat.

"Not sure it's a good idea," Taylor said quietly behind her.

She turned to him and smiled. "It isn't," she said. She should've told Liam no while she was still in a position of strength. Her rejection would make him furious. A lot of movers and shakers had witnessed the exchange. Backing out now would look like chickening out, and that would make Liam the winner.

She walked to the table. Her high heels clicked rhythmically against the hardwood floor as she approached. The last time Ivy had been in this room, she'd worn a simple dress, but today she was turning heads. She wore a three-quarter-length black evening gown with a frilled hem. A side slit exposed her left leg up to her hip and the lace top revealed her bare shoulders. She held her cigarette in a holder in her right hand and in her left she held her silver clutch that matched her elaborate diamond earrings.

She sat down at one of the places at the table and put her purse on top of it.

"Ten thousand," Liam called the buy-in. "No limit."

Ivy acknowledged his words with a small nod. Ten thousand tickets' worth of chips was provided to her. There were some hushed conversations behind Ivy's back, others deciding whether or not to join the game. The buy-in was high, but the promised reward was tempting. It could be anyone's lucky day.

Liam got up and approached Calista and Sarai. They spoke to each other in whispers. Calista eventually agreed to join them at the table with a nod. She came over, her head held high, and sat down in one of the empty seats. She glanced at Ivy and smirked. Sarai trailed behind her and slumped into one of the chairs at the table, avoiding eye contact with others. Stacks of chips representing ten thousand tickets each appeared in front of them.

The first hand Ivy got wasn't good so she didn't bet aggressively. The flop, the first three community cards, and turn, the fourth community card, didn't give Ivy any advantages. When the last card, the river, was displayed, she had lost the hand.

The next few hands weren't great for Ivy either. She won only once, while Liam's stack of chips only seemed to grow. What were her chances of beating Liam? The room suddenly felt warmer, drying her lips. Only fifty-two cards, but the combinations seemed endless. What had her teacher said? *Watch what others are doing. It's not just about the cards. Feel it. Be part of the game.*

Sarai was more animated now, looking around, glancing at everyone at the table, including Ivy. She was enjoying the game. Calista seemed nervous. She grabbed a chip off the stack and played with it. Liam looked relaxed sipping his whisky, but he folded at the first opportunity and Calista won the hand with a pair of sevens and ace high. He also ordered and paid for a fruity drink for Ivy, who hadn't asked for it. She slid it away from her and asked the waiter for a glass of water instead.

Ivy examined the back of the two cards she received from the dealer on the next hand. She recognized one by a scratch on the back of the card. She must have had it in an earlier hand. A king. She lifted the corner of the card and peeked at it. Yes. A king, but of a different color.

"I'd like to request a fresh deck," she said to the dealer before the next hand started.

She heard people whispering behind her.

"As you wish, ma'am," the dealer replied.

Liam stared at Ivy gravely. "Something wrong with your cards?" he asked.

"As a matter of fact," she replied, "there's something wrong with the kings."

The dealer collected the cards from the table and picked a fresh deck, opened it in front of everyone, and dealt a new hand with it.

Liam tapped his finger on the back of one of his cards in front of him, waiting for the flop. The change of decks had clearly made him nervous. Calista folded on her turn, but Ivy had to fold as well. Her cards were too weak to win anything. The river showed up and Liam won with two pairs, ace high.

The man to Ivy's right stood up. "That's it for me," he said. He no longer had any chips in front of him. He'd put his last ones into the middle, and the dealer moved them towards Liam.

The next few hands came and went with some small wins for Ivy. The cigarette in her holder was finished, but she didn't bother replacing it. There was already a ton of cigarette haze in the room, but it wasn't enough to conceal Calista and Liam's glances at each other. Nor that the two of them had the largest stacks.

The number of people at the table started to thin out. Those who didn't want to increase their bets further left the game, minimizing their losses.

On the next hand, the man to Ivy's left bid high, pushing the rest of his chips into the middle of the table. Calista looked nervous again as she tried to decide on her next move. She played with her chips. Liam folded confidently before the River was shown. Calista won the hand again with three fours and an ace.

From the total of eight people who had initially sat at the table, only four remained. Ivy was left in the company of Liam and the Tari sisters. Calista once again played with her chips. Was she signaling to Liam to fold again to take advantage of the cards in her hand? Whenever Calista fidgeted with her chips, Liam behaved strangely, raising aggressively or folding unexpectedly.

As Ivy predicted, Liam increased his bet, but folded when the river was shown.

"What do you have, Calista? Is that an ace?" Ivy said before Calista could reveal her cards. She folded instead, her cheeks red. When the hand was over, she collected her chips and stormed off. Sarai sat with her head low, avoiding eye contact with Ivy. Was she laughing at her sister being caught cheating?

"Were Calista and Liam . . ." a lady behind Ivy whispered. "Disgraceful." Ivy didn't hear whether or not anyone answered her question.

On the flop of the next hand, Ivy had a pair of nines. She could win with that if Liam and Sarai had nothing, but Liam bet aggressively. Ivy looked at the stack of chips in front of her. She had a little more than what she started with. It was hard to count her opponents' chips. Sarai's stack was similar to hers, but Liam had four times the amount. The turn brought Ivy a third nine to add to her pair. Three of a kind. It was a good hand. Both Sarai and Liam were betting heavily, but the odds either of them had better hands were quite low.

Ivy lifted her head and met Sarai's eyes. It was brief, hard to notice, but her gaze hung a little too long. She was telling Ivy something, but what? Was it intimidation? Ivy wouldn't fold because Sarai wanted her to. Not when she finally had a fairly good hand.

The river showed up and Sarai was the first one to make a move. She hesitated, biting her lip. She took one more glance at Ivy, then firmly said, "All in!" Sarai pushed all of her chips into the middle of the table. Liam glanced at her, slowly counted his chips to match her bet, and placed them in the middle. He then turned to Ivy and sneered.

They were working together, squeezing her out. If she wanted to stay in the game, she'd have to match Sarai's bet. She'd need to bet almost all of her remaining chips. There was still a chance that Sarai had something higher than three of a kind. Ivy eyed Sarai sitting opposite the table and Sarai glanced back, her eyes shining. The Tari sister was up to something.

Ivy matched Sarai's bet. Only a few chips remained in front of her. *They are bluffing,* Ivy repeated to herself. They had to be.

The last betting round was over and Liam immediately turned his cards over. He had a low pair of fives, queen high. Ivy turned her cards anxiously over as well and showed her nines, three of a kind, but there was muttering in the audience. Ivy gazed at Sarai who hadn't shown her cards yet, but both Ivy and Liam's cards were clearly visible. They were too eager to learn who had won and ignored Sarai, who was supposed to show her cards first. Everyone looked at Sarai, who wasn't moving. She focused her eyes on Ivy again for a moment, then, with a straight face, said "Fold."

"Bitch!" Liam immediately leaned over towards Sarai. "I know you have the winning hand! Why did you fold?" He reached for her cards, but she slapped her hand down on them with a thump, staring him down.

One of the onlookers gasped. "Did he really just do that?" someone said rather loudly.

Liam's face was red. He breathed heavily as he sat back down. He unbuttoned the top of his shirt violently and took a large gulp of his drink. He nodded to the dealer that he was ready for the next hand.

All of the chips in the middle of the table were now being pushed towards Ivy. She stared at Sarai, who got up from her seat, looking relaxed with a small smile on her lips. The sister unhurriedly stepped away and mingled with the crowd of onlookers.

It was just Ivy and Liam left at the table now, playing against each other. The room was eerily quiet. All the other games finished. Everyone stood close to the poker table where all the action was, not wanting to miss the final hand.

Ivy started with a small blind as she had the dealer button. She put a small number of chips into the middle. Liam posted the big blind, doubling her bet.

The first two cards Ivy got were an ace and a queen of hearts. A good hand. Liam put in a larger bet and Ivy matched it.

The flop, an eight of spades, an ace of clubs, and an eight of clubs. Two pairs with ace high. There was a chance Liam had an eight. Three of a kind would lose her the game. The odds, however, were in her favor. Liam bet more and Ivy had no reason to fold. She matched his bet.

Turn. An eight of diamonds. Another round of bets. A quarter of Liam's chips were now in the middle of the felt. Ivy smiled at him, then swallowed silently. A call that fast and that aggressive had to be a bluff. Right? She had a full house, aces and eights. She had the winning hand. He couldn't possibly have four of a kind, could he? Ivy matched Liam's bet again.

River. An ace of diamonds. Liam stirred in his seat. "All in! And . . ." His face was glowing and his eyes shone, even though he wasn't physically smiling. He took a small statue out of his pocket. It was made of blackwood and looked like his beloved horse, Eclipse. The atmosphere in the room changed and everyone gasped in surprise at the amount of the bet, and the player's confidence. Liam put it beside the pile of chips in the middle of the table.

"What's that worth?" a woman asked behind Ivy.

"A million," another woman replied. More whispers erupted.

"What are you betting?" Liam asked Ivy.

Full house, now ace high. Was this really happening? Ivy looked up and scanned the room. Everyone's eyes were on her. They were waiting for her to make her bet, an equal one. Ivy couldn't back down now, she'd be humiliated.

There was only one thing that she had that was equal to the horse in value. Ivy picked up her clutch from the table and opened it. She took out a small golden key from her purse and put it on the table beside the chips. "The key to the Leggett factory in Covedale," she said.

She regretted it instantly.

A hushed murmur went through the crowd.

Ivy had only been thirteen when she'd first stepped into the Leggett factory's dim hall. Women and other girls had sat bent over their desks, arranged in straight rows. The sound of the sewing machines filled every inch of the space. That day she had learned to sew. With the strength of both her legs, she'd pressed the large, heavy pedal, setting the sewing machine in motion. Her small hands felt the smooth fabric as it glided between her fingers and disappeared underneath the fast-moving needle. Sewing had come naturally to her.

The factory hadn't just been hard work, it had also been smiles. There were hidden laughs when someone made a joke about their supervisor, risking being fired. On paydays, after their shifts, Ivy would go with the other young girls to the Covedale market for some kettle corn. She remembered the wild rose liquor, sweet on her tongue during the games of dominos Ivy occasionally played on her days off. So many memories, and they all had a special place in her heart.

What had she done? There was a lump in her throat as she swallowed. Mark. The one and only person she had truly loved. How could she do this to him? The factory had been his gift to her. A gift he'd given her on his deathbed. Leaving here in shame would be the least of her problems. Living in Covedale would be out of the question. She wouldn't have the strength to watch the factory workers walking to work each morning. Ivy would have to sell her house and move somewhere else, but where? There was no place on the face of the earth for someone like her. How would she ever forgive herself?

Folding was no longer an option. The only thing that could save her now was winning, but the cramps in her stomach told her that it wouldn't happen. Her heart raced. Cold sweat left her body through every pore. "I call," she said. It was like ripping off a bandage.

Liam smiled widely and immediately showed his cards. An ace and a six of spades. Ivy released the breath she'd been holding in.

The audience discussed the hand with each other.

"Full house. Ace high," the dealer announced.

"Liam has won," someone in the audience said.

"She could have four of a kind," another voice added.

"No chance," a man commented.

Ivy glanced at Liam's hand again on the table. He didn't have an eight. She swallowed and closed her eyes for a moment feeling her tense body relaxing. *He did not have an eight.* Her factory in Covedale was safe. With trembling hands, she slowly turned her own cards over. The corners of her mouth lifted in a small smile. "Full house. Ace high," the dealer announced with no emotion in his voice. "It's a tie." He immediately busied himself splitting the pile of chips into two equal groups.

"Unbelievable!" someone shouted.

"One in a million," another voice added.

"One of them was cheating," an annoyed woman said.

Liam jumped up from his seat. "Deal again!" he shouted at the dealer. A vein twitched on his neck. "We're playing again!"

"No, we're not." Ivy got up from her seat. The house would split the money and put it in her account. She didn't wait for the dealer to finish his job. She grabbed the golden key from the table. "Keep the horse," she said to Liam. She put the key in her clutch and smiled at him.

Ivy turned her eyes to Taylor. There was a look of relief on his face. It hadn't been a good idea to play, and they were both glad it was all over.

Liam stepped towards Ivy threateningly. "Sit down! We're not done," he ordered.

A murmur erupted in the room. "Oh, no!" a lady in the crowd gasped.

"What is he doing?" someone else added.

Another patron stepped closer to the table, placing himself between Ivy and Liam. "Let's have a drink," he said to Liam, and steered him towards the bar.

Taylor stepped forward as well to shield Ivy in case Liam tried something stupid.

"What a shame!" a lady commented at the scene. "So disrespectful."

Ivy smiled at Liam. He looked pathetic with his red face and messy hair. "Goodnight," she said and turned away from him. If Liam replied, she didn't hear him.

The crowd moved away from the table. The game was over and so was the excitement. Someone commented on the late hour.

Ivy caught a glimpse of Sarai between the guests. Sarai had a full smile on her face, happy about Liam being shamed. Ivy then turned back to Taylor and hung her arm on his elbow. Ivy welcomed the support as her legs hadn't yet regained their strength. She'd been a fool to put Leggett on the line, but it was safe now. Ivy would never again jeopardize anything that was so dear to her, no matter how much pressure there was.

# 28

CAT WATCHED THE MONITORS around Max's bed. *Why did she insist on staying and watching over Max at the clinic?* she wondered. He was still unconscious. Dr. Lott said that he might sleep for some time, but he assured her that the patient would make it. Max needed to rest and recover. Some of his internal organs were damaged, as she'd suspected, but it was mostly soft tissue injury that would heal with time. The doctor was confident that Max would make a full recovery.

Initially, the clinic wanted Cat out of the windowless room. They told her to go home, but she insisted on staying. She had no home besides the empty base, and now Max wasn't even there to keep her company. The staff eventually let her stay after telling her what to do in the event any of the monitors made any noise.

She finished her small stroll around the room and sat back down on the hard, uncomfortable stool beside the bed. She grabbed Max's hand in hers. He was warm.

Max had risked his life for her and Seb. Cat didn't know what had motivated him to do so, but without his intervention, Leo might not have been distracted and he could've seriously harmed Seb or even killed him.

She glanced at Max's face as he laid there motionless. Why had she saved him? He hadn't been able to walk on his own. She'd practically carried him to the chop-jet. She hadn't wanted him to die. A natural human reaction, sure, but why was she worried that his condition might worsen and that she might not be there?

The information that Mafdet couldn't be removed had been a big blow to her. She'd cried for hours. Cat had lived in hope that once she delivered the device to Oliver, she'd be able to go her own way. Start a new life. That was all she'd wanted, even if it meant going back to Sābanto.

Cat's mind raced, trying to make sense of her life. She watched one of the monitors beside the bed as it produced a line that spiked with each beat of Max's heart.

It was the perfect time to ditch Max, but part of her didn't want to. It felt natural to her to stay here. Was it fear driving this? She feared waking up alone in the middle of the night, eating her meals alone while watching the news on a display. She imagined herself sitting up with a bottle of cheap wine or whisky and drinking herself to sleep. There would be no one there to stop her.

That was the reason she had stayed for so many years with Tom. She'd been a coward not to leave him even though he'd hurt her over and over again. She should've left and never looked back. Why wasn't she doing that now? She was repeating the same mistakes she'd made in the past. Max was no different. A part of her wanted to leave; the door was open, and no one was keeping her there, but she weren't moving.

Cat kept Max's hand in hers as she lay her head down, pressing her cheek into the back of his hand. She closed her eyes. She was exhausted.

Cat is lying on her bed in a small room at Sābanto. It's dark, except for a faint light seeping through the window from the lamp outside. She can't sleep. Her mind wanders, replaying scenes from the past. Cat thinks of Tom, Riverlea, and Violet. She listens to the quietness of the house and hugs her pillow closer to her chest. She buries her face in it. It doesn't have the smell she expects, but she imagines it does—that it smells of Max. Cat feels his invisible arms embracing her. She wishes he was here with her. Somehow the heat of his body transfers through the pillow, warming her up. She feels safe and at peace as she drifts off to sleep.

A faint movement under her cheek woke Cat up. She didn't know how long she'd been asleep, but her neck was stiff. She brought her head up and looked at Max. He was awake and had his familiar grin again. Cat smiled at him, got up from the stool, and stood above him.

She could see him better that way, and he wouldn't have to strain his eyes looking at her.

He was trying to say something.

"Doctor said you need a rest," she said. "And that you'll be fine."

The nurse told her she could wet his lips, so she went to the sink on the side of the room and wetted a prepared towel with cold water from the tap.

"The boy?" Max asked. His voice was a little raspy.

"Not a scratch, but that was foolish of you to step out like that. Leo almost killed you." She returned to his bed, cleaned his lips with the wet cloth, as she talked, and wiped his face.

Max thanked her. "Leo was impatient. He would've killed that kid."

"You saved Seb's life. I don't know how to repay you." Cat smiled.

"I'm sorry for everything I did wrong—" Max said, but Cat bent over him and pressed her lips against his.

"Save your strength," she said. "I've been thinking about us. My answer is yes." Cat gazed into his dark eyes without saying another word as his face brightened. She then kissed him again.


Sophia cuddled beside Oliver on the sofa upstairs, feeling his warmth. "I'm glad to be home," she said. She kissed him, then grabbed his hand and looked down at it. "I've been hard on you lately. I'm sorry," she said. "So much has changed, and I was confused."

"No need to be sorry." He stroked her hair.

"When I was in the cabin, tied up for the night," Sophia continued. "I had time to think. I didn't know if I'd survive to see Matthew again." She pressed his hand to her chest. "But I knew you'd come and save me."

"You know I love you," Oliver said.

Sophia smiled shyly. "Yes," she said. She put his hand down and gazed at it again, massaging his palm.

There was something from that day at the cabin that Sophia was afraid to bring up. She couldn't explain what she'd seen. When Oliver had opened the hatch to the cellar to rescue her, she hadn't recognized him at first. Her hair had stood on end at the sight of the face she thought she knew. There was something strange, wild, in his eyes. For a moment she'd thought it was Leo wearing an Oliver mask.

She didn't know who her husband was. Her father had warned her about him, but she hadn't listened. Sophia had never inquired about Oliver's past. It bothered her now and she could no longer ask her father for advice. She couldn't believe what Leo had said about Oliver. It wasn't possible that her husband had killed her father. There had been an autopsy. Doctors had inspected the body. They'd said it was a heart attack. They wouldn't have lied.

She toyed with the ring on his finger. Oliver was different from Leo. He cared too much about everything. He could've killed that young man who had locked her in the basement, but he hadn't. Oliver wanted that man to go to jail. He wasn't a killer. He'd never been fascinated by violence. She would've noticed something like that. Oliver played by the book, but for some reason he hadn't done so with the girl. The girl, Violet, had killed her own brother, and Oliver had spared her from jail. He'd lied to the Sābanto men who were investigating the crime scene and said that it was Greyson who'd killed the girl's brother. Why? Did he still feel something for her? She couldn't push Oliver away anymore. Not into the arms of that whore.

She didn't think letting the crime go unpunished was right. The killer girl should've been paying the price, rotting somewhere in jail. Crossing Oliver about it, however, would be reckless. How would she explain a sudden and unusual interest in the girl's fate, or her lack of trust towards him? She didn't think she ought to present her opinion on the matter. There was no doubt the kid was his. She'd never mistake those large blue eyes, but Oliver had been oblivious to the toddler when he'd seen him. What more could she ask for? If she showed interest, it would make him interested as well. He might ask questions, dig more, and find out the truth. Knowing Violet's secret about her brother's death also gave Sophia leverage over the girl. Something she could use as a threat to keep her out of Oliver's life and make sure she'd never destroy Sophia's family.

"Ruby," Sophia said, pointing at Oliver's ring. "We could replace the dragon's eye with a ruby." Then it wouldn't look so cheap anymore. She looked at him and smiled.

Sarai called Ivy a few days after the game. "Wanna do something?" she asked without much enthusiasm in her voice. "I'm bored, and ordering the servants around has lost its appeal."

Wasn't being bored a good thing? Ivy lay on her back with her legs dangling off the side of the bed. The phone bud was in one of her ears, and a small box which contained a microphone lay on her chest.

"Thank you for your help," Ivy said.

"At the game?" Sarai replied. "Liam and Calista were long overdue for some payback for how they treated you. I apologize. It was shameful of me to allow myself to be dragged into what they were doing. Dumping some chips on you, the ones Liam gave us for the game, was the least I could do."

"Thank you," Ivy repeated.

Sarai had taken a brave step towards breaking out of her sister's control by taking Ivy's side at the game. She was finally able to stand up for herself and had apologized multiple times for taking part in tormenting others. She had spooked the horse together with Calista, which could have killed Ivy. Could Ivy forgive Sarai? The wounds ran deep, and it would take time.

"Liam was mad," Sarai continued. "He and Calista had a shouting match outside of the chateau. All the guests heard them blaming each other." Ivy listened, playing with a strand of her hair. "The news about them colluding spread quickly," Sarai continued. "Calista doesn't speak with anyone or go anywhere anymore. She's locked herself in her room and doesn't even allow the maids in. She barely touches the food they bring her. It's a madhouse here. Everyone's trying to help her, but they know she's been shamed for life. There are rumors that our parents might send her away to one of our properties overseas. Being away from anyone she knows would apparently be good for her."

"How are you dealing with all this?" Ivy asked.

"Me? I'm doing much better," Sarai replied with a small laugh. "I had no clue how much Calista's influence had weighed on me over the years. I'm glad to finally be myself. If I lose any friendships over this, it only means that they were never my friends. They were all Calista's friends."

"Time might help her," Ivy commented. She was feeling a little sorry for Calista.

"I don't know," Sarai replied with a negative tone. "She no longer has a place among the popular crowd. No one's interested in spending time with her. I don't think she'll be invited to parties or dinners anytime soon. Our parents haven't asked me my opinion, but if they do, I'd tell them to send Calista to a convent or something. Speaking of going out and socializing, Mrs. Ouellet is furious."

"Why's that?" Ivy asked.

"The number of visitors to the Château de la Belle Cascade has plummeted, and those that still come don't bother with the games. A rumor spread that the casino was in on marking the cards, because Liam is a co-owner," Sarai said. "She's facing financial problems with her main income disappearing literally overnight. She not only told Liam and Calista never to show their faces at the chateau again, she's also asking Liam for a huge amount of money as compensation for the lost business."

"Stands to reason," Ivy replied and stretched her arms out above her head on the bed.

"Liam is not in a position to pay," Sarai continued. "Coal sales are down. People are turning away from him and finding smaller suppliers. They say he's cheating them on price and quality—"

"His horse is bringing him money," Ivy said.

"Leaving Liam with the horse was brilliant. Did you know that he bought it behind his father's back? Liam couldn't use his own money, 'cause his father would've known. He borrowed it. I don't know from where, but there are rumors Liam was asked to pay everything back in full."

"I don't pity him," Ivy said.

Someone touched her hands and she looked up. Ivy hadn't seen or heard anyone come into the room, but Taylor's eyes were looking at her from above and he was smiling widely. He was wearing the expensive cologne she had bought for him in Clamerton. She smiled back as he massaged her palms. Ivy was glad he never brought up the fact that she'd almost lost the Leggett factory in Covedale. He hadn't criticized her decisions, but had gone with the flow and trusted her judgment.

"And you shouldn't," Sarai said. "He's looking for a buyer for his mines to pay his debts. I think that will ruin him even more, but it might be a choice between money and life. No one knows who else he owes money to. Either way . . . wanna catch a bite in Clamerton sometime?"

"I'd love that," Ivy replied.

"Let me know when you're around," Sarai said. "And say hi to Taylor for me. He seems like a good guy. More up your alley."

"I will," Ivy said and pressed the bottom of the speaker to disconnect. She glanced at Taylor again. "Sarai says hi," Ivy said. She sat up in bed and put away the phone on the nightstand. She then turned her body around to face Taylor who sat beside her. They kissed. Ivy's hand held his cheek, then traveled down to where his heart was. She gently pulled away from his lips. "Sarai said that the Menken mines are up for sale." Ivy smiled. "I think I'll buy them."

Taylor gazed at her, but said nothing.


Cat wanted to convince Violet to stay in Covedale. She was sure someone would have an opening for some cozy position as a maid. Violet, however, had already made up her mind about returning to Sābanto, and Cat, still on the wanted list, asked Amy for help to ensure Violet was assigned to the safest compound. The least she could do for them was give Seb the best chance to grow.

Violet didn't speak much about what had happened in the cabin. Cat sensed that her stay there hadn't been pleasant and didn't press her for details. She couldn't imagine how Violet must have felt after her brother's death. The scar of that moment would never heal. When Cat had met Greyson, he'd seemed like a nice guy. A little confused, maybe, but she would never have believed Greyson would have been capable of murder. She had read him wrong.

Cat peeked outside through the small window of Oliver's chop-jet as Amy landed it in one of the Sābanto compounds. Cat was risking being apprehended, but she had to say goodbye to Violet. She didn't think Sābanto would dare to search Oliver's chop-jet, but she stayed hidden in the vessel while Amy interacted with the compound staff just in case.

Cat turned to Violet. "Are you sure you want to go?" she asked again.

"I can't stay. I gotta go back," Violet said.

"I guess this is it." Cat's eyes became moist. They hugged each other. "Please take care of Seb," Cat said. She bent down to Seb and squeezed him tight. She'd miss him. She'd miss them both.

"I will," Violet said. She looked sad despite the small smile she'd put on. Cat handed her the assignment card for the Sābanto compound. "G3." Violet read it. "A different place."

"They no longer had space in your old compound," Cat lied. She couldn't send her back to the same place. The riots were escalating and it wasn't safe. "I made some arrangements."

"I'll go grab ma things." Violet took Seb's hand and they walked into the other compartment of the chop-jet where they'd left their bags. Cat had gotten some money from Oliver, and with Amy's help she'd purchased some items for Violet and Seb as a goodbye. She'd gotten fresh clothes for both of them and some scented soaps for Violet. She also hadn't forgotten to get some toys for Seb. It was his second birthday and she gave him a tiger plushie to replace the monkey he had lost. Cat couldn't let Violet go back empty-handed.

While Violet was still in the other room getting ready, there was a knock on the door of the chop-jet. Amy walked over and allowed Robert in. The moment he saw Cat, he got angry. He pursed his lips and scowled. "What do ya think you're doing?" he asked bluntly.

"Nice to see you too." Cat walked over and gave him a playful punch on the shoulder. "I don't have much time to explain," she said.

"What do ya want?" His face was close to hers. His fists were tightened.

"First, this meeting never happened," Cat said, which angered Robert even more.

"I don't need more trouble!" Robert fumed. "It's enough ya broke ma nose and almost got me fired."

Oliver had shown Cat Robert's file in Sābanto. She was glad he'd gotten to keep his job. He'd testified he had nothing to do with Cat running away and they'd believed him. The broken nose had helped his case.

"I'm sorry. I didn't want to hurt you, but I had no choice. I did it to protect you." Cat's own words reminded her of Max and how he had justified his own actions to her. Maybe there had been another way, but in the moment she'd had no other ideas. In the end it was for the best. Eventually Robert would see that the pain had been necessary and forgive her.

"Who was that man you ran away with?!"

"That's irrelevant." Cat took a step back.

"Is it? Everything was perfect until he showed up!" He narrowed his eyes.

"Please, I need your help—" Cat said softly.

"Ya kidding me, right? Why would I help ya?" Robert shook his head.

"I'd like to place someone in your protection," Cat said.

"Wait, is that why I got transferred to a bigger box?"

"Is that what they call them now?" Cat laughed. "I need you to keep an eye on someone for me."

"What if I say no?"

"Please?"

"I won't play your stupid game," Robert said.

"Cat. I can go somewhere else." Violet said, coming out of the other room.

Robert noticed Violet and the boy beside her.

"Seb?" he asked. The kid escaped his mother's hand and ran towards Robert. "Hey buddy," he gave the boy a big hug. "Ya've grown."

"You know each other?" Cat asked. She'd never considered that there might be a connection.

Robert picked Seb up in his arms and walked up to Violet. "After I helped ya both off that truck last summer, I looked for ya, but I couldn't find ya. I forgot which compound I saw ya at. The registry had no one named Violet with a child. I thought I'd never see ya again."

Violet stood speechless. Cat came behind Robert, saving her from answering. She put a hand on his shoulder. "Should I assume that you've changed your mind?"

"I'll take care of them." Robert looked at Violet. "If they want, of course."

Violet didn't look fully convinced, but she nodded. Robert bent over and grabbed Violet's bags from the floor. He then looked at Cat with cold eyes. She didn't hold it against him that he wasn't ready to forgive her. She would've been equally mad in his place.

There was not much time left. Cat had to be on her way soon, back to the base, but she couldn't leave Violet in Robert's protection unless she got one more hug from her. "I'll miss you," Cat said. "Everything will be fine. No one will hurt you anymore."

Cat watched them leaving the chop-jet. Violet gave her a last look behind her shoulder and smiled shyly. "Bye Violet," Cat mouthed without saying it out loud. It would be too dangerous to visit Violet and Seb in the future. It was their last goodbye. Cat wiped a tear from her cheek with the back of her hand.

Anita scanned The Jungle in search of anything unusual. Flashing lights were shining various colors at a large group of people swaying to the beats of bass-heavy music. The long bar to her right had all its seats occupied by girls and women in dresses that bared their shoulders and neatly dressed men of different ages.

Anita had no idea why she'd accepted the invitation to join some of her friends from Clamerton for a night out. They were talking about their recent stay in a resort by the warm, crystal-clear waters of the Mediterranean, shouting at each other over the music, but only a few words reached Anita. She was in her own world, disconnected from the others. The local clubs and restaurants were of no interest to her. They only offered cheap entertainment, deafening music, and naked waitresses.

Anita's phone buzzed in her pocket. She took it out and glanced at the display. There was a new text from a number she didn't recognize. *Call me. I have a story for you.* She read.

"I'll be outside," Anita said to her friends, but they didn't hear her. She got up and followed the exit sign on the wall, pushing the heavy door open.

She stepped outside into an empty alley and shivered from the cold air against her skin. The door closed behind her, separating her from the loud music. She called the number.

"I hope you remember me. It's Oliver Conway," the person on the other side of the phone said. Oliver Conway. The last man she'd expected to hear from.

"What do you want?"

"I might have a story for you," he said.

A story. Oliver Conway had a story. She found it amusing.

"How do you know what I'm looking for?" Anita asked.

"You know about the list—"

"That's not a story."

"There's more to it," Conway said.

A young man opened the club door behind her and exited. Anita followed him with her eyes as he walked away. She waited until he was out of earshot before she continued the conversation.

"And?"

"If you help me get this on air, I'll give you exclusive access to the information."

Anita laughed. "I don't think you have anything that would interest me, and even if you did, what makes you think I'll agree?"

"If your contempt for Menken is stronger than your prejudice against me, I think you will." Anita opened her mouth to say something in reply, but Conway added, "Call me when you make up your mind." The phone clicked, indicating the end of the conversation.

Anita looked around. The alley was deserted. A shiver went through her from the cold dampness of the air. She turned towards the exit door. There was no handle on it or a way of getting back in. She hugged herself, turned left, and walked towards the main entrance to The Jungle.

Anita had come to Clamerton following a story about Conway and Riverlea, and she'd achieved nothing. She'd chased a ghost, something that either wasn't there or that she couldn't get a grip on. Each turn brought her to yet another dead end. Her career was stagnant and the story she was currently working on was far from being ready. It lacked a connection to the average citizen, which made it irrelevant and unimportant. No one would care about it in its current state. She needed something that would ignite the story.

Anita stopped at the end of the alley before she walked out onto the street. She looked at the lights reflecting off the surface of the wet pavement.

She couldn't accept the story from Conway. He didn't do anything for free. There was something in it for him. Whatever the story was, it was furthering his agenda which was . . . what? What was he up to? Even though she thought she had investigated the man as thoroughly as possible, she still had no answer to this question. It felt obvious that there was a catch, a consequence of which she wouldn't learn until it was too late. She didn't want to be complicit in any of his crimes. She would never forgive herself for accepting such an offer. 'No' was the only answer she should give him.

On the other hand, finally knowing what Conway was up to was tempting. Perhaps she should grab the story and get closer to him and his plans. If she said no, he would just go and find someone else. Maybe he would reach out to that sleazy Victor who'd worked with her at the office of The Citizen years ago, who wouldn't hesitate to steal this story from her. Saying no wouldn't stop Conway. Whatever evil he was planning would happen whether she was there or not. 'No' would only push her away from the center of the action. What did the story have to do with the list and with Menken Mines? *Damn.* If it was about the number of worker deaths, she couldn't leave it to Victor.

Anita took out her phone and hit redial.

"I wasn't expecting to hear from you so quickly," Conway answered with satisfaction in his voice.

"I'm in," she said, and hung up.

What have you done? Anita sighed as her stomach churned. She wasn't being smart. She should've thought more about the consequences of this agreement. Spent at least a night on it. If people began to associate her with Conway after she aired the story, she wouldn't be able to criticize Sābanto anymore. Was that Conway's plan? There was no turning back now. She'd suffer the consequences. *That was stupid, Anita.*

She stepped onto the sidewalk, but instead of returning back to The Jungle, she turned the other way. The hotel she was staying at was a block away. She cursed to herself as she walked.

When she got back to her room, she poured herself two fingers of whiskey from the bar, compliments of the hotel, and looked at herself in the mirror. Her dark skin and black hair looked familiar, unchanged, but there was something Anita noticed deep in the reflection of her brown eyes that she found new and alien. She realized that she had lost something important to her that she might never be able to get back. "Look who you've become," she said, before gulping down the liquor in her hand.

# EPILOGUE

I T WAS THE END of summer already, and the wind blew Cat's hair as she ran down the path on the island. She'd woken at dawn to go for her routine run. Finally, after so many years, she felt happy. She stopped for a moment at the lookout point with the silver ocean stretching out in front of her. It was going to be a beautiful day. She smiled.

She didn't stand there long, just long enough to release the tension in her muscles. She continued running along the familiar path through the island greenery that led back to the building.

Max was already waiting for her, sitting on the steps in front of one of the white Sābanto-style houses that Robert had referred to as boxes, with a cup of coffee. Milk and sugar, just how she liked it. The doctor had released him from the clinic weeks ago, but he was still recovering his strength. Once he was back in good health, he'd promised he'd train with her, and she looked forward to it. With Leo dead, she might not need those bō skills anymore, but there was no harm in keeping them fresh and ready, just in case.

"How are you feeling?" she asked and sat down beside him on the step.

He embraced her and pulled her gently to him. "I'm fine," he said and kissed her hair. "I hope you had a good run."

Cat brought the hot brew to her lips as Dr. Lott came out and sat with them. There was a cup of coffee in his hand as well.

"Good morning," the doctor said, and they returned the greeting. "Do you know what the meeting is about?"

Cat shook her head. Oliver had requested a meeting today. He wanted to discuss something, but he hadn't said what it was.

"I guess we'll find out soon," Max said, pointing with his chin at the chop-jet landing down in the field in front of them.

They all entered the house and sat down, and Cat distributed the rest of the coffee to Oliver and Amy. They'd made extra and kept it warm, anticipating their arrival.

When everyone was seated and ready, Oliver spoke. "I was thinking about what happened in my house," Oliver said. "Leo abducted Sophia, and no one noticed anything. Someone lied, but I wasn't able to catch them red-handed."

"Sophia went willingly to meet with Leo. She could've paid off the staff," Cat said.

"What if Leo was in my house?" Oliver said.

"What are you getting at?" Max asked. "Better surveillance?"

He was right. Kidnapping had nothing to do with them, so why did Oliver insist on their presence at this meeting?

"A person I thought I could trust," Oliver continued, ignoring the question, "made a deal with my enemy."

"What do you suggest?" Cat asked and took a sip of her coffee.

"I spoke with Amy about her experience with the device," Oliver said. "She saw every step of what was happening, and I watched the replay afterwards. I watched both of your feeds, how you took down Leo, and how Max risked his life and saved that kid."

"And?" Max said.

"This . . ." Oliver said, pointing at Cat and Max, "is what we might need to get rid of Friends."

"I don't get it," Cat said.

"We still have some control," Oliver added. "We can't control the laws or the employers, but we could control the workforce."

Cat gawked at him. "Stop talking in fucking riddles," she said.

"We know of every person who lives in Sābanto," Oliver continued. "We know who the Black and Green Shirts are. We know their histories, and families. All of it is documented. We know where we are sending our workers, which factories and mansions. This knowledge is our power."

Max frowned, then asked, "And what do we do with it?"

"The device," Oliver said, turning to Bruce. "We can replicate it. And Dr. Lott did it."

"Yes," Bruce said. "The blueprints for it were very detailed."

He leaned forward before anyone could add anything or ask any further questions. "Hear me out," Oliver said. "How about we create an army to fight Friends?"

"A what?" Cat asked.

Oliver turned on the display. "Look at this," he said. Everyone's head turned towards it to watch the news.

"We've received exclusive footage from The Citizen," the anchor started. "Please note that our special report includes sensitive content that might not be suitable for some viewers."

A car stopped in the circular driveway of a vast mansion. It was one of the new vehicles, a new luxury line featuring all the necessities of a comfortable ride in style. Only a couple of these had been produced so far.

The news played on the display inside the car. The anchor was discussing something urgent. "This is horrific! It doesn't even compare to what we saw during the war."

The images and videos were hard to see. They were dark because of the quality of the video and what they were showing. "That is where the workers work and live," the anchor was saying. There was a terrible sound coming from the display—the noise of the machines and the men coughing. "Only twenty-four hours of breathing fresh air per week. The death toll is at seventy percent of workers."

A porter ran up to the car and opened the door. He wore a tailored uniform, and white gloves covered his hands. From the car, a woman emerged. Her bright red pumps lightly stepped onto the ground as she stood. The porter bent over and showed the woman respect, but she didn't notice him. She didn't even glance at him; it was as if he wasn't there at all.

She walked towards the house, her bodyguard following a few steps behind. Her strides were sure and easy. The tail of her long red dress swayed slightly as she walked up the stairs to the front door.

The door opened as she approached. She didn't even slow down. She stepped inside and took off her fox fur, exposing her bare arms. The back of her dress was open, showing her skin down to the waist. The garment was an example of the finest craftsmanship.

The display was on inside the building as well. Everyone was interested in the latest developments around the world.

"Miss Gibala, a reporter with The Citizen has distributed this everywhere," the anchor continued. "She is not revealing her sources, but every newscast in the world is playing these videos. The message is obvious. Mr. Menken made us believe his mines were safe. They weren't. He lied to us. In light of this news, World United will no longer be providing subsidies to Menken Mines, and many major company shareholders are withdrawing their investments. No one wants to be associated with this crime. They've sanctioned Mr. Liam Menken, the owner of the discredited mines, and ejected him from the mining association."

A servant girl curtsied. "They're waiting, ma'am," she said, and the large, double-winged door, perfectly carved with ornamental roses, opened wide in front of the woman.

In the background, the anchorwoman went on. "The value of Menken Mines, a corporation that was once world-renowned, has crumbled. The owner is in ruins."

The woman raised her hand and removed the pin that held her fascinator on her head. A cascade of copper-red hair fell down her back. She handed the hat to the servant without looking at her. She then raised her hand to signal to her bodyguard who had followed behind her to remain in the hallway as she stepped forward and continued to the next room. The door closed behind her.

Inside, several men sat at an immense mahogany table. Only one of them, the one closest to her, got up. The others were surly and uncomfortable with her presence, averting their eyes.

"Miss Roberts. With the purchase of Menken Mines and your existing ownership of Leggett Manufacturing," the man said, greeting her awkwardly and with some reservation, "you're now a key player in the corporate world. We'd like to congratulate you and offer you the seat at our table that was previously occupied by Mr. Menken."

"Thank you for inviting me," Ivy replied. "It's an honor."

The man nodded and invited her to the empty seat. "Welcome to Friends, Miss Roberts."

# SĀBANTO

Sābanto is an English loanword in the Japanese language, written phonetically. Japanese doesn't have a natural V or a hard R. The macron over the A means it's an elongated sound, imitating an R. The word means 'servant'.

Books in Sābanto series:
Book One: *The Crimson River*
Book Two: *The Copper Briar*
Book Three: Coming Soon!

Please visit www.ewaanderson.com for more information.

# ACKNOWLEDGMENTS

First and foremost I would like to thank my readers and fans of Sābanto. Your continuous support and encouragement created a tremendous impact, which allowed me to keep going. As I hold the finished manuscript in my hand I realize I couldn't have done it without you.

I am especially grateful for my tireless beta readers, Dawn Kewell and Deb Smith for their help making the book better. Your suggestions were invaluable in having this book see the light of day.

English is my second language, and I couldn't have published this book without the help of Lara Dwyer, who spent countless hours fixing the manuscript.

Many thanks to my family for enduring my obsession with writing, especially my husband Ian for his constant encouragement and help in getting the book through the editing and publishing process.

Last, but not least, rest in peace Dr. Brooks.

# ABOUT THE AUTHOR

Ewa Anderson was born and raised in Warsaw, Poland. When she was eighteen, and with very limited English, she immigrated to Canada. She took the challenges of living on a new continent and learning a new language as an opportunity for growth. Living in Canada as an immigrant increased her awareness of the importance of belonging, acceptance and diversity in society, which she tries to relate in her work.

You can follow Ewa at
www.ewaanderson.com